THE MAN WHO MADE
FRIENDS WITH HIMSELF

CHRISTOPHER MORLEY

THE MAN WHO MADE FRIENDS WITH HIMSELF

A NOVEL

DOUBLEDAY & COMPANY, INC., GARDEN CITY, NEW YORK, 1949

Personal Book Shop
1.80
8-5-49 hm
10-26-49 ee

The lines from "Here in My Arms" are copyrighted, 1925, by Harms, Inc. Used by Permission.

FROM RICHARD TOLMAN'S MUSETTE BAG

◆§ I give to thee who knowest all my wayes,
My crooked winding wayes, wherein I live.
> George Herbert (c. 1630)

◆§ The writer's power to transform anything whatever into any symbolic representation is subject to self-imposed limitation: an object or event that fails to fit the given context is thereby destroyed. . . . Between the work and the writer the relation of dependence becomes absolute; but it ceases the moment his work passes into the public domain.
> Bulletin of the New School, New York (1948)
> (Précis of a course of lectures by Jean Malaquais)

◆§ The Dream knows best. The Dream, I say again, is the responsible party.
> De Quincey: Dream Fugue, The Vision of Sudden Death (1849)

◆§ With the exception of the violently satirical, and the violently sentimental specimens of the art [novels and romances] we find there the closest imitation of men and manners; and are admitted to examine the very web and texture of society, as it really exists.
> William Hazlitt, Edinburgh Review, February 1815. (Review of
> The Wanderer, or Female Difficulties, by Mme. D'Arblay.)

CONTENTS

CHAPTER 1   WENDING WAYS, 3

CHAPTER 2   THE GREAT ANXIETY, 9

CHAPTER 3   DOMESTIC INTERIOR, 14

CHAPTER 4   I GET ON WITH MY KNITTING, 17

CHAPTER 5   I TAKE THE TRAIN, 22

CHAPTER 6   A SPADE A SPADE, 30

CHAPTER 7   TOLMAN'S LAW, 36

CHAPTER 8   GRAND CENTRAL VESPERS, 47

CHAPTER 9   SHARPY'S OTHER SNORT, 58

CHAPTER 10   FILTER THE AIR, 67

CHAPTER 11   SUMMER YCUMEN IN, 79

CHAPTER 12   IN THE BROODHOUSE, 85

CHAPTER 13   ½OETRY, 95

CHAPTER 14   CASE HISTORY, 101

CHAPTER 15   BURN THROUGH TO THE STORY, 108

CHAPTER 16   IT ALL HAPPENS TO ME, 122

CHAPTER 17   MONOLOGUE, IN BED, 128

CHAPTER 18   FORK IN THE ROAD, 135

CHAPTER 19   SHARPY SHOOTS THE MOON, 144

CHAPTER 20   REALITY GOES OVERBOARD, 153

CHAPTER 21   MUSETTE BAG, 164

CHAPTER 22   HAILSTONES IN THE CHIMNEY, 175

CHAPTER 23   LET ME GIVE YOU A LIGHT, 187

CHAPTER 24   CHILD OF GREED, 199

CHAPTER 25   DEFENCE IN DEPTH, 208

CHAPTER 26   THE TRESTLE, 219

CHAPTER 27   PLENTY OF TIME, 233

CHAPTER 28   COME TO NOTHING, 241

CHAPTER 29   THE VASTY HALL, 252

CHAPTER 30   POSTSCRIPT, 272

❧ THE MAN WHO MADE

FRIENDS WITH HIMSELF

TOLMAN & ELSE
AUTHORS' REPRESENTATIVES

MEMORANDUM FROM MR. TOLMAN

To: ZOE

(Monday, 2300)

You always smiled about these memo-pads the printer gave me. I never had much reason to use one. But while I was on vacation, as ordered, I made a bagful of notes. I'll bring them to town tomorrow.

It seems simple as I look back. It never did at the time.

Remember, I said once "If anything ever happens to me . . ."

You said: "What do you mean *if?* Something's always happening to you. You're the most happenstruck person I know."

I continued: "I'll leave a scenario in the safe, in a folder. Give my love to Miss Tally when she opens the safe."

I was rather touched, because you didn't say what I expected; only looked at me with that narrowing of the eyes that means danger. So I had to go on:—

"It's turning out different. I thought it was going to be my detective story. But I had no idea I would be myself the Crime, the Criminal, and the Detective, all in one."

"You're wonderful, you really are. Split three ways."

1

"If you think long enough about anything, no matter how small, you can find big meanings in it. Even in me."

You were rather touched, maybe, because that wasn't what you expected. But you said in your tone-of-voice I'm never quite certain what it means:—

"Love, lover, and the beloved, all in one?"

I wanted to say, "I was never able to starve myself of love." But I said nothing. Everyone has his own small triumphs, and needs them. Here are my notes, as far as they go. If the time is yet, print them if you wish; do any editing you think wise; I hope you'll add a few scholarly footnotes, I love 'em. But no publisher (not even **Calamine**) can afford all the space needed between the lines.

If any ideas, high or low, are expressed, they are my own, and not necessarily my sponsor's. Height and Depth are the same, turned inside out?

A demain,

R.T.

W ENDING WAYS

❧ From the curved and wooded privacies of an upland suburb, commuters come striding down toward the train. Wending Ways the region is called, plotted about the Turn of the Century by some devious-minded schemer. Everything was turning then: it was fine for picturesque, but those pretzel-twisted roads make motor traffic dizzy. Study a map of Wending Ways (the cynical Mortgage Company printed one) and you'll say that only brains, or intestines, could be so screwy. It looks like a curly sponge on top of a straight spinal column. The spine is the taut and well-trimmed backbone of Railroad Avenue, from the neck of our forest headland down to Salamis Station.

From the convolutions, or convulsions, of their sylvan retreat passengers converge briskly into the trunk nerve, the marrow of their duty. Here are sidewalks, civilization, and sun; we straighten our minds to the purposes of the day. There is a slight, very slight, down grade; helpful when catching trains and going to work. It keeps us moving. Railroad Avenue is a delicious walk in early freshness. The mind is alert, yet at ease. Thought also feels a gentle downward slope. (I can think like anything when away from my desk.) The mind notices things comfortably, without studying them. It has Free Enterprise.

Gluttons of morning air know there are only a few hours of God every day; say from 9 to 3, reversing the L of the clock.

About 3 (A.M. or P.M.) the angle turns from acute to obtuse; the Book of Lamentations begins; the Adversary spreads his hand upon all pleasant things.

In those lovely mornings one thing puzzled me: how often I saw the same man walking ahead of me at exactly equal pace. I never noticed where he turned into the main road; simply he was there in front. There was something I liked about his light-foot going. My own movement had more conscious effort, perhaps due to the heavy bag of papers I always carried, but our progress was even. I used to wonder about him. I experimented (in those morning minutes of pure speculation) to find ideas to label him. The mind, a secret little drugstore, likes to compound its own prescriptions. I called my unknown neighbor detached, self-contained, serene. I called him (that was an era of anagrams) MPNA, the man who pays no attention. Mostly I thought of him as That Man.

Perhaps, I pondered, he was one of the Electric Set?

During the Penultimate War—what my neighbor Sharpy Cullen calls War N-minus-One—people learned to walk. Even the superior clique on the Electric Side of Wending Ways trudged to the station on foot. Our suburb lies between two branches of railroad. The sooty old steam trains at Salamis are nearer but fewer. The electric line at Marathon is three miles off, but cleaner and quicker. So there are two lobes in that brain-shaped woodland, two social classes: the Electric Set, businesslike and brokerage and smart; and we simple Steam Folks who take it as it comes, often a little late. But when there's a blizzard the steam train can sometimes plow through while the electric voltage has been shorted by sleet.

There are other symbolisms too. The electric line crosses an appalling high dangerous trestle, only too plain an allegory of our civilization. On that "funambulous and narrow track" (Sir Thomas Browne) I close my eyes as I do during sessions of Congress. Also, at Marathon, the cars run stealthy through a deep ravine so you can't hear them coming. But the steam train at Salamis is terraced high on Hapsburg Hill, its proud com-

4

manding whistle-chord brays across the valley. It gives you at least a minute's warning, or thrombosis.

I used to brood these things on my walk to the depot, but I have no notion of writing an essay on commuting culture. It would be unsalable anyhow, and my earning business is selling other people's pieces. What sociologists see, after giving the data a brisk raking, is only the hair that got left in the comb.

During the War, under gasoline restriction, some of the Electric Set kept pioneering from that other neck of the woods, to share our rude routine on the 8.37. Perhaps the stranger in front was one of those.

&6 I have a habit of walking fast. I've struggled against it, as I have thought of struggling against several other habits; but when I forget myself my pace quickens. I overtake someone, and we are enmeshed in meaningless palaver. Sometimes, to avoid this, I try diversionary tactics, zigging and zagging from one side of Railroad Avenue to the other; but that gets conspicuous. Specially troublesome are ladies hightailing along to catch the train. They patter hard not to be overtaken; they don't want to make chatter any more than I do; but sometimes we can't help it. My private theory is that women should be kept locked up until 10 A.M. It amuses me how little influence my theories have had on the conduct of the world.

There was a day, as I noticed myself walking faster, it struck me that the man in front was going faster too; intentionally. One may have one's own innocent reasons for avoiding people, but still it's a shock when you find them purposely avoiding you. My artistic instinct was piqued, for my habit is to speculate about people. Behind my professed business as a Literary Agent ("Authors' Representative") I am seriously a private detective; perhaps the most private ever because I do my detecting in secret and without fee. Even my best friends have no idea of this; that's why they are my best friends.

That morning—the morning I first became suspicious of

5

the greatest of all crimes—I may have been fatally expansive and sociable. I have never been entirely cured of the disastrous habit of being genial to strangers met by chance. Also, I had lately brought to a happy solution one of my most curious cases: the long baffling malady of the Radio Announcer who had morbid occupational jocularity. He not only corned off a falsely affectionate cajolery, an audible smirk (which outraged millions of possible customers), but worse than that his producer put in an echo-effect, which vibrates spurious overtones in the caves of the air. The only solution was to get him off the mike as fast as possible.

My success in this (I sent ten thousand return-postcards to Listeners asking them to gripe; I got 70 per cent replies; few philanthropies have ever been so cheap) may have induced in me an opiate satisfaction. I had been going over my notes and decided it would be rash to publish them. The great upsurge of resentment against commercial radio had already begun in fiction; and I'm not a historian, needling people from behind. Historians needle people in the aftermath, where it hurts most, but has least effect.

"You see," (as the doomed Announcer always began his processionals) if radio psychoses were well and truly exposed it would be too brusque for our irritable civilization. So I chose to do what all philosophers prefer: evaluate my data, and lock them up. But it may be that my study had caused a pathological jocularity in myself.

So I admit it: I had a weird impulse to catch up with the stranger and pass him the Time of Day; even, what would be worse, the Time of Life. I had been strangely attracted by the shape of the man's back, his odd way of appearing and vanishing (I never saw him on the train) and his half-sideways carriage of the head as though wary of being approached. Now, to my own surprise, I was thinking of interrupting him, snaring him in some trivial dialogue. I even knew, with horror (there is no horror like one's disgust of one's self), what I was getting ready to

6

blurt: "I think we ought to say Hullo; I've been investigating you for quite some time."

The other would be courteously startled. Then (I am a good deal of a pedant) I would explain the literal meaning of *investigate*: to follow in someone's footsteps. I would add, kindly, as an old-timer, "This is better than going by Marathon. Stay tuned to this station."

I would rush on, of course, not to abuse his privacy; explaining that I had to stop at the Post Office; just shouting back, as a piece of news, "What a gorgeous morning!"

But, mercifully, it didn't happen. The stranger went faster and faster. He got to the station first, and disappeared.

It was a gorgeous morning; crystal weather; the first blessing of spring. The season came early, just when we needed it so. I had taken my first cold bath; as I used to say to Sharpy Cullen, I was at the top of my apex. I was talking to myself inside myself; the kind of soliloquy a dog must think when following his tracery nose. Bathtubs brim with poetry, in the anguish of stinging water and friction towel I found Herrick: *Wash, dresse, be brief in praying.* . . . I was so keen to be out I skimped the toothbrush. Mealie, my colored Amelia who housekeeps me, was troubled because I didn't eat my scrambled eggs.

"I don't need them," I said; "not with all those forsythia bushes in blossom. Breakfast is too wonderful to spoil it by eating. If you don't eat any breakfast, breakfast-time lasts all morning."

"You better fortify yourself," she grumbled. "Aren't you goin' to have a Hard Day at the Office?"

That has always been a valuable catchword; the businessman's alibi for everything. He has had, or is going to have, a Hard Day at the Office.

As a matter of fact, I didn't think so. I didn't even think it was going to be a hard day in my mind. There were no serious

7

appointments; there was plenty of futile paperwork and correspondence to keep me unconscious. I wouldn't need to think; just live along. It wasn't going to be one of those significant days when everything seems to mean more, or different, from what it appears.

THE GREAT ANXIETY

᪥ When did the Great Anxiety begin? I sometimes asked myself while walking to the morning train. It was a happy mile, felicitous for thought. The world did not impact upon me until I got to the Post Office and picked up my mail. I prefer to collect it myself, rather than R.F.D., because obese and laxative robins nested in my mail-box at home. At the P.O. I can throw the second-class, and letters about Causes, in the waste-basket. Ruthlessness begins at the Post Office. The only pushover for Causes is he who has none of his own.

The Great Anxiety; the Sense of Guilt. It wasn't just in myself, I saw signs of it everywhere. It wasn't only political or economic. In my work as Literary Agent I could see it in the scripts of my clients. Much of their stuff was uneasy and feverish. Even the most inept writers are hypersensitive to storm warnings. The Coast Guard knows when a gale is coming.

All decent people were weary; the world was in a bag's end, and not a sleeping bag either. Overtired men were flying round the earth, in overloaded planes, to try to patch the seams. Tired men weigh heavier than fresh. Sometimes I said to myself (my best audience) that my notion of a perfect day would be to sit in a very hot bath rereading Veblen's *Theory of the Leisure Class*. It is the second most dangerous book in American literature. (The first, of course, is *Moby Dick*.)

9

The emblem of man had become the question mark. It was an era of Quiz Programs; but the most valuable of all such would be the personal solitary interior and reflexive catechism each man might put to himself; to his own perishing soul. Man was not only tired but insolvent, both in morals and economics. He was bitterly aware how few hours he can live without food, drink, rest, shelter, and hilarity. He was pooped: mind, body, and estate.

Fortunately some of my troupe of clients were good old ham practitioners, and brought me thick slices of percentage. I was never one to snarl at increment. Even among the apostles someone had to hold the bag.

The world goes into a slough (or Great Grimpen) at aliquot intervals; but always, as that cynical snob Henry Adams insisted, in swifter progression. Thank the Devil (the Great Concealer) for hiding the formula from simple men, who otherwise would fear to shave. The chief danger in these periods of poop is the medieval sin of Accidie: sloth, fatigue, languor, lethargy. Only the very happy man can know the depth and intellectual beauty of Despair; but I said to myself, those fatal mornings, I better take out Accidie Insurance.

It was not only my profession but my passion to think about these matters; a career in which there isn't much competition. It was odd that I, Dick Tolman (a simple, carnal, comic soul), should grieve myself to do so. But reading pieces in the papers, listening to the impudicities of radio, I could see that few others cared. I noticed odd phenomena. Liquor and cigarettes and psychiatry flourished as never before. Only the humorous maga-zines dared mention starkly somber topics. Women, whose be-havior instantly reflects social alarm, were hurrying to clinics for beauty and success. There, according to the advertisements (the Domesday Book of our life), they were steamed and greased and swaddled, rocked in heartbeat rhythm on rolling stretchers of aluminum. They, even more than poor blockhead man, yearned to clamber back into the stupor of the womb.

There were more bad words printed in books than ever

since Chaucer or the Old Testament. The smartest women were wearing a sideswipe hairdo that dated from the Wife of Bath, but didn't know the jokes that went with it. Yet they loved to believe their minds were fashionably foul! Delicious creatures, but they had never heard the wonderful mocking wisecracks of the fourteenth century. On the whole I preferred they shouldn't, unless I myself could tell them. Sometimes I did.

Fortunately these symptoms were noticed only by a few underpaid students or ushers of "English," which also means an off-axis rotation. My own wisdom, if any, was to remember that everything has happened before, and will happen even quicker again. I thought of my untroubled neighbor, vanishing before me so fugitive and serene. He would put in an appearance, and then (in another of the pavement's diamond phrases) take a powder. He simply blew. But why, these gemlike mornings, should he go to Town? Why indeed should I? Rather, like pure idea, stay inside the brain, the shady skullscape of Wending Ways? As one of my syndicated poets wrote (I do quite a traffic in corn-sirup):—

> How comfortably in the brain
> Unwritten madrigals remain.

But of course, I had to go to the Post Office.

There were more pamphlets and mimeographs than ever before. I tear them crosswise three times (makes eight fragments) before throwing them into the tin waste-basket (which is too small). Once I tried to rent a private P.O. box to receive mail under another name; but the Government wouldn't allow it unless I got two neighbors to testify that I wouldn't use it "for purposes of deception." Sadly I admitted that was exactly why I wanted it.

I was aware, and probably everyone else was inwardly aware, that we are in an era of diminishing returns. Man is bored, disgusted, and eager to destroy himself. He is crippled by his vast burden of consciousness; the only animal on whom this horror has been laid. Man is too witty to survive. As they used to say,

11

let's face it. Zoe murmured, in one of her mischievous moments, I can bear anything if my face is turned upward.

I was sorry it had to be me to meditate thus. I am not a thinker. I had, at that time, a madness to listen again and again to news broadcasts. I imagined that names and facts so gorgeously mispronounced couldn't be exact. Irony, the sterile goddess of defeat, troubled my tenderest mind. The world was unbearably fair; Meaning spread luxuriant around me, appealing to be enjoyed; and I trudged and grudged like a salesman of crape. Like a minor poet (which in my high moments I am) I was outraged by the dreadful paradoxes of mortality. Why should the village utility-man be called Hegel, and his truck say COAL AND ICE? The Hegelian antithesis, I would mumble, and be cheered for an hour. A mind so easily tickled is hysterical, I would reflect, and be damned for a moment. Why is black, I would ask myself, not only the suit of woe but also the convention of formal frolic?

"You see," or if you don't it's my fault (no one but I knows how I'm condensing), I was getting ready, reluctantly, to say good-by to Beauty. Lady Mary Wortley Montagu said (of Henry Fielding; I wish I could have been Fielding's agent): "He has known more happy moments than any prince upon the earth." So had I. A man who has not known exquisite and absurd happiness is no fair reporter of human doings. Distrust him. That is why I conspue the Henry Adamses; I cleave to the old clo' men of philosophy, the castaway or displaced Prosperoes like Einstein, who said, "I can't explain my equation to you, but I'll play it on the fiddle." Prospero found his truth on an island. On its offshore reefs the great surges of human selfishness collapse in silver foam.

I was having a wonderful time telling myself that I was Through. (Language, the varied vulgate of common men, is our greatest glory.) All that is left to me, I said, hoping for inspired contradiction, is Surrender. I was ready to admit defeat, but I wanted to do so gloriously. Sometimes, on those tramps to the station, I was really godlike. I was young Keats, writing to Frances Brawne: "How I shall curse myself tonight, for having written you so cold a letter." I wanted to write the world a letter, but it must not be cold.

I was even so stricken that when important publishers would call up, while I was at my late supper, and proffer me my fortune and theirs, I would lose my temper and snarl. It wasn't American. I wasn't an American any more; I wasn't even a reasonable Literary Agent. I thought of inventing Patriots Anonymous (like Alcoholics ditto) to cure victims of the destroying tipple of nationalism.

Is it possible, I wondered (I am still walking to the station), that after being tricked, lied to, fouled and muted upon, the human mind might be ready to reassert itself? Can lure and learning teach us once more, the simple sweets are true? I must ask Zoe.

I hurried for the train, which I didn't even have to catch. The train was my daimon, my drug, my Locomotive God. Craving silence, I boarded a caravan of noise. From the cigar store, where I got the morning paper (in a momentary suspension of disbelief), Chaucer, Montaigne, Keats, Coleridge, Hazlitt, Wordsworth, and Father Gerard Hopkins rushed out. They swarmed round me like Notre Dame tacklers, tried to pin me down. I reversed my field, swivelled my hips, threw them off, sprinted for a gain of 40 yards. I made first down in the vestibule of the smoker. I was aboard the train.

I didn't see my evasive neighbor. I was happy in my own fatal achievement. But I shall curse myself tonight.

This was a modulation, to suggest some of my private frequencies. Now I must flash, or flush, backward.

Domestic Interior

∙§ The best detective stories ever written usually began with a scene of domestic interior: Holmes and Watson on either side of the Baker Street hearth. My own was different, but comforting to me. Amelia, my colored cook-general, is probably a shrewder detective than any of us. She is a natural psychiatrist, full of the dark wisdom of her race. When I'm alone (I usually am) I sit with a book or newspaper at table, and Mealie never speaks until the coffee is served. Then, if she feels a need for talk, she wedges open the swing-door to the kitchen and washes the dishes very quietly. Open also is the wide easy-swinging door of her generous mind. She says that putting the hands in hot water is good medicine. "It take the blood down from the head, where blood got no business to be."

Often I consulted her about cases that puzzled me; or we discussed household problems. Perhaps something faint, dim, almost imperceptible, a subwhisper of unhearable sound, murmured in my ear. It came between the lines of what I was reading, like the unknown stanza Coleridge was about to scribble when the Person from Porlock . . . I had to stop chewing, even stop thinking, to catch it. "Mealie, is that plumbing gone wrong again? Or is it just the end of the world coming?"

Mealie, who hears everything, went into her act. "Did seem to me like I hear kind of a whisper. It's mighty confidential, wait till I turn off this tap."

14

I held my mouth open to tense my eardrums. We both listened. Yes, a dull disturbing undertone, something just-not-silence. I was reading poetry that night—I do, about once a week, to take me back to reality after the folklore of the evening papers.

"There was a roaring in the john all night," I said. "But at my back I always hear, Time's wingèd chariot hurrying near."

Mealie said: "That ain't no laughing joke."

We have plenty of topics. For instance Chiropody, the piebald philoprogeny cat, had slain the great fascist rat that bedevilled me so long. I had read how scientists baffle rats by putting them through random sequences of shock—like commuters—until the rat collapses in Accidie. It is a political fable; but this great rodent had never been frustrated. The creature had a passion for binders' glue; he came into my study (piled high with copies of clients' books) and gnashed off the backstrips. I christened the cat Chiaroscura, for her mottled equation of colors; but Mealie found that name difficult and changed it to her own personal concern, Chiropody. Mealie's feet, she said, didn't keep up with her torso. But she approved the cat. "She a good chaperone for this house, half black and half white."

Maybe it was a day when I stayed home to read MSS. "I hear you squeak the cork in that gin bottle befo' midday. If you eat a fittin' breakfast you wouldn't crave gin befo' lunch."

Or I was in the garden, raking and burning leaves. Full of zeal at the wrong moment, I scrambled a huge pile, a gusty wind was blowing, the blaze spread furiously. Mealie had to rush out with a bucket. "Mr. Tolman, what for you set such a big fire? I repute you always a smart man. Build a small fire and buhn it in control."

Wise, competent, dogmatic Mealie! She had no idea how I enjoyed watching her strong black-pink hands in the white suds of the dishpan; manipulating the china with skillful quiet because we were enjoying our talk. Sometimes, if I wanted her to take a day off, I would give her a bottle of rye to take home at night. She never turned up the following day. She must have

15

wondered (as much as I do myself) what was really my business? I think she imagined The Law, because she used to say on the phone, "No, ma'am, The Counsellor ain't in." Once, in one of my grievous moods, I told her I couldn't take any calls because I was working on an epigram. Later, planning a dinner party for the Cullens, she found in the cookbook *Epigram of Sweetbreads*. "What-all this epigram you labor with? Sounds to me some kind of cutlets."

Even at epigrams merely verbal Mealie is more gifted than most. Darkly shining as a well-fumed briar, she is straight human grain all the way through. A Counsellor-at-Heart, perhaps. When we burned the corpse of the slaughtered rat she said "he was incriminated." Best of all, I overheard her say to Salmon (her son) who was helping wash up, "What I like about Mister, he got no antisemitism for colored people."

Come to think of it, I had a psychiatrist at each end of the day's work. That will take time to expound. Being so expertly taken apart, I might have been better purged? Perhaps it was only on the train I had a chance to be Myself? With all its horrors, the commuters' train gave me the only infrangible solitude I ever knew.

I GET ON WITH MY KNITTING

◌◌ Except on paper, I'm shy. I am bald, swarthy, busy, and evasive; I think it likely, by my extremes of emotionalism, that my genes are mixed. I like to think that being a mongrel makes me a good American. I can bring tears to my own eyes when I can't do it to anyone else's. My favorite prejudice is that I'm completely unprejudiced. Alas, anyone without prejudice is practically dead, or practically God.

I'm specially shy about my knitting. When neighbors come to call, unless I know them well I hide the bundle of wool in the fireside settle. They would think it precious or quaint. Sturdy souls, stamped and embossed in the rigid suburban matrix, they have little to be shy about.

But the kittens, *Shall* and *Will* (I call them that because so few people know them apart), find the ball of yarn trailed outside the bench and begin giving it pattypaws. I might as well pour the visitors a gin-and-ginger and resume wool-gathering. I explain that I'm making soakers for my expectant nieces. Those sweet girls are, as the Germans say, *guter Hoffnung*, of good hope. No nation that has such lovely genitives can be completely wicked.

My life was difficult because I loved words. I perceived their terrible power; I tried not to mollify their meanings. Their overproduction and misuse are the stigmata of our perishing culture.

17

I learned to knit, for self-salvage, during the Peace of Nerves. People were fatigued and falsified, smoking and drinking too much, dancing and gambling and reading too much. Knitting rested my eyes and kept my mind from picking and stealing. If we had more knitters, we'd have less jitters.

I have a silly habit of jetting impromptu rhymes when my mind is at ease. The neighbors probably think the tall glass beside me, as I purl and cast-off, is plain water. It often has in it a good royalty of gin, the only drink imperceptible to all but the participant. One night when Sharpy Cullen was here, confiding his troubles at his age (any age after fifteen was a dangerous age for Sharpy), I had been reading a translation of *The Odyssey*. I was startled at the number of punts Homer kicked in the end-zone, over the heads of young students and most of their profs. Musing over my wool, I said "The nymph Calypso is a bit of a dipso, she can't keep up her drawers they slip so."

"The wish is father to the thought," said Sharpy. Then he added, "I say that more in sorrow than in anger."

I was in my Baker-Street mood. I said: "You've been associating with a bald man who has a little beard and less morals."

Sharpy rapidly visualized his usual companions, and denied it.

I knitted several loops to give myself build-up, and then flattened him. "I mean Shakespeare. You quoted him twice in two sentences. You're an old cornchandler without knowing it."

That is what I call counter-detection. I detect upon the sleuths themselves. When stupid people murder stupid people I'm not much interested. They're better dead anyway. When intelligent people murder themselves, or are nullified by inertia, or stereotyped by publicity, it's serious. When I see a whole civilization committing suicide . . .

All one can do, with my temperament, is find it a witty epitaph. I haven't found one yet, but I practice by pricking poor Sharpy with etcher's acid. When I say ironically, "Quick, Watson, the needle," I mean the knitting needle. When I say earnestly, "The real detectives are the poets," I mean that the

18

best way to tune in on great poets is to be a small poet yourself. When I say sadly that my mind, like Kubla Khan's casino, is "a pleasure dome with caves of ice," I mean all sorts of things. Then, by natural sequence, I go out to the kitchen and cube Sharpy and Betty Cullen another drink.

My life, like all lives worth the difficult long while they endure, was full of delicious stratagem and subterfuge. I was a fugitive from chain-reactions. I learned, too late, that men live only by reckless imagination. I can say this without shyness because I am not fanciful. I fly in terror, on the endless downhill vistas of the mind, from the upland of the Brain. At least, my only credit, I know what I'm flying from. I hurry away from those awful fantasies of Rilke and Kafka and the other mid-European writers who felt the worst before Americans even knew there was such an illness as feeling. I see thousands of people on the streets, unconsciously in flight from the places where their number is up, libraries and bookstores. Colleges and chambers of commerce are for the immature.

It was middle-Europe, the navel of the world, where the anxiety came from. The navel is always where trouble begins; there we were severed from unconsciousness.

The neighbors thought I was unmanly because I was that hermaphrodite creature a Literary Agent, and occasionally a small-time publisher. They could not know that I took up the profession of Authors' Representative because it gave me a chance to offer my own verse to magazines under other names, without distress. The only fun in publishing is when no one knows who wrote it. As soon as anyone knows who wrote anything (from the Ten Commandments on) nuisance begins.

Probably some of the neighbors thought I was unmanly because my wife left me, long ago. That always bothers the chambers of domestic commerce. Why would she leave such a worthy man? Once, as I was turning the chubs of a soaker, I said to Mr. and Mrs. Cullen: "My wife left me because I kept a diary."

There was more to it than that; but even that sparse allusion filled poor Betty with wild surmise. If anyone was going to issue a White Paper on Husbands, Betty Cullen could do it. Like many official documents, the paper would better stay white.

Betty wanted to discuss this, but I stalled her. "Let me look at my notes," I said. "Increase once at each end of needle in every 10th row, till 82 stitches on needle—6 rows plain— then cast off 5 at beginning each next 12——" She was so interested in this woollen algebra she forgot the other topic.

So I sat, full of widowers' pique, by my greenwood fire, dropping embers of ill humor. The fire itself was a symbol of my spiritual fuel: hurricane wood, self-chopped, ill-seasoned, sooty in the chimney. The soot crusted so thick and scaly I had to throw handfuls of salt up the flue. My goodhearted neighbors, who are a sort of chanting chorus to my theme, defended themselves by assuming I was merely jocular. I doubt if they guessed my deep conviction that man's only triumph is the Sacredly Absurd. (Kipling. An Authors' Representative is always conscientious to identify the Author.)

Shall and *Will*, identical kittens of the progeny cat, wrestled with my shoelaces. I cut out the toes of old socks and the armpits of stale shirts and rolled them into a pendulum ball (on a string) for their jungle-gym; stronger than valerian or catnip. It was their radio program, intoxicating and delicious.

I was always a pushover for any kind of symbolism. I kept two stools (strong cane-woven antiques from the Catskills) in front of the fire, so I could fall between them. My life was like that; my Holy Land was always partitioned. I worked mostly in Town, and slept mostly in the Country, so I saw the worst of both. I kept moving my office uptown because I wanted the number of my street to be bigger than my age; but after I had made northing as far as 50 I ceased to care. I was the kind of man to whom embarrassing things happen; and what is so embarrassing as to grow older? Mingling tides of Manhattan commerce caught up and surfed over me; at the time of my trouble I was imbedded in wholesale jewelers. The pavement was so choked with them, looking at precious granules through their loupes, I had to walk in the street to get to a restaurant for lunch. I consoled myself by saying that I am a kind of jeweler too.

I went bald before I got up to 30th Street. I think it was good for me, gave me a sense of erosion, like mountains and gutters and the T.V.A. Nothing is so important as drainage? Perhaps it helped me to be a detective? It made me universal, gave me the torture of uncertainty grown people ought to have? So I found comic what the zealous American herd believed serious and hopeful. I found tragedy and collapse in our farcical zeal. As Sharpy said to Betty Cullen, on their way home, to detour her from what she was evidently thinking, "Dick's values are all wrong. He doesn't know that what they call Par Value in the prospectus has nothing to do with the offering price."

"This is the Century of the Common Stock," he added. Sharpy was one of the Electric Set.

So, fair warning, came horror and despair. A crime has been arranged, and will shortly take place.

I TAKE THE TRAIN

᪥ I've commuted from
Salamis these many years; no one would guess how I love it. That
little plaza isn't the neat-pin suburban parking-lot of the Electric
Set. It has a few grim prickly shrubs (littered with bubble gum
and candy wrappers) to remind us (if we have time to be reminded) of boys who didn't come home in 1918. It's grotesque
and sloppy enough to be all America; it has everything that makes
this great handyman among nations comic and well-meaning and
terrible. The ancient depot itself, until it was remodeled after my
death, was the foulest and stuffiest between here and California.
The *Men's* had the corniest graffiti ever pencilled; there's a high-
school near by. One of those progressive vocational high schools
that prides itself on facing the facts of life. I know about the
Men's; I was in there one time, just before the train, and the
door-knob came off. I yelled and banged and kicked, but I missed
the train.

There's a grade-crossing (history is full of them) with a deep
step down that has agonized many an arthritis. There's a bar-and-
grill and a cigar-candy-stationery; a Hand Laundry and a Negro
Bethel. There's a firehouse with a wonderful old bronze alarm-
bell (silvered and no longer used) and a sledge to smite it, hanging from a scaffold outside. There's a navel-European pants-
presser and a branch of the hopeful village library. As John
Donne said, in the most Men's Room poem ever written about

22

America, there's everything: "Before, behind, between, above, below." There's a police booth, and an open space alongside the gravel walk, room for the shabby old fawn-colored mail truck. The sign says:

RESERVED FOR U.S. GOVERNMENT

How much understanding and forgiveness it takes to love anything; or vice versa, to be loved.

No one would guess, as I trudge my uncomely way to the gravel path beside the tracks, how I process and thrill within. Middle figure, middle age, who could suspect me of ecstasy? The Middle Ages were fine for cathedrals but difficult for individuals. As my profession requires, I am all things to all. If trapped in converse I can say what's necessary; but as one of the oldtimers of the village I have earned the privilege of oddity. Not for me the agony of the young commuter (this was one of my most curious cases) who Wasted a Whole Day because he did not know how to say good-by to a Talker he met in the train. I taught myself, long ago, to enter the car from the rear (so no one sees me coming). I choose a half-seat with someone I don't know; preferably a narrow person. No highest churchman could have a life more full of private ritual. All men need their own decorums; those who haven't achieved any are on a one-way trip to despair.

Apparently absorbed in the morning paper I walk to the far end of the gravel platform, take a look at Hapsburg Hill in daffodil sunlight. Then back to where I know my smoking-car will stop. Now, on a clean purged morning, is my great moment. The engine blows her melancholy stave, the chord of first and second mortgage, as she rounds the bend. I always say the same versicle to myself as she thunders near: *Her cranks akimbo, blowing steam; blue morning on her lens.*—Then I turn my back, partly against cinders, partly to control my crisis of devotion. Like the poor lascar in H. G. Wells's dynamo story, or the neurosis Wisconsin poet of the Locomotive God, I might worship too much. I want adoration, not sacrifice.—But perhaps there has to be sacrifice?

23

You see why I'm a part-time detective. My devoir is to study the queer things people think. In my better moments I know that what I feel everyone feels; what I suffer everyone suffers. The newspaper I carry is only a screen, to get me modestly aboard the train. It is not my métier to offer opinion on political or economic ideas. I am only competent in the terrible secrecies of human beings.

In the lovely and sordid old smoking-car I nurse my fat briefcase on my knees and go through my papers. Or perhaps I study the advertising cards, the Holy Writ of our time. I love them so, they make me sad, as true love often does. The mannerly suggestions of funeral directors (All Rites, from $200 up) grieve me to think that the most exquisitely comic affiches will be appearing a generation hence and I not here to relish and disregard. There is Whiskey for Men of Distinction, which I shall never live to taste. There are mammals in three shapes of cups; and my favorite, the machine shop that cries *Everything sharpened that needs an edge.* That's me.

It would take time, and I don't know how much time there is, to meditate the full peculiars of commuting. One happy phase —and rare, in the infatuated sociability of the American folk—you get used to knowing people only by sight. How peaceful that is. Better still, as one gets older (and one does), you see them ageing too. One incredible fellow used to ride my trains, a tall assured youth with a thin accipitrine profile; he always grabbed double seats for his pals and they roared with laughter and pinochle all the way out from town on the 5.03. I used to think (I was pretty grim in those days) life or love or liquor or something will get that goy, or guy. Then for years I didn't see him, I think some Depression intervened. Suddenly he reappeared, an old old man. He was in the Club Car (a Pullman, by subscription only) and I saw him playing backgammon with a banker. He was wearing a banker's hat, and carrying one of those thin Vuitton attaché cases, too shallow for anything but certificates and debentures. (You can't carry MSS. in a briefcase like that.) Then I knew that destiny has its cruel way. Even in the Club Car one can't do

24

things just to pass the time; while we're doing so, time passes us. I take my own time seriously.

So I know my fellow-passengers only by guess and by God. They amaze me often by casual things they say, casual bundles they carry, their patient fidelity and good humor, the daily discipline of their collars and stockings. As we stand in line to leave the cars, stumble out (Watch your Step), shuffle up the bright footworn treads, disperse to our incommunicable doings, I try to divine how guilty or innocent each may be.

It must be noted that our railroad service had schizophrenia. Halfway to town one changed pace at a nerve center called Jamaica. Not, as in Massachusetts, Jamaica Plain, but Jamaica Complicated. Here, like diplomats in the old carbarn of the State Department, unknown dispatchers had godlike or childlike power to shuffle us to and fro. At hours of affluence (as the linguistic French call Rush Hours) we were bespoken through Public Address megaphones and told what to do. We piled onto a baresark platform and jousted our way into a different train; motivated by excitable electricity instead of soothing old steam. Usually there were no seats. If one were moderately courteous he stood in the baggage car. Often there was a coffin in it, one end marked HEAD. We didn't mention it; only thought, in our somber way, it's better to be buried where one falls.

The passengers changed, and the mood changed too. From there in, New York City took charge. In hot weather the train went mad through the tunnel. Socrates or Santayana would have been jittered by that part of the ride. It was a rocketing rioting reeling roar through the East River bottom. Evidently no one was troubled by it but me; but I always got to Penn Station a little crazed. Hot putrid gale scoured through the long steel boxes, people tossed from leg to leg, sickened in the rush. Then, as I staggered up the laboring stairs I would sometimes see the Man in Front above me. Agile he flickered up the treadmill, nimble, negative, and neat.

But of course, to philosophize the matter, I had to hold them all in my mind; including for instance that sweetheart of a

25

girl (I guess I really mean woman) who always got on at East Allison. She also climbed on hinnuleo ankles, her little nylon heels lifting bravely in slippers, up the long stairs, and disappeared. Gallant were her hats and diversified; always her jacket slung over her shoulders. That is woman's craving for a cape, but the dressmakers insist on putting sleeves on it. Women loathe tubes on their limbs?

I could guess, from the vigor of her make-up, pretty close to the number of her next birthday, which was coming fast. She was a detective story I'd have loved to read.

But I'm in Penn Station, where the torque of hurry is golden rope round everyone's throat. Every great Terminal (rail, ship, or air) is Nuremberg Trial for those who collaborated with the great fascist, Time. I'm a little mad, and cry utterance, like a saint or a sadist. I plow through the crowd and always think of someone's line in *King Lear:* "A little to disquantity your train." I thrid those bottleneck estuaries where twice a day the tides of human duress obey their mongering moon. Words, and my occasional sense of being their foreman, are my best medicine. My super-detection is compassed on the study of words, men's unconscious confession of glory or guilt. I care not if they come from low or high, from near or far, from Stratford-on-Avon or Hogs-on-the-Marne (Léon Bloy). All words men ever said are my pleasure.

(Strange to think, the words we need may be so close, waiting in the dictionary at hand. Only a few hundred, timed and chosen by the perfect chooser, could change the tilt of the world. Churchill, magnificent old stonehenge, did it many times.)

I abandon the pretence of being the calm, the placid, the ironical détaché, the innocuous bystander. Suddenly I feel the joy of orderly flowing mass; I'm crowd-happy. But how lethargic they move. Through my veins runs New York's ichor: Hurry, Hurry! Quicker, quicker! I minnow through the shoal. Sometimes, darting ahead of some ridiculous slowcoach, outflanking a hobbling sciatic, I ejaculate cries of pantheism, on the chance they may perplex those left behind. This, I am aware, is a virus, unworthy of the Quaker forester, author of *The Fruits of Solitude*. I have

26

often imagined a copy of that book, lit and showcased in a shrine, in the station named for Penn.

But what then, I muse (mind running hot, clear, and fast), what keeps man alive if not his competitive aggressive propagandive instinct?

It keeps his rivals alive too. Going past the newsstand I feel a blood pressure. The least prick of pain horrifies me, instantly I struggle to rationalize. Partake of the competitive spirit up to the point where its comedy (or tragedy) becomes personally noticeable. Then retire at once, as does a well-bred verb, to the perfect passive participle.

I knew an old Quaker who even tried to train his dogs to non-resistance. Every dog is a power politician by nature. But even dogs can sublimate: they don't bark at the milkman.

Speeding through the tunnel-passage to Sixth Avenue I see people in an underground restaurant eating lavish belated breakfasts. How absurd people look, eating, when you yourself are not hungry. How absurd they look hurrying, when you yourself are at ease. How absurd they must always look if you are a god. Only the gods can weary of comedy, because they get too much of it. Being in New York is like being in love, it puts ideas in your mind. I croon one of my unfinished liturgies:

> . . . as tragic as comic can be
> That I who am so unimportant
> Still seem so important to Me.

In the harlequin mood I rush up to the Seventh Avenue train. There is a crepitant echo on those tiled walls. Hurrying upstairs is always a spiritual tizzy, because the doctor told me it might be fatal. What one blurts out on upstairs really comes from a breaking heart. In the swarm of that high-colon immigration at 33rd Street I cried aloud:

> Monday to Sunday, to and fro,
> A Gulf of Fundy, ebb and flow.

Another word came to me—I wasn't quite sure what it meant, but it seemed appropriate. Even the logothetes must sometimes

27

have used words first and looked them up afterward? My word sounded wonderful, I boomed it on the echoing stairs: *Fundibular!* It isn't in my old Webster, nor in the two-volume Oxford, but it must mean going through a narrow channel, throat, or funnel. A history of us all? I chanted it, *Fundibular!* in the white sepulchral larynx of the subway. Did the Man in Front hear it as he singlefooted into the Car Ahead? Probably not; he was intent on his own drastic affairs. But it did me good. Anything devotedly absurd does me good; literature is too merciful and rarely exposes the dancing particles inside the mind.

I have been in a pure felicity, between stations, wondering what happens when Moby Dick meets Spermaceti Belle.

Even literary agents are too merciful. I would take Saint Matthew, or Matthew Arnold, or Arnold Toynbee, or even William Penn, and plant him for twelve hours in the fundible of Penn Station; halfway between the newsstand and the *Ladies'*. That, I think, would make good copy.

After the partial privacy of the train comes the complete blissful anonymity of the City. The Great Dispersion: here are several hundred souls from the Salamis Branch, decanted like strong cognac into the thin soda of New York. This, that, and other ways, they spread to their weird burdens. I say to myself (except in fireworks moments whom else can one tutoyer?) the line of Ronsard: "Into the woods then with their girls and salads." Into the city with their wormwood secrets. So I thought as I followed, panting, my lightfoot unknown. He was bound, I hoped, for his own devotions, with his own little flask of oil and vinegar. A bulging girl sat hamsandwich against me in the subway, I was tempted to warn her that her cosmetic was deadly strong; I even thought how I could do it without offence: "That's not a perfume, that's an effluvium." Also one of her nylon seams was askance, but fortunately she scrambled upstairs faster than I could. She skipped across to the sluiceway of an office building. What is it about 42nd Street that makes it the causeway of the Lost Cause? Is it the stubborn bulk of the Public Library on one side (last stand of the Art Preservative) and the grim frivolity of

28

Uptown on the other? At that crossway, they finally decided, traffic can make No Turn.

I crossed, rallentando, and walked up Fifth. Down and down toward me, flowing, flowing, unstoppable till all things stop, lovely fatal traffic. Like the river in Joyce's *Finnegan:* "Weh, oh Weh! Silly to be flowing but I no canna stay." Resigned and swift and still moves the stream above the falls: going where no one wants to go, doing what no one wants to do, but saving its face between high façades; saving our Great Stone Face.

I love my walk up Fifth Avenue. Every face, every person, I think hopefully, is a thrill seen only once; *hapax legomenon* as some old Wisconsin professor used to tell me. Rag-tag-and-bob-tails of semi-scholarship float through my mind; I see the gentle downstream of our doom. I see my drugged enchanted fellows gloating on delicious windows; all secretly sick for the joy none have had since —— fill in your own date. The first proof of Old Age, I remind myself, is when you like to think that other people aren't having the fun you had; but perhaps they are, all the time.

The whole bloody world, I say to myself, is become a Studio Audience, waiting for an usher to hold up a placard to tell it when to applaud.

So, because I'm on my way to my office, where I shall have to buckle down, I take my time. I only ask an hour a day, how moderate it seems, to think in my own stupid way, about my private dreams.

As I turned off onto my own street I saw the Stranger in the distance. For a decimal of a second we met eye-on, but as usual he had an air of intense purpose and showed no sign of recognition. All right, old boy, I thought peevishly; go ahead and toss your own salad. I hope there's more vinegar than oil. I wondered, is That Man following me, or am I following him?

A SPADE A SPADE

◈ For my private business, what Quakers would call my *Concern*, an office is only a front or screen. It's useful for mail, telephone calls, figuring income tax, and salmon (please, not tuna) or egg-salad sandwiches sent up from the Coffee-Clutch in the lobby. Of course I keep a keen well-shevelled young woman there to type letters and make memos; this is Miss Tally, short for Tagliaferro. I often call her affectionately (I am very affectionate) J. F. S. She drew an immaculate blank when brains were being distributed, which is what makes her worth 50 a week to me. She still doesn't know that J. F. S. means Just For Show; she still thinks, or believes, that I am seriously a Literary Agent.

Miss Tally likes me best when she thinks I'm a publisher. Since life fell apart, some thirty years ago, to be a publisher (of no matter what) confers social status. The world shows its reverence for print, as it shows its reverence for every high command, by ignoring it. I achieve the dignity of publisher without the embarrassment of customers. Every other year or so, and always under different names, I print a pamphlet of my own verses or aphorisms in an edition of 250 copies. That is as large a public as I can afford to have gratis. Miss Tally signs and mails them. I never number a limited edition; it only annoys the recipients of the larger figures. I was amused when I got one from my young client Urban Block, which said: *This edition is limited to 250 copies of which this is number 249.*

So my office is always strewed like Vallombrosa with duplicate galley-proofs. This makes an impression of serious futility on some of my clients; and leads them to suppose I am more naïf than they will eventually learn.

In my early days I had a rolltop desk; I've often wondered why they went out of favor; you could hide things in them. When I moved above 30th Street it collapsed, I had to get a flattop, and Miss Tally could read everything on it. Then I bought an iron safe, second-hand on Third Avenue, because painted on it was a scene of swans on a lake and blue Alsatian mountains behind. I always liked the Victorian instinct to transfigure iron reality with romantic decalcomania. The contents of my safe are just as absurd as the picture. I was embarrassed one day when Miss Tally forgot to swing the door shut before an important client entered. I'm sure he expected to see it stuffed with MSS. and contracts and loopholes, including his own. It contained only a Complete Shakespeare, the 2-volume Oxford Dictionary, and a bottle of gin. Those are all I need as springboard in my kind of business.

From Miss Tally I get a pretty accurate notion of what's going on in hairdo, nail polish, vanishing cream, wisecracks, and foundation or uplift garments. America has such a passion for mammals, you'd think they were something new. How firm a foundation, ye saints of the Lord, should be the favorite female hymn. These matters may or may not be urgent in my affairs, but I like to be polyglot: what Sharpy Cullen calls femniscient. Miss Tally has an eager and loyal heart; on the phone or at her counterbalanced typewriter-desk (which poises as beautifully as a contractor's derrick) she gives a convincing performance of a hardboiled Literary Agent's harderboiled Girl Friday.

Like the gravedigger in *Hamlet* I call a spade a spade. So I may add that Miss Tally's greatest value to me is her total immersion in the lifestream of her own time and class. She swims in it, irregardless (as she would say) that anything different ever was or would be conceivable. Therefore she offers a pure gelatine or emulsion on which I can expose startling negatives. Sometimes I let her go early so I can take an afternoon snooze on the couch. (An office that doesn't have a couch for naps is only a jail.) She has to go to a movie, which confirms all her social fantasies. Meanwhile I probably read a few pages of Saintsbury—the learned, the lepid, the lingua-franca Saintsbury, the deepest-breathing critic of our lifetime; his sentences, like his beard, often reached to his waist—and pass into the desiderated doze. I like to think that even the lively Miss Tally, with all her concinnity (Saintsbury would call it), uses that same divan for siesta. Once I came back when she didn't expect me; the ottoman was gently concave and warm.

Still-and-all, as Tally says, we manage a good act. After stenography, a sandwich and a salvo of gin, we might almost be characters in one of those fashionably wise-cracking detective stories. Then I pull myself apart. I have to impersonate several careers.

I was getting ready to impersonate a man who has done a good morning's work. Some of it really is; trying to protect writers against themselves is resented by all concerned. If the dictation is difficult I do it walking to and fro; I have worn a diagonal path across the office rug trying to think. Few have ever walked so far fro and so little to. I was trying to convey, ironically, to one of my profitable clients that he was editing too many anthologies. Much to Miss Tally's agony I was doing this by improvising a verse to shame him, something like this:—

> Why do your own wash? Use the laundry,
>   My experience has shown
> I get from other folks and sundry
>   Linen better than my own.

In one of the long pauses of composition Miss Tally spoke up.

"I'm sorry to interrupt, Mr. Tolman, but you had so much on your mind, I forgot. There was a man here to see you, just before you came in this morning. He left a package for you, said it was important. It got covered over in the third draft of this Calamine contract."

32

"What is it?" I asked irritably. My mind was intent on the severe problem of rhymes for *laundry*.

"Looks like a script." She handed me the package. "But he said it's not to be opened."

"What nonsense; or is it a new kind of trick to rouse the poor agent's curiosity? *Thus is the poor agent despisèd; Troilus and Cressida*, somewhere in Act Five."

The parcel, very neatly wrapped, was correctly addressed to Richard Tolman, Literary Agent. It was the usual 9 x 12 size of literary property in the raw, but heavily inscribed ONLY TO BE OPENED ON AUTHOR'S INSTRUCTION. Moreover, it was sealed with great crusts of wax and carried a notary public's rubber-stamped identification of that morning's date and hour of sealing. More preposterous still there was no name of the author or sender.

"Didn't he leave a card, or his name and address?"

"No, Mr. Tolman. He made me sign a receipt for it, but he wouldn't give any name. I tried to make him wait, I said you'd be in any minute. He was awfully attractive, he really was cute. You know, sort of shy, but underneath you could see he was so sure of himself."

I was tempted to seize the big shears and slice open the wrapper, but Miss Tally seemed oddly earnest about this absurd episode.

"He said he put his trust in your professional honor," she remarked. "He took a gander round the office and saw the safe, and said 'Tell Mr. Tolman to put it in there until the time comes.' "

"Damnedest nonsense I ever heard," I grumbled. "This isn't the Library of Congress. Suppose it really is something important? It might be the text of the Yalta conversations, or the proof-corrections by wireless in Churchill's Memoirs. Or never mind what."

"I told him the safe didn't mean anything, you only use it for Shakespeare and a bottle of gin. He said to put this halfway between them." She took the package, deftly spun the traditional

7-7-3-4 combination, and set it inside the shelf. I always envy the graceful flexible way she can haunch down, sideways. I've told her never to open the safe except when I'm in the office.

"What kind of guy was he?" I asked as she went back to her notebook. "Young or old, thick or thin, wolf or sheep, true or false, sweet or sour?"

Tally seemed puzzled. "Oh, about your age; but definitely sweet. He didn't look like an author somehow; more like an actor."

"Why would an actor be in a hurry so early in the morning?"

"Maybe he wanted to get back to bed."

I took two or three strolls across the trodbare rug while I meditated what not to say.

"Let's get back to dictation." There was a long pause while I tried to return my mind to the laundry.

"He acted like he heard an alarm clock ringing somewhere," was Miss Tally's casual comment as she sat with her long-pointed pencil poised. If I ever look at that pencil and imagine it waiting for my inept words to run obediently off the machine-shaven point, I'm licked. I'd had enough to agitate me that morning.

"Linen better than my own . . ." repeated Miss Tally, to prime the pump.

"Forget it," I said. "Cancel it, delete it, erase it. I've got to go out, something I forgot. Go on with the Calamine contract."

As I put on my hat and coat I saw her obediently running long downward stripes of pencil through the birdfoot of cryptogram.

"I'll get lunch while you're out," she said sadly. She is feminine enough that my bad moods are her trouble too. Poor child, she also needs her sense of achievement. But she seemed vague, possessed by something beyond our crisp routine.

"He said, Yet is not the time," she muttered.

Pushing the elevator button always gives me a sense of return to geometry or incentive capital.

"A screwball, but beyond doubt," I thought. "Any responsible person would say, The time is not yet."

34

I dismissed it from my mind. Just one of those things.

I was enormously busy going down in the elevator. I was thinking, as I watched the operator's faithful dexterity, don't ever forget: good people are just as busy in innocent work as bad people in wicked work.—If one could find out what people are thinking when they're not supposed to be thinking——

TOLMAN'S LAW

~§ When I'm bored, or anxious, or anything troublesome arises (if it's worth troubling about), I say "I must consult my partner." When I say partner I mean ELSE, that strategic ampersand on my office door. It isn't an anonym, that's really her name, Zoe Else. She's more than my partner; financially she's my sponsor. Intellectually, something much more complicated. She'll be amused, in these notes, to see me try to speak with such counterfeit reserve. So cold a letter!

I never phone her from the office; her only phobia is that someone illicit might learn her unlisted number. Only very confident women feel that way. Even shrewd little Tally doesn't know that when I say I must go out, it means I'm bound for the booth at the Celebrity Bar, to call Zoe.

Women are the true detectives. Zoe Else divined my real worth and encouraged me in my left-hand or sinister profession. She has made herself a lot of dough in her own work; it was my bewildered simplicity, I guess, that suggested to her to be my financier, my beamtipper, my clear conscience. Often we rage, wrangle, and rasputin with ourselves, but when I need to know she tells me. She rarely comes to the office; she says she couldn't bear a safe with swans painted onto it. I know what she means. She means she couldn't bear the screen I have put for Miss Tally to dodge behind when she pulls anything up or down. Zoe would say, or more likely not say, that she loathes anything overt. So

36

when I phone her I do it outside, which keeps it always what ecstasy should be, a conjure, a conspiracy. The only other woman I ever noticed her getting matey with is Mealie. They understand each other perfectly.

I call her unlisted number. It strikes me that a lot of people must have learned it somehow, so often when I phone the wire's busy. But hearken, I say to myself, hasn't she a right to her own life? Even if it's only (as I hope) the Naborhood Market or Liquor Store? We all have that right, and how rarely exercised. So I wait, sitting one-ham on the padded bar-stool, and surprise the barman by finishing the half-bottle of soda plain.

When I'm full of thalamus and thyroid, or just plain human hungry (which few are coarse enough to admit) I consult my sponsor. She can be harsh with me (as I can with myself, so I don't need it as much as she thinks), but she knows when I need help. She gives it first, afterward tells me why I shouldn't have needed it.

I went to the bank; Miss Tally must have her cash envelope. While waiting for the teller to disburse those complex payroll accounts that are always in line ahead of me, I was saying Zoe's mystic number in my head. I'm always afraid I might say, when I get to the window, Give me Eldorado five 20's five 10's, and five one's (or some such anomaly). If there were any record of the things people think to themselves while shuffling in line at the Prune Exchange Bank, historians would be appalled. Historians are appalled anyhow. I remember how grieved a wiseacre at Columbia was when I said that the two greatest ghost stories came from Cambridge and Oxford. Cambridge, the Ghost Book of Montague Rhodes James; and Oxford, the Study of History by Arnold Toynbee.

I wondered, as I was dialling in my head, if Zoe would be chez-elle. Usually, if I'm going to call her, I do so earlier. Then, because I'm an old and substantial depositor at that bank, I thought why should I be so timid? Humility, or the pretence of it, is my besotting sin. Damn all, I said to her once, I don't need to be so humile.

37

"Any other man," she retorted (what other man? what should she know of any other man?), "would have said humble, and meant it."

"*Humile* is what I said. It isn't even in the two-volume Oxford; but it's in Webster, at the bottom of the page among the *Obs.*—I'm obsolete too," I murmured.

She was in. She sounded a bit dour, said she had a hangover. She amplified it: "I was trying to grease with honey the poisoned cup of life."[1]

"Who was Honey?"

"Don't be waggish."

"I'll be right over."

"I hear you say it," she growled. "I'm not up yet so I couldn't escape anyway."

"I have to report to my sponsor, don't I?"

She clanked down and I bustled along in excellent spirits. A little snapping and snarling on the phone often means extra kindness later.

She was drinking coffee in her, I guess they call it a housecoat? I used to say *peignoir*, something to wear while combing or being combed, but Zoe said that was archaic. As it goes nowadays or nowanights, it has a practical zipper-track all the way down the front, accurately bisected. Women are so evenly divided.

She turned away from me at the door, goddessed across to the coffee table, and poured me a cup in her most austere demeanor. But it was my special mug, a good sign. Her great beautiful porcelain eyes looked like oysters.

"You look terrible," I said. "Like the Apparition of Mrs. Veal."

It is sound strategy to give a woman a chance to use her resources of repartee. Zoe can always double in Bartlett.

"And you, I suppose, are Corporal Trim."

Evidently she didn't love me. There was no reason why she should. She placed my coffee mug exactly in the white ring where I had once been careless with a highball. That circular stain was

[1]Actually that was a quotation from Lucretius, but Richard didn't get it. Z. E.

38

dear to me, and to her too, but she didn't mention it. When sponsors don't mention things, don't you either.

"I sent off the State Income Tax," I said. "I even thought up a greeting card for Mr. Hoskins." (He is our office tax-adviser.)

"The best friend that I ever had
Is the Income Tax Consultant:
Sharp pencils and a yellow pad
Make him exultant."

"I wouldn't get too pixy with tax experts," she said gloomily.

"I send greeting cards to everybody on every possible occasion, I'm so afraid they may have forgotten me."

"I dare say you're right."

Maybe it was the April noon, or the wagonload of affirmative daffodils I had seen on the street, or escape from the office, I was suddenly in high fettle. I knew it by mischiefs that came into my head and I didn't say. I didn't say (because I had said it before), "If I were raising a really noble woman, I would insist that the first time she goes in unto, it should be with an English professor. I mean, a professor of English."

She would have said (in fact did say, the first time), "And if she can't have an English professor, poor soul, I suppose she might make do with a literary agent." Or she might have said "Tolman on Natural History," or "So you wanna lead a band." Whatever she might have said, it would be subjunctive. She takes it away on the downbeat. Half a dozen women like that could run the world and make it go. When earnest and conscientious man admits himself stymied there will be a few realistic women left. They will crawl out of the radioactive wreckage, and begin looking round, on all fours, for someone who can bear and rear facts. I was thinking this, in silence, pretending to sniff my coffee. All I could think of as a gesture was to take off my wristwatch and wind it. It made a horrid faint little buzz.

"So you didn't wind your watch last night." She was sitting in the carved Biedermeier chair I associate with her more somber attitudes. She has a formal way of silk-swishing one knee over another. It sounds, at high noon, slippery and cold. I've always wondered how women feel before noon, and so have they. Is that why they behave so rigorous, I mean with their coffee? A whole generation of them have grown up who don't even know what it tastes like with sugar. Zoe keeps a bottle of saccharine for me; but only for my coffee.

I can tell, by the slippery textile sound, there's nothing under the robe; I mean, nothing but knees.

"I was pooped," I admitted. "The Long Gyeland Railroad; the Calamine contract; and so on. Tell me, there isn't any legal responsibility for unsolicited manuscripts, is there? And anonymous too."

Wonderful woman! It would have been so perfectly in character if she had said "Ask the American Bible Society." She said nothing; she was trying to build my character, not hers. She went to her cellarette, got out a bottle of cognac (which she never pronounced coneyac), and poured an amber inch in my mug.

"My sweet," I attempted. But it didn't have the right chest-tone. Not at noon in the midday. Not the sort of thing one says to one's sponsor, sitting on the edge of a straight chair. I'm moody about the chairs I sit on.

Silence. She assimilated her black coffee. Those chintzy robes go all the way from neck to ankles; even her feet, eloquent outposts of emotion (I believe like John Donne to begin from the feet), were muffled in rabbit-fur slippers. But I have sometimes a blessing of silence too. I drank my boosted-coffee faster, and noisier, than she did.

For courtesy she had to speak first. "I suppose you're in trouble? Always original."

I saw she was going to make me fight for what I wanted. Without even bothering to uncross her legs (I resented that) she leaned forward and poured herself more coffee. Evidently she was in her Hypatia mood, perched high on some cabala of her own. But watching desperately for a sign, I noticed she left plenty of room in her cup. As though absent-mindedly I filled it with a slug; even more absently I poured another for myself. I always squeak the cork putting it back in; never when taking it out. It's a sort of code. We have so many codes sometimes I can hardly break them myself.

I waited a while. Even Bisquit Dubouché goes into slow potion when slacked by a lot of coffee. But as Mealie's sonnet says (one I haven't written yet), "Build a small fire and burn it in control." I could see Zoe getting a little sore. She narrowed her eyes, then pulled the halliard to slat the Venetian blinds against the blaze of noon. Perhaps to force me to some gesture, she started the victrola—whatever record was left on the turntable from the honeygreasing session.

She has a right to do whatever she chooses; she's my majority stockholder. But no matter how humile I know a cue. Even man, biology's minority stockholder, can recognize it.

I switched off the machine.

"I wish you hadn't been playing Berlioz last night," I said.

There was a flash of almost admiration but she lowered the beam at once.

"Murder will out," she said; but in quite a different register.

I assumed, without any trouble, my most irritating pose. It's my instinctive imitation of that I hope mythical English Professor. "A very interesting and misunderstood saying. It doesn't mean that murder necessarily is discovered; it means that murder *wants* or *wishes* to be discovered. Exactly what we mean when we say a dog *wants out*."

She was a different person. This time it was she who reached for the bottle. She squeaked it. "The cork wants out."

"A woman who quotes Chaucer," I said, "can be forgiven anything."

"I didn't know I *was* quoting Chaucer. I hate intentional quotations."

"To quote anybody shows you know that other people were real too."

She looked more and more like Zoe.

"Why you old sweetheart," she said. "You make me think

things I never thought of before. No one can do more for anyone than that."

(It is a fact, we can have more sport with some minor assiduity of grammar or philology than most people with a tureen of Spanish fly.)

All sparring spent, we were approaching simplicity. "Listen, Zoe, I came for truth, not witcrack."

That, she knew, was code. In real trouble we go back to cognac, or gin, eked out with a little Shakespeare. The reason I keep that copy in the safe, when she was disturbed about the epicene phases of the Sonnets she went through them and normalized the pronouns. When Shakespeare seemed to be wooing a man (as he was) she changed all the hims to hers.

"Okay," she said. "Benedick. Act Five. *Much Ado.*"

I raised my eyebrows toward the sofa. Without more ado we knew exactly what we didn't need to say. Still there are ways of not saying it.

"I've got to do a little falling on my own sword," I bleated.

"I hope you've sharpened it."

It's the opposite of what I am told they do in psychiatry. She lies on the couch; I sit in a chair behind her, turned away, so neither can see the other. But she's the analyst and I'm the patient; for a while, anyhow. If she falls asleep (sometimes she does while I maunder) I know everything's all right. If what I tell her worries her, she stays awake. The formula is:—

> If I'm lousy
> You stay awake,
> If you get drowsy
> Everything's jake.

We call that Tolman's Law; it has solved some of our toughest cases. I said to her once, I can't lie to anyone when she's horizontal. (Faces are so lovely sideways.)—The conjugation of *lie* (she whispered: Zoe has a penetrating whisper) is very anomalous. Is it lie, lied, lied? Or lie, lay, laid?

"Use two question marks," I suggested. "For us both."

42

Now it's too late, and I've been looking through that copy of Shakespeare in the safe, I see how many fatally appropriate things I might have quoted sideways. That time we spent the whole night quarrelling: how gloriously savage she was, anger and misery all down her wonderful pale thighs, crouched and muscled for angry leaping, whether to or fro. Then in the wet grisly morning we woke and yearned one to another until she remembered we were still angry. I should have said, sonnet 90, *Give not a windy night a rainy morrow.*—Probably all we did say, either one of us, was *Skip it.*

One more squeak perhaps, to take the coffee taste out of the dregs, and she lay down quickly. I pulled the beige blanket over her, so I wouldn't think of her as anything but sponsor; and I took the straight hard chair, averted behind the sofa. I turned my thoughts away too. *The Sofa*—William Cowper— the Stricken Deer—died in 1800—couldn't bear the nineteenth century—the nineteenth was the Common Man's chance for a Century but he lost it—Cowper went mad too—I refuse to pronounce him Cooper—that professor of English probably did——

She shrugged herself comfortable under the heavy blanket. "Tell me about it," she whispered.

I knew now that I had been pushing myself too hard all morning. Goodness, those forsythias alone were enough to have exhausted one's acceptance for the day. Here, at the sill of candor, the stupidest of everything came blunting down on me. No, my sword wasn't sharp enough. Because the Calamine contract had only offered 40 per cent of book club rights to my client that was all that came to confession.

"I find I'm only about 40 per cent interested in most of what I'm doing," I mumbled. "Worse still, so is the author. What happens when you have a transaction in which each party is only $\frac{2}{5}$ interested? Do $\frac{2}{5}$ and $\frac{2}{5}$ make $\frac{4}{5}$?"

She was slow to answer; at first I thought, hopefully, maybe she was drowsy.

"$\frac{2}{5}$ and $\frac{2}{5}$ make $\frac{4}{25}$," she said. "Frustration doesn't add, it multiplies."

"You mean that I'm only about 16 per cent efficient."

I could almost hear her not saying "You don't need to tell me what I mean." But her not saying it released me from nervousness. How wonderful, and maybe how rare, to watch kindness coming softly up over the sharp horizon of a woman's mind. Anger is so much more sudden and spectacular.

"16 per cent efficient would be miraculous for a steam engine," I mused. "I suppose it's not good enough for a human being."

She remained silent. I wanted to turn round and see what she looked like. Even under that woolly blanket I might have guessed the general (evenly bisected) outline. But I didn't. I have my victories too. I burst like a clown through my paper hoop.

"I take the train to Town, it goes through the tunnel faster and faster. Shockingly, terribly fast, it roars and screams down that horrible tube. Fundibular! Even the engineer I'm damn sure isn't in control. It reels and rolls and rocks and riots. It's not right anything should go like that. You know my motto: everything is everything. Any and every mortal experience is a parable of everything else. If a train goes like that, then the Department of State, or *Pravda*, or the C.I.O., can go like that too. People's minds can go like that. Economics can go like that. Proofreaders and parsons and senators can go like that; bowels, loins, ovaries —but even the Fallopian tubes have a slow-down device?"

"Just the opposite, I think."

She may be right. She knows more physiology than I do, because (as I enjoy telling her) she has more? Perhaps that's not so; but what is? Man is more complicated than woman can afford to admit.

She knew what I was thinking. She said (it's one of our codes), "Let's not be morbid."

"I am morbid," I said angrily. (I hadn't even noticed anger creeping up on me.) "I'm a sick man; everybody is. When I got to Penn Station I was so shattered I had to go to the bathroom. I mean really; a nickel in the slot."

44

Zoe murmured something, so gently that I didn't hear; but I guessed the purport. Only God knows what terrible things nice people say to each other. You can't reach the frontier of comedy until you have passed the formal black-and-white customs turnpike of shame.

She was so eloquently silent that I broke my rule and looked backward to reassure myself she might have gone asleep. She hadn't. Her stoic attitude (even the heavy rug couldn't hide the truth that she's bifurcated) showed me how tedious man's reminiscence can be to an intensified female. I decided, which is fatal to analysis, to cut it short.

"I don't seem to be good at saying things today. I could write you about it. When I get home I'll write you a letter."

"I'm damned if you will. You're going to take me out tonight. We'll go to the Grillparzer Club and give you a good purge. Your mind needs a blockbuster."

Somehow that did break the block in my thinking. I struggled through.

"When I take the train," I said, "I see a man who enchants and fascinates me. He's unique among commuters because he minds his own business, he pays no attention to anyone, he won't even nod or say Good Morning. Even if the morning really is good he won't say it. You know how I am, I admit it's silly, I'm accustomed to people liking me, or at least pretending to. They say hullo and we spill a little innocent chatter. We say things we don't even believe, just to be folksy, then fly apart like United Nations delegates. I figure it's the tax one pays for being a member of the human race. Then I see this silent evasive godlike creature. I think he rides somewhere secretly far ahead, introvert and incommunicado. He dances before me up those graveyard stairs, celeritous on his own concern, too pure to say me howdy. He makes me conscious of myself, and that's bad. Usually, in my dumb routine, I get along swell without conscious mind. This bird looks and acts the way I'd like to but was never smart enough. He makes me feel ashamed, and that's not good for me. Is it?"

Zoe was silent long enough for me to feel that it probably is good for me.

"It's not just on the train, either," I continued. "I see him crossing streets, going to the office, on the way to the bank, questing a taxi, always when I'm full of busywork. It has me worried."

It's dangerous to make any kind of statement to Zoe; she asks the culminating (or fulminating) question.

"What has?" she said quietly.

I did something that is very unprofessional for a Literary Agent. I quoted without giving credit. I quoted Miss Tally.

"He looks so sure of himself."

Zoe said nothing.

"What has he got that I haven't got?" I blurted. "In this demogorgon democracy, how can a man be as happy as that?"

Zoe said nothing, and after waiting a while I broke the rules. I kneeled down beside her to hear her verdict. I leaned my head on her until I feared it might be too heavy, but still her breathing was shallow and unperturbed.

"How can he?" I repeated, putting as much tone as I could into such short syllables.

"Is he real?" she murmured. I think she was almost asleep, for she whispered from the upper sternum and without any mammalian surge.

That really shook me. Did she mean, had I dreamed or invented a phantom? But she knows that I have no invention and no imagination.

"I think perhaps he's more real than I am," I mumbled sadly.

"Tell him to come up and see me sometime," she breathed.

GRAND CENTRAL VESPERS

&ℐ Zoe had work to do that afternoon; she had appointments with patients at her office (she's a psychiatrist, and a very successful one) and I knew that must involve a special make-up and a perfection of severe *tailleur*. She is too professional to tell me anything about her practice or her patients, nor would I wish to hear it; but one gets one's notions. I suspect that powder and liprouge and fingernails and shoes and skirt and bust, all the technology of gender, must be adapted to the woes and weakness of the customer? Even Pontius Pilate, I suppose, put on a special robe to give judgment?

So I left while the sun was still making Venetian stripes on the tawny couch. Reluctantly, because if anyone lies down on it she looks like a tiger. But I was nervous, and therefore polite. Analysis needs more than a couch and a blanket, and Zoe (bolder than old privydocent Freud) isn't afraid to be divulged herself. Naturally she was angry when I began dithering. "That wasn't much of a sword to fall on," she said. "The way to the heart is with an ice-pick."

"I'm sorry," I admitted. "I guess this wasn't the time of day to be analyzed. High noon! Anybody'd ought to be at their office."

"I know I've got to be at mine," she said.

"Well, I'm sorry——"

"That's twice you've been sorry. Once was plenty. You can phone me after work if you feel sociable."

47

A retort came into my head, but I didn't say it. I wanted to say, I know why women are bad tempered in the morning. They know they're a day older.

She got a backdraft from it, though, because she softened a little. I was glad, for the sake of her patients.

"I didn't mean to be sharp," she said. "It was my own fault, I listened to the morning housewife programs."

"That sort of thing can poison you for hours," I said, but I waited at the door so she could have the last word.

"Try to forget yourself. You need a vacation."

I saw that wagonload of daffodils again, and in a florist's window branches of dogwood freshly sprinkled. On the dogwood twigs are crystal drops (I said to myself), And beer is made from female hops; The daffodil has a golden ovary, And give my love to Madame Bovary.

I could hear Zoe ribbing me. I don't know anyone, she said once, has more fun thinking verse than you do. It's a pity the pleasure is so restricted.

As if that mattered. I was in a joviality, I usually am if I've been only partly analyzed. This is going to be a fight, I thought; a fight with my most resolute opponent, myself. All my habit would drive me back to the office, to reconstruct the Calamine contract. But what I wanted was just to slow down for a while. I skirmished merrily among the high-class pedestrians of Madison Avenue, wondering which might be patients of Zoe's. If I went back to the office I would be interrupted by all sorts of people whose affairs were important to them. I thought of going to a movie at the Janus Theatre ("always double feature") where the seats are costly and sedentary. The trouble with You (I said) is you're just Not Smart Enough. You lie down like Kipling's toad and let the harrow rasp over you. The only way to be smart is to go and look at people in worse trouble than you are. I went, as I sometimes do in the dark night of the soul, to Grand Central Station. I sat on one of the benches and watched people who Had to Go Somewhere. I didn't have to. I could send Tally's envelope by messenger; if I didn't phone the office, she would close up at 5 P.M. and leave plenty memos. If I didn't phone Salamis,

48

Mealie would feed the cats and put in slow oven a dish of spaghetti (baked with scrapple and cheese and oyster sauce; I oughtn't to eat it but how wonderful it is at midnight). I could sit on a recurved bench (carefully shaped to keep people awake) and watch the men of distinction buying news-magazines. The news they were least likely to think about was what might be happening in their own minds. A desert island story.

I had a momentary temptation to go to the News Reel where New Haven commuters try to forget their troubles; it is a perfect place to sleep; but I might see something dire and important. The greatest Director of all had the wonderful idea of putting himself in as one of the crowd, just crossing the scene as if by accident. It was a godlike idea until people made a stunt of it. Richard Tolman only lives once, I said; he can't afford to be an act.

There's no place you can be so surgically antiseptic as in a railroad station. I sat there, dangerous as a million units of penicillin, and ground myself to powder. Zoe has taught me I can afford myself no pity. Until one knows how much trouble there can be in the mind, one cannot guess how much beauty also. I paid no attention to my neighbors in misery on those rump-burnished benches. Study your own anguish before you presume to relieve others'. If you have no anguish of your own, hurry to find one.

I took the liberty (with myself) to think over some of the thoughts I had been suffering. I thought (since one is first of all professional) of some of the authors whose Agent I never had a chance to be. Can I make up for it now? Ecclesiastes, Ronsard, Blake, Hazlitt, Saintsbury—my Pentagon Building? Isn't it wonderful to be alone when a Literary Agent can really be literary? I'm much too busy to go back to the office. It was in Saintsbury I first read the perfect lyric by the ill-christened poet (James Hogg):—

> Love is like a dizziness
> It winna let a poor lad
> Go about his busyness!

Zoe once played me a black bauxite ballad on that theme. How unbelieving she was when I mumbled that an Ettrick Shepherd said it more than a hundred years first.

Perhaps that is woman's great strength: She knows that nothing has happened until it happens to Her. I meditated briefly about Woman.

She sets the trap before she knows what the bait is.

She has an early spring; Man prays for a late autumn.

I was happy thinking (as Hazlitt said). I'd rather have Hazlitt's and Saintsbury's and Housman's scrap-baskets than most of the complete Works of later critics; the only trouble is that we *do* have their scrap-baskets; but let's not start an argument. I live a long way This Side Idolatry; even Chaucer and Conrad could be corny.—It isn't possible to convey how happy I was. In writing, or at least in print, Horror comes through. Felicity absents itself a while. But now I seemed to have the most wonderful of all gifts, a fresh pad of mind, on which nothing had ever been thought. Something no diplomat or historian can ever have. I astounded myself by thinking, Life *does* begin at fifty-plus. Any joy or triumph you have then isn't just biology or imitation or the green grog of youth; it's the accumulated power of one's own intuitions. If a mind has lived to be fifty-plus, without making too many disreputable compliances (place the quotation, Zoe!),[1] it can begin to be useful.

I have reserves of thought because I didn't begin thinking too early.

Forget Yourself, Zoe said. I really was trying to. What Penn Station commuter except me ever came to Grand Central, just to watch how the Other Half perishes? There is an iron curtain between them (the subway shuttle); and the only purpose of a curtain is to conceal the fact that people are the same on both sides. I saw the citizens of the clock skimming across their thin ice of Time. As when I came out of my office and saw the skaters on ammonium ice at Rockefeller Plaza. Unknown garden gods had set out beds of precocious crocus, and under that

[1]Check! Dr. Johnson on Milton's brother. Z. E.

C.O.D. spring, haunches of grace still twirled in lifting kilts. Those people on skates were as lyric as Yeats, and boys on the streets as eager as Keats. April skaters!—winter lingering in the lap of spring. Everything that ever happens is just a modulus of what some agonized poet said long ago.

I sat fighting for the Waking Dream. Anyone can dream in sleep; it comes by hazard from Apollo or Apollyon; assuages or deterges the soul with cunning disappointments of delight.

But in dream unslept, man guesses his harsh gravelly truth. In conscious life man is equal with dog. He is so overtrained he cannot do his civil duty unless taken out on the leash. He is taken out in millions, especially before wars and elections.

At that moment I saw a parson, in decent sable and starched dog-collar (I couldn't see the leash) bustling toward a train. He halted at the hobgoblin newsstand. I saw him buy, without blenching, a news-magazine. I wondered if like me he would read to fortify his disbelief? What train would he be taking? *The Wolverine?* No, that's later. *The Advance Commodore Vanderbilt?* (And give the countersign.) Could a man of spiritual kidney take a train so brutally named? *The Pacemaker*, perhaps: it's cheaper, and he might think it was called the Peacemaker?—I followed him to the train-gate. It was *The Commodore Vanderbilt.* —I said happily, To hell with the Public. —I've been told that the Commodore never actually said so, but it's one of the most truly spiritual apothegms ever invented. —As soon as a Person becomes part of a Public they're both doomed.

I was still fighting against Me, but I am Me's only mouthpiece. One is almost helpless in a civilization that has to live in labels and do its singing in commercials. I prayed my cleric wouldn't read that magazine, but I knew he would (between here and Utica) and perhaps snap his judgment. He would be at South Bend ("Stops to discharge passengers") at 7.22 Central Time next morning. That, on the New York Central, is one of the Stations of the Cross.

I went to the Commodore Bar and asked for a double Martini.

I was feeling Romish (I can feel all sorts of ways), and I said to the barman, "I want an encyclical onion." It's the only word there is for the pearly volute of the bulb. He thought I was being fresh; I was only being accurate. Never be that; people dislike it.

By trying not to think of Myself, I was doing so more and more?

I thought of Zoe, peeling her patients like onions; stripping off the semitranslucent shells of their resentments. But what do you find if you peel an onion too far? a shrivelled little gland of gristle.

"A double Martini always fills my mind with double meanings." I said this to the whitecoated bartender, but he was too priestly to thaw. If I were a barkeep—I am, in my profession, a sort of literary barkeep—I would pay most courteous attention to any solitary customer. When a man goes to drink or worship alone it means he really needs it. I looked around, I was sorry that ladies aren't allowed to stand up at the bar.

Pull yourself together, I soliloquized. Zoe doesn't like you when you go free-wheeling. Woman likes to be an experiment in free-enterprise, but not outside her own gear-shift. Or do I mean outside her own differential? What do I mean? Isn't it rather wonderful to be somebody who doesn't always know just what he does mean? Zoe chaffs me for my silly delight in impromptu verse, what we call ½oetry .Of course, because she —perhaps every woman?—is an expert in prose. Do women compose extempore lyrics? Why should they? They live them. They walk the calendar with ticking feet. It's too grim to put anything down on paper. There'll always be someone who hasn't got sense enough to destroy it. What's paper meant for? To destroy. *"To destroy!"* I mumbled (I felt like shouting it, but I mumbled it in the deep voice that everyone has for himself.)

The bartender said, "I beg your pardon?"

"Everybody should beg everybody's pardon," I said coldly. If he could high hat, so could I.

52

◣ Perhaps I did achieve the Waking Dream. Mockeries fell away. Outside the revolving glass door (turning like a peeling onion) I could feel other people's afternoon mount steadily up the hump of tension. None of my business, I said calmly, what happens to people in Grand Central. They came pattering in squads and spurts, up from the deep Lexington Avenue subway. The steepest stair in Manhattan; I remembered an old friend of mine (an unsuccessful poet, swag in mind as in belly; I was his Agent) who fell dead at the top of those stairs. If I fall dead, let it be on the way *from* the bar; not on the way *to*.

I could see, like the shadows in Plato's cave, thousands of eidolons pour by, flitting and refracted by the quartered glass door. I could hear the bundles of fresh editions thumping on the big newsstand outside. I could see the papers, still sticky with pressroom static, snatched off by the devotees of Just Not So stories. Through the circling lens of the door it was like rushes of a minicam film. Afternoon, the clockwise dramatist, was beginning to tingle for second-act curtain. The tomtoms of the press were beating tattoo on the tight little drumheads of men's minds. I could forehear the radio programs that would lacerate them when they got home. Still I don't mock. Singing Commercials are just as amusing, just as worth collecting, as the Old London Street Cries that sentimentalists cherish. Preserve them on records, historian; play them again a few years hence. *On rira.* I pray that people may always be able to laugh. It's what makes them people. Surely it's only sheep that always have wool pulled over their eyes?

The barman was more sociable now. He saw I was stretching out my duplex Martini longer than his Grand Central peasantry do three singles. The bar always respects a slow methodical drinker. He saw me watching the Finnegan's flux of populace, drawn and quartered by the spinning door.

"Let me recommend to your attention," I quoted, "the singular epidemic among the sheep."[2]

He was courteous, but not amused. There was no reason

---

[2]"Silver Blaze." *Memoirs of Sherlock Holmes*, 1893.

why he should be. It's silly to quote either Shakespeare or Sherlock without putting a tag on it. But he polished the counter and stood by as though waiting for a cue.

The Iron Curtain was lifted. I saw the enemy rush by, converge, echelon right or left, double onward in ragged platoon. Graceful and grotesque they weave the saraband of crowded places; the well-tempered clavichord of death; craving and achieving disaster in frenzied unanimity. What unconscious choriambic beauty when thousands caper their courses trying to keep out of each other's way. The great silent cry eddies above them: Don't let me think anything I haven't thought before! It's like an anthill. No one should be a historian or even a Literary Agent who hasn't lingered (brushing off his shins) to watch that basic horror. They antennify or evade without gross collision. Glorious insect life! Like the Ancient Mariner, I blessed them unawares; and the carrion of self-consciousness dropped from my neck.

Did you ever pour a kettle of boiling water into an anthill, thinking, Well at least I've put them out of their soulless cominform misery?

The bar was jammed with customers. I was trying hard to love them, with my elbows close to my ribs. People are so disastrously big. Because I had been knitting soakers for my greatnieces, I was thinking how excellent it would be if people stayed about the size of new babies; say the size of rabbits.

I should spend more time with myself because I have such wonderful fun. I was thinking about that seventeenth-century zealot who put a pan of burning coals on his head and skirmished London streets crying Woe on the anxious folk. My own strategy was more subtle. Instead of balancing a redhot skillet on my skull, which must be difficult, I keep it inside. I prayed a secret prayer of thankfulness for my divine Zoe. I kept it chaste, and washed out visual images. Oh great god Terminus, I said, loud cheers that her mind is as desirable as her body. I wasn't awfully sure about Terminus—I think he was a kind of boundary bust in Roman religion?—but he felt worth praying to.

54

The barkeep found time to pause opposite me, and I agreed. "This is almost as bad as Penn Station," I said politely.

"Sure has ants in its pants this time of the afternoon," he admitted.

I remembered my Oxford Dictionary. "It's fun to watch them formicate."

"I beg your pardon?" he said.

I felt talkative. (A wonderful feeling it is.) "If I were designing a railroad terminal, I'd put in a little chapel somewhere, where folks could pray."

The barman went down the counter to rattle a vase of ice. It sounded like Manhattan or Rob Roy (every cocktail has a different sound in the shaker. Certainly it had the dull impact of vermouth). I thought he was too lofty to answer me, but he came back presently.

"My kind of religion, I can pray anywheres," he stated.

It was getting to that time of afternoon, the barroom vespers, when customers strike like trout at any brightly feathered lure.

"You got something there," said the man next me; but the austere whitecoat was not to be drawn. There is great wisdom in the old tradition of the saloon: never talk religion or politics.

"There's a chapel down in the Lower Level," my neighbor addressed himself to me. "They call it MEN. You put a nickel in the slot and get all the privacy you need. Of course people can see your feet, but nobody can't tell from the look of your feet what kind of prayer you're praying."

The man on the other side of me rose from his deep foam of beer and snapped at the hook. "You can't pray unless you kneel," he said. "Suppose you kneel down in one of those booths, the attendant would see your feet turned the wrong way up and he'd drag you out. He'd think you were committing suicide."

Rob Roy leaned across in front of me. "Nuts," he said. "Posture has nothing to do with prayer."

"I bet I know where you commute to," said Beer. "You're one of those Quakers from Chappaqua. That ain't real religion, that's only ethical culture."

55

I was paying my check, near the rotating door, when I saw my mysterious Stranger, William Wisp Esquire. He floated or flitted outside, with the peculiar light agile weaving gait of the Long Island traveller—more graceful, more quietly desperate, than the motley herd of the Grand Central stampede. (Greater pains beget greater prowess.)

I followed, bumping a little in the cross-flow, the great tidal rip of the main concourse where currents of travel wallow and churn together. I had glimpses of him in the mob; his warily tilted head, his nimble nonchalant passage. I could see he was heading for the caverns of the Shuttle; that meant he was taking the classic, the traditional, the incorruptible and ultimate 5.33.

Was I slightly pickled? William Wisp, I follow thee, I said in private liturgy. I could imagine, here and there in the shambles of Manhattan, the faithful congregation of the 5.33 speeding through snares and springes toward their caravan of escape. I was shaken by a horror of the city, a horror of multitude and mellay, a horror of strain and stress. Thirty miles away the blessing of silence and stupidity was waiting; the yellow pollens and powders of April. So I mumbled to myself (in the Shuttle) and, always professional, decided to make Oona Knox, one of my emotional writers, take out some of her too copious alliterations. There is nothing that annoys me so much in other people, and how I love it inside my own mind. Each man kills the thing he loves, when someone else does it. I was in terrific spirits, watching my wrist, when I got to Penn Station and saw I still had time to send a telegram to Zoe.

The Man in Front darted down the stairs to the train. He would get a seat; I would have to stand in the vestibule. Think fast, Tolman, I said to myself, as I seized the yellow blank. Should I say I had been taken ill? I felt rather as though I had been Taken Well. No, Zoe might think that was a transposed gag. Psychiatrists are all too cute in twigging what never occurred to you. They start two meanings above par. My telegrams are instinctively decimal:—

56

SORRY TONIGHT IMPOSSIBLE JUST REMEMBERED SOMETHING
IVE GOT TO DO.

"Eleven words," said the Western Union girl. "I'VE is two,
what they call an aperstrophy."

I rewrote: SOMETHING I MUST DO LOVE.

"That's much better," she said. "Never forget Love."

SHARPY'S OTHER SNORT

◦ঙ "Guess I *will* have another snort," said Sharpy Cullen.

I hadn't offered it because Sharpy asked me not to encourage him. "Stay me with flagons" used to be his cry—like a good suburban vestryman he had picked up a number of rocksalt crystals from the Song of Songs which is Solomon's. Then he decided we were all drinking too much, and adopted what he called the doctrine of rinse. "Just use it as mouthwash," he said. "You don't have to swallow it. Rinse it around and then eject it—quietly, behind your hand, into another vessel. That way you're good to your gums and teeth, and save your kidneys. And you get almost as much kick."

Good old Sharpy, he used to come up every few months with a new theory that would solve everything. It was like Napoleon who tried to learn English when he was ulcerated on St. Helena. He wanted to find out what the English had that he didn't. Isn't it the truth, after we're licked, and it's too late, we try to learn life's language?

"Pour it for yourself?" I asked.

"You do it, old boy. I'm just relaxing. —Protéger la bourse." That is his Franco-American for the bird's second wing.

One of Sharpy's charms is that business (Uncle Sam's business) took him twice to France; in the curious traffic of the quartermaster corps he learned more human give-and-take (and

58

less French) than most Long Island Quakers. I like it that he was really shocked when a Fifth Avenue store opened a Female Falbala across the road from the old eighteenth-century Friends' Meeting House at Marathon. Like a lot of the outbred Hicksites Sharpy had gone Anglican (perhaps to appease Betty), but he still worried about his long row of ancestors planted for eternity opposite that modernist bazaar. He used to go inside the burial ground, secretly, to see the prim little stone of Aunt Abigail, an old vixen who went to earth there aged ninety-six. "Sleep well, old gal," he would say. "Never mind these smart young suburban wives in sunsuits just across the pike. They're having a damn sight worse time than you ever had, old Plural Petticoats."

"May as well protect my investment," he said as he sucked a generous draught of gin and ginger.

"That's what God might say," I suggested, "if He decides to wipe out the human race."

"Not bad," Sharpy admitted. "Who'll take over? The termites? Rats? Fungi?"—He was silent while the gin gently explored his channels. We were on my screened front porch where early moths were flickering at the wires. He moved his chair to see through the panel of clear plastic in the middle of each screen, so the view isn't blurred by the mesh. It's my own invention, as the White Knight said, and Sharpy always compliments me on it.

"Still and all," he said, "God might miss the human mind. We really had something there? I get quite surprised by the things I find myself thinking."

I enjoy an occasional evening with Sharpy. He knows my dislike of anything sudden, so he never telephones. I have expounded to him my theory that the telephone instrument is full of a kind of Graafian follicles (or Fallopian tubes? I must get those straight), and just one random stimulus sets up a whole breeding of calls. He is Public Relations for a big association of steel pipe makers, sometimes he has to stay home to write paregoric on labor problems, a tough job. He tells me

59

(these evenings when we take our wigs down) that Betty always says she'll get out of the house so he can work undisturbed. "But before she goes to Town," he says, "she throws around half a dozen phone calls on impulse, and then skips. Just about time I get concentrated the backwash begins to come in. Never prime the phone unnecessary."

So Sharpy doesn't phone. He writes a postcard (it's astounding how few people know there are such things) which takes two days to reach me. Intravicinal mails in Wending Ways are mercifully costive. (I never give a lift to one of the local postmen when I see him canting along with his leather bag, it would only mean someone would get something he doesn't want, that much quicker.) Sharpy's postcard says he has a mind to come and *visit* with me, wonderful Americanism for chewing the fat. If I don't repudiate he comes on the date suggested.

He knows I have taught Mealie to say, to any casual Person from Porlock, "Mr. Tolman he never call back. Thass why he so peaceable." Less Porlock and more Sherlock, one of my private runes.

Like many American businessmen, Sharpy is a frustrated monk, and more sensitive than his pipe tycoons would suspect. His incredible energy for having fun is a pathetic symptom. Perhaps if he had put more zeal on his business than on his fun he'd have had more fun? He often tells me that I know nothing of the Durable Satisfactions because I am not a Family Man; but I notice that two or three times a year he finds a desirability of making a long business trip into the hinterlands. On safari he always seems to fall in love, or be fallen in love with; which necessitates later tours—to protect his investment? If it weren't for those gaming trips, he says, he would never have any really helpful deductions in his income tax.

I was curious that a man of Sharpy's age could be fallen in love with so often. He says it's because he never travels by plane, which either kills you or tightens you up. A night in a sleeper, he maintains, makes him as supple as a kitten. I think he's been influenced by the advertising. Even a hypnotist couldn't put

60

me to sleep in a sleeper. If I have to go anywhere I always go by plane; except, of course, over the Blue Ridge.

"The American Graveyard," he says.

"Nonsense! The great American graveyard, intellectually, is the printing press. If airplanes crashed as often as newspapers we'd abolish the atmosphere."

He broods on that. Nice thing about Sharpy, he's willing to listen to what you say and figure out how much of it you mean.

"Printing," I continue, "is about 500 years old and is still only bearable by careful choices. It's a long adolescence."

Sharpy is always accessible to biological analogies. That is where historians are weak; they don't realize that we are only cave men who have lost our cave.

"Wending Ways is as close to a social cave as you're likely to find," Sharpy says. "Take me, for instance," he says, and pauses, as any mature person does before confessional.

I had sense enough to refill glasses and keep quiet. I took out my knitting.

"I saw in *Life* magazine how some of the best cartoons ever drawn were on the walls of those primeval Spanish caves. Our social ideas, what you and I say to each other without benefit of clergy, are just our cartoons scratched on the walls of the cave? What is human life but a comic strip? Zounds, isn't that what the New Testament keeps telling? You gotta keep needling people who think life is important? Listen, Dick, when my mind is alerted I know life's trivial. It's hard on Betty and the kids, but most of the time I just eliminate. What is it I mean, one of your dictionary words? Nostalgia? Neuralgia? No, I mean peristalsis?"

Wonderful is the great rotary press. *Life* and *Time* (magazines) were Sharpy's Yale and Harvard, as Moby Dick said. Every man must dig his own crop where he plants it.

Such are Sharpy's cries of truth and pain when he comes to spend a stag-at-eve. I try to keep him talking, for fear he'll sit down at the piano and play the old songs they didn't dare use at his college glee club. To hear Sharpy do a bel-canto of *The Blasted*

Blooming Sparrow, or *I'll Go No More a-Roving* (the Harvard version) is to defrost the New England icebox. Also it leaves my piano charred and ringed.

Thank editors, thank even literary agents, there's no publishing the kind of thing two old commuters, in the glory of middle-age and middle-drink, say to each other. It's a black market in candor. Sharpy was telling me, with gentlemanly abstentions, about some doll he shacked up with in Assignation, Kentucky. He kept mentioning the number of her room, which seemed to have mystic significance. He was annoyed when I said she must have a different room by now?

"If you would fall in love with some of your neighbors' wives," I said, "and several of them are all set to be desirable, it would save you a lot of travelling."

"That would be practically incest. I always draw the line at anything that might embarrass anyone."

"No mature woman is ever embarrassed."

"They can be terribly annoyed." He paused to ingurge some ginball and I saw him dropping overboard large jetsams of autobiography. Even in the confessional, tongue should not choose to run.

"I used to try awfully hard to be wicked," he said. "I don't know how, virtue kept butting in."

"You're quoting Boswell."

"Oh, Zounds," he growled. "That's why I loathe you literary guys. Anybody says anything you know it's all been said before. That must be a terrible handicap? You and your Oxford Dictionary."

"It has some wonderful *lacunae* in Americana," I said. "Aren't you crazy about *lacunae?*"

"Of course I am. First things I look for. No wonder you keep it in the safe."

Sharpy is a Harvard man, but not severely (School of Business, non-grad), and so fair game for riding. He says they flunked him for thinking *Ve Ri Tas* was three words. "I thought it was

62

Russian for *I love you*. Now I don't believe there *is* any Russian for that."

Sharpy slid deeper in his chair. He enjoys a striptease of the mind, vulgar, varicose, and vernacular. "Say, what for gin is this? It really sends me. I'm feeling no pain."

I'd have loved to tell him that both those phrases—to be sent, and to feel no pain—are quotations from Keats. I'm glad I didn't. Sharpy was climbing a high mesa of meditation. I wish I could always remember, never ride hobby on someone else's horse. One man's fun is another man's fury. Also it's tough when a man of fifty-five (Cullen) has to be cued by a man of twenty-five (Keats). Quietly I sluiced him about thirty more cents' worth of the $3.25 gin, and stood by.

"Why *should* I feel pain?" he exclaimed. "I don't got the temperament for it. Zounds, I've had my share? Why shouldn't a man of almost your age relax himself a little? Twice I pull myself out of treading the mill and go off to make Europeans happy."

"I'm sure you did; several of them."

He was pensive awhile. "You weren't ever in Normandy, were you? Boy, how we highballed those camions up the Red Ball Rout."

"The Norman Conquest in reverse. Give it eight or nine centuries and history does the gipsy switch."

"Centuries! Give it eight or nine years. Who was that funny old man, one of the historical Adamses, talked about Acceleration? I don't read that sort of thing any more. I drug myself. Why not?"

Sharpy lost the thread. "What *do* you read?" I asked.

"My week-end's pretty crowded. I mow the lawn, go to the liquor store, check up the car, and drive the laundry down to the washerwoman. Then there's my news analyses, those mimeographed dope-sheets they put out in Washington, tell you the real murder and Molotov on what's happening. Boy, is that somber reading! Then I open up Betty's Book Club cartons for her. She says they break her fingernails. I gave up literature

63

when they started packing books so you have to open them with a chisel. You read books before they're published, don't you? Funny kind of a job. How do you know what to think about a book unless you can read what they say on the paper cover? It must be a terrible strain?

"Show you how dumb I am," he continued. "I see a man on the train, only man who never reads newspapers, he carries a great thick book and he certainly gives himself the complete works. Even when we get held up by some block in the tunnel, he goes right on reading. One day I sit in the same seat with him and after I finish my *Wall Street Journal* I sneak a look at his literature, called *Modern Library Giant*. That sounded good so I went to a bookstore and asked for it. What do they tell me: there's a whole slew of books called that and how do I know which one I want? The chapter he was reading was called Pride and Prejudice, and I thought maybe it would have some dope on Labor problems. I was on my way to Assignation, Kentucky."

Sharpy bridled; I hadn't seen anyone do that since I last read Jane Austen. But the loveliest thing about Sharpy is that, unawares, he is of the eighteenth century. Most of us Americans are, sure and serene if not persecuted by new ideas and instalment thinking?

But it makes us terribly vulnerable in a cold war of nerves.

"It was really funny the way I met that dame," Sharpy confided. "I was riding in a daycoach smoker, having a quiet drag for myself on a cigarette. In comes this gal from another car, so happens she sits in the empty half of my seat. Maybe I looked more genteel than most of the drummers in that coach. It was Kentucky hot, they were all sprawling around in shirt-sleeves and legs on the seats, so on and so forth. The windows were open and there was a hell of a draught, the burning end of my cigarette blows off and goes down her neck. Inside her blouse, right in the gully. She lets out a yell, and I practically tear open the front of her clothes to put out the fire. As a matter and fact I had to spit on it to put it out. I didn't like to go scrabbling into her bosoms. I always have plenty saliva ready for action.

The kids at school used to call me Spitball Cullen, but that was the only time it really got me anywheres romantic. —You can't be formal with a lady after you've spit on her breast."

He exhaled a memorial sigh, and took a long painkiller. "It was embarrassing," he said. "I got some cold cream from a lady across the aisle, but most of the men in the car suddenly remembered they were Southern cavaliers and wanted to help. The conductor and I had to make a screen while the other lady soothed the place. —She still has a little scar there, but not generally noticeable. We used to call it Our Little Cicatrix. She said she thought of me every time she took off her bra. At least I hope so."

I kept on with my knitting; Sharpy Spitball Cullen studied the pellucid emerald sky. I was getting a little weary of his sentimental journey, but glad for him that he could unload. In every man's life how much is indescribable; or, if described, unbelievable; or, if believed, brutalized. But woman, I thought, poor dear, in whom can she confide? Don't they all have a little scar-tissue in the happy valley?

"I should go to bed early tonight," Sharpy grumbled. "I've got a tough day tomorrow."

Sleep, Death's promissory note, I thought. I didn't want Sharpy to leave; now he was well emulsified I might be able to say some of my own anxiety.

"There's a man I see at the station," I said. . . .

There was a roaring and sprinkle of gravel—my new load of bluestone, not yet settled by summer rain and washout—and a smart convertible coupé came ripping up the short steep drive.

"Cheese it, the coop," said Sharpy. "It's Betty. Pull in my horns, Dick, I'll have to go."

Poor old boy, he didn't go in time. Because, after Betty (who had double-spaded her competitors at the Ladies' Bridge) had a drink, Sharpy was fluked enough to soliloquize on the Management of Women. "I always tell them," he said, " 'Listen, Babe, lie down and take a good rest. Get off your feet and quit spooking. Women can do terrible harm if they're allowed to run loose. They always want to do as they would be done by. They want to Play House. Why don't you take a nap?' "

Betty cased him with one aluminum look. "Sharpy, come home and get a good rest."

"Yeah?" said the doomed Sharpy.

"You said you were going to have a hard day at the office tomorrow."

"And a Hard Night before that."

FILTER THE AIR

                                            ⋅§ There is always one pluperfect day in April that I think of as Shakespeare's birthday; which I reckon by opportune weather, not by calendar. A day of pure transparence, when you can see, as in Fitz O'Brien's old story, the tiny nymph of naked beauty inside her crystal drop. ("The Diamond Lens," *Atlantic Monthly*, 1858.) Days like that I take a little literature with my reading and even sulphadrug myself with a few shots of the Sonnets.

I'd love to have seen those tenacious little babyfingers in the cradle at Stratford. It would have been odd to foresee what they would do when they got a good grip on a quill.

My nieces (the Twins, Gin and Ginger) were here for their annual visit, with their infants, so I was thinking in terms of proliferation. In an April garden, all infancies are beautiful, even baby poison ivies. The ferns come up in little question marks, then lengthen to pastoral staves or crooks? The whole process of living is so full of analogies that the commentator has to hurry to say his wisecrack first. It takes a brave man to go out in the garden and just watch.

But no one can take a vacation more vacant than I can. That annoys the very people who bade me take it.

April sharpens her colored pencils and writes fresh palimpsest on the wrinkled brown parchment of last winter. Sometimes a Cold Front comes down suddenly, a blanche or blench of frosty Presbyterian ozone from Canada, most bipartisan of climates.

"Just the same," says Sharpy, who goes up the Saguenay every summer to fish, and feed gnats, "Canadians are lucky; they wear ear-muffs half the year."

April should be like *Aucassin and Nicolette*, dappled with impromptu lyrics. "Thus say they, thus sing they, thus tell they the tale." I mosey about my ragged garden, and when I am doing nothing I hate to be interrupted. I quote, or invent, verses for myself. If the phone shrills like hyla pickeringi or Mrs. Pikestaffe, I hide behind the woodpile and let Mealie deal with it. That is build-up for her, and sometimes it's good even for an Agent to play Hard to Get.

Days when old Topsoil the jobbing gardener comes to mow and trim are one long hide-and-seek. I keep curvetting round the garage to avoid being talked to. Topsolito can stretch Good Morning into ¼ hour, a regular Thomas Wolfe among soliloquists.

"You can't blame him," Mealie says. "Every minute he spend in social conversation worth to him about two cents cash. If you not slick enough to duck, it's you own futility. Hard-laboring man, his time and life and forty grandchildren, he deserve every two cents' worth. You can always sneak sideways, they ain't any man got so many hiding places in one acre of ground."

"It cost me thirty cents to hear about his wife's bladder trouble."

"It's those Europeans drink too much wine. Thass what hygienic about colored people, they drink nothing but hard liquors, pass out before they do themselves harm."

"Mealie, did you phone the plumber about the noise in the pipes?"

"He say those pipes is pledged to rumble. We got to get harden to it."

My idea of a vacation is when words—my own, or better men's—come to me with delight (and not for sale). One of the few times cool genius has reached us in print, in our age of cat-fever, was the opening lines of Eliot's *The Waste Land*: I was mumbling them, down in my own waste land, the vegetable patch too shady to yield anything but half-grown onions, savoring the linking and suspending participles:—

> April is the cruelest month, breeding
> Lilacs out of the dead land, mixing
> Memory and desire, stirring
> (*The Dial,* copyright, 1922)

"Put the papers on the sun-dial," one of the great gnomes of literature.[1] Bleach the ink and printing out of them. How does our paper-work face up to the challenge of open air and sky? It was in April I had strength enough to throw away ten years' accumulation of expired insurance policies—against fire, and theft; wind, storm, and lightning; 80 per cent collision or upset. I am a believer in Comprehensive Coverage, and in Theft (Broad Form), and Personal Effects and Civil Commotion, but life (my life anyway) was too short to read those clauses in small type.

Put the whole of life on the sun-dial in April. Reckon by sunlight only. Oysters go out of season, and poets in. Away with the buckram men——

"And in with the Bock Beer," said Sharpy. "What are buckram men?"

"Wonderful Elizabethan term for stuffed and boiled shirts."

Sharpy and I have arguments. I like his well-honed commercial mind. He ribs me for having so much fun out of dictionaries. I reply, words are wonderful bait. He knows what I mean.

We were arguing one day about Franklin Roosevelt. Sharpy always calls him, without malice, the Great Finagler. Sharpy says *finagle* doesn't imply reproach, simply means to attain by stratagem what might not be attainable by frontal attack. We looked it up in the American Dialect Dictionary (copyright, Thomas Y. Crowell, 1944) and found the first instance given was "c. 1915–1922 at Bryn Mawr College." This amused us, because my highbrow nieces went to Bryn Mawr; and Betty Cullen to Beaverbrook Co-ed, where, she said, the better ethos was pooped by a lot of crude young men.

"You certainly get comedy out of the most unlikely places,"

[1] "The Five Orange Pips." *The Adventures of Sherlock Holmes,* 1892.

Sharpy said. "Some day I'll buy that complete 12-volume Oxford Dictionary and have the bulge on you."

We poured more white-collar beer.

"One thing I envied F.D.R.," I said. "His intimates say he was a great President because he could fall asleep the instant his head touched the pillow."

"Some Presidents sleep even sooner than that."

We swapped a number of wisecracks along that line. If one knew the casual social gags of any period of history, how historical historians might be?

Sharpy said he was embarrassed when someone in the Electric train asked him what were the Four Freedoms, and he could only think of three: Free Will, Free Trade, Free Speech——

"Don't tell me you forgot Free Love?"

"There's no such thing as Freedoms. Even rock candy has a string in it."

So it was April (Broad Form) and a little Civil Commotion thrown in. April, the chrysalis of next year's filthy January. Frogs sharpen their knives in the mire, commuters hanker for canned fruit juice, Orion limps down the western sky. I didn't want to interrupt Sharpy, who had gone off into a long looping parenthesis about Labor Unions, but I would have liked to renew my argument with A. E. Housman. "Orion plunges prone," Housman said (More Poems, copyright, Jonathan Cape, 1936), but I myself think it supine. Orion staggers backward, like the twentieth century.

It was April, whose colors (in this latitude) are pink and green and yellow; April, when man gets his poor little dividend of being animal. They have threshed out his brute simplicity so almost nothing is left of it but scribbles in the railroad station. It was April, when the afternoon sun falls on the typewriter paper, and any word you put down has competition of 93 million miles. It was April, when 1000 cheeping baby chicks arrived at the Post Office. That was an error; the local animal-husband and grain-&-feed had only ordered 100. There were 900 displaced chicks, like smuggled Semites on the sandy shore of Palestine, refused admit-

70

tance. The chicks were lucky: they can live three days without food or water, and our heroic little P.O. put all other business aside until it could reship those living yolks back to western Pennsylvania. The tycoons' club car was held up at Salamis depot until the cartons were loaded aboard. A vice-president of the Clambake National Bank wrote to complain.

I repeat, it was April. Man was too big for his britches; children too long or too short for their bicycles. My vacation got off to a quick start, because my nieces, those frolicsome twins, made their annual visit. Once a year they get bored with their husbands, their parents, can-openers, book clubs, rubber nipples, and homogenized milk. They come to stay with me and pick up the soakers (Oxford calls them *pilches*) I've been knitting. They go to movies and barrooms while Mealie and I dribble apricot juice over the babies' chins and walk them round Wending Ways. I even invented a precaution signal for a baby carriage, a red semaphore that lifts on a lever and warns ASLEEP! when a talkative neighbor comes along and wants to do pattycake. My neighbors, especially Sharpy, think it comical for a barren old bachelor to be a great-uncle. They have so little comedy in their stricken lives they welcome any absurdity in mine. I was pushing one of the babies down flat (supine) for the fourth time, to try to seduce him into a nap, when a censorious lady paused at one of our Stop-signs. She gave me a Hokinson glare. I could see she thought I was Irgun Zwei Leumi, abusing a Moslem babe.

It was April. The first dulcet Sunday afternoon people drive out from town in their new sports cars, and get lost in Wending Ways. That's when my friend Fr. Balmacaan, at the Roman church, preaches his sermon about our village where there are fifty convertibles and only five converts. They park in the marsh or grimpen in front of my house, because (as Mealie says) they wouldn't think anybody lives here. They drive looking sideways because there is always a girl with a windblown bob in the front seat. They pause under the splintered willow (whose long veronica tresses were dishevelled by hurricane) and I wonder should I go out and tell them where they are. But maybe they don't want

71

to know? Then the dark young man, who wears dim lilac slacks, gets out and fusses with a sort of compact. I see it's a light-meter. Now I know why she was combing her hair a moment ago. He is taking her picture. He stands backing the sunset and I see a pink patina where he is getting bald. That kind of young men get bald early. So did I.

It is what Kafka said. You don't need to stir from your place, wherever it is. Just sit there and watch: the world will roll with ecstasy at your feet.[2]

So my nieces were here (with babies and portocots) and Mealie hung prismatic strings of minuscule linen on the line. Like all youngsters who were in college about the time of Pearl Harbor, Gin and Ginger know life only as a continuous struggle; they never had the old mammalian lethargy of milk-and-cheese-fed Wisconsin. Their ironical cry, as things get more and more difficult: "Is this what Peace is Like?" "I didn't know Peace would be such a strain? Was Peace always like this?" I love women with a sense of irony; I wish I could remember which one it is (Gin or Ginger?) who spoke of the depressing view from her Italian East Side apartment. "Nothing but strings of wash," she said. To which the other (Ginger, or Gin) replied: "I always think they filter the air."

"And you, my good gals," I say, "filter the air for me. You keep me in touch with reality."

"But it's a wonderful street for hot weather," said the East Sider. "There's an embalmer at one end of the block, a gelateria at the other, and frozen foods in the middle."

"And I hope elbows on windowsills all the way along," I said. "That's the kind of block I like."

I read aloud A. E. Housman or Somerset Maugham (they're grown-up girls) while they do my mending. Was that why they put on buttons so big I couldn't get them into the opposite holes?

I can't understand, one said, how an old bachelor can burst so many buttons off his pajamas?

I let my nieces stay only two weeks; long enough to realize

[2]The Great Wall of China, p. 286. Martin Secker, 1933.

72

that other men can be quite as annoying and tedious as their husbands. When they are here I am on my best behavior, I wish they were on theirs. I still think it isn't wise to rub a child's gums with the juice of Oldfashioneds. One of the babies, eager to get more, fell (in straps) over the gunwale of its carriage and almost strangled.

The only answer in parenthood, I tell them, is always be one jump ahead of both child and husband. Especially husband. They say, why didn't I warn them before it was too late? My infuriating answer is, it was none of my business to tell them anything. I was already a crypto-defeatist when they were still in rubber breeks.

Their Mother, I tell them, was my Babysister, a northamerican word for simpleton. Naturally I love them, and their legitimate issue, but without ruth. I think it quite possible that humanity intends to go on, but I will have nothing responsible to do with prolonging such confusion.

"I wonder what they think about you," said Sharpy, "in the fifty weeks a year they don't see you?"

"They idealize me. That's what I need. I require to be idealized."

"I'm sorry you've got to go tomorrow," I said to the girls. "I shall miss those tweaked-up strings of garments, hanging on the line."

"We sure have filtered your air for you," they said.

"Uncle Dick is really cute," they said. "It's a pity he's an old bachelor."

"He would have made some woman a wonderful ex-husband."

"Or a wonderful widow."

I quoted Elizabeth Barrett Browning, which isn't often done these days. "A curse from the depths of womanhood, Is very salt, and bitter, and good."[3] This tickled them. They called for another snort and drank E. B. B.'s health.

"What wonderful poets the Brownings would have been if their readers had any sense of humor."

[3] E. B. Browning: *The Curse.*

73

"It's dangerous," I suggested, "to make assumptions about other people's senses of humor."

"That's what I revere in Uncle Dick," said one; "he has none."

The other, whichever it was, really discharged a guided missile. "The world lost a great comedian when you decided to be funny."

"Dick thinks we just married a couple of goons from North Philadelphia," said one of them. "But Chelton even writes me private poetry, the way a husband ought. Some of it is so fluent, I can't help thinking he might have practised his lyre on other dames? It took him some time to realize that women get cussèd at regular intervals, but then he wrote me the most delightful takeoff on sterile Housman:—

"The moon that moves the oceans
    In cosmic ebb and flood
Can mischief women's motions
    With lunar tides of blood;
So, if you find me bitching,
    Reproach not me too soon
But rather, those bewitching
    Compulsions of the moon."

"I don't think poetry should be so physiological," said the other twin. But that may have been because her husband works for International Business Machines, and certainly never writes intravenous lyrics. He has on his desk the framed imperative THINK; we believe it rattles him.

"It's at least as good as some of poor Housman's posthumous reliques," I said. "Do you remember,

From the wash my laundress sends
My collars home with ravelled ends. . . .
Copyright, 1936.

I haven't any patience with literature unless people can have fun with it, among themselves."

74

"How I loathe that word *literature*," they cried. "Isn't it only what people would have said to each other if they'd had the chance?"

"And then they went ahead and said it anyhow."

"It was wonderful until it became a business?"

"That's what's so grand about Philadelphia: there hasn't been an income-bearing poet in Philly for about a century? People in Philadelphia write poems for their wives and paramours and for fun."

"Some day I'll tell you about Philadelphia," I said. "I have a client there who is a poet. His name, very misleading, is Seldom Frank. He has just sent me his annual catharsis of *Elevenses*, free-verse poems with the syllables all counted. Seldom has never been the same man since he was walking by the Town Hall in New York and saw they were having a Round Table on 'How to Repackage Your Personality.' But whatever package they put him in, he was bound to ooze somewhere."

&§ The girls weren't much interested in Seldom Frank, nor was I. Of course I'm a snob, ever since I took English 88 at college. I still think that Thackeray, for long haul, and Max Beerbohm, for medium-haul, and Pearsall Smith, for short-haul, were the best writers (in English) of the past century. And for mixed passengers and freight, any distance, the deliciously acrid Maugham.

It's agreeable to have around, for a few days, handsome young women of whom one never thinks in terms of sex. Perhaps they're a little bored with biology, since they found it got them into such endless kitchen police. I suggested that, and they said, "Uncle Dick is just a chartered libertine."

I was nervous that evening; I had a queer feeling someone was spying on me, looking through the windows. But Mealie hadn't spring-washed them yet and I couldn't be sure. "Chartered libertine" was a phrase they had probably picked up in their Alumnae Bulletin, so I read aloud to them ("familiar as his garter") that great passage from the first act of Henry V. They were really startled; maybe it was the first time poetry had ever pierced their tight bandages.

"You take literature seriously, don't you," said one.

"Sometimes," I said. "I'm like those babies of yours, just learning to drink out of a silver mug. As a child I was taught to drink out of a silver mug; and, in literature, I still prefer to."

"You get your fun out of it too," one said. "I had hysterics about the contract you drew up for that British lecturer. Poor soul, he had to travel First Class in a Name Ship."

"Sure," I said. "Forthright commercial candor. That's so he could be interviewed. They don't interview anyone in cabin class."

Maybe it was Shakespeare who was peering in the windows that night? He has looked through most of them. But I was getting weary. One of the heavy 4-engine planes went over the house; they converge over Wending Ways because we are near the Clambake Fix where they make navigational check and disperse on great circles. It must have made a vibration—my house is easily shaken—the clockwork rabbit in the pen, which I had wound up all that wet afternoon for the children, fell sideways and resumed its tragic little tinkling (without benefit of copyright) Happy Birthday to You. As if by signal, there was an answering squall from upstairs. The babies were awake. One, or other, had kicked out of cocoon.

"Oh, God," said the girls. "I haven't had a real night's sleep since Butch was born."

"Bed is only a place to pass the time between feedings."

"If you once allow your sleep to be interrupted," I said brutally, "it goes on for twenty years."

"I'm sorry we're going away tomorrow," they said. "The boys are coming to take us home."

"I knew that," I said. "I saw you cleaning and straightening bureau drawers. Women never do that except when they're desperate."

I put the cats away and started to untwist the telephone wire; these are my overt gestures when I think it's bedtime. My telephone bill goes up from $15 to $45 when the girls visit. Their husbands, quite properly, call them up from the road, Binghamton or Wilkes-Barre, usually to ask where their laundry is. Then the girls call back to explain how they haven't had time. I often wonder what women think about when they're not thinking about laundry?

"Cat's in the cupboard and can't see me," I quoted Mother Goose. I turned out a lamp, another hint. The girls were looking round at the neighbors' lights. They quoted one of my family runes:—

> How late the lights are bright
> On Saturday night
> Said Mrs. Grundy:
> People are getting tight
> Just out of spite
> Because tomorrow's Sunday.

There was another yammer from upstairs. The girls fled to the icebox to chauffeur the nippled bottles. I heard them clatter out saucepans and inflame the gas. I heard the meter clicking in the cellar. I have a sharp ear for the tenth of next month.

My Stranger slipped in (I always leave the front door ajar, so if I frighten a rat he or I can escape). "Never tease the young," he said. "They are ashamed of being young, they think that truth is something they haven't yet had a chance to learn."

"And never tease the old," I retorted. "We think truth is something we missed by going round the wrong corner. There are too damn many corners?"

"Tease no one except yourself. Remember even if they're your nieces they're still women. What makes women beautiful, they have strong sense of decorum, but no sense of shame."

"I don't think I know what you mean?"

"Of course not. Language can't keep up with human feeling."

"But feeling loves the hot breath of language on its neck."

The girls were flagellating themselves in the kitchen. I joined them, I thought I'd have a glass of milk too. I picked out a bottle of the lesser lactation. "But I still think," I said, pointing to the brown rubber teats on the warming flasks, "they might make these things more lifelike."

Summer Ycumen In

⟨§ I wanted to square my-
self with Zoe, after the way I had behaved. She buttoned up, or
battened down, a lot of Oedipus complexes or paranoid defences
or inkblots or ego-involvements among the distraught, and was
able to get away for a long week-end. I couldn't have been happier if I were an English professor. We were nicely relaxed; even
Mealie noticed it. "Ain't nobody soften him up the way you do,
Miss Zoe," she said. "He's been awful sposmadic lately."

I suppose that was why Zoe began looking for new worlds to
analyze. She suggested I take her over to call on the Cullens; I
had mentioned Sharpy so often she wanted to see him. Maybe
she was a little bored with me; we were so well squared you could
feel the corners. Also it was long June, those endless terrifying
twilights. I was so full of silence I just couldn't retain.

"I guess you're right, we need a little proletarian relief. What
is it you crave, extraversion, masochism, or narcissism?[1] I'll phone
Sharpy and tell him we're coming."

She said it would be more scientific to catch him bent over.
I didn't approve of that, it was contrary to the code of Wending
Ways; but we did. We walked, in the loveliness of a golden sky;
I was nervous, because I don't like to put the stethoscope on a

---

[1] Richard's use of professional terms was always comically random. But that
was part of his innocent confusion, and I have made no attempt to correct. Z. E.

neighbor without warning. But I could see that Zoe, by reaction from nimble wench, was in her delphic or pythoness mood.

I tried to warn her. "It's Saturday," I said. "The kind of man Sharpy is, an executive, he's likely to be off soundings. I forget what you call it, compensation? or selective forgetting?"

Zoe is too smart to crack back. She just doubled ahead of me up the hill. You were wearing, I mean she was wearing, a canary yellow cotton thing with a white froth at the hem; makes you think there's a petticoat under it, but when she sits down you see there isn't. I would never be certain about a woman until you see her walking, from behind. "My mistress, when she walks, treads on the ground."[2] Everything about her that is movable, moved.

"Lissom, honey," I wheezed. "Don't get too far ahead. You're so lovely when you oscillate. Or osculate."

"Okay, Webster."

"You can't say that. It's a serious legal problem, Federal Trade Commissions have ground their hearts out on that. Can you call a dictionary a Webster unless it's lineally descended off of the original publishers? As a literary agent——"

She said a dual noun that I hope to believe she doesn't use to any of her patients. Just then I saw Sharpy, out watering his garden. It was our great Rose Year; not since the French poets of the thirteenth century have there been such roses. It was the last rubric of a crimson civilization.

As a detective I could tell that Sharpy was alone and in a good mood. He had the hose-nozzle set for a wide gentle spray. When he's peevish about anything he hoses a straight stream. I knew Betty must be away, because he was wearing his horrible old gray dressing gown, flapping wide over grizzled chest and shins.

"You didn't tell me he's a Franciscan," said Zoe.

That's really what he looks like in that dreadful robe.

"It's what you'd call autokinesis," I said. "He wouldn't dare appear like that if his wife were home."

He had his Tom Collins on the sundial, drained it as he saw us approach. "Waes Hael!" he cried. "Don't be frightened, lady,

[2] Sonnet 130.

80

I've got on my shorts," and flung wide the bathrobe to prove it.

"I wish you could say the same," I whispered to Zoe, but we made a mannerly gambit up to Sharpy's well-swept crazy pavement and I made introduction in form.

Sharpy settled us on the terrace, in a rattle of ice and a scrape of chromium chairs. He boasted how his clumps of tiger lilies were coming on. A little too late he refrapped his gown. It has a roll collar, and he has replaced the worn-out sash with a fathom of clothesline. Hence the Assisian aspect.

"Sit down, kids," he said; which was charitable. "Betty's babysitting in Marathon while the young cocks throw folk-tales. If my grandson ever writes his autobiography it will begin, 'The first sound I remember was the clatter of ice-cubes.' "

He pointed to the gin bottle, and escorted Zoe into one of those wheeled and hooded chaises-lounges; the first thing that playwrights buy when they aestivate in Bucks County, Penna. They mustn't be left out in the rain; nor should playwrights, except maybe Mr. Maugham. Zoe wriggled herself deep in the hutch-wagon; while I had both hands busy, Sharpy pulled down her skirt for her. He collapsed into a steamer-chair, and I had half a mind to pull down his. But I didn't want anyone to think me prudish; which of course I am.

Zoe, recessed in the poltroon chaise, was in a mood of deep freeze. So I said what was required: "Did you ever see such a heavenly day?"

"What is so rare," said Sharpy, "as a Day in June?" He can be very annoying.

So can I; and more intentionally.

"An interesting example," I said, "of Lowell's vestigial scholarship. When he said so rare he didn't mean infrequent or scarce. He meant Elizabethan usage, exquisite or perfect or tops. Like when we were kids we said things were slick; and then years afterward we said everything was swell. When we said hot dog! it didn't mean frankfurters; it meant life was impassioned."

"Oh, rare Sam Johnson," growled Sharpy. "I remember that from my English at Harvard. Hot-dog Johnson."

"Tolman is so wonderful when he prates," said Zoe, in her coolest tone. "He's a pedant. He should have been an English teacher."

Bitching mallecho! Her torso was shadowed inside the wrinkled canvas hood of the stretcher; her top-of-the-bottle legs were gilded by the late slope of sunset. I never noticed before how sunset glow creeps always upward.

Sharpy, in his crude way, was all Khayyámed about his roses. Mine aren't so good as his, because he sprays them and all I ask of mine is a line for a poem: *The labile sweetness of the rose.* A flower, I think, should have to fight for itself the way I do. No one ever dusted *me* against aphids.

"Have a drink," said Sharpy.

His house is on top of a plateau, besieged by dwarf cedars and giant mosquitoes. We looked off above the trees where a great silver-meringue cloudscape was creamed and curded Andes-high. The leaves of ragged scrub-oaks were black against the goblet clearness overhead; they looked in profile like little reaching mittens. I wished I had brought my knitting with me, but it annoys Zoe, she thinks it's epicene. I could see by her neatly crossed ankles that she was enjoying herself and feeling observant. I hoped Sharpy wasn't going to tear himself wide open.

"Everything smells *Oh rare* tonight," he said. "Bad sign. Air's too clear. Weather likely change tomorrow. Usually does, when moon's young or full. That's why I'm tired of keeping a dog."

"I don't follow that," said Zoe.

"Every time I tap the barometer old Fleabag barks. She thinks it's someone at the door."

"Even dogs have their established frames of reference," I said.

"Anchorages, we call them now," said Zoe, crisping like a head of lettuce in the icebox. "Every phenomenon exists for the purpose of fooling someone."

"It's nice to know animals get fooled too," said Sharpy. "Or birds. Take seagulls, there was a whole formation of them over here this afternoon. They always spy on me when I'm working in the garden. Betty says they think I'm a dying porpoise."

"Isn't it the capacity to be deluded that makes the arts possible?" I said.

"You've got the foetus of an idea there," Sharpy agreed. "Which of the senses gets fooled easiest? I mean sight, touch, smell, hearing, tasting, or what have you?" (Zoe shuddered at the "what have you." She likes her small-talk up to date.)

"I'll give you smell," I offered. "Remember when the Japanese beetle was so bad, you always had a lot of those traps with chemical stuff that smells like roses in heat. As we came into your garden just now, I thought: Sharpy has got out all his beetle traps. But it was the roses themselves."

"Correct. If you don't watch out you get to confusing the actual thing and its synthetic imitation."

Out on the terrace was the Cullen week-end reading, in a rolling magazine-wagon. "Good man," I said. "Man of distinction. Remember that, when you look at the four-color advertising."

"I get lots of funny delusions in sound-effects," he said. "You know, Miss Zoe, when the wind sits one way I can hear the steam train puffing out from Salamis depot; that train Dick is so crazy about. But sometimes, in my den at night, I can't tell is it the train pulling out or Betty coming downstairs in mules."

"I see you lead a rich complicated life," said Zoe.

"It's too rich. I have trouble getting rid of my wastes."

"Lots of us do," I said, just to keep him going.

"A beautiful spring like we had this year," he continued, "laylocks and dogwood and pink hawthorn, we're not good enough for it. And the neighbors' kids riding round on their bikes; suddenly grown lovely and shy and impudent. What have we got in our corny routine that's decent enough for them? Utilities Pooped? Industrials Gaga? Rails Sidetracked?"

There was a silence, the tall glasses ebbed.

"I'm glad summer y-came in," Sharpy said. "Spring was too beautiful, it frightened me."

83

I knew what he meant. The shining puberty of April and May; the year in that swelling stage when her skirts are a little too short, or her legs a little too long. Spring, like any blossoming female child, has her exquisitely awkward moment.

Like everyone, struggling and in secret, perhaps Sharpy is a poet. There are millions of people who don't have to get their poetry from print.

"Sharpy," I said, "you're a man after my own heart."

"Not a bit of it," said Zoe. "After *his* own heart."

"I think I hear Betty," said Sharpy. "I better go put my pants on."

IN THE BROODHOUSE

      ↝ I've always been fond
of Betty Cullen; but I don't have to live with her. I suspect she
was once carefully trained not to say what she thought; so she
got out of the habit of thinking, but not out of the habit of talking. Marriage to Sharpy, whose taste runs all the way from
Hymns Ancient and Modern to fescennine limericks, must
have cost her many a second-degree burn. Like most semi-smart
suburban wives she developed a protective lacquer of frankness,
a repartee as rough as it was ready. It was no more a part of her
self than the oxblood varnish on her nails.

  As women broaden in the beam they also broaden in speech.
But to be married to Sharpy might make almost anyone a Wife
of Bath, or a Lady of Macbeth.

  Then Betty found herself overtaken by woman's crowning
chore, the part-time care and feeding of grandchildren. She was
back in the old human broodhouse. Myself, celibate, unfertile,
and unattached, observe these matters with monkish calm. I am
a natural referee, a kind of sensual and superficial santayana (a
name I use as a common noun to suggest anyone content to let
the world go to hell in a handbasket). The astounding devices
and taboos of human multiplication are no more serious, to me,
than the social life of ant-cellars. A man among broody females
is as helpless and luxurious as those leafmould beetles that live,
as contributing guests, in the chambers of an ant-labyrinth.

There is a great ant-metropole in my garden and sometimes I dig it up for study. The toiling ants enjoy a pause that refreshes by licking a syrup that exudes on the beetles' hair. The beetles, when bored, use the ants as taxis and ride round the town on their backs. These pselaphid beetles, by acting dumb, get the best of it. They enjoy the ant-cavern because it is dark, moist, convenient, and well thermostatted. On their own feet they are slow, and crawl like sanitation trucks, eating up the dead or wounded workers. Sometimes they go a bit gaga, break into the nurseries and devour some of the larvae. Just so does man, the clumsy beetle, parasite himself on woman's fierce instinct and urgency.

Or is it the other way round? What does it matter which way it is? I take the dim view of history. It will never really be written except by some old indignant lady of quality. The Queen Ant sheds her gauzy wings when she breeds larvae. So will my Queen Historian when she breeds ideas. The more Old Women they are in spirit, the better history they write.

When you think (I said to Zoe) what women have done by using just a little bit of brains, imagine what might happen if they used them in full.

Women, she replied, are too smart. They know that men don't like intelligent women; and women need to be liked. Unfortunately they've got no one to be liked by but men.

And they would tear the whole world apart for the sake of being liked, I muttered.

She said that I had an obsession for generalizing about sex. It's a sign of an imposed inferiority, she said.

Leave us proceed from general to buck private, I suggested. You forget You and I'll forget Me and that makes us Us?

The saddest of the Forgotten Men, she pronounced, was the one who forgot himself; his own worth and dignity. This contradicted what she had told me before, but I was heroic; I didn't mention it.

I always wonder, I said, what frame of mind is a psychiatrist in while he's writing his book? I've placed several of them with publishers, and they do very well indeed. In fact I get a pleasing 10 per cent on several popular textbooks of human woe. They say a lot of wisdom but why do they pass us through such a Heaviside Layer of jargon? To hell with affectivities and cognitive reactions. And when you want to make anything plain, you have to call on some artist who said it better, in a story or a poem. You remember what William Blake said?

"No," she vetoed.

"A 1000 times No," said Sharpy. Zoe shuddered again, but I was not pleased. When a man shudders her twice, a woman thinks she better take him in charge. I wondered if Sharpy was Maladjusted.

Betty came back from babysitting—which returns woman to the simple sweetness and horror of the viviparous treadmill— and was properly peeved to find her home invaded by parasites; and Sharpy, the old underground beetle, evidently in a mood unbecoming a grandfather. He had squeezed himself into a suit of white ducks and looked like a Southern Senator ready for filibuster.

"Hello, darling," he said, in the infuriating accent of one who never calls his wife darling except in public. He made it worse by one of those brush-off superficial kisses. "How are the little bundles of drainage?"

"Pour me a drink," she said.

"At least the oldest," he explained to us, "is big enough to Attend to Himself. That's something.—Here you are, my dear, slosh it down. Good for varicose veins."

"I hope Miss Zoe isn't easily offended," said Betty patiently. "I don't suppose there's another vestryman in America whose conversation is as raucous as yours."

"Miss Zoe is a voodoo woman," said Sharpy. "She's used to incantations. You make me think of my Spring Poem."

"My good man, spring is over for you. Didn't anyone tell you?"

"Dick writes poems for the equinox, I don't see why I shouldn't. What has Dick got that I haven't? Present company excepted."

87

Silence was unanimous. I wished the shadow didn't hide Zoe's face; I could feel her analyzing like a house on fire; someone else's house. Betty's silence had even more projection.

Sharpy was well primed. He continued: "Days I work in the garden really blow my tubes. I see roses and squirrels, rabbits and seagulls and Jap beetles, all doing their stuff to perfection. Zounds, what form and pattern and outline! And I have to whip off to Town and plunge into some foul merchandising muck."

Sharpy never showed a purer profile against allover darkness. He was practically filibursting the white suit that starched him in.

"What's *wrong* with human beings?" he shouted. "Why do they spoil things so? Every animal is a natural artist."

"And vice versa?" Betty suggested.

"How about the poem?" said Zoe gently.

"Yes, I forgot the poem. Wait a minute—yes—

> "I can't act like a beadle
> When all the birds go tweedle."

He paused and hurdled a belch.

"There's more of it, but it's evaporated."

"You blew it away," said Betty.

I couldn't resist an impromptu suggestion:—

> "I don't feel like a bailiff
> But much more like a caliph."

Sharpy was annoyed. "That's the Good Naibah. Crab my act, steal my show, flush my plumbing.—Wait, I got it:—

> "Things can't be wholly wrong
> In a world so full of song."

"You've been reading Robert Frost," said Betty. "Sharpy sneaks a look at my poetry books while I'm out. What way is that for a man to behave?"

Sharpy can always roll with the punch; like the time he got off the train so grogged and there were no taxis. He tottered

88

to that smart liquor store in Marathon that advertises We Deliver At Once. He bought a bottle of gin and one of vermouth
and had himself delivered with them. He said he would find the
ice at home.

"I know it's not as nifty as those sonnets of Dick's," he
said mildly. "My poems are just personal roughage. But give me
credit for the Galvanized Pipeworkers Decision. Quoted in the
Supreme Court. That was my real sonnet."

"Strictly from Portuguese," I wanted to say, but didn't. Zoe
helped me not to. I saw her leaning forward out of the spinnaker
bulge of that skiff-on-wheels.

The evening was getting anxious, both outdoors and in.
Huge fleecy clouds were turning and sprawling like uneasy sheep-
dogs. "The glass is falling," said Sharpy.

"Fill it up again," Betty chirped.

Sharpy wanted to know if he could put Zoe on the electric
line at Marathon before it might rain. But he turned just enough
sideways for me to see his left eye.

"If it's going to rain, maybe I won't go," said Zoe.

Betty whittled herself to a point. "Miss Zoe can spend the
night with us, if that would be convenient."

But it's no use needling Zoe. It's like needling a haystack;
you only lose the needle.

The dialogue went on, with a good deal of iota subscript.
Finally, I suppose on reasonable provocation, Betty said:—

"I can't imagine anyone living in sin with Sharpy."

"Nor can I," he retorted. "But I can imagine sudden flashes
of mischief. It isn't really sin unless it gets tedious."

I have a feeling he had to pay for that later. Nothing has as
much backfire as a husband's wisecrack. But Sharpy could always
get away from Betty by going to bed.

"What do you think," flashed Betty—a sure cue she didn't
care what I thought—"of a man who really likes to do the housework?"

I bulged with tact. "I'd subscribe to the Theatre Guild
matinees and let him do it. I was doing housework today, and

I surpassed myself. Dodie Pikestaffe telephoned, you know what an earbender she is. I took it as long as I could, and then I said, quite innocently, 'You'll have to excuse me, I hear the phone ringing.' "

That was my attempt to change the conversation; which Zoe, the psychiatrist, says one should never do. Let it flow, and purge itself, she advises. But intramural squabbles are hard on the guests, and I honestly tried to cleave the current. Like the time I crossed the Great Divide between Alberta and British Columbia; Kicking Horse Pass I think it's called. A little ripply creek comes down and splits, one side to the Gulf of Mexico and the other toward the Pacific. A small flatiron-shape stone is the actual divisor. It looked to me hot-tempered Mexico was getting more than its share, so while no one was watching I shifted the rock an inch, for fair play.

But Sharpy was the Kicking Horse himself. He caracoled right back. "I was thinking of the Garden of Eden. Housekeeping was pretty simple until Eve took it in hand. The very first week-end she decided to clean things up. No wonder she gets griped. She has only about twenty-five years to keep her temper."

"And man keeps his twice as long," said Betty. She blew a long caustic sneer of cigarette smoke, both mouth and nostrils, and dubbed out the fag with perfectly timed disdain. No director ever staged it better.

"I don't understand these distinctions," she said. "I thought you had forgotten there are two sexes."

Zoe fixed me with a curfew eye. I rose.

"Aw, say, do you have to go?" said the Cullens, in two quite different accents. We did, and there's still a crease in Sharpy's right-hand fender to prove it. It was tactful to let him drive us back, it gave him a High Barbaree or Low Bohemia feeling. There are so many trees in Wending Ways, you can't whitewash them all for Sharpy when he drives with one eye. And it's touching to see the big baboon pulling himself together to go back to kindergarten and stand in the corner.

"I'm sorry Betty was browned off," he said sadly. "Brown

90

Betty. You know how it is. Women *have* to take things serious. They have such an unfavorable balance of trade. Too much invisible export."

"You don't mean what you think you mean," I mumbled, pushing him back into the car.

"Not sure *what* I mean, but I'll think about it."

"I know exactly what he means," cried Zoe. "Night!"

"I hope so," he growled, jet-propelling some of my new gravel.

◄§ Zoe and I got into dressing gowns and had a grand palaver. We were in form for it; to pursue Sharpy's metaphor, there was a balance of trade to re-establish, because I had exported too much and she too little.

"Poor old sweetheart," she said; I discovered she meant Sharpy.

"I wonder what he thinks he's chasing," I asked. "He must have some sort of spook in his head to act so off the beam? He ought to belong to that club I heard about in Chicago. The members wear buttons with the initials C.A.I.C.—That's really something you could use in your work."

"My kind of work, I have more than I can use already."

"It means, *Christ, am I confused!*"

"It sounds the least exclusive club in the world. Don't tell me you were blackballed."

I have learned to invent a kind of grimace, perhaps a tic, to register the unanswerable. A pang faintly edged with smile.

"I'm glad you're so nice to Sharpy," she said. "I think I can tell you what he's pursuing. You."

"What the devil do you mean?"

"The poor soul believes you have found the answers, or the certainties, that he lost somewhere. He thinks you've Got Something. I even heard him say—it was while you went indoors—he was thinking of commuting on the Steam train."

I was appalled. If one of the Electric Set was thinking of

changing over he must be badly shaken. Suppose he wanted to sit in the same seat with my hardwon solitude. Was I unconsciously acting as a kind of phantom (like my own Man in Front) for poor Sharpy? If the sense of horror had infected that busy soul it had reached far and deep indeed.

Zoe, by turning some of Sharpy's dumbcracks inside out, had taught me more about him than I had guessed in casual years. Maybe it's not fair to exercise this cold-turkey psychiatry on simple folks; some of it's damnably true?

Zoe went after Sharpy like a factfinding commission; like one of those Displaced Psychologists who throw Greenwich Village into a perpetual state of seminar. But I had a nervous feeling that some of her observations were intended to duplicate meanings for me. A night in June can be rare, but not when you spend so much of it talking about Sharpy. Even Zoe can waver under alcohol, and when she got technical I guessed we had both had one nightcap too many. She said (I knew then she was tight) that Sharpy was full of Instinctual Id. Her suggestion was that Sharpy should draw the cards, but Betty should play them. Maybe she said he was Infantile Regression, or Imbalance, or Cultural Lag. She had a Greek name for it. Maybe she was teasing me, but I was still on my feet, though there didn't seem to be enough of them.

"You scientists certainly have fun beating around the bush," I said.

"If the bush is burning, that's the best you can do." She yawned. "Is the bed made up?"

"Which bed?"

"The other one."

"If it is, Mealie's going to be in trouble." But that was only bravado.

"I want to think about Sharpy," she said.

"How's for thinking a little about me?" I babbled.

"You can Attend to Yourself," she quoted. "Sharpy is only a symbol."

I piled blankets and sheets on the guest-room bed, which

hadn't been made. An unmade bed (Mealie knows) is also a symbol.

I'm sure Zoe is a good psychiatrist, she goes off so easily into unconsciousness. Later, the weather turned cold and wet, and I went into the guest room to put a blanket over her. Even an analyst looks innocent and helpless in sleep. The extra conversation, or the extra drink, had put up what Zoe would call a Threshold; my own, and I stumbled over it. Everything had come back, as it always does, on my solitary self. Everyone except me could slip off into perfect nothing: Zoe, Mealie, the kittens, perhaps even Sharpy and Betty, had found oblivion. They were no longer verbs and adjectives; they lay like unconscious nouns. Why must I still fight, or shadow-box, for peace?

I was almost proud of myself for being so difficult. Only those who know insomnia know God? I tried to weary myself asleep by composing a verse:

> Most of what psychiatrists know
> Was said by poets long ago:
> What mumble-jumble they can make
> Of what was plain to William Blake.
> Is there an analyst in the House?
> Page Walter Mitty, or Mickey Mouse.

Sharpy is right: life is too rich for our thin blood. Blood only thickens when it's dead. What a wonderful title, *Dead to the World*. The great titles, like the great truths, happen by accident. That is why artists are so embarrassing; they have no more conscience than an anthill; they'll take the least grain of chance and process it to their own purposes.

I must have been really exhausted because I had a professional sort of dream. I was hurrying through a great crowd in a Grand Central Concourse. I wanted to look at the constellated ceiling but people catching trains don't have time to study the zodiac; and always, just ahead of me, was a man who kept slipping away in the throng. He wore an overall, like a filling station attendant, with a name stitched on the back, but every time I

93

thought I was going to be able to read it, someone got in the way. The last three letters looked like MAN, but even more disturbing he was carrying a paper parcel exactly like the mysterious MS. in my safe. I thought I could recognize the seals, the notary stamp. Had it been taken back, and now hurrying to some rival? I tried to scream, "Hey, that's mine," and could only croak. The vision fled into a subway burrow and disappeared.

I waked sweating and half out of bed. I guess I really do need a vacation. I was ashamed to tell Zoe, but I phoned the office in the morning, just to make sure the parcel was safe.

½OETRY

᷈᷈ I put Zoe on the train —my train—but I was staying behind. I gave her an upward hoist, and reached her the little overthreenight bag.

"This is the only time I don't resent that long step up," I said.

Zoe is too smart to leave on a sentimental note. "Quit pulling the bull over your eyes," she said. "Have a good vacation. You don't know how I need it."

The train gave a rough backward jerk; just ill temper, I think, because I wasn't taking it; but the brakeman caught Zoe in his arms. There's always a brakeman coming through when Zoe is in the vestibule. He's the one they use in the mathematical problem: if the train is moving thirty miles an hour, and the brakeman walks forward at three miles an hour, what is the speed of the brakeman? Almost anybody, including Sir Isaac Newton, would say thirty-three m.p.h., but Einstein proved it isn't so. And I could trust Zoe to prove it to the brakeman, but I could see him chivalrously taking the bag to carry.

"Let the bag walk and carry the lady," I cried ironically.

Fortunately it was my favorite brakeman; the one who has quinsy and can't answer back. But Zoe can.

"Never mind about having gin for lunch. Write some half-oetry. Send me honest reports."

The train shogged off. I could see them staggering forward into the car. I suddenly wondered if my Stranger was aboard.

I was happy because Zoe left me with a barb sticking in. It's good for us both. She knows that when I'm typing and try to write the word *poetry* it always comes out ½oetry. Psychiatry has a word for that; I forget what.

Serve her right if I do, I thought. I went across to the stationery-cigar store and bought a clean notebook. SPIRAL COMPOSITION it said on the label, one of those exercise books with a twirly wire binder. *Lies flat in Perfect Alignment.* Let's not think about that, I said. Then I remembered that the Hand Laundry had some washing of mine, and went to pick it up. I was tickled by the tag, which said:—

Wearing Apparel in this bundle was done by Ironer No. 5. Your opinion of her work would be appreciated, as she would like to do her work as nearly perfect as possible.

I slid into my old car and brooded a moment before tossing an ampere. So I'm going to have a Vacation? I circled twice round the loins or pelvis of Station Plaza, and then up the spinal meninges of Railroad Avenue. It's the Harley Street of Salamis, there are six doctors, a hospital, three dentists, an osteopath, a masseuse, and a back entrance for the undertaker, all in one quarter mile. I told Zoe that my idea of a vacation would be to visit them all and ask each one what was wrong with me. Then I could cancel their advices and take treatment for the worst common denominator. Probably impetigo or gin-and-tonic, both fashionable in Wending Ways this year.

Zoe said: That would be unethical. There's nothing wrong with you that I can't take care of; except your teeth.

I drove so slowly that the traffic light (at the gullet of Wending Ways) was green. (It turns red if you hurry.) I would soon be safe in the curly brainland of the woods. Perhaps I was like Kafka in *The Burrow*, that appalling story; the most dangerous picture ever written of high-mind-pressure. It even frightened

Zoe: I wouldn't dare intentionally recommend it to anyone—least of all to a psychiatrist, swimming bravely in the undertow of other people's horrors—but I left it lying around one night, open on the table. Zoe took it to read herself unconscious. Poor darling, she has to do so much of other people's thinking for them, how desperate she must get when she does her own.

Later, but not much, she came into my room and crawled into my bed. She admitted she couldn't take it. "I'm human, all too human," she said.

We nearly had a quarrel, afterward, arguing was that Schopenhauer or Nietzsche? Zoe and I can argue about almost anything, but we decided to attribute it to Eisenhower and laughed ourselves asleep. But she always sleeps first; a kind of tribute. That was the only time she ever said "I adore you." She denied it the next day.

I would have liked to give her a curtain-lecture about Kafka. Beaten and bemused, man can't carry such voltage. He would rather destroy himself (as he's doing) than admit simple answers, simple truth. And anything that ever is true has always been true, if you can interpret it for yourself. Like the royal jelly on which the queen bee is fed, simple truth might prolong human life twenty times. Why do you suppose Sherlock Holmes retired from Baker Street to "segregate the queen"? He was hunting the secret of longevity. Aren't we all? But until they get that panthotenic acid (the anti-gray-hair vitamin) into capsules we'll earn our longevity the hard way; by thinking more thoughts in the same stretch of time. As for Kafka's *Burrow*, you can give it a dozen meanings: it could be the Mind, the Id, National Security, Chastity, Wending Ways, or the Church. I was thinking this as the light changed. I had to accelerate: a huge tank-truck, jangling its tail of chain along the highway, almost clipped me from behind. I speeded into the Black Forest of the brain. "I fled him down the labyrinthine ways," I said to my old good friend, the suave and never-failing gear shift. For a while I just drove round those twisted roads to see what was going on. Spiral

97

Composition. I felt, as Ben Franklin said, snug as a bug in a rug.
But I went on from there, in ½oetry:—

> I feel
> Like an eel
> In a creel,
>
> Full of doubt
> Like a trout
> In a drought.
>
> Don't squirm
> Like a worm:
> Be firm!

I stopped the car and wrote that down in my spiral notebook.
I want to be as faithful as Ironer No. 5.

It was June, it was cirrus June ("roundish and fleecy cloud-
lets," says the Shorter Oxford). Would they precipitate in
verse:—

> The least last latest trivial thing
> Is what empowers me to sing:
> The labile sweetness of the rose,
> Or peonies, pepper to the nose;
> How, on your memory, imprint
> The sharpness of my backyard mint?

The mint, most ambitious of succulents, pushes up between
the kitchen steps. Zoe used to lie there, in perfect alignment,
blazed in noonday sun. If you can imagine a kitten five and a
half feet long, smelling golden-sweet as spoon-bread, she was
that. Watching Zoe sun-tranced on the kitchen steps I realized
no one had ever written a poem about Woman. I didn't tell her
so, she would want me to write it. She was quite correct in calling
me a crypto-defeatist. I know, even if I don't admit, when I'm
licked. So, since The Tempest, does the English language. And,
I hope, English professors.

I drove around and around; I even went over to the smarty-pants Shopping Center at Marathon to see what was doing. If any historian with conscience would just spend one day in studying his home community with his own eyes and ears, what history he could write. Imagine! What a historian Mealie might be. And how wonderful is a suburb during the day, when all the men are drained off. They are only dregs. Summer, when the children aren't in school, is woman's hell.

Over at Marathon, which is several brackets above Salamis in social Schwärmerei, the baby carriages are all parked outside the bars about 11 A.M. That is something the wastrel husbands in town don't guess. The Little Woman at Home begins drinking long before He does. I don't blame her. Indeed I don't blame anyone. I only wish I had a dictaphone laid on, to hear what those femmes say among themselves. They haven't had any breakfast because they had to do formula for the children; the modern doctors think women's breasts are just sculpture, not nourishment. So our frustrated young maternals, having had nothing but squall and cold coffee, are famished by eleven. They roll the curricle or stroller to the nearest bar, and horse down a Hamburger and two Manhattans.

I parked under an alley of lindens, besieged by bees. They were even dropping their elixir on my head. It was too parable, like being the Only Man in Wending Ways while all the husbands were In Town. I'm wasting my Time, I said; and drove home, where I tore up a lot of unanswered letters I had treasured for months.

Man is mad if he thinks there's such a thing as a Vacation. On my way home I met the laundry truck. The driver gestured me to stop and cried "We found that pair of shorts you lost. What do you think, Mr. Allibone was wearing them."

All I said was, "They were too large for him."

But I don't resent anything for Mr. Allibone; for years I had a pair of his pajamas, heavy South American silk with his initials on the pocket: E. A. A.—Edgar Allan Allibone.

A man who has his initials on his pajamas must be uncertain of himself? Surely you should know who you are by bedtime?

I was about ready to put it into Spiral Composition, how sylvestered and chaste everything looked. The children were exhausted for the moment; United Parcels in pause; young wives out for their midday dram; even some of the neighborhood dogs were getting gray on the muzzle. Oh blessings of senescence! Then, coming innocently to my cottage, Mealie was in misery. "That there kitten, he ruff up his tail, and get caught in the vacuum cleaner. God in Brooklyn, the mo' you try to keep things simple, the mo' they get amplified. I bite it off and put bandaid."

That was the night I heard that low anxiety sound again. My sleep isn't as good as most people's, because I'm afraid of it. It gives me horrid lightning flashes of simplicity. I saw the Man in Front, sneering at me along the road. He was behind a clump of cedars (the same that snows down and breaks off on the electric wires in winter) and waving to me to Go Back and not Take the Train. I was frightened. He threw a stone at me that made a bleeding gash on my forehead. It was so real, I had to go and look at myself in the bathroom mirror to see if I was bleeding. I wasn't, but it took me quite a while to pull together.

I couldn't tell anyone about That Man, I think he is dangerous.

CASE HISTORY

✍§ I promised to report. I'm trying, as you advised, not to think of myself. The duty that should be men's: Don't be a screen, be a lens. But why should I be imbedded in such endless analogy? I went walking in the guts of Wending Ways, I took my old bamboo cane for punctuation; when people see you walking with a stick they feel shy about interrupting, they see you're walking seriously. I found a man emptying goldfish into a pond. One of the lakes suddenly dried up, no one knows why, all the goldfish had to be rescued and carried to the other pools. They had accustomed themselves to a warm emulsion of mud, and now the handy man of Wending Ways, in rubber boots, was goosing and tickling them to swim out into pure cool water. Some of them turned belly-up at once. It was a parable of the goldfish of the mind? How many of my thoughts, conditioned to tepid slime, could live in clean cold element?

Since I saw you off on My Train I have a feeling you're far enough away so I can write to you. Letters, like prayers, should have no expectancy. They should be sent to such infinite distance that no one can be embarrassed. Like Keats's letters to his brother and sister-in-law in Kentucky. They were the divinely casual dysentery of the day. Wouldn't it be awful, except for professors of "English" (the damned euphuists), if George and Georgianna's replies to J. K.'s letters were ever printed. What answer could there be to *La Belle Dame sans Merci?* There is no answer to beauty but silence.

"Nature is also a language," said Hazlitt. (*The Indian Jugglers*, earthworm literature—you can cut off half of it and the other half is still alive.)

᷍ᴥ It was horsinine to take a holiday? The mind, after oscillation, takes time to come to rest. Also, as you used to say, I've been phased by the moon. It got so bad I had to wash my mind by reading Keats. I try to hold some of his letters in mind, for antisepsis; like I hold the toothpaste foam in mouth while I take my bath.

Phased by the moon: how unfair when she is still there in the morning sky. You went through with her listerine-color last night, and then wake up and she's still in the high aloft before breakfast, just a shaving. It drove me, in the tub, to ½oetry:—

> Slice off the buttered moon
> A shaving in despite
> More like, in morning white
> Cross section of French loaf,
> O ribald pantaloon,
> O idiot, fool and oaf,
> What you forgot all day
> Remember night by night.
>
> I wish that I could utter
>   The thought now in my head:
> The moon last night was butter,
>   This morning, only bread.

That helped me through my bath. The weather was so hot I took the bath hot too; it seemed to me that would reduce elemental conflict. There are enough frontiers of antagonism already without bath cold-porcelained up against the heat.

I saw That Man again. Can he be taking a vacation too? He was going down one of those curly roads that I don't know the name. I know that I don't know the name because United

102

Parcels asked me, and while I was trying to think, T. M. disappeared, behind a clump of birches. I guess he doesn't like me. He was wearing a white tropical suit and looked rather like the birches, but he grows straighter up and down.

If Keats and Kafka could write journal-letters why can't I? In a manner of speaking, I am one of your patients, am I not? I'll mail them anyhow, it will give me something to do; and nothing is going to go wrong with my teeth because I hold the foam in my mouth while I'm in the tub. Remember the time you thought I had epilepsy? But you could write me just a postcard, one sentence, to give me a diagnosis?

P.S. I send some addressed postcards, just in case.

POSTCARD

Your vacation is doing you good.

Z.

Zoe Mou: I'm going to write this but I shan't mail it. I'll send you a postcard instead. Almost anything on a postcard sounds like an epigram. I used to send myself postcards to the office to remind me of things, but I gave it up because Miss Tally thought it was queer. She thought I ought to be able to remember things from Here to There.

I'm *not* going to mail this; I'll give it to you some time when you're in the tub, seethed in foam. I never saw anyone who gets a tub as sudsy as you do. Life with Lather.

You could see if I mailed this (why should that innocent pack-rat bear my burdens?) I'm in an ill humor. I'm angry. Who calls me up but Sharpy Cullen, says he wants your address. He says he needs analysis. He says he has been in a very low state and needs help. I know what Sharpy means by help. I need it too. He says he hunted the phone book and couldn't find you. I told him you have an unlisted number, an unlusted number.

103

He said he (and Betty) were fascinated by you they thought maybe I'd get hold of you (what a phrase) some night & we could have a party at Nighty-Night or the Grillparzer.

Then we could all go home separately, I suggested. That was irony.

I don't think Sharpy likes irony unless it's his own. Few of us do.

I went over to the beach today, and lay on the sand, and I smell of salt. Funny thing about poets, how few of them ever seem to have gone swimming. But ½oets do. O Zoe Mou, listed, or lusted, how wonderful you were in swimming. I realized then you are not a person, you are the Life Force, which will always be an Unlisted Number.

P.S.—I didn't mail this, but (what a fool) I phoned Zoe and told her the gist of it. Never tell anyone the gist of anything. As Hobbes said, it is nasty, brutish, and short. Gist is livable, not tellable.

POSTCARD

I have no intention of being a Life Force. You be that, and have fun.

Z.

I thought I told you something beautiful. I guess I didn't say it very well.

Mealie knew. "When I hear you talk like that, all hickups, I knew Miss Zoe goin' comb your hair for you. God in Brooklyn, Counsellor, you can't be so impersonal like that with a beautiful female woman. Listen, black, white, or piebald, they got to be hanselled. How kin a man live to yo' time-and-life an' suspect so little about sex? Sometimes I suspicion you ain't worth trudging for. Even kittens fluff up their pelts to hear the way you carry on. Oh, I know, you full with literary dudgeon, full of deep sea stuff. Come to land, Mister, crawl up on de beach."

104

The slow summer sun chases me round this table. Will it never go down and give me peace? I can't even try to tell the truth; men loathe it so. Yet still I think, there might be some decency in trying to give a picture of a breaking mind? Your specialty?

Cowards do away with themselves in the bath, like that fellow in the French Revolution. But no chance: I was gently soaking when Mealie banged on the door. "Scramble eggs might float, I serve them in the tub?"

I wasn't angry, I was just trying to think?

POSTCARD

Of course you were angry. You're angry at life because it frightens you.

                                                    Z.

Zoe Mou: I read in the paper that hurricanes begin to be dangerous when they develop a rotary motion, that's when the Weather Bureau goes out and seeds them with dry ice. They drop small pellets (or postcards) of pure zero into the disturbance.

Mealie better take a vacation. She doesn't like my simple arrangements.

MEALIE: I figure the way Miss Zoe act up last time, you goin' to live bachelor a while-and-some?

ME: Could be, Mealie.

MEALIE: I figure now's opportune for fixing up. I never did like that habit to keep a bottle gin and a Baby Talcum on the shelf in the Powder Room.

ME: I get chafed; one way or another, they're useful.

MEALIE: I don' like that. Gin for old men, and baby powder for infants. They ain't nothing there for young middle folks, like—well, like callers.

ME: You better not let Miss Zoe hear you.

MEALIE: Nobody ain't never hear me until I'm ready to

speak my speech. Talkin' to you ain't speechmakin'. This just fables in the family.

ME (beginning to get an idea): So you finished up the baby powder? I knew I oughtn't to go to the beach today. I knew you'd be into mischief.

MEALIE: They still powder if you need it.—Set down, Counsellor, take the nerves off your feet. We got silvers of veal tonight, and noodles like they cook at the cigar store.

I had horrible heartburn about 10 P.M., I took a hot bath with half a carton of Table Salt. Then I had an H. G. Wells nightmare, great striding hostile giants were walking all over Wending Ways and I took refuge in a cavern just below Sharpy Cullen's house. O, the rich accuracy and Detail of Dreams! Things we didn't know we knew!

If all the dreams that all people had at the same time were put together, which of course they can't be (there isn't time), wouldn't you think things might be simpler? But I am shy to ask what you really think, because you're not here when I need you. But did you ever have a dream so vivid you had to get up and walk round the room and look at yourself in the bathroom mirror (one of the luckiest mirrors I know, yours, sweet soapy girl) to make sure it was a dream?? Two question marks.

They've put a post box up in Wending Heights, but no one knows do the pack-rats really clear it or not? There is no label on the front, and the slot looks rusty to me. If you don't get this, they don't collect.

POSTCARD

I got it. Quit stalling.
Z.

I was stalling. Of course; how could I tell you how low and licked I've been? The anger, and the comedy, were both part of a sickness. I told you I was sick. I never should have taken a

106

vacation. It takes a very strong person to do that. I never pretended to be strong. I told you, I am a lyric poet without a lyre.

I've been in that dreadful state where everything I see is significant. I can't even watch the dogs or the delivery trucks or the school children go along the road without seeing their meaning and beauty and pure unspoiled intent. I see the kids (especially the girls in their sun-suits) and how can I avoid noticing their growth and beauty? All of a sudden they begin to grow in all directions at once. That never happens to a boy? But girls, how can they ever get over what happens to them, in the glandular years? No wonder women go for psychiatry. They have a laboratory in their own persons. They never get over it. But how they love to be told what a tough time they've had. If I were you I'd charge them double. You probably do. But I never interfere with your private professional austerity. "Come down, psychiatrist, from the mountain height; what pleasure lives in height? the shepherd sang."

BURN THROUGH TO THE STORY

          ❧ I knew I was feeling better when I found myself singing in the tub:

> After the ball is over,
> After the break of morn,
> After the dancers leaving,
> After the stars are gorn . . .

As a conscientious dealer in literary property, always after humming that in the tub I add "Copyright by Charles K. Harris."

I was laughing about the time we tried to sleep under the two-switch electric blanket. You said you were too cold and I said I was too hot and we were both wrong.

I said, We must have got our wires crossed somehow.

You said, How do they do this sort of thing?

I said, It's what they call ohms, units of resistance. You're just full of them.

You said, If we have a nice rainy day we can play in the attic.

I thought it was perfect just to be talking, so I said: Some day I'm going to write a story about a man who was Dead to the World.

You said, I hate autobiographies.

I said, Why, you live on them, only you call them Case Histories.

You said, You're not a writer, you're just an agent for writers.

Nux vomica, I said, and if I weren't so fond of quiet conversation . . .

You said, The only story you could possibly write would be what happened to yourself the day before, and who would be interested in that?

I thought, but didn't say, Miss Tally might.

That was the time I got partly under the hot side of the blanket and partly under the cold, and woke up with a stiff neck. I griped a good deal about the neck, but then I was sawing wood and dropped a log on my toe. My toe was so sore I forgot all about my neck. You said that was allopathy.

If you take time to sit down and think it's remarkable what a lot of queer things you remember. No wonder people fly madly to fresh woods and pastures new for their holidays. As Miss Tally would say, "No wonder people fly; period." I know you detest that locution. You said it had become an automatism. But don't all the logotypes of the public become so? Poor harried souls, the more automatism the better? Do ants and termites say anything original?

I'm having fun. I'll make a go of this vacation if I have to fight it out all summer. Miss Tally phones every other day to tell me what's happened in the office. I tell her what to do about it. The Calamine contract went through! Never be feeble with publishers! Oh Forcible Feeble (2nd Henry IV). I was tickled by one of those subway advts for some troupe of Models; you never travel subway so you wouldn't see them, the *Meet Miss Subways* cards. Here was a picture of Miss Unetelle, says she is "An avid reader of Shakespeare, has a complete collection."—The one-volume Oxford? Aren't people priceless when they talk about things they know nothing about? That made me happy for several hours.

I think I'll ask Miss Tally to come out some day and take dictation.

Urban Block, the young author whose name sounds so

Town Hall and civic, says one of the Reviews has broken his release date and is printing a brutal notice. I said, of course, it's unforgivable to break a release with an adverse review; the publisher hasn't even sold NYC yet. What's even worse, Urban says, the review didn't explain that the book is about homogenized sex, which would have meant a sure 5000 copies from the jobbers.

I said we would sue for $100,000. If we only got a compromise verdict of $5000 that's more than the book would earn? It was rather enjoyable, for a moment, to get back into professional routine.

Urban was annoyed with me, I told him the only reason he is so keen about homo-hominy is, he hasn't explored the alternative.

I consulted Sharpy (we had a snort together tonight) and he was aghast at the complexity of the literary business. He said, Well at least you can't break a release on Steel Pipe. He says there's a serious shortage of same.—I described Urban to Sharpy; his comment: "He sounds like something snapped at him when he was an infant."—Probably a safety pin.

Keats also found it difficult to take a holiday. He went alone to some Island to try to collaborate with himself, but he said the "continual burning of thought" got him down. He wrote an Ode to Psyche, and what the psychiatrists could do with it. Good night.—

᪥ Here is a man, I said, in the crudest circumstance, with a black mammy for tendance, and a couple of bioenergetic kittens, a murmur in the plumbing, and a woodpile that isn't adequate if the Middle East petroleum breaks down (watch it). Why should anything he thinks be worth while (worth whose while?) in such gloomy and glimmering light? Was there ever a landscape so poorly staged for truth? Out of soft suburban plastics, a picture of human ghost in its divine despair? Im-

110

possible. I ratch round, and I say (coward), Why here? Why Me?

And I answer (I always beat myself down, you put me into the habit of it), any place on earth is strange and sweet enough. The pavements of Piccadilly or the banks of the Irrawaddy; Middletown, Indiana, or the Chicago Loop, or the Seventh Avenue Subway—Truth is no respecter of places. But Truth is helpless without someone sensitive to Truth. Like those beetles on the waterpond, you can bend the surface tension film but you dassn't break through.

Bend the surface film just far enough, but don't slip through. And art (even poor Urban Block?) is the enlarged shadow on the sandy bottom, the shadow of the skimming water beetle. Life is suspended on that film of illusion. Break film, break all. Physical death is nothing; the really Blessed Event, release from our carnal horror. Keats, that great unconscious courage, was not afraid of it. He begged for it, escape from the tension of the mind.

Maybe I'm the only man who was ever smart enough to fall in love with a psychiatrist? Because you can tell me what I mean even when I don't quite know myself.

Sometimes I have to take a snort of gin to get a running start. Like those planes Urban Block told me about, on Pacific Islands: the ambulance runs alongside them until they're airborne. I use a glass of gin as ambulance.

POSTCARD

Give me a briefing on this Urban Block.
Z.

I was embarrassed, I was walking in bare feet on the front porch and Sharpy Cullen brought the parson to call. I poured them an ambulance and soon we were all airborne. Sharpy drank a health to the Dow-Jones averages and we talked about hay fever. I said that three things always made me sneeze: roses, rye whisky, and——

Rev. Pikestaffe (a very plain man) interrupted quickly and told how he broke down during the most profitable wedding he had to perform this summer; the local radio station was going to air it, but they had the altar so bedizened with roses he could do nothing but sneeze. All the listeners heard was sternutations. I said, that was the kind of indignity God sets before his children to grieve and pester them. You've got to fight your way over a little barb-wire kidding before you can be salved?

I had sense enough not to belabor them with what I was really thinking. It had been put into my mind by one of Sharpy's shrewd accidentals. He said, the cork makes a different squeak when coming out and going in. Made me think, how much sweeter is the sound of a zipper (on a house-coat) going down than going up. Quite a different cadence, a descending aperitive tonality. Invitation, not recessional?

I think of such matters because I'm lost in Few Men's Land. I used to read Ronsard, and wake up with sweat on my neck, now I guess I'm non-objective.

> I used to burn
> But now I smoulder
> That's how I learn
> I'm growing older.

The host, when I'm the host, always drinks twice as much as the others. I griped Mr. Pikestaffe by talking about Palestine. I said, which is it they're really worried about, the Holy Land or the Oily Land? I reminded him that the State Department had recently moved to that part of Wash'n called Foggy Bottom. I said, the accidents of news report are more significant than keeping up with the Dow-Joneses. I told them of my winter hobby, making a temperature-graph of the drip from front-porch icicles. You'd be surprised how low the thermometer has to get before the icicle quits dripping. At 31 degrees the drip from an 18-inch icicle is still about once per second. The liquid gravity flux is still stronger than frost-potential. There, I shouted, is the whole history of the old political parties. The great frost has begun, but they still drip.

Zoe, I am the only political thinker there is, because I see these questions in terms of physics, ecology, and oecumenical behavior (like termites or water beetles or erosion).

One reason I was pacing gloomily up and down the porch: Miss Tally brought out a lot of stuff from the office, including a pamphlet about Bacterial Warfare. You should see the agents of horror the scientists are studying, where the pest begins. They discuss the varying "suitability" of all sorts of toxins (tocsins?) for annoying (or being annoyed by) an enemy. Botulism isn't so good, because it might be difficult to get enough saboteurs into a canning factory. Rat-bite fever not so good neither, difficult to transmit.

(The bobtail kitten, *Shall*, fought it out with a rat, in the woodshed, I found them both mutually dead. I buried them in the same grave, they cancel out perfectly. Whyn't I suggest to Sharpy that he and I be buried same way; he the indicative and I the subjunctive? Man has as many moods as a verb?)

POSTCARD

You are beginning to break up, using *like* as a conjunction. See Fowler's *English Usage*, p. 325.

Z.

POSTCARD

As regards you and me, anything as long as it's a conjunction.

R.

Man, who invented Plato and poker and paper towels, is now degraded to reckoning the diseases his fellow-man might unload on him. Or epizootics on animals too. Here are some of the ways the next war might be influenced: Dysentery, Fowl plague, Swine fever, Hog cholera, Mumps and measles, Tomato canker, Potato rot, Cucurbit wilt: "the use of infected insects over fields of cucumbers would seem practicable," or they might try psittacosis and rinderpest. For the influenza virus "impregnated house-dust still retains considerable activity." I better tell Mealie that. As a medical woman you will be pleased to hear that Mumps is most prevalent among Southern Democrats, but neither measles nor mumps are very good bacterial war because the enemy would use shock troops that had already had them.

What do they think they mean by "troops"? In any other War everyone will be troops.

Man himself is a disease? A rinderpest on the planet?

But every disease throws up antibodies, often very different, such as Tristram Shandy and Mahatma Gandhi. I know you don't think rhymes are comic, but still like Kipling (as Kipling?) I enshrine on shrieking circumstance the Sacredly Absurd. Nobody ever started a war by thinking things funny? I find Stalin's moustache just as comical as Hitler's. Hair is always funny. Hair is the Life Force's way of italicizing a joke. You should have seen Miss Tally's sideswept coiffure, the latest thing she assured me. I might have known she'd go frolicsome if I stayed away from the office.

᎑§ I walked down to the station (without my briefcase; I took the old bamboo cane instead) just to see how it feels to watch the 8.37 pull out and not get aboard. I really had to anchor myself not to jump on; I saw That Man, he rides up front, maybe there's another smoker there I never knew about? I didn't try to catch his eye, but I let mine roll round ready to be caught if he felt like it. He didn't. He's the damnedest unfolksy guy I ever saw.

When I got back, Mealie—part Dark Angel, part District

Attorney—was laying for me. She pointed (that long dark wash-pan-wrinkled forefinger, like a canned frankfurter) to the ghost of a burned cigarette I had laid down on a book and forgotten. A gray ash-mummy of a cigarette. "I save that to show you what you do, thass what they call fire hazard. Only your lazy luck that didn't buhn through to the story."

I'll give you three guesses what the book was. Remind me to remind you. At least I left a scar on the cover. I'm trying to burn through to the story.

P.S. I predict a postcard from Z. No woman can bear suspense? And question-marks (??) are the old old men of punctuation, bent over with burden.

◄§ Summer is a wonderful time: some of the big plugmen of radio are off the air. But they announced a program "that will keep you in stitches." —The whole damn world is in stitches. Oh boy, wait till they take them out. As Miss Tally said, with her adorable innocence, "the situation has deteriated." She meant the office, she said the In-Basket was overloaded and the Out-Basket was empty. —I said "Let's go to hell in an In-Basket."—

I knew, after seeing the ads, she'd be wearing an Angel-Cake bra, and she was. —All I really intended was what the King suggested to Laertes: a pass of practice.

> POSTCARD
>
> I hope Miss T. is taking care of herself. I don't know what the book was, but I know what it should have been.
>
> Z.

Mealie was in the Lucknow (so I call it, because of the Relief of Same) and I had to answer the doorbell. The usual question, "Can you tell me where Cullen lives?" It was Railway Express, a new driver, poor fellow.

I made my usual answer: "I've lived here twenty-five years and I'm so dumb I don't even know my own address." —That's true, because one year at Hallowe'en the high school kids twisted the street-sign and nobody has ever known since which is the Larches and which is the Aspens.

Well, who does know where he lives? At the crossing of In-Basket and Out-Basket? At the gully of Angel Cake and Treacle Tart?

Bend left, then right, then left, I said. You'll see the name on the mailbox, Approved by the Postmaster General.

Have a drink, I added. The Postmaster General has been a good friend to a lot of Displaced Robins. They all nested in my mailbox. They're much worthier than Southern Democrats and the Poll Tax.

He thanked me, but said No, he was on duty, and he was short-sighted. If he took a drink his eyes would refocus and make trouble.

I wondered what Sharpy and Betty were buying, they had no business to be buying anything, not even on Acceptance terms (those were the Days; ask General Motors, ask Free Enterprise) but Railway Express was off on his toes.

POSTCARD

Quit biting your nails.
Z.

I felt it my absolute duty, when I saw Tally's sideslipped hairdo, to ask her to stay overnight. She would have been humiliated if I didn't? What really embarrassed me was that Mealie put out all the best embroidered guest-towels and Tally never used them. She only used the container of Sweetheart Suavity Tissues, as instructed on the radio every morning. Poor baby. Isn't it wonderful to be so docile?

You wouldn't believe, though, slender and narrow as she

116

is, how much enthusiasm she has. I told her it was opening the safe that always tickled me. We had a joke about that . . . it better be private.

I know, professionally, there's no such thing as privacy. Still, it's comfortable.

&§ What a pity to be Grown Up; you have a theory for everything. It should be just Delicatessen. *Deliciae meae puellae.* How lovely the body is in Latin. English is such a muffled and muzzled language. Latin goes after meaning like a dentist. I ought to go to the dentist.

You got me into the habit of frankness; I suppose that's the occupational disease of psychiatrists. But it really was rather tender about Miss Tally. I led up to it by dictating to her, without telling her to whom I was dictating. It was, I think, just the right mixture of Ode to a Nightingale and Kin Hubbard. We emptied some dull opiate to the drains, and gradually she got the idea I was dictating to Her.

She tore out the page from her notebook and folded it up very small and put it in her bag. She said "I'll keep that so I can read it again some day. Just let me phone my sister that I won't be home tonight."

Later she said, "I always thought it was going to be Sam who would do this to me first, but he's so serious about it."

And who, I asked, is Sam? I bet he's an English teacher.

She looked up from inside my elbow and said "How did you know? He teaches English Literature at Van Houten High. We're going to be married next fall, if he gets a raise."

Well, I was 50 per cent right, what? If Sam doesn't get a raise, Tally will.

&§ Miss Tally put a new ribbon in my typewriter, which I had postponed so long. My notes were coming out so pale I could hardly read them myself. A woman who will put a new

117

ribbon in the machine, that's what a man like me craves most of all. I am too wise to remind you—even a psychiatrist mustn't be reminded of Herself—what you said one time: "You regard Woman as a drug." —Worse still, I said "Woman is only a man with more complicated drainage." —You said, in your most metallic tone, "Wait and see, old boy, wait and see."

➻ Miss Tally was terribly uneasy until she could get back to the office. January 2 of the Year One must have been a tough day for Eve also. Mornings are always painful. I could see Tally was bashful, so I stupefied the craving cats with a can of sardines and drove her down to the early train, just my raincoat over my pajamas. She picked up the paper and the mail for me, I didn't want to embarrass her by getting out of the car in my bare ankles.

Miss Tally brought out the office mail. That accursed advt I ran in some of the papers—you remember, in a moment of frenzy we agreed we should Go Out After some young new authors?—that advt has brought in some excessively alien corn. Here's a letter I got from a young woman in Kentucky. She has written a book of poems and would like me to "look it over and criticize it." She adds, poor sweetheart, poor chimpanzee, "I know I proceed with three strikes against me: I am young, pretty, and a woman. . . . I plan to motor to New York some week-end to discuss the book with you."

I hastened to telephone a reply to Miss Tally, to head her off by wire. But I showed the letter to Sharpy, knowing his sentimental interest in Blue-Grass.

Sharpy said, If she thinks that's three strikes, what would she say to a base on balls?

➻ The merciless sunlight of afternoon falls across my table; I try to hunt for beauty, and comedy (the cruellest of man's frailties) burns me down. In an office in town, at any rate not

118

in mine, I don't see afternoon sun. A double negative, and so am I; I have denied both sun and moon, and mucked about by lamplight. Myself was the only friend I might have had? —*Summer afternoon*, old Henry James used to mumble, the most beautiful syllables in human tongue. I am pleased to see H. J. rediscovered by zealous young men, who couldn't possibly have understood him when he needed to be understood. He needed to be understood, and was, by magnificent great ladies, laced and corseted and Dressed for The Day, ladies of careful coiffure and culture, ladies who would bare their breasts sooner than their ankles (quite right too) and still defended all bulwarks with lacy fringes of fascination.

Think of the woman who took dictation from Henry James. How she must hanker for simple declarative statement.

&§ Something else must have snapped at Urban Block. He is tho upthet he wants to come out and talk things over.

And Mealie is in trouble. She says the station-master caught her son Salmon writing dirt on the wall at the Depot. "They put the snatch on him because he defoul railroad property."

"What did he write?"

"Never mind. No novelty to you, I bet."

"He should write it in a book, I could make his fortune."

"That ain't no laughing joke. Don't think I don't see some of that drainage literature you leave round."

Poor Mealie, then she broke down. She says the Colored kids are corrupted by the Polocks, and the Polocks by the Wops, and the Wops are corrupted by the Commuters. Everybody corrupt everybody else and a decency woman got no life at all. Now the judge put Salmon on probity and he can't play basketing ball next year.

I said, Bring him up here and let him mow the grass for me, that will work off some of his metabolism.

"He always did have too much. I had such hanker for can salmon before he was born. Now they segregate him and he's

119

licked. You know, Counsellor, it don't mean nothing when they write that washroom stuff. It just to get rid of a notion. That's a nice good boy, I used to wash him for bed every night and he smell sweet as a pohk chop."

You never know how bright tears are until you see them on a black face. I couldn't figure anything except to give Mealie a snort of rye.

But life can be very complicated even if you stay home? "We-all get snarl up in a woolsack," said Mealie. "I don't mind to weep in the dishpan, tears is warm, ain't they? But everything seem so good and likely when it happen."

Didn't Marguerite in *Faust* say something like that? That's what is cruel about literature, it says things before they happen. So do dreams; I've had some honeys. You know the big sandpile down below Sharpy's house? I dreamed it was on fire, and I dug into it with my hands to try to quench it, and uncovered a perfect corpse, and recognizable. Yes, in *D*etail; not, as they say on radio, de*tail*. What is this Franco-American push for accenting the ultima? How could sand be on fire? You use sand to put fires out.

POSTCARD

Don't mind Tally, or even Asp in Blue-Grass, but lay off Urban.

Z.

Frank Xerxes Mullaly is the Wending Ways road commissioner. He'll be up for re-election, and he is attentive to the residents' appeals for more sandpiles. We have slippery winters, and Frank is careful to distribute, during the summer, convenient dumps that can be used to sprinkle grades and curves. He himself, like Sharpy, lives on top of a steep hill so they keep it in mind. Me, living in a hollow (lower assessment), I don't get much sand until it washes down off their slopes. Then I go out with a broom and sweep it into a ginger ale carton, which Mealie uses to housebreak kittens.

Frank asked me if I'd let him put a new sandpile at the edge of my woodlot; he didn't say but I knew he meant, that would be sure votes from all the families along The Wend and Alameda. And, if he kept it off the roots of my dogwood and birch trees, it wouldn't do me any harm. I always thought a sandpile the most romantic of all objects. I might go out sometimes in the moonlight and play in it? So I pretended to be won over by good-citizen feeling.

The point of Sharpy being there was that he also consented, a couple of years ago, to a sandpile on *his* property. It was pie for Sharpy; warm afternoons, while Betty is making slenderizing resolves in the tub, Sharpy takes his grandchildren to play in the village sand. I don't know anything funnier than to see him sitting there, reading the *Iron Age* or the *Metal Pipe Journal*, while his grandbabes rump around in the yellow gravel.

I haven't been doing so well, Zoe Mou. I have a strong craving to come back to town. I have a horrid feeling that almost anyone, except you, is going to phone me tomorrow. I am a little pooped after Sharpy and Frank Xerxes Mullaly. But for several hours I didn't think of *anything*. Maybe that is what friends are for, to keep one from thinking.—How are you getting on with my analysis? Do I get passing grade?—I think tomorrow I'll go over to the beach, take dictation from sun and sea and sky. Always a pushover for triple alliteration. How does that show up in a Thematic Apperception Test?

I T ALL HAPPENS TO ME

MR. TOLMAN:—

Sorry you fixed to go to Jones Beach today, everything happens, wouldn't you know. They unload truckful sand on the woodlot, I try to fight them off but they say they got authority. The kitten crazy about it, better than ginger ale cartoon. Miss Tally foam from office, say that Calomel contrack is as good as legal and Mr. Urban Block on superchief to California, he has a redcap call me from Penn Station. You get Mr. Block care conductor train number 37 Room A, car 742. Maybe Altoona about 10 o'clock Pensilvania time where they slow down for some horseshoe.

I foam cancel lamb kidneys Marathon Market because we don't have to cook meat for Mr. Block? But that not everything. Take time, we got scallop-cheezburger on the stove, let simmer slow. Miss Zoe foam, and that aint hay. She say she happenchance on Miz Cullen somewheres East 59 Lexington. Miss Zoe say Miz Cullen push her right into the endzone but she allow nothing except nobody can't have her home number. I agree you can't harris a woman like her. Cats fed, if they behave hungry it just an act. Same with Mr. Cullen, I think. He foam sorry he upset highball inside our piano, I say I swage it up with washtowel and some still sweet. Thanks for Old Grandad, see you after tomorrow. Turn off oven before you go upstairs.

MEALIE

I found Mealie's memo when I got home—tired and clean and salted from ankles to armpits. It struck me that Mealie writes better prose than Urban Block. I guess Old Grandad collaborated. The only writing worth my while is when it's unconscious.

122

I ate the scallops, and gave some to the cats, even if they were only acting. I went to bed. Phone rang about 11 P.M. but I didn't answer. At that moment I meant more to myself than anyone could mean to me.

It takes guts to disregard the phone. I don't often, but try to console myself: our silences are sometimes the best of us. It might only have been Urban Block calling from the station bar at Pittsburgh? If it's really important, I'll hear soon enough, too soon.

Again I think of Mealie: when she's angry at me, and likely she has plenty of occasions, she makes a point of dusting the books in the shelves just outside my workroom. I can hear her (like that dishwiper in the Bible, wiping them and turning them upside down)[1] and breathing hard, just to annoy. I hold myself in as long as I can, then I yell, "Mealie for Someone's Sake will you please quit that."

"I just want to know, do you feel I should quit?"

"Mealie, have a snort and betake yourself home. I need nothing, I want nothing, I am nothing."

"Counsellor, I just want to know you feel like yo'self. They sardine toast on pantry shelf. Also liver paste. Cats is bulging fed."

I kept silence. Then, as she goes down the road, I look after her. She has the most wonderful backward heels, you have to watch to see which way she's moving. She walks heavily with the burden of being Mealie. I pray just a small shy prayer for the good of Mealie, I hope she does for me, and I need it.

I looked out from my window, and the new sandpile (cold wet sand from the Harbor, in a hot night?) was also steaming in the fresh lemon-lollypop moon. I know I saw That Man skipping away, out of sight, behind the sandpile. Must he take his vacation just when I take mine? Maybe he is an F.B.I. or a Secret Agent? But I'm always doubtful about Secret Agents, they show so little secrecy. They used to come here to check up on Gin (or Ginger?) was she loyal to U.S.A., had she ever shown subversive

[1] 2nd Kings, XXI, 13. What is a home without a Concordance? R. T.

tendencies, would it be all right if she worked for the government overseas? To which I could only reply, "I hope so, she's been over there a year and a half already."

I smoothed the crumbs off the sheets, and took a drink of water, and went back to bed with (Never Mind What). My numbskull, my Nepenthe, is the Corn of the 90's. I have it all, from Sherlock Holmes to Churchill's comical *Savrola*. The university library, which has just caught up with that sort of thing, is begging me for it. But I keep it in my bedroom, partly to annoy Zoe. She is too young to need anaesthetic. What are Cutcliffe Hyne or Anthony Hope to her? But to me, they are what Old Grandad is to Mealie.

So I go to bed with a detective story. Maybe people who don't have to be beaten asleep were never really awake?

⊷§ I was hoping Zoe would answer: *Pretend I'm a detective story*. What she wrote was:—

```
                    POSTCARD

        I suggest you do more knitting.
                       Z.
```

How expert she is with nails and vinegar. But maybe she's right. I'll get even by knitting her something for Christmas, the sort of scarf old ladies used to call a *cloud*, or a *fascinator*? I sat out in the sun by the woodpile, middle ground between the ants and the termites, and watched the cats and did my woolgathering with the pattern diagram in front of me. It *is* good vacancy, no doubt about it, but maybe the mind abhors a vacuum; such queer notions push in.

I imagined a dialogue with Zoe when I give her the scarf for her proud and pretty head. I have to think up something to humiliate her, she can do it to me extempore. I might say, I wanted

124

to knit you a pair of underpants for cold weather, but I couldn't remember your shape.

I was half asleep, and three-quarters happy, when I heard the phone in the house. The kitten heard it too, she hissed and shot her fur, I knew it must be Urban.

Mealie bawled: It's that Master Block on foam, he wants advice from Hollywood. He say they make him advances.

Tell him I'm away. Tell him to mail me the contract.

He say it ain't that kind of advances.

Tell him I'm in New Hampshire. Tell him what Gertrude Stein said, Okay is okay is okeydoke.

He say there's big agents in Hollywood sitting on his doorstep.

Tell him that isn't a doorstep, it's a gangplank.

I try to tell him, Counsellor, but he make with a frenzy, say he reverse charges.

Tell him he reverses everything.

He say he cancel you by register mail.

Tell him good-by.—He doesn't need an agent, he needs an alienist.—The most depressing thing about the young poets is that they reached a *fin de siècle* mood before the century was half over.

The cats calmed down. One reason, maybe, why animals are happy, they only think of one thing at a time. Man's trouble is being forced to think of so many things at once?

The cats noticed, long before I did, that Mealie was frying liver. So I folded my tent, like an Arab—I don't see them folding their tents much?—and silently stole indoors. With fried onions! Nothing alleviates the horrors quicker than a slab of liver and a sprinkle of circumcised onions.

Of course they come back later, boring from within. But still, Zoe Mou, one reckons by parentheses of ecstasy rather than by the long bagpipe squeal of endurance?

You said take a vacation. You said accomplish myself by doing nothing. You said report what happened to me inside. It is my inside, but at least partly your responsibility.

125

I believe I have led, and now gently retreat from, the happiest life among all men I have known. I grabbed and guzzled it sometimes, without delicacy or dignity. In those burning wastelands of the night, that purer men never endured, I've had my willywaws. But take it by and large, all and sundry, we have lived our own, our very own, absurd and vulgar joy. We have cried, in moments not exceeded by Shakespeare, nor Shelley, nor Tally, plain expletives of mirth.

The night turned cold. The fire burns low in the hearth; just one marigold stripe between two crumbling logs. Neither gin, nor baby powder, avails me now. The night rocks with the harsh mockery of cicadas and low-rolling stars. This is Evident Doom. Even misery, if told cheerlessly enough, could be a kind of triumph?? I have done my duty in merchandising slop. Suppose, by some uproarious chance, that MS. in the safe were what I always dreamed—pure and shapely as an icicle—a dagger of despair.

◆§ I was thinking of an imaginary man (all my imaginary men are very like Me?) who ate canned tuna and bottled mayonnaise and frozen asparagus, and still thought of himself as a gourmet. That is the literary history of America?

Okay, okay, okeydoke.

◆§ A wonderful day. The phone didn't ring once. I went for a walk through the woods, trying to imagine myself a sort of Wending Ways Thoreau. That's the occupational disease of a Literary Agent: you keep trying to vaporize a dream-fugue of the last Author you've read. On my vacation I read only authors from whom I couldn't possibly make any professional profit.

Suppose Thoreau had a telephone at Walden, how would he have got along? What would he have said if he could see the Concord telephone directory? Call Concord 1775. He would have broken wind heard round the world.

I could hear Zoe saying, Since when did you want to be a

kind of Thoreau? He wasn't a man, just a vegetable gifted with bad temper.

It was lovely in the woods, over in that part they haven't developed yet. The mortgages hang on the trees as thick as Spanish moss. I congratulated myself that I was really purifying; I had got through half the day without thinking anything vulgar; then I remembered I just had. It's a pity I approach my devotions by the footpath of low comedy. You should be a great classic, well morticianed, before you can do that. When I think what vulgar thoughts some of the great writers had, I am glad I wasn't their agent. Suppose you had to try to sell Chaucer or Shakespeare or Montaigne to a Magazine Women Believe In?

I saw Betty at the village drug store. It was just when the school kids are having their noontime sandwich and soda and Comic Book. That is the hour when the station master keeps the Men's locked, for fear of fresh inscriptions.

I said to Betty, Have you ever thought of the Village Drug Store as America's social safety valve?

"I've never thought of anything," she said. "I wouldn't dare."

POSTCARD

Does anything happen to anyone else? Or does it all happen to you?

Z.

127

Monologue, in bed

§ I am trying to look at Wending Ways with a clean eye, as if I were my own guest. As if I were tailing myself like a detective. My own modest routine suddenly strikes me funny, or even ominous. I am amused by Mealie's placard set out on the front steps to instruct the newspaper boy:—

LEAVE PAPER AT KITCHEN DOOR
DON'T RING BELL MR. TOLMAN SLEEP

The village goes about its small doings quite unconscious of scrutiny. There is a clamor of children, bark of dogs, gear-shift of United Parcels (our all-year Santa Claus) rumbling up driveways, the rattle-and-suck of someone's cesspool being pumped out. (O sound of fear, Unpleasing to suburban ear.) The bee at my window nuzzles into the pubic pollen of the rose.

Is it fair, or wise, or safe, to creep up on an organism—even a village, or a mind—and watch it live??

But what I would give to see it, say, through Hazlitt's naked eyes.

Why should anyone wish to live longer than Hazlitt, or Shakespeare? They both got as far uptown as 52nd Street (check this, Miss Tally?) and I dare say it amused them.

128

⋘ Every screech of child and yap of dog at least shows that life goes on; though I tremble and put a stopple in my outboard ear, I am still alive to be troubled by it.

Mealie comes out and finds me in the woodpile. She hates to take telegrams on the phone, she thinks Wesson Union is a cooking oil, and like any good woman she can't find a pencil.

It's a kindness for me to quit chopping wood a few minutes, it gives the catbirds a chance (they have been sitting almost under the ax) to beak out bugs and woodlice from the mouldering tulip logs.

"Oh, God," I grunt. "Telegrams always mean trouble."

"Counsellor so right. Recollect that flush of telegrams from Hollywood, and when they send you the contrack you said it was just rape in 5000 words."

"He wouldn't need that many words," said Zoe.

"Counsellor too good for a world like this," said Mealie. "He got a mind that's fleshy, but pure. How he hate to go through the motion of selling things. Like when my poor husband try to barter me to the black market in East Allison, for a case of bourbon. Trouble was, I never did crave that bootlegger."

Mealie wanted to make a hollandaise sauce, to stagger Betty Cullen. Then she found we didn't have a lemon for juice; I was too lazy to go down and buy one. I said let's use one of my ascorbic pills, equals (according to Squibb) ½ dozen lemons. We did. It was a great success, but I thought Betty puckered a little about the chaps.

⋘ I was walking around the roads and saw the RFD man delivering his grim load of *Time, Newsweek, Look,* and *Dow-Jones Average* (or whatever it is) in the mailboxes. I gave up my box because it was full of robins' nests, but Sharpy's mailbox is full of mares' nests. He got on one of his phobias, and Zoe ticked him off. He was grinding his teeth about the mailboxes; he didn't know, until RFD went through and people stencilled their names on the boxes, how the Electric Side had been taken over by "foreigners." Some of them must be United Nations? He growled off a list: Milchendraff, Assmanshaeuser, Uomobono, Homerescu, Feuchtendirndl, Zenzenpfennig, Potosi-y-Lefferts. Lefferts he didn't mind so much, he said it was an old Long Island family. I suggested Borden-y-Sheffield as a highly desirable name.

I was wondering whether he knew that Tolman is also, if you strip it down to its genes, outside the Blue Book.

You said, "In America, no name is a foreign name."

There was one he mentioned that I haven't seen, but Sharpy said he saw it on a mailbox and laughed heartily: Doppelganger.

Evidently where That Man lives? I saw him strolling the other side of the pond—he doesn't seem to go to Town so often now—and I wanted to ask him, but he silently slipped away. Perhaps he's an Ayrab? That would please Sharpy. How God must laugh to see His Children tearing each other to pieces for love of Him.

I had a notion to go to Quaker Meeting at Marathon next Sunday (First Day) but they might be folksy with me at the front door. When I am really worshipping I like to be left alone, even by God.

◄§ I saw a Blue Moon. It comes about ½-slice through July, when a humid pink sunset flushes the upward reflection of roses wet with rain. It looks like a capital D of Stilton cheese. You know those semicircle cheese-knives, like garden-spuds, that cut through a blue Stilton and leave a little wisteria-colored mould on the blade?

For ½ hour or so, fresh-sliced, the moon is faintly blue. Maybe only while it gets tincture from the roses. All flowers, at that season, are cruelly procreative in suggestion; but the implications of the roses most of all.

I saw a stocky bee, very like a Minnesota halfback, plunging head-down into the roses as though looking for holes in the Wisconsin line, and finding them. Exactly similar to football pants he had great yellow pollen-pads on his working thighs.

Everything, as we know too well, is a parable of everything else; but fortunately nice people pass away without guessing it. They can yammer and yelp about the beauty of a rainsoaked expectant rose without ever guessing what the gardener or the bee had in mind.

The mystics who pursue the Perfect Rose
Must bear the puncture of the Perfect Thorn.

I can't vacation indefinitely. Miss Tally sends me scripts to be read, and I employ my hour-glass technique. Years ago I picked up, in the village capharnaum (no, Miss Tally, not in the Oxford; try Larousse) an old New England hour-glass. It was what the Congregational minister used to put on the pulpit and turn over when he began his sermon. This one must have cost the congregation a few extra grimaces, it takes 62½ minutes to run through. I start it sifting when I begin to read; if, by the time the sand has vanished from glass bust to loins, my mind wanders, I return the MS. with thanks.

Me, I like books that encourage the mind to wander. My thoughts are natural vagrants. Digressions, as Irrev. Laurence Sterne said, are the sunshine of literature. But that doesn't mean Tolman & Else deal with them professionally.

◄§ I had the most ridiculous dream: a bunch of high school kids on a scavenger party (very popular around here) arrived late at night asking for a manuscript by Urban Block, who was publicized on a radio program! This was a literary scavenging party, arranged by their English teacher who accompanied them as chaperon. So (in my dream) I gave them one on condition they wouldn't return it, but in spite of their anxiety to get away I made them sit down and talk about books. I said, "The kind of book I'd like to write would be Chekov's Note Books," to which one of the kids replied—I thought it the perfect answer—"I don't see how anyone could write that except Chekov."

She wore the cunningest little muslin blouse with black ribbon looped around her Brussels sprouts, and I offered her a job when she graduates. In my dream.

POSTCARD

Please don't write a book. If you did you'd put in it everything you could dream of, including the kitchen sink.

Z.

Did you send me that postcard or was it part of my dream? But what a wonderful title: *Including the Kitchen Sink*—or should it be *Kitchen Stove*? I might suggest it to Seldom Frank.

That was the night I had eaten myself to sleep with Huntley & Palmer biscuits, to strengthen British exchange. I can't conceal these things from Mealie, and I heard her muttering "Counsellor sure is God's gift to mice."

Speaking of mice, Urban Block telegraphed "Have appointed you my literary executor."—I replied "Executor of what?"—It seems he has been "signed" by some director of B-pictures. What is the whole earth just now but a B-picture?

⪜ It must be queer to make a profession of tipping people's minds this way and that to see what spills over.

Some minds don't need much tipping. Like those brimful Martinis at the Grillparzer Club, you have to bend over the bar and lap off the surface tension.

But what about That Man who slips in and out behind birch trees??

Slipping behind trees was the first American art. Remember Fenimore Cooper?? But Chingachgook or someone gets us because we step on a twig.

The artist is always taking cover. What he shows outside the trunk is to draw the critics' fire and make them waste their powder.

As he grows older he goes deeper into the wood, where the

trees are thicker. Like a dying dog he scratches little tentative holes to lie in.

The smartest of all the hide-and-seek artists is Death. We don't even hear him call, "Ready or not, here I come."

Birch trees aren't big enough to take cover behind. Even Death isn't big enough.

Death is hiding from you, until you've done your utmost.

Death is a great artist who has only been reviewed by 2nd-rate critics.

Well are you or aren't you going to get some sleep?

I have my own bedtime story, about the Squirrel That Didn't Sleep. When it came time for hibernating he was excited about something and didn't feel sleepy. (If squirrels don't hibernate, my story is no good, so don't tell me.) After all the rest of the tribe were well dozed off, warm in their curly tails, digesting their fat, in the hole in the tulip tree, the Schizophrenic Squirrel was out and around, looking very haggard. Having put it off too long, he couldn't sleep, so he had to beg at people's back doors all winter.

He consoled himself by saying "To the artist every door is the back door. That's where the grub is."

I asked somebody at the Natural History Museum, Do squirrels hibernate? He made a statesmanlike reply: Some do and some don't.

◄§ I took a photograph once—years and years ago—of an old riverside town in central France. It was sunset, and the fortressed medieval burgh shone golden-gray in a slumber of light. There were two bridges across the stream, and I took a chance on a picture from the ugly modern one. It shows the old walls steeping up from the ravine, birdshot with gillyflower and gorse; the high-pitched roofs, the three-towered church on the hilltop; the promenade of linden alleys where the aperitive citizens (steaming with vermouth) walk in their dusty black pants and call their shrill children (shrilldren) to French heel.

133

But the river, "waters stilled at even" (D. G. Rossetti), lay so motionless that the reflection is clearer—more "real"—than the town itself. The hemicycle arches of the ancient bridge are doubled in dark circles. Actual mortar and stonework, even those ridiculous French china insulators on the telephone poles, even the tight-shut windows of the awful stonebedded room where I lay that night—France has been through many darknesses, no wonder she has a horror of Night Air—are more clear, more visible, than the details of the living town. There, in a glass of truth and tranquillity, was Doppelganger Town. So is that evening view on the Armançon River, remembered by no other, equal art-and-mystery. It took me more than twenty years to learn it. That is not long, in the pursuit of truth?? So I can tolerate a hundred Urban Blocks, gaping through washroom windows, on the chance of finding one student of still waters.

I'll have another try. Night now. . . .

◄§ An aspirin encouraged my legs to numb. I can't go to sleep until my legs go first. The bed-lamp was searing my eyes. I closed them, so I would have an excuse to take off my spectacles. The pillow was hot, damp, and compressed. I thought furiously how many people swim off into nothing on their soft swansdown or squirreltail. Can't I afford as good a pillow as anyone else?

Never get angry in bed. I pulled the clothes together. I scrambled myself to sit and looked sourly at the long mirror. I had it put there for my nieces. For me, the shorter the mirror the better. I don't reflect as well as an old French town.

The monologue I prefer is uttered in a congenial bar, with a hand (my hand) on a congenial knee (your knee).

It didn't take me long to imagine Zoe's reply to that. "You are never so tedious as when you are about to be taken short with an epigram."

134

FORK IN THE ROAD

◄§ It was twilight on Sharpy's terrace, he and Betty were sprawled in commuters' flop. I dare say Sharpy had sold long through-put of pipe for he was mellow, and Betty always takes her cue from him. I came around through the garden, not wanting to bother them with a doorbell. "Don't get up, don't get up," I said. "I'll help myself." I could see a jug and glasses on the iron table, which proved to be iced tea well knit with rum. I got an impression that there was someone in the hooded chaise-longue, but I could only see a pair of legs, in trousers, so I didn't pay much attention.

"You know each other, don't you," said Betty vaguely. If she mentioned a name I didn't catch it. (Doppelganger?) When you've lived as long in Wending Ways as I have, everyone assumes you know everyone. That amuses me as I'm only just beginning to know myself. I think we both growled something, but I recognized his evasive attitude. It was That Man. Naturally I was standoffish, and paid no attention. At least, I thought, now he'll have to speak to me.

Sharpy was definitely mellow. "What sort of a day?" he asked. "Tell us something to liven us up. We're ½ooped." (I must have confided my typewriter trouble to him in one of our hairdowns.)

"A lovely day," I said. "I'm really beginning to enjoy my vacation. I've written a ½oem. I'm going to collect my erotica into a little book to give away next Christmas. I've got a good title: *Loose Leaves*."

"It better be ½rivately ½rinted," said That Man.

"Think of having a neighbor who writes Erotica," said Sharpy. "Who is Erotica? What's her address?"

I thought Betty looked tense, and I hastened to soothe. "Just piping songs of pleasant glee," I said. "Like William Blake."

"Piping?" exclaimed Sharpy. "That's my business. Poacher, lay off."

"Songs of Innocence," said Betty. "What would Sharpy know about that? Please, let's not have any Songs of Innocence. We've just sung lullaby to the grandchildren and sent them home. You should hear Sharpy do Mother Goose."

"You prefer Songs of Experience?" said the other, in his provoking tone, from the shadow of the cabana chair.

"Let's just grope to and fro," I suggested.

"Who is this author of yours, Urban Block?" Betty asked. "I heard on Hollywood News, he's writing a book on The End of the World."

"He better hurry, he'll miss the deadline," said Sharpy.

"Sharpy is trying to speed up sewer-pipe to take care of us when we all go down the drain."

"Now just relax," mumbled Sharpy. "Take it easy."

"130 million people rushing to the precipice and shouting to each other, Take it Easy."—Did I say that, or the other man?

"If there isn't enough rum in that tea, say so, Sharpy can muddle it up."

"I got through the whole day till now," I said proudly, "without a snort. I kept saying to myself, Filthy stuff it is, I loathe it."

"Keep saying that till sunset, you'll be all right."

"I'm interrupting you," I said. "What were you-all talking about?"

"You wouldn't believe," said Sharpy. "I was arguing that a woman oughtn't to sleep lying on her face. It makes such a hump in the bedclothes."

136

"You shouldn't generalize on one instance," said Betty.

"Maybe I don't."

"That wasn't what I was talking about," said That Man. "I was getting ready to say, this is the time of year I get ready to reread Hazlitt."

That really shook me, because I had been thinking so much of Hazlitt, liege lord of grace and ill humor. Hazlitt, like Tybalt, king of cats. The affectionate scorpion!

But I wasn't going to be pushed into cordiality too easily.

"What hypocrites you literary people are," said Sharpy. "Hardly a year goes by without your intending to take down the belovèd works of Hazlitt. My reading is functional. The *Iron Age*, and Kieran's Almanac."

"My reading is ruined," said Betty. "I can't read novels now without figuring out the ages of the characters. When they get to be fifty, I really feel anxious for them."

"It's the first down-payment of autumn. That brings out the colors in people as well as in foliage." I think Doppelganger said that; I wish I had.

"And the color of the leaves in autumn would be nothing without the feeling that accompanies it."

"Yes, Hazlitt said so in the greatest of his essays, *The Indian Jugglers*."

"I'm having fun," I said. "Is it all right for anyone to have as much fun as I'm having?"

"The only time I ever really had fun," said Sharpy rashly, "was under another name."

"When was that?" Betty asked.

"I don't remember."

"It isn't like Sharpy not to remember anything like that."

"Like what?"

"But wouldn't it be wonderful," someone said, "if one could just once go somewhere without taking his accursed Self along. His damnable Id."

Betty sounded shrill. "It must be wonderful to have so much you don't choose to remember. I always wanted to be like that."

137

"All you need remember, my dear, you were born and raised a gentlewoman."

"That was a long time ago; and curses!"

"Time is all that matters. There isn't as much of it as there used to be."

"I used to be the youngest person there ever was," Betty lamented. "It never even occurred to me that ——" (There was a pause.)

"That what?" said Sharpy, the fool. He was pouring himself a drink; we could hear the rum chuckling into the tea, or vice versa. "Oh God," cried Betty fiercely, and turned away with a handkerchief.

Sharpy went to fetch sandwiches. That Man and I didn't say much, but either he said to me, or I to him, I'm not sure: Wouldn't it be incredible if you could tell the true fiction-facts of just One Day. If it was a sunny day, how incredible the fury of the sunlight. If it was rainy, how wonderfully wet was the rain. If it was muddy, what lovely malleable mire and muck.

"You remind me," I said, "of poor Urban Block when he sent in the script of his play. He writes good dialogue, but it's all on one side.—By the way, did you leave a script at my office a while back? What am I supposed to do about it?"

Betty, fluttering her handkerchief to dry, said unexpectedly:—

"I think Sharpy is the most Christlike man I've ever known."

"Maybe he didn't have enough competition?"

"I resent that."

"You should."

"While Sharpy's in the kitchen," Betty whispered to me, "let me tell you: don't be griped because he wants to meet up with Zoe. He wants to tell her he's worried about You.—He loves you, Richard. He admires you. I think he even respects you, which is more than I do. You've got everything he never had a chance to have."

"I feed my cats and pay my taxes and insurance. I even gave the village the right to put a sandpile on my property."

138

"What's this about paying things?" said Sharpy, coming out with a tray. "Never pay your life insurance till the due date. You might be lucky and die the night before. The great nerve systems of insurance are in Hartford or Philadelphia, where death is less of a shock."

Betty said to me: "If you didn't make your troubles so amusing you'd get more sympathy."

Sandwiches toned us down to make sense. I compared Betty (in my mind) to an atomic bomb. Anybody who had patience to watch a woman carefully, guessed the secrets of atomic fission long ago. You can't bombard uranium (woman) with a slow neutron (man) without causing explosion. Scientists lie prone, with muffled heads, twenty miles away. I didn't say this. I said:—

"Have you noticed the terrible increase in unsealed mail, the $1\frac{1}{2}$ cent stuff open at the end? I find myself throwing more into the waste-basket than ever before. Is that my personal degeneration, or an oecumenical disorder?"

"Oecumenical?"

"Nothing in modern business is so cruel and cynical as the traffic in mailing lists. By crossbreeding and conspiracy of mimeographs, a poor soul who once bought a bag of bulbs finds himself, years later, called upon by a salesman from a bond house. Imagine! Ghastly for us both."

"You're always beefing about something," Sharpy said. "Have another drink."

"No, thanks; I'm tapering off."

"You're topering off."

"We sound like the Hartford Wits."

"Who were they, did they start the insurance business?"

"I'm sorry your friend had to go," I said. I'm not surprised, I thought; Sharpy and I were getting painfully waggish. "I liked him."

"Whose friend was that?"

I looked more closely; there was no one in the chair, only a blanket.

"Run you home?" asked Sharpy.

"No, thanks, I'll walk. Like Prospero, to still my beating mind."

"You do give it a beating."

Sharpy saw me to the driveway. "I'm going to get a good rest," he said. "I don't have to work tomorrow."

"Take care of yourself," Betty called from the terrace.

"Let's take care of All Ourselves," someone said.

&§ I love to walk those curly roads at night, in the dark blueprints of the mind. One is alone, but aware of neighborhood. On the Electric Side, even after 2200 hours, there are sabbatical shrills of euthanasia, people trying to forget the handwriting on Wall Street or the sharp comments of their teen-age children. Lighted windows are montaged by foliage. Strong shafts of dazzle plunge into the stubborn oaky woods as guests wheel their varnished hydramatic convertibles (or vermilion and syrup station-wagons) to face the gravel swath. They waver home by fluid drive. The death of the gearshift saved many useless lives in Nassau County?

Walking alone in this sylvestered cerebellum of the suburbs (damn that three-handed alliteration) we can be shabby or sincere as we please. In the burning season there was horrid rumor of a peeping Tom who flitted round houses gaping and drooling. A shadow, a shrill gargling laugh, and he was gone like a columnist. Probably his palsied brain couldn't rationalize whatever it was he saw—he couldn't see much in Wending Ways. The young, pretty as magnolia trees, couch in the attic where they applaud their buds and miracles of form, and fall confidently asleep. At ground level, where poor Toms patrol, they would only observe Sally Garden Malabone opening a conjugal can of soup, or Ben Kesselring caulking the cellar with a homespun insulation, or the Christlike Sharpy triumphing over the purse-proud paperhanger. Rarely the lurking spy would ever catch these good citizens at anything but the most conscientious concerns. I, as voyeur, would want to know more than that. I would be not just peeping Tom but peeping Thomist. I need to learn enough to be a god, even God's minister of the trivial.

So I meditate, muse, and mumble. I trudge by the ponds and the little lisping brook. Thoughts come swimming: here and there a lusty trout, and here and there a grayling; or an underpar goldfish. I am heavenly alone; which I cannot relish except by reflex from company. In the dark dialogue of my brain, God ignores me. He ignores us all (did I say this, or did someone say it to me?) so we may come to Him at last by vanity and pique. Not by Tennyson's wide altar stairs (how characteristic of Tennyson!), but by our own pitiable scrambling.

Maybe I don't like to be Alone after all. After so many things I've done, so many people I've been, and been done by, I feel rather like a roomful of persons, and I need someone to act as chairman—I better hurry and get home where I can call myself to order——

"Have you heard from Zoe lately?" said That Man. He took me unexpected; he was waiting down by the pond, which was sucking and clucking in the muddy night. Considering how rude he has been I was really suave.

"Yes," I said, "I had one of her sardonic postcards. All she said was, *Genesis I, 24.* That was a backdraft about Miss Tally. I am a creeping thing, after his kind. Zoe is life itself. She forgives everything and forgets nothing."

"She has wonderful fun ribbing you," he said.

We were at a fork in the road. Our varicose veins of travel, in Wending Ways, wriggle apart under real estate pressure. I wanted to say, as one would to any unknown neighbor, "Which way do you go?" so I could then announce "I have to go the other."

I was annoyed at his assuming knowledge of Zoe. So I hesitated. What is so anger-making as a stranger suggesting that he knows someone (even Hazlitt) as well as you know you do in your own way? I changed the topic.

"You used not to pay any attention to me," I said. "Since why the change?"

"Things are more serious," he said. "We need help. I think we better spend an evening together. Zoe would come too."

I should have been surprised; but in the Wending Ways of the psyche, at that midnight hour, there is no surprise. All falls into proper frontage and plot. That Man has a pleasant voice— I appreciate it after years of radio misery—an easy lifted tone, with deep register in the heavier vowels and diphthongs. I have heard Zoe say, she can tell what has happened to a patient by the tone of his voice. If he throws the accent away, hurrying for hysterical or commercial stress, he has been frightened into trauma by some sponsor. I know when people are lobbying for something; I've even caught myself at it. I envy people who have never caught themselves. When I get comic my voice rises too squawky. I could have been a wonderful demagogue if the idea hadn't bored me. That's my grievance, every kind of success always seemed vulgar and tedious. Mass emotion, even in the publishing business, is degrading.

I crossed my teeth and ground my bridges, or whichever, and said in a low controlled voice:—

"Suppose she does rib me, who has better right?—Which way are you going?"

I must admit he had the rudiment of decency. He didn't say, as most good naighbahs would, "Either way, it doesn't matter." On my side of Wending Ways we have a sense of Milton's cloistered and fugitive virtue. So he said "This way," and I could say "That."

But he added, "Who is this man who is writing a book about the End of the World?"

I hate to be pursued on a casual remark. Question marks are the most damnable of punctuations, and sentences ought to fade off (as they did in dear old falsetto H. G. Wells) with four dots. . . . So I said, "Well, good night all. That was just a manner of speaking. Urban Block has a great deal of manner in his speaking. We know the world won't actually come to an end. There'll always be a few termites, or termagants, left."

"But it does," he said. "The only world that matters, the

142

world each of us carries inside his own mind. *That* comes to an end. Maybe very soon."

There was a wild whooping siren over Wending Heights. Great booming buzzards of sound-wave swept across our shaken woods. "I think I better hurry," I said. "Might be fire on my side of the village. I hope the cats are all right."

"I hope it's not my manuscript," he said.

I thought I heard his footsteps following, but I didn't turn to see. There *was* a peculiar sort of glow around my sandpile, but not what you could call a fire. They must have scooped up some phosphorescent plankton or putrid shrimps when they dug that sand from the harbor? I scuffled the pile with my foot, but the shining still hovered. I could see it light up the whitest limbs in Wending Ways—my birch trees.

I even picked up a few grains and rubbed them apart in my fingers. Either they, or I, were faintly luminous.

"See the world in a grain of sand." I thought I heard that in a voice of mischief, but when I turned angrily there was no one.

Please don't be calm and competent with me about this. I know what he meant; thank God he didn't say it. The crime is against one's self.

SHARPY SHOOTS THE MOON

AD EANDEM, as Milton used to address some of his 100%oetry. I was thinking in the dark and middle of the night that a good many of my reports have been too scherzo, or too schelmisch. I wasn't trying either to shock or amuse you (one would be as hard as the other?), only trying to come clean.

I didn't know, till you forced me to take a vacation, how seriously split I am. Milton: *When I consider how my life is split.* I've been rereading Milton, trying to imagine myself back at Wisconsin, which is something he couldn't possibly have imagined. You said once, how you must hate literature, to have gone into the publishing business. And I replied, How you must loathe the mind, to have gone into psychiatry.

You were properly sore. I squeaked the cork and you said, A psychiatrist can't afford to drink with her patients.

I said that of all the Career Women I'd heard of, from Cleopatra to Urban Block, you were the one that still remained a woman.

You said that it was always tragic for a woman to be intelligent.

I said, Maybe it's tragic for a man too, to be intelligent.

You said, How would you know?

We both remember what we said after that. But anyhow,

The important thing,

144

Each single mind must somehow integrate and dominate its own experience? I'm trying. It's the little habits of routine that show how we get partitioned up? I've taken time (splitting night from day) to consider. I sleep half on the couch in my study and half in the room upstairs. Even my train service breaks in two. I wanted to be a writer, and now I'm only a broker for other people's tumid stuff. Even my dictionary comes in two volumes. I'll tell you what's funny—I had to phone Miss Tally to check on this—I imagined her opening the Currier & Ives safe and pulling her wide draggletail skirt up over her slimmy knees—I'm rather particular about knees, and I think the dressmakers are wise to keep most of them in ambush—What Did the Dressmaker Have in Mind?—I had to check with Miss Tally, the word *schizophrenia* isn't even in the Oxford Dict. That's what I love about Oxford, and about England. You couldn't possibly have a psychic split over there; they know England is always integral and always right.

One winter evening I was enjoying the bare tracery of my big oak tree against the sunset. Mealie came to call me for supper.

"That tree is certainly beautiful," I said.

"It's because you look at it so much. Everything is beautiful if you look long enough."

That reminds me of another of Mealie's sayings. "You got a black woman to clean your house and a white woman to clean your mind, everything in between is just fog."

How is it that the things that happen to me are always exactly what I needed? I can hear you answer: You're so damn needy that anything that happens fills a long-felt want.

If you don't reply, I have to invent your answers.

I am mailing you some more postcards.

◦§ Life has been too summersweet to make notes—and I was still brooding on your remark (I forget when?) that sometimes I seem to be talking to impress some unknown listener offstage—that is the Listener I've always been waiting for??—

I don't like to refer again to English Teachers, but how right was that chaste old coot who tried to teach literature in college. He said once, "Never make a business of what you love."

One of those impudent hypermammalian Minnesota girls (all caloried up with steaks and starches) said "But Professor, aren't you doing just that when you teach English?"

He replied patiently, "Well said, Froeken Yustaffsen. But I hope it may be overlooked, it's a business with such small turnover."

It's true I never heard of a college prof dying of ulcers; they come of high feeding and fast trading. It's only 2nd-rate people who die in their entrails? People who really have hearts and brains, that's where the hemorrhage comes?

Even that swiving Swede (she was like cream cheese bursting duplex out of the churn) was taken aback, which she should have been used to.

Now you've got me pressure-cooking, remembering things I didn't know I remembered.

Do you include these innocent memoes in your Domesday file of clients' histories? I hope they're in code, so they can't be identified. The one thing the human being is most afraid of is being identified—yet it's the only thing worth being born for?? But suppose, in case of fire—a good title, IN CASE OF FIRE— I had to laugh, I saw an advt in the papers, some fire-extinguisher company learned something had gone wrong with their chemicals and asked customers to turn in various numbered tanks of defective acid. I feel sure some of my extinguishers are in that lot, but should I do anything about it? I'd rather relax. Fire is God's child as much as I am, or more. The sandpile at the bottom of the drive flickered again, with an eerie blue flame. The Road Commissioner (who has an answer for everything, as village officers must) said bubbles of marsh gas must have got sealed up when they excavated the sand from the harbor. He blames it on Sharpy Cullen or garbage. I am too old to blame anything on anybody. I just say, it happened. I retire upon my private religion (it's good to have one; yours, I know, is your code index). All sorts of queer things have been made the symbols of devotion: birdguts, plaster images, cows, cats, flower arrangements, mistletoe berries, stone cromlechs, Trotsky's goatee and Stalin's sickle moustache, F.D.R.'s long cigarette-holder and Churchill's thick cigar. I don't think mine is any worse than others: the deliberated arrangement of words, to suggest the astute disarrangement of thoughts.

If people don't know man's enjoyment of life and his agile evasion of testimony, why have they lived at all? Even the kitten doesn't swing on her sock-and-armpit trapeze any more. She spends her zeal in the sandpile, where she scrabbles and frolics. There must be something there even more corrupt than socks and shirts.

Sharpy and Betty and I had our annual game of Hearts, for the benefit of the local hospital. For my money, Hearts is the only card game worth playing; losing tricks is the criterion, not winning them—unless, like the great mahatmas, you win everything, and die in peace by someone else's hand—to take everything is called Shooting the Moon—and, as in politics, all depends on your discard. So we play Hearts once a year for our hospital contribution. It is a cutthroat game when played by three, and I take care that Betty gets my discards, because she knows Sharpy's technique. It usually works out that we pay, among the three, about 250 Dollars to the hospital.

Sharpy actually did shoot the moon (which cancels one's deficit) on the last hand, so it left me paying $110, and Betty paying $95, and Sharpy zero. Like a good fellow (since he might be gallstoned to the hospital any day) he put in $15 to even up.

I wouldn't have known about poor Sharpy's calculus in the bladder except that we were in a gay humor and I recited at random that old seventeenth-century doggerel,

> May I govern my passion with absolute sway——

(Anno Domini will take care of that for you, said Sharpy ——)

> And grow wiser and better as strength wears away,
> Without gout or stone, by a gentle decay.

147

This put Sharpy into a tizzy; he had already been to the hospital (which I didn't know) to have his bladder "visualized," but what agitated him was the doctor saying "Don't let the patient smell food before 10 A.M."

Then you better not have Mealie around, I said. Sharpy handed me his discard—three low clubs, which I knew meant strategy—and said, You don't know what trouble is until you go to hospital. Before they X-ray, they give you a fat-free supper at 5 P.M., a dose of paregoric, capsules of dye for coloring matter, and then they tell you to sleep on your right side.

He never could sleep on his right side, said Betty. That's the side I sleep on.

Betty, perhaps thinking of the cold side of the bed, made a foolish discard. She must have handed Sharpy just the AKQ of hearts he needed, and he set forth for the Moon, like Jules Verne.

I guess I was in a very annoying mood. When Sharpy took and kept the lead throughout, I quoted Wordsworth: "We have given our Hearts away, a sordid boon."

Betty burst into tears. "You are so horrible," she cried. "You make me think of sophomore English, when I was crazy about poetry, and thought life was like that."

I know you loathe cards (except in an index) so I sign off. But somehow I learned more about Betty. Sharpy was too pleased about winning the game to learn anything. Be wary of your discards.

P.S. I'm still thinking about Betty and what she said. That's why I'd never be a good reporter. I've told you how I lost a job on a newspaper because I took too much time to try to find out what really happened??

Betty said, I wouldn't blame any woman for leaving any man, men are so mercilessly faithful.

I said nothing.

She said, "You seem to infer that you don't think so."

148

I said, "I would leave any woman, at any moment, if she said *infer* when she meant *imply*."

There was a crash in the pantry, I felt sure that Sharpy had dropped one of their old Tuscany platters. Betty shivered like an overbred spaniel (she looks rather like one, with that Gozzoli bob) but as with spaniels you can't tell how old she is unless she shows her teeth; which she is too mature to do. Her mouth gets a little pulled sometimes (just fatigue) but she's too smart to openwide her dentures.

Betty said tersely, "You are a beastly snob. Night now, I want to see what crashed."

I continued saying nothing. I'm not like that scribble on a poster at the station, where I read: *Jane loves John*, and then the rejoinder *Jane loves anyone that loves Jane*.

Sharpy appeared at the kitchen door and barred the way. "Better not go in there yet. Have a drink first." He beckoned me with a man-to-man wink. "Wait awhile, Dick. A nightcap before you go."

"I *want* to go in there," screamed Betty. "I can break something too."

"Achtung! Schpitfeuer!" said Sharpy. "I knew something would go wrong if I shot the moon."

"Couldn't I just throw something, or smash something, or scream something? I shan't sleep if I don't know what's broken."

"We won't any of us sleep," said Sharpy. "There's going to be a thunderstorm. I can always tell by watching Betty, she's better than a barometer."

"I didn't sleep last night either," Betty apologized to me. "It was that damn dog. This humid weather has got her run ragged with fleas. She sleeps outside my room; to protect me from Sharpy, I suppose. She's been bathed and combed and dusted, but all night long she whines and scuffles and goes thump-thump-thump on the floor like Henry Wallace. She scratches the screen, and what a gooseflesh sound that is. She doesn't know what it is that torments her."

"A perfect picture of the world today," I said. "The states-

149

men scratch hard in Berlin and suddenly they feel an itch in Vienna; chafe that and soothe it and here's a twinge in Trieste or Korea or South America. Growl, scratch, whine, thump; dog and statesman both in a tizzy."

"Nothing for it but a hot bath and a scour to the hide," said Sharpy, pouring the highball. "Don't think we won't get it. So don't worry about a little thing like that Venetian platter."

Betty trembled, like the State Department when someone breaches protocol, but kept her divine vocative to a mutter. "I don't worry about anything when Dick puts it into universal terms."

"Even a hot bath won't give the statesmen the rest they need," I said. "The poor brutes are trying to make a system work that hasn't been workable for a long time. It went down the drain, or into the crater, one summer day in New Mexico."

Old Fleabag, the dog, came in and quested the cat-smell of my trousers, and exported a few parasites.

"Dick always gives me something to think about," said Betty.

"So does your pooch give me," I said.

"Maybe there's something in the universe that resents thought," said Sharpy. "I know I find it difficult."

The moon, as I walked home, was worth shooting. The birch trees stood up in slanted clusters, like white china muddling-rods in pools of absinthe.

Doppelganger was there, of course. I heard his light step, just off-syncope from mine; he must walk on his toes like a dancer? Why do I always have to be the text and someone else the glossary? I felt tough and tired and middle-elderly; I wouldn't even pass him the time of night. I was only thinking to myself, but he answered me.

"God bless old Sharpy," I said. "I never knew, till I got my bottom on gravel, what a wonderful guy he is. I really think I love him. He's heroic. He's unspoiled, and no double-exposure."

150

No matter how fast you talk, there's always something left over in your mind. I was stupidly hoping maybe Old Doppel would say "You're sort of heroic yourself." Of course he didn't. It hasn't been said since it eased the right-hand thief on the Cross?

I don't remember now, did he say, or did I think, "Maybe it isn't till life shortens up on you that you give it full creative attention?"

"Excuse me a moment," I said. "Stop for Necessities." I went behind one of the argentine birch boles. The phrase is a local gag of ours; there's a Shopping Center in Marathon that has a big sign STOP FOR NECESSITIES. In Nassau County that simply means small wares, notions, household goods. But all the diuretic foreigners on their way to Lake Success think it means Comfort Station. That Man waited for me. He must be something more than a commentator, for I saw him scratching his ankle as if he had a burr in his sock. What could be more literal than that? It's like the horror I always have when I see women on the street reach down under to secure their caout-chouc gear. That was what first suggested to me, they can't be just the disbodied angels I was taught to imagine. You must deal with God, Woman, and Yourself, on even terms. Woman and Yourself are the thieves on either side of the Cross?? I only thought this, I wouldn't know how to say it. Language is muscle-bound when it comes to the truth.

My mind felt as bright as moonlight; brighter. It felt like the point of a trowel, polished with work in the coarse loam of living. Or maybe like the point of a bayonet, when we were taught (in 1917) how to let the sandy dribble out of a dummy.

"One of the things I like about here," I said, "it was laid out with so many wendings, there's frequent chances of taking the other way."

"A parting has been arranged," he said, "and will shortly take place."

I used to think of you, I thought, as the Man Who Pays No Attention. Now you pay too much. You, the cause of all my horror and weakness. You, the disease of despair that crawls up my nerves and glands and brain. You, in the dark repartee of the mind, turned my dull and happy habit to a gyro of——

"Don't say it," he said. "You're like Sharpy's little grandchild when she fell and scraped her knee; but she couldn't cry, she had a lollypop in her mouth. She wanted to cry, she yearned to howl, her face was wrinkled with woe, but she couldn't. Spit out your lollypop, so you can cry."

And what is the lollypop?

He was gone. I got home, refreshing myself with the professional thought of all the authors in the Middle West who are half-writing novels half a million words long. Maybe I'll sleep after all.

Wouldn't we yearn for nothingness, if we were quite sure we could come back from it??

Reality Goes Overboard

~§ He came so quietly I didn't know he was there. I was sitting at my desk, trying to fit together a few jigsaws of neglected work. Then the phone rang, one of those continuing savage trills that mean Long Distance— probably Hollywood, the longest spiritual distance there is. I leaped like a man stung by a Black Widow; as I went into the living room he got up from the couch—

"Hullo, Doppelganger! I didn't hear you come in. Excuse me a moment, I'll just answer the phone."

"Don't," he said. He really has a way with him; a very quiet way.

"It sounds to me like Trunks," I said. I picked this up from one of my British lecturers, it was his comic way of saying Long Distance. "I know the sound of that bell, it may be Person-to-Person."

It was really absurd. I kept trying to get to the phone, and That Man weaved to and fro (extraordinarily light on his feet, only looks at you sideways) and always prevented me. It became —I was angry at first, then enjoyed the becoming—a kind of ballet. I found myself inventing patterns far beyond pedestrian compass. Even compasses have two exquisitely counterpointed legs? The phone was ringing fiercely, maybe even profitably, but Doppel interspersed it with ironical sayings. "Charge, Urban! Reverse Charge!"

I began to get the idea. The words that came to me—and when they come, you have to accept them—were "Throw reality overboard." I shouted them, and he seemed pleased. The phone, unanswered, dribbled off. We capered and sashayed impromptu figures, yet each always knowing how the other would move. The cats bristled, and so did Mealie, but we cut them off from access. We uttered fancy dialogue and danced it out. I didn't have time to think my thoughts, but I know I kept getting ready to think, we were Shelley and Keats. "You know how it was," I screamed, but no one heard me, "Shelley tried to lend Keats money, and he wouldn't take it. A dying man doesn't accept a loan."

It was all double exposure, because as I danced like a dervish I could also see myself sitting at the desk, sunk in stupor under the lamp. Then sometimes it seemed as if Sharpy Cullen was at the piano, improvising blue serge music, and Zoe Mou with her chaise-longue legs was sometimes on the couch watching or directing the ballet—and delicate little Miss Tally appeared now and then, trying to offer me an inbasket full of papers—and Mealie with a tray of hot sausages, followed by chafing cats—

There are only two ways of calming yourself; either by tearing up papers or by having a snort of gin. I had used both medicaments. It was like this:—

TOLMAN:	I must answer the phone
THAT MAN:	Leave it alone
T	Then I'll turn on the radio
TM	No, no, no, no
T	I haven't answered my letters yet
TM	File and forget; file and forget
T	But then what can I do?
TM	Just a little while, be You.
T	I haven't a clue, I don't understand
TM	Pit it up in Poppa's hand.
T	Are you the crime or are you the criminal?
TM	I'm subliminal. I'm symbiosis.

T	Wait a minute—you're neurosis. You're a fairy, or the ghost of the Oxford Dictionary.
TM	I'm Life's unwanted child.
T	I'm deuces wild.
TM	I'm the other half of one-half oetry—
T	Give me time to find a rhyme. I never played this game before. Don't expect anything showy—Zoe— all I want is one-half Zoetry. Gee whiz, there she is.
ZOE:	You didn't answer the phone, so I came.
T	When I am dead, let gent or dame 　　Put in no calls for me, And hastily delete my name 　　From the directory.
TM	When you are dead, old vagabone
T	By cardiac, or cancer?
ZOE:	I'll carve your stone with a telephone 　　And the simple text, DON'T ANSWER.
T	Taciturnity to my relics. Sir Thomas Browne.
TALLY:	Did you want me to take that down?
T	Bless my soul, and here's Miss Tally
TM	Join the schizophrenic ballet
ZOE:	Analyze, analyze!
TM	It must have been a couple of the same guys.
T	Here's old Sharpy, man of sin
ZOE:	All Wending Ways is coming in
TM	If you're desperate enough You can really do your stuff
TALLY:	Will you preside at a meeting to prevent this attempt to control American Thought and Expression? At the Gold Room in the Savoy Plaza.
T	I can't even preside at my meetings with myself.
TM	I *am* American Thought and Expression. Leave me be.
T	Aren't you eager for the Cause?
TM	Willy waws, willy waws.

155

ZOE:	I'm the phone.
TALLY:	I'm telegram.
TM	I'm the fuses that were blown.
T	Damn, damn, damn, damn.
MEALIE:	I'm the cat, have I been fed?
TALLY:	I'm the script, have I been read?
ZOE:	I'm the tissue of the brain
TM	I'm the little sudden pain
T	I'm the early morning train
MEALIE:	Hoooo, hoooo, who-hoooo—
T	Monthly ticket, can you stick it?
	To and fros, to and fros,
	In the heat or in the snows
TM	To New York, every week,
T	You're the cork
TM	I'm the squeak
T	Can you solve my problem, buddy?
TM	I am God's own understudy.
SHARPY:	When does the drinking begin?
T	Gin, gin, gin.
SHARPY:	After the dancers leaving,
	After the stars are gorn
T	Sharpy is full of corn
SHARPY:	All psychiatrists have big feet
	Om—tiddleompom—pom—pom.
ZOE:	Oh Death where is thy sting?
T	Oh Time, thy mustard plaster?
TM	When every little thing
	Moves faster, faster, faster,
ZOE:	Give me a snort. I feel Bacchante.
T	I'm Boccaccio.
TM	I'm Dante.
ZOE:	You're being littery.
T	I'm being jittery.
TM	Alighieri, known as Dante
SHARPY:	Swing the bell, Dixie Belle,

156

TM	Wrote a 3-part capstan chantey
	One part Heaven, two parts Hell.
T	Beatriechy
SHARPY:	Or Barbara Frietchey
T	Knew exactly what he meant
ZOE:	Hell takes 67 per cent.
TALLY	How do you spell Beatriechy?
T	Put the papers in the folder,
	That English teacher's getting older.
TM	Throw Reality overboard
	Laughter is the overlord.
T	Thank God this hasn't been transcribed
SHARPY:	Too much imbibed
T	I've got an ulcer, or a cyst,
	I've been pressure grouped—
TM	You're on someone's mailing list,
	That's why you're pooped.
T	I'm the mind that contemplates,
	Sometimes differentiates—
TM	What, in these United States?
T	I retire, withdraw, refuse
ZOE:	I'm the Ayrabs
T	I'm the Jews
TALLY:	I'm the cherubs in the News
SHARPY:	Congregation in the pews
CATS:	Mew, mew, mew, mew
T	Who are you?
TM	I'm all the things that trouble you
SHARPY:	Excuse, excuse,
	While I go to the Double-U.
T	I'm the hyperthyroid gland
TM	I'm the pressure in the blood
T	I'm the Holy Oily Land
SHARPY:	I'm stick-in-the-mud.
	I am Drink
	I help you not to think

TM	I'm Prejudice I never miss, I'm anti-Other, That, and This.
CATS:	Hiss, hiss, Sssssss!
TM	In one sentence, insult triple, I sneered at three kinds of pipple: I said Wop, and Kike, and Pape—
MEALIE:	How did colored folks escape?
ZOE:	Three rousing sneers
T	No laughing joke
SHARPY:	I hope you croak, I hope you croak.
TALLY:	Let go of my leg. Of my leg, leggo—
ZOE:	It's the involvement of the Ego—
MEALIE:	Tapioca, corn mush, sago—
TALLY:	I'm sorry to interrupt you, Mr. Tolman, here's a wire from Urban Block—he says they wouldn't take him in Hollywood, he's too virile.
TM	He is virile like a squirrel Hark, hark, the dogs do bark, Pantywaists coming to town
T	The double curve We don't deserve For skirts are coming down
TM	Clown, clown, clown.
SHARPY:	Urban Block? and who may he be?
T	He's a ganymede; an ephebe.
ZOE:	They won't know what you mean.
T	I mean, epicene.
TM	I warn you, America Doesn't like esoterica
T	Presto, a manifesto!
ZOE:	Individuation.
T	Mispronunciation.
ZOE:	Differentiation.
TM	Adaptation. Sublimation. Self Preservation.
T	Inflation.

158

TM	Principia Mathematica.
BETTY:	Sciatica.
TM	Symbolism.
ZOE:	Embolism.
T	Milk and hooey. Prunes and prism.
MEALIE:	Counsellor, he win.
SHARPY:	More gin, more gin.
T	Mealie, as a working wife,
	What do you think about it?
MEALIE:	There ain't no happiness in this life,
	You got to be happy without it.
SHARPY:	If the whole world's on the slide
T	My own fault for being snide?
SHARPY:	Where can he find
	A comfort station for the mind?
T	Man is doomed, for being a dope
TM	There still is hope, because
	Though there is no peace, there never was.
MEALIE:	We've got to be peaceful without it.
SHARPY:	When I was a soldier boy before
	I was far from being a hero
T	And what's the score
	In another war?
TM	The score will be Zero-Zero.
ZOE:	The only song that's worth to sing
	Is, everything is everything—
TM	Birds and insects, crops and weather
	Coefficiented together
T	It was not wing nor claw nor fin
	Made this earth a loony-bin
ZOE:	Notify the Next of Kin
T	This is madness on the verge?
TM	It's a purge, it's demiurgic.
T	I'm allergic.
ZOE:	He's psychosomatic.
T	It's a rainy day, let's play in the attic.

ZOE:	That's an infantile regression.
TM	It's occupational therapy
SHARPY:	O sweet cookie!
	It's a roll in the blue-grass in Kentucky.
BETTY:	You better come home if you want to be lucky.
SHARPY:	The pianist do not remove, he—
MEALIE:	Mr Cullen sure is groovy.
T	I should have climbed; instead, I slid—
	It's just my wicked instinctual Id.
SHARPY:	Let your mind run,
	It's good clean fun
T	But not, I fear, for everyone.
TM	Let's not be controversial.
T	Let's be a singing commercial:
	It's galluptious, yum, yum, yum,
	It's compulsion, give me some.
SHARPY:	What a truthpaste.
	Sag, sag, sag, sag,
	Tolman's mind is in the bag.
ZOE:	He has insecurity feeling.
SHARPY:	Tolman's mind has a low ceiling.
T	Life is just a bowl of soup,
	See the clown jump through the hoop
TM	I am Middle East in fission
	I'm uranium partition
SHARPY:	I am guts and germs and gism
TM	I'm anti-humanism
T	Slow it down. I'm getting wheezy. My lungs are full of fuzz.
SHARPY:	Take it easy.
T	But who does?
TALLY:	I've got some memoranda yet—
T	File and forget.
TM	File and forget.
T	Still I think that I outstomped you—

160

TM	It was a wonderful impromptu—
	Reality went overboard.
SHARPY:	One closing chord. I'll go no more a-roving,
	With you, fair maid.
BETTY:	I hear you say it.
ZOE:	What delights the mind, enjoy it.
TM	What terrifies the mind, destroy it.
ZOE:	Life is a chain of command
T	And man is the weakest link
SHARPY:	When you can't understand
	It's better not to think.
	Drink. Drink hearty.
BETTY:	Thanks for a most unusual party.
TALLY:	I don't think I got very good notes, Mr. Tolman,
	but I'll send you a recap.
SHARPY:	Miss Tally has a beautiful kneecap.
TM	Night. Be seeing you.
T	I can do without it.
TM	I doubt it.
	(Taxi horn outside)
MEALIE:	Cats in the cellar,
	No calls on foam,
	Taxi's yeller,
	Ah'm goin' home.
	Counsellor, if you say so I put Miss Tally on that
	last train.
	(I tried to catch Zoe's eye; she kept it to her-
	self; I don't blame her—it's a lovely eye)
ZOE:	Me too. I mean also.
	Unlisted numbers
	Are good for slumbers.

They were gone. I was alone; yet not chemically pure alone. Some of the poor old piano keys were stuck down where Sharpy had beaten them. There was still shapely impression in the sofa cushions—I might measure them for Zoe's winter knitwear?

Not really alone, I said to myself. Alone takes time. Forlorn. The very word is like a bell. . . . The telephone rang.

I didn't answer. It sounded like that Hollywood operator again. What a life they must lead. Of course out there it was still only the shank of the evening; not even up to the kneecap. I was afraid to go near the instrument, it might noose me with its constricting tensile twist. Only pain and bad conscience could make such mortal coil in telephone wires? I went out through the kitchen into the moon-phased night.

The night was a warm blonde—like that Hollywood operator. I could hear her skirling me, and the cats also who still smelled sausage. I thought for a moment that the lisping cats were Urban Block, who also purrs when he first smells Hollywood pork and B-pictures. He might be a great pixy-poet and still I don't favor him. In moonlight my blue gravel comes pale silver (like a publisher at forty).

I am a coward: I had to fight not to rush back into the house and answer that screaming phone. But I knew what would happen. The con-carne tamale voice (from Hollywood) would ask for me, and I would say He has passed away; we buried him this evening in a filing case. You must have the wrong number. How are the abalone steaks this evening? Is it sheep-shearing time in Southern California?[1]—There would be a pause while the poor gipsy shrugged up her dress shields and reseated her comely chubs in the saddle-chair, and pushed a fresh kleenex into the uplifted sierra nevada. Then she would say, Will you excuse it please?

I did; I mean I would; I was alone. The gravel sparkled gray, my battered old roadster sagged sideways in the garage (I had a flat, and too idle to call anyone about it; I have told the local garage that I have such arthritis in my hands that I can't change a tire. I took my cue from Somerset Maugham who said, in that grand book [I wish I were his agent] never do anything that

[1] It was one of Richard's gags to quote this famous first line in that old novel *Ramona* (1884) and say it was a history of the movie business. Z. E.

162

someone else can do better for you. This makes Zoe very angry when I tell it.)

And then I wasn't alone. My crunchy gravel, my magnesia moonlight, my gerundives of desire, all the lovely dance and song and Border Ballet—on the border between self and sanctity—vanished. The moon phased white with horror. I was under the great overhanging dangerous limb of the big oak tree.

By the clump of birches, below the wood-lot, That Man stood with moonlight on his hat. He wore one of those ghastly cigar-store summer hats, white linen with sweat-holes and a green celluloid shade. He might have been a birch tree himself; "his hat was of the birk." Why should he spier and spy on me? Why pretend to be as lovely and loin-white as a birch? Why not leave me alone? When I needed him he ignored me. When I craved to be alone he was the Great Silky. Is a man to be mocked in his own house—even in his own mind?

Pale fume was above the sandpile; the sandpile that breathes and symbolizes the whole zoology. The tree-men had been here; they terrify me, they climb to brittle heights and they aren't allowed to use spikes—only Nazis and Communists, the delirium tree-men, use spikes in climbing the Tree of Life?

They had sawed off a great oak beam. I seized it, and as he stood there in his merciless silent rebuke I let him have it. I heard his skull split.

So reality goes overboard, I said. I hope you like it.

I got the shovel and buried him in the sandpile.

"Will you excuse it please."

Musette bag

⏎ Having buried my tormentor in the sandpile, both climate and weather were wonderful.

It cost some thought to compose that sentence. Anyone trained in syntax reacts violently against the Detached or Dangling Participle. I write it to compliment Zoe, who sometimes accuses me of being only a Dangling Participle in our great mortal storm. She says that Fowler's *Modern English Usage* (Oxford, 1926), classic of lingo and stingo, is also one of the most useful textbooks in psychiatry. People (she says) can only think in words—words are pushbuttons—and by their use of words you can twig what is wrong with them.

After the sweat, swink, swank, and swami of my ballerino evening, I had a sense of purge. For several days I was what is called happy? How long, I don't know. I didn't count time, I don't dare to any more: there is endless of it, but so little my own. I went back to my tested narcotics: gin, knitting, and my old college textbook anthologies of English poetry. In those happy days cautious editors ended with Matthew Arnold; the wilder liberals tiptoed on as far as Meredith and Swinburne. It never occurred to us that literature had anything more to do or say. Good God, Zoe, do you realize—I mean, do I realize—I was in college when Swinburne and Meredith died.

164

I carried those two shabby books, *Manly* and *Hidden Page*,[1] out to the iron table in the garden. In later times the educational publishing business has become a sordid scuffle or shuffle, to see who can fastest compile the current fashionabilia. It's hard, now, to know which is prose and which is verse. But it's not the poet's fault if the world won't give him ½eace enough to write ½oetry?

Maybe I was doing reconnaissance for a sonnet? I happened to open one of the books at Matthew Arnold, and (not to read, just to get the vibration) I laid *Hidden Page* (page 708) beside me.

Mealie came out just then, all Ethiope with triumph, carrying the corpse of a rat she had trapped under the oven. Mealie will set traps any time, which I shudder to do, but will never unbend the grinning carcase from the heavy wire spring.

"Here that big temerity rat, he try once too many to ration off cheese from egg noodles. You unstrangle that spring, I incriminate him in your griddle." She means my precious outdoor picnic grill.

Go away, Mealie. You remind me of that story R. L. Stevenson loved: the Scotch minister who was suddenly called on to preach. He snatched one of his old sermons from the shelf, but in the pulpit he found the rats in the manse had eaten the first three pages. "Never mind," he said, "we'll just begin where the rats left off."

"That a sermon in itself," said Mealie. "You fling him over the hedge somewheres neighbors'. I always displeasure to take hold on the tail, it shuck off in my hands."

I resumed Matthew Arnold where the rat left off. The line I happened on was probably the most unpromising opening of any sonnet ever. I cackled to read it:—

Who prop, thou ask'st, in these bad days, my mind? Incredible; yet by the increment of miracle that often does raise

[1] *English Poetry*, 1170–1892. J. M. Manly. Ginn & Co., 1907. *British Poets of the 19th Century*. Curtis Hidden Page. Sanborn, 1904.

sonnets from the dead, eleven lines lower he threw a forward pass and scored the goal:—

Who saw life steadily, and saw it whole.

Which is what I was doing, for a few days or hours. I was copying, in what I call my *Musette Bag*, extracts for the private anthology I compile for Zoe. It is soothing to turn one's mind toward the past, to fix it on those whose ardors and endurances are long gone by, consumed into the general humus of the arts. I was pleased, but didn't want Zoe to be, by one of my troves (London *Times* Lit Supp., Oct. 28, 1944), what Shelley wrote to Thomas Jefferson Hogg, after Hogg had made a pass at Harriet Shelley:—

I attach little value to the monopoly of exclusive cohabitation.

Musette, in French, means bagpipes, and some of the notes in my little windbag have an ironical squeal. I hope to print it about 1950, when irony will be welcome?

I brooded about this, and found it an excuse to consult Zoe by phone. She was crisp. She advised me to turn down the agency for newspaper syndication of a famous book, in pemmican form. Parboiled to brief aphorisms.

"Certainly not," she said. "Everybody would read it. It's literary strychnine. Deadly nightshade. Use only in minute dosage for nerve stimulant."

I babbled: "It's the best job of social haruspication that's been done in years."

There was a silence. Perhaps she was looking under the bed for the dictionary. She keeps it there because that's where words really come flowing into my mind.

She couldn't find it; she probably looked for a double r. What's the use of a dictionary if you can't spell? She said, defiantly, "I don't care for condensations of condensations. You get your feet wet in the dew."

"We need the business," I said cowardly.

166

"Suppose we don't sell anything. You can live on me, can't you?"

That was that, my beautiful. Zoe said once, I'll couch with the dictionary and put you under the bed. But I still think, the delicate way to woo a woman is with words?? What are so intimate, what come so far from within?? Medical diagrams of tubes and afferents don't give any notion of a woman's behavior? Zoe never loved me so much as when I said she had a wonderful brisket. She said that was what cattle have; but she was pleased. It's a pity men give women so little comedy. That is what women are created for?

⁊ I was detached, remote, midweek godlike; practically posthumous. Maybe hot weather and cold baths had to do with it. In the shudder and sting of Long Island's frigid water the belly, like a bagful of snakes and bladders, retracts its coils to resiliate. You're the doctor, Zoe: don't tell me if I'm wrong. The water should be so cold, as the Scotchman said, I don't know is my name Angus or Agnes.

I was having fun with my natural trivialities. I decided, instead of printing ½oetry, to make my Christmas pamphlet this year my long meditated *Census of Solecisms in Radio*, analyzed by time, announcer, sponsor, and network. These sweet golden crimes against syntax put me into an ecstasy. I rub my long, thin hands together like Sherlock Holmes and quote the noble Churchill's note on a State Paper: *This is the kind of English up with which I will not put.* (His Majesty's Stationery Office, 1948. Crown Copyright Reserved.)

If I can't tell you about things that tickle me, what's the use of telling anything? Minuscula of discrimination are what make life bearable?? The pedant needs his joys no less than the psychiatrist??

It was the season when the garden is patriotic tricolor: red hawthorn, blue iris, white dogwood. I felt like declaring war on something, but I met Sharpy at the supermarket which was

167

equivalent release. He looked unusually vague. He asked: "—Was I very tight at your house the other evening? It's a bit blurred in my mind."

It seemed he had been avoiding me. I can hardly blame him, I had been avoiding myself. I was a Dangling Participle while Mealie had her summer attack of the To-and-Fros. What I thought was distant thunder was Mealie hauling furniture in the room over my study. Something in the livery of the burning sun rouses all Mealie's follicles of achievement. Already at breakfast she is on fours scrubbing the kitchen. When her great kilted beam comes me rumping in through the swing door I flee. Never interfere with a woman in her domestic orgy.

"You go in garden," Mealie orders. "Out there you can be fanciful as you please. Vacumating man coming to treat the rugs. I bring you salmon-on-rye and ice coffee in tremoss bottle."

I thought I had my silver mug concealed, but she noticed the bend of my elbow. "What you carrying there?" She sniffed it and did a double-take.

"Lucky thing we got two liquor stores in the village. I'd be shamed if either one knew how much gin you buy."

She trots out again presently, bringing my sunglasses.

"Now you can set in sun and read dirty books." (Mealie has a fixed impression that anything in typescript is obscene.)

She catches a glint of light where I had smuggled the gin bottle behind the grape vine.

"God in Brooklyn! I like to know who knock you down this way so you guzzle gin before lunch. I'm goin' cook you a message of fried onion, that give you something to agonize on, you won't hanker nothing else. Either that or I foam Miss Zoe on you."

I retreated under the hickory tree where baby caterpillars sprinkle. Tally had come out to take dictation, but so many caterpillars fell down the sinus of her blouse she said she'd rather sit in the sun.

There's something wonderful about Dictating in the Open Air. You fight past the qwertyuiop½, that line of typewriter

168

keys that stands like a Normandy hedgerow against the poor D-day infantry of composition.

"Like Moses took the Ten Tables," says Tally.

"He only meant Nine of them," I reply. "Like a political poll, he allowed 10 per cent for error."

Mealie has her prejudices. "Miss Tally a right comfortable little shape, but she only an interloper."

An interloper now and then, Is relished by the best of men. I didn't say this, there's never any use getting into argument with Mealie.

வ§ I made a note in the Musette Bag; I attributed it to Kafka, because Zoe will never look it up. I said: "If I were going to write anything it should be more than a book. It should be an ordeal." What a quote for a book-jacket, I could see it printed on the wrapper:—

"More than a book, an ordeal."

That was when I decided to give Zoe, instead of knitted breechclouts, a book that would really shake the needles off her Christmas Tree. *Shakespeare's Bawdy*, a study and glossary of his virtuosity in Schmutz. Fortunately restricted to psychiatrists and English professors, as I will say in my inscription. It really belongs in the safe.[2]

I discovered I was lonely for my nieces. The Cullens tell me I know nothing of life because I have no children, but I notice they find grown-up children sometimes cramp their style. But with nieces, and especially twins (Shakespeare was fond of twins too), their pure and sure condescensions can be ignored. They make life sweet for me because the things they say are so far above their husbands that those worthy young men would never smile. I took them over to Marathon one afternoon to see a baseball game on the television set in the Super-Bar. By

[2]Where I found it later, and removed it, not to contaminate Miss Tally. By Eric Partridge; London (Routledge), 1947. Z. E.

some diffusion of focus all the images were double. Each player, each bat, each ball, was irradiated in a duplicate picture. The batter, preparing his stance, waggled two bats and four buttocks; he struck a double ball and ran with four legs.

"They must have known we were coming," said one of the twins.

"Maybe it's a doubleheader," said the other.

Those are the tiny triumphs of mortality that I hold like jewels in my heart. Thank goodness, the things that amuse me don't amuse anyone else. If they did, there might be an epidemic of suicide. Perhaps that is exactly what there is.

"I don't read the papers," said one of the girls. "With a baby to tend, I can't afford to burst out laughing."

I was reproaching them (I really was shocked) for having gone through college and never read *Tom Jones*.

"When I was at college," I said, "we all read *Tom Jones*, even the engineering and dairy-farming students, because it was kept in the lock-up case. It was forbidden. A pity, too, because it's such a Squire Middlewestern kind of book. Sort of animal husbandry. But you gals, majored in English, how come you could go through a college course and never read that gorgeous hybrid corn?"

"We majored in *Poetry*," they cried indignantly.

I felt like Urban Block, the time he slipped on an idea and strained his mind. It had to be taped up by the nurse.

I put down an excerpt for the Musette Bag, based on one of our conversations, when I was telling the girls how little sleep I get:—

Fortunately most people don't have to eat crackers in bed to get to sleep. Perhaps a bedful of crumbs is the mark of a saint.

R. Tolman.

Come lovely and soothing Death (Walt Whitman). "Year that trembled and reeled beneath me." Doom is all around me. Let me feed, like good old Topsolito (he has just had his teeth out) on soup, spaghetti, and mashed potatoes. Let me feed on Shelley and Swinburne and Matthew Arnold. Let me ride philosophy's bony crupper behind Santayana, Don Quixote of our age, who never learned life's vulgar slang but only its Castilian. Zoe, you should have woman's purest privilege: thou shouldst be wooed all over again, and by a —— man than me?? (I left the blank for her to fill in.) A man less like an English teacher?? I grinned to remember what Zoe said when I told her that Tally is going to marry one.

"She'll have a wonderful time with his euphuisms."

My old Austrian Grandmother used to say, when we got hopped up about something, it's just *schwärmerei*. Glorious word. I can think of plenty topical translations of it, but who am I to climb up on the scaffold?[3] Zoe—her grandmother also came fresh from navel-Europe—knows what I mean. Those who don't know are no patients of ours.

&§ I explained to Zoe how patriotic the garden looked, so she came out to spend the Fourth. She was beautifully cool and clinical. As we walked in the terror of that midsummer beauty I pointed out my private landmarks. There was the lawn where one of my neighbors, with a bad heart, thrombosed himself by mowing the grass in hot weather. After his death the family sold the house, and it stands empty and untrimmed. "The long green grass is his memorial." (A good navel for a sonnet, but I didn't say so. Sometimes people have an allergy for sonnets that haven't been born yet.) Zoe was silent. Perhaps she was analyzing.

"Here's where the Pikestaffes live. They had the most ridiculous old sheepdog. During the War he was fed on table scraps, and when canned horsemeat and liver came back, after five years, he was afraid of it. When he smelled it he growled and bristled and backed into a posture of defence. He thought it was a squadron of the mares of Parthia coming down to attack the Pikestaffe household. I explained to the Reverend

[3]"Cooking with gas" was his usual translation. Z. E.

what a good sermon that would make. After being fed so long on cereal and substitute, when the real guts of doctrine were offered them, the congregation were terrified. Grover Pikestaffe said yes, it would make strong preaching, but let's keep it to ourselves."

"Poor Richard," said Zoe. "What an almanac you live. You've fenced yourself in with so many private fantasies, fables, symbols, you're practically cancelled. You're worth a fortune to a psychiatrist. I mean a disinterested psychiatrist. I don't know whether it's ego-involvement or disintegration; or impairment of restraint? It would be fun to run you through a few ink-blots."

"What the hell are they?" I grumbled sourly. "Maybe I'm just an ink-blot myself."

"Watch yourself among all these double meanings," she said. "Things have a meaning of their own beside what freak you choose to impose on them. Those children, dogs, goldfish, grass, et cetera, what do they care how you symbolize them? Be careful about double meanings; the second meaning might come true."

"I'm sorry," I said. "I can't help it if I do sometimes think things that are beautiful."

"Come behind these birch trees, you helpless old ape."

I didn't like the idea of the birch trees, whiter than women and emblem of death in the old ballads; but one doesn't debate about privilege.

"What's going on here?" said my Stranger. It isn't right to hide behind birch trees wearing white clothes. Birches, growing in clumps, lean radial from the root like ideas.

A light must have been turned on chez Sharpy, for we were suddenly caught in a shaft of brightness.

"What's going on here?" said Sharpy, lumbering down the slope.

"We were just having an argument," I said. "I thought Doppel was under a ton of sand."

"Never argue with Dick," Sharpy said. "He can argue the cocoanuts off Brigham Young."

"I'm only an ink-blot."

"Never mind. Come on in. I've got an eraser."

&§ I sit and think, especially about people who never had the curse of sitting and thinking. . . . as Keats said, "Until the whole wide world to nothingness do sink." Keats, poor boy, and with full reason, had the posthumous sense. The sense of Something Coming.

Even if wiped out, which they so methodically plan, human beings maybe justify themselves by what they have invented against such drastic odds?

But I'd rather wipe myself than be wiped??

Don't ever forget, Zoe, our double question-mark is the most loving double meaning we will ever have??

I am sorry to be bashful; the quality women most resent?? I didn't mean to be thinking about women at all, it was those damned caterpillars in Miss Tally's blouse. At least they perished going uphill.

Zoe, once you said—once to me, I mean; it may be a stereotype for your patients—"If you show life the least courtesy, you'll find its arms around your neck." I could add to this, but I love you too much. How were men cursed with this horrible hunger for life, they can't imagine how civilized Death can be?

Time smoothes away everything. It glosses our most intimate agonized memories into peace and prose. I found an anecdote in my Keatsiana.[4] Someone visiting Madrid, about 1880, saw at a reception a stately, massive, elderly placid Señora. She looked like a female Castle in Spain. His host said, "Do you know who that is? That is John Keats's baby sister." The whole icy cascade of human irony is in that episode.

I was glad Sharpy had seen Zoe again, because now if he and I should get to talking privately he would know what I was talking about. That, if not abused, is man's kindest charity to

[4] Perhaps in Colvin's *Life of Keats*, which Keats so much prefers to Amy Lowell's ditto. It never occurred to Amy how she would have terrified him. R. T.

man. I wrote him a couple of postcards but Betty said he had been Detained in Town. Finally they came over for a drink. Sharpy was in an off mood, and started badly by saying that Betty was angry with him.

I said, just for something to say (and to give Betty a chance to bristle), "A man who hasn't made a woman angry is a failure in life."

They were silent. Then Betty:—

"Considering all the opportunities he must have had, it's unlikely."

"I don't know why Dick talks such whistleberries," said Sharpy. "He hasn't the faintest idea what a long patient persistent career it is to live with a Good Woman."

Betty blew. "You can't say that about me," she screamed. "I won't endure it! I'm *not* a Good Woman, and I never was; and I don't intend to be."

What Sharpy inferred or implied from this outcry I would not examine. I looked steadfastly at the pleats in the summer drapes that Mealie had hoisted. Betty was streaming and gargling; Sharpy seized her by various flanges and impelled (or implied or inferred) her to their car.

"We better get home," he said, and trod the starter.

The car was almost mute; only a faint moan. We had to get Yakle Horowitz, the kindly mechanic, out of bed, to diagnose the silence.

"I'm sorry, Mr. Cullen," he said by flashlight. "Your generator's burned out."

Yakle pushed them home, bumper to bumper. The last I heard was Betty's hysterical laugh, sliced up by the birch trees.

HAILSTONES IN THE CHIMNEY

§ I have had an anxious time with Mealie. Her boy Salmon, who got himself into some kind of trouble, has disappeared. I didn't hear about it until I noticed my orange juice tasted bitter. I always drink it carefully, to be sure not to swallow any pulp or seeds. (Orange pips I believe are fatal, as they were in Sherlock Holmes.)

"You didn't put salt in by mistake?"

Mealie said she might have wept in it, and told me about Salmon. "He just run off and vanish. Been gone four days now and no sign."

"Have you told the police?"

"I'm allergy to policemen. Folks like us, less we get public the better."

I felt guilty; I had forgotten about Salmon. Of course I've been very busy, what with prickly heat and postponing the dentist. I phoned the police myself. Naturally they asked if I had any suggestions, and I told them the little I knew. I concealed from Mealie their remark that they could hardly search every station on the Long Island Railroad.

A sergeant and his fellow patrol came round in their smart little car to ask questions. Mealie was terrified, but also flattered. "God in Brooklyn, they send two cops, they must figure it take more'n one shammus to overpower that boy. He always been

175

athletical, I wish he get into something with social standing, like prizefight. Way he act now, he just one more jigaboo."

Later was one of those hot spongy evenings as we get (I've been fowlered off the adverb-conjunction *like*) and a recurring thunderstorm kept rolling around and accomplishing nothing. I could see Mealie was anxious because she rushed to the phone when it rang. Usually she won't do that: "My mother tole me, never talk on foam in a thunderstorm."

She cautiously held the receiver so far from her ear that it took a little time to understand. "She say Person-Person in Philadelphia."

Better, anyway, than reversed charges from Hollywood. It was Seldom Frank, who said that Philadelphia had discovered James Joyce and he was founding a Germantown Branch of the James Joyce Society. Would I take a life membership for 100 dollars?

"For whose life?" I bleated, cringing as javelins of lightning quivered into Wending Ways.

"Two dollars a year, or a hundred for life," he repeated.

"I don't expect to live that long, especially in thunderstorms. Our bosky acres are being ripped to pieces. *The Tempest*, Act Four, very appropriate."

"What?" he said.

"No," I said firmly. "But I'll give you a motto for the society: We stew in our own Joyce."

He was griped, and rang off. The storm stumbled eastward, the air cooled in dark drip (indoors as well as out: there's a leak in the flashings of the shingles and my powder-room is one puddle). I sent Mealie home in a taxi and prepared for a peaceful evening. I was all ready to knock myself out with something really stuporific, good tedious trudging stuff like (as) Austin Dobson's 18th Century Studies or Pearsall Smith's carborundums from the English Aphorists. I had been so busy all day (I don't remember at what) I hadn't even put on socks and shoes.

I decided to drag a mattress into the living room and sleep on the floor where there is always a creep of cool air. It was only about 9 P.M., but I regard that, socially, as the iron curtain. Old sobersides Austin Dobson looked good sedative, better than luminal. I set out my books of mercy, I spread and smoothed a sheet on the mattress. Then I added, just in case, proofs of an English detective story, which I had to read for business. I disposed myself to think at large. I thought. . . .

I saw right away I would have to do some editing on the English detective story, for U.S. readers. I have my own system, I always change barley-water, kedgeree or fish-pie, and treacle pudding, to buttermilk, clam chowder, and apple betty. No one has ever complained.

I found, with anxiety, my thoughts were getting personal. It was frightfully humid and my neck oozed. I had a grand idea: I have some new sheets of desk-size blotting paper. I sliced a long strip for an absorbent collar which I fastened round my throat, with that tie-pin you gave me. I turned from the detective story to Dobson on Swift and Stella. I was almost feeling like Swift (the Journal is much more mischievous than the profs ever told us)—I was thinking, I couldn't tell my despair to anyone else, and only to you because maybe you share it——

And who comes me chapping at the door but Betty Cullen. I was embarrassed, because a mattress and sheet on the living-room floor looks loopy, or lupanar. In the Electric Elite people would rather toss wakeful on their proper beds than sleep where they're not supposed.

But I welcomed her with my well-known courtesy. If I was going to be humiliated I might as well get it over.

"What is this," she exclaimed. "An assignation? Or have you a sore throat? Of course a bachelor's sleeping arrangements are his own affair. I understand, I am very broadminded. You know my father was a bohemian too."

"But not a bachelor," I insisted. "Have a drink; I've only got rum."

"Do you think I better, in this warm weather? It makes me so sticky I can't get my girdle off."

177

"Keep it on. Where is Old Sharpy, after curfew? Detained in Town?"

The smooth white freshness of sheet-on-mattress (I am fussy about a well-crimped sheet) shone up at us in the lamplight. I had set the desk-lamp on the floor upstage, and Austin Dobson was propped at the comfortable angle against a sofa cushion. It really is shame-making when one's innocent little mise-en-scène is exposed to outsiders. I have always tried to explain to Urban Block or any other clients who hanker to write fiction, it's not necessary to invent anything; the interpretation of what actually happens is intricate enough.[1] . . . I was wondering if, at my present timing and living, I know what really happens and what doesn't? . . . I missed some of Betty's remarks.

". . . on a Retreat," she said. "Someone in the vestry, one of the Pikestaves, must have been working on him. He's at a monastery up the Hudson. He sent me a circular about it. They've got him jobbing in the cellar, for God's sake!"

"The wine cellar?"

"There's nothing there but empty hogsheads. They're going to make bookshelves out of them."

"I never thought of that: bookshelves with curves? They can put the folios in the middle, and the little 24-mo breviaries at the ends."

"He says the Great Silence extends from Compline until after Breakfast."

"Alas, my dear, it extends longer than that."

"I suppose you were having a little compline of your own," she said, looking at Austin Dobson. "But you shouldn't read lying on the floor, you'll have presbyopia. I saw a piece about it in the paper. Is that a kind of religion?"

"Just old man's eyes. I've seen enough anyhow. I don't need to see anything more."

[1] I always quote to them, but in vain, the immortal first chapter of Conrad's *A Personal Record* (copyright, 1912). Without digesting that neither writer, reviewer, publisher, nor agent, has begun to earn a life. The "accumulated verisimilitude of selected episodes!"

R. T.

"Nor Sharpy neither," she said angrily. "I always know, when he gets spiritual zeal, he's building up mischief. The big lout, I bet he's fixing to make a beast of himself."

"Dr. Johnson said when a man does that he gets rid of the pain of being a man."

She meditated while I poured her a lenient rum and water.

"I shouldn't blurt in on you like this, but being alone in the house in a thunderstorm gives me short circuits. I couldn't even call up Sharpy at that monastery, he'd be in his Great Silence by now."

"Perhaps he'll be struck by lightning," I suggested. "I knew a monastery in Canada that was built on a ridge of iron-ore, it was a regular switchboard for high voltage."

"If there was iron there he'd have them digging it up to make pipe.—Let's talk about something pleasant. I don't know which smells sweeter, this rum or your bowl of roses."

"I think the roses are stronger," I said.

"Oh, the heavenly things." She buried her face in them. "They make you want to die, the world is so lovely and we mess it up so."

"Die of a rose in aromatic pain," I quoted. "I was just reading, Pope got 'aromatic pain' from the Countess of Winchilsea."

"Goodness; I didn't know it was catching. I thought it was just this damp weather."

I explained, and put in a plug for the most perfect poet who ever lived. "I didn't say the greatest; I said the most perfect."

"I suppose Popes were always infallible."

"Sometimes too perfect. He rings a little mechanical bell at the end of every line, like a typewriter."

"Why can't we always have conversations like this?" Betty cried. "This is the kind of thing I really buy, Dr. Johnson and Pope and Austin Hobson. When you and Sharpy foregather you are so coarse. I must say it's sometimes very apt, but men get vulgar at the wrong time of life. Do you suppose I could send a telegram to Sharpy at his Retreat? I thought of a wonderful wisecrack, it would really wring his withers."

"It must be good," I said. "His withers are tough."

"I'd have to have more rum, or more roses, before I could tell it. Make it rum; roses have thorns."

"Rum has thorns, too."

"What is that book there, Aphorisms by Smith? I was hoping you'd lend me something to read. What are aphorisms?"

"The thorns of literature. But what is the Western Union thorn to stab Sharpy?"

"I got it down to ten words," she said proudly.

"Then you're an aphorist at heart."

"*You shouldn't make sewer pipe you should pass through it.*"

"Eleven words," I said. "*Shouldn't* counts two, it's an aperstrophy.—You can send it on my phone if you want."

"No, no," she said impatiently. "I've got it off my chest now." She was looking over the preface of Pearsall Smith's *English Aphorisms* in the hasty searching way of those who think that a book, some book, almost any book, might solve their problems.

"Maybe I'll borrow this, I might make with aphorisms myself. It would give me something to do while Sharpy fashions barrelstave bookshelves."

She leafed over the pages with woman's feverish inquisition.

"I get the idea; you can say almost anything if you make it short enough? Who is this Chesterfield, writing scruples to his son?"

"His son was a bastard. The noble lord couldn't give the boy his estate, so he gave him a piece of his mind instead."

"Warning him against his father's enthusiasm? That's foul about men, they enjoy something and then make shame for it. —I'll say for Sharpy, he never apologizes."

"You don't want to read a whole book of aphorisms," I said. "It's like eating a meal of bouillon cubes. Modern bouillon is all chemistry and few beef. Try Pope's *Essay On Man*."

"Oh rare!" she exclaimed. "That sounds right up my alley. I could write one myself."—She looked at the volume I brought.

180

"Hell, it's poetry. No, I prefer aphorisms. Here's what Dr. Johnson said—say, how wonderful if someone brought these things up to date. I can imagine him saying 'I would spend my life driving briskly with a pretty woman in a Mercury Convertible.' "

You don't get anything out of literature, I realized, just lying alone on a mattress and reading yourself into a presbyopia. The way literature comes through is when you've got a woman around to double it down to her own business and bosoms.

"Men are such prigs," I thought, and unconsciously said it.

Betty was delighted. "There's a word I haven't heard since my mother died. What is a prig? Is it the same as a Tory? They used to elect them to Parliament? Prigs is prigs?"

"I'd have to call up Miss Tally and get the dictionary out of the safe, to be sure. Offhand, I would say he's a social account-executive. Correct in a small way and tries to sell it in a big way. Like a man I saw mentioned in the business pages of the New York *Times*: he used to be a paper-box maker, but now he's a packaging consultant."

"Like a man who used to be a literary agent and now he's an authors' representative."

"Touché," I admitted.

"Of course I know, in business, you have to give yourself the kind of label people will buy. It's what Sharpy calls 'consumer pressure.' But don't you think our packaged civilization is pretty wonderful? Sharpy and I had a shack on a lake in the Berkshires. We practically lived on packages. We had a baby Sears Roebuck icebox, and canned soup and canned liver paste and canned beer. We had cartons of paper towels, and marshmallows and tomatoes in cellophane. We had everything the Consumers' League sneers at, and we loved it."

"What kind of grub does Sharpy get at that monastery? Old Hudson Valley buckwheat, ground by ye ancient millstones? And a flitch of bacon, smoked from the rafters like a Spanish saint?"

"If he comes back and sneers at my can opener I'll kill him. He kidded me once because my can opener was never rusty, and I told him his corkscrew isn't either. If your corkscrew isn't too rusty I'll have another swatch of rum."

She dredged a little rum and water (more, by my providence, of this than of that) but I could see that she was far enough off first base so she'd have to slide for second on the pitcher's wind-up.

"Still I'm thinking," she said. "Our civilization is a sales package. And now Sharpy says the Soviets, who just pick up things off the dump as they go along, are going to bully us out of it."

"The Soviets," I said, "are mostly dung, Doukhobors, and Dostoievsky."

My habit of treble alliterates leads me into some dangerous traps, but Betty didn't notice. She was looking again at Pearsall Smith.

"These aphorisms really say what they think. Here's someone called Hazlitt: *The least pain in our little finger gives us more concern than the destruction of millions of our fellow beings.*—That's horribly true. I've often thought that myself. I bet everybody has thought everything. We have disgusting minds, don't we."

"I know I did, until I learned to yield gently to temptation. —Of course to do that you must first be tempted."

"That reminds me of Sharpy in France," said Betty, but was interrupted by borborygmus. "Pardon," she said; "I was too nervous to eat tonight and I've got a little gas. Even the stomach has its own aphorisms."

"Betty," I said, "you're swell. You're swollen. Maybe it's good for you to have Sharpy in retreat?"

"*Il recule pour mieux sauter.* I learned that at Beaverbrook, before I knew it was an Essay on Man. Is that an aphorism or an epigram? What's the difference?"

"Maybe one is a prig and one is a Tory. An epigram is a hard-shell clam; an aphorism is a glass prism. But what about Sharpy in France?"

"He said he went over there to see if their lives were as irregular as their verbs. He read in a textbook that the French are superfluous people, given to dancing, light wines, and light women. Don't you love our envious American hope that other nations are so much wickeder than we are? I do get awfully depressed about the American psyche.—I'm smelling your roses again. I'd forgotten they were like this. They just crept up on us while we were asleep. Like Stalin, or cancer, or Sharpy. We always forget, don't we. I've got to go home."

"Drive easy," I said; and then, quoting the great admonishment of radio: "Remember, the life you save may be your own."

"I think you've saved mine. I'm almost over the hump."

"It was good catharsis," I said. "Latch onto a can of soup when you get home."

"And go to bed with chemical cubes—— Where's that book?"

I gave her the Aphorisms. We had got as far as the screen door.

"Storm's over," I encouraged her. "The fireflies have come out again. I like to watch them during the rain, they shelter low down in the shrubs but they blink back resolutely to the blazes of lightning."

"Like aphorists, I suppose," she said bitterly. "Damn philosophers and prigs, were their own lives any happier and better than anyone else's?"

How womanly it is to ask the unanswerable at the moment impossible. A whole aperçu flashed into my mind, it would have been fun to expatiate. I thought of the Johnsonian gloom, the frenzy of Hazlitt, the cotton-wool chasms of Proust, Keats's bleeding lung, Emily Dickinson like a spinster moth in her barren virgin garden behind a poison-hemlock hedge. I was about to say, "Pearsall Smith's was; always on the run from any kind of responsibility. He began as a beautiful young Philadelphia prig, and he fought his way up to the paracme. . . ."

I was about to pull Betty back indoors and say Wait a minute, I want to talk. Then a yelling siren went screaming through the hinderlands of our woods. Someone's house had been struck by lightning? Even the cats on the cellar stairs set up a squall.

Betty also. Her lovely defeated dewlapped face brimmed with tears. "I'm frightened," she bubbled. "I'm terrified. I can't go on, it's too dangerous. Too much la-ightning—and con-su-mer pressure. It might strike once in the same place. I didn't tell you, I heard hailstones come down the chimney. What good are hailstones if the house is on fire? To hell with aphorisms, they're just cold little hailstones in the chimney."

The siren of the fire truck decrescendoed somewhere beyond. Betty flung my precious book into a wet rosebush and scrambled into her car.

I gave the cats a can of jellied consommé that Mealie had iceboxed. It's always amusing to see them get it gummed in their whiskers, but it calms them as Austin Dobson does me. I looked up his dates, too, as my mind works on a calendar. 1840–1921. . . . I thought about Austin Dobson and his 1890 overlap of moustache. I thought about the sandpile: no sand or gravel is heavy enough to bury human hunger. I better have another look at the sandpile, to be sure.

Out on the wet drive, the air still heavy. Rainspouts gargling, fireflies morseing about. They were sparkling like young English poets on their first trip abroad, looking for an American agent, so they could sneer at him. There was more storm to come, I could tell by a sort of Third Party feeling in the air. My ivory-groin birch tree was curtseyed, drenched with social purpose like a Canadian novelist. (I have to think of things in terms of my own trade.) It's a pity we have too much lightning in our climate and not enough fireflies. Pearsall Smith, old flittermouse from American biliousness, said his joy was to dance with the glowworms. I retrieved his book: probably the only one ever thrown into a wet rosebush full of fireflies. That pleased me, and would have pleased him. I like to have pleased someone. . . .

No one nursed on Matthew Arnold (I said to the flopping roses) ever outgrows him; yet he did outgrow himself in some wonderful poems, old moody dancer on redhot moral ploughshares, trailing a faint spice of macassar oil in those indoctrinated whiskers. I wasn't sleepy any more, I was having such unexpected fun I sponged off the roses with my face. "The roses, as all roses should be, were nose-high," wrote E. V. Lucas in his pleasantest vein. (*Windfall's Eve*, Methuen, 1929.) When I took the *Aphorisms* back into the house I looked up Arnold's dates. 1822–88—couplets again. Then I had another small rum, and got a shovel to dig. I hope I sometimes have imaginative dominion over experience (Pearsall Smith got the phrase from Santayana; *The Life of Reason*, 1914) but I also know one has to use tools.

As I went down the drive, in a night so stormed and sweetened, there wasn't an insect in the garden I'd have changed places with. Rum, rheumatism, and rebellion, I said. My mind is an alcove of irrelevant echoes, but isn't it wonderful, in a world of insect teleology, to be Tolman, the Man without a Purpose, the Neo-Nincompoop. There came to my mind Arnold's rose-garden dirge—

> My life was turning, turning,
>   In mazes of heat and sound. . . .
> Tonight I shall inherit
> The vasty hall of Death.

I changed the pronouns, as Zoe taught me to do. I can rewrite anyone's poetry to advantage except my own. *It* is a paltry little anonym. Pronouns rise in dignity (and pinpoint effervescence) from *it* to *him*, from *him* to *her*, from *her* to *You*. . . .

Me is the most sensitive of all. That's why I left it out. I'll have to pay plenty for this anyhow when Zoe analyzes it. The hunger-cry (which is literature) should be short and savage, not long and lugubrious.

P.S. This, I add, is not a love letter but a Letter of Love. I had thought of nothing else for so long, and found it shattered into debris of beauty and ribaldry. Could those broken bits be put in pattern together, a stained-glass window worthy of Chartres. Be patient with all vulgar cries of mirth and pain. They wouldn't be so sunset if there weren't pain behind them. Even the most perfect stained-glass windows are held together by curly veins of dull plumber's lead.

Perhaps the worst dishonesty is to say "I thought," when what I mean is, "I'm thinking now. . . ."

LET ME GIVE YOU A LIGHT

⎈§ Moist close-packed con-
voluted darkness; perhaps Wending Ways is really (*really?* If
we're going to bicker adverbs, there's one to examine??)—is
Wending Ways "really" only a blueprint or mortgage map of
the brain? These precautionary sandpiles scattered through the
woods, are they anxiety-dumps or little deposits of prudence?

How ironical, therefore how human-likely, if Salmon were
buried in that sandpile, at the very foot of the overgrown lawn
I wanted him to mow. I could see his beautiful young tawny
body choked and fouled in the brown-sugar gravel, only a few
yards from where his mother worked and wept. Really, or not
really? Or was he strangled and suffocated in our sand-dunes of
social silt?

If you and I, from first pang of self, had to keep an invisible
forearm raised against power, would we not also scribble muck
on the walls?

I thought more kindly (for a moment) of my screwball
clients; I could see they were trying to struggle up from moraines
of debris; trying, in their haggard mood, to suggest the despairs
of man. Alas, it is not enough to be sorry; you must be an artist
as well. An artist can be an artist in fewer words than he realizes.

This was in the few steps going down the drive, my shovel
on my shoulder like a work-battalion.

The sand was dense and heavy as one of our historical

novels, but I dug bravely. With method too; I shifted the whole pile some yards to one side. There was nothing in it but a few desiccated starfish. I kept myself going by muttering "Ozymandias, king of kings . . . the lone and level sands stretch far away." (A very irregular sonnet, incidentally.)

I paused to pant and sweat. I picked up a dried starfish, thinking at least it ought to be an asterisk referring to some footnote, and there was That Man sitting on the mound.

"You might have spared me some labor," I said. "You're the one I was digging for."

"I spare you nothing. Catch your breath and let's have a talk."

I threw down the shovel, which was shiny with friction. The cigarettes in my breast pocket were damp and bent, I could hardly raise a light. "I suppose the exercise was good for me," I said peevishly. "I thought I was going to have a nice quiet evening curled up with a book."

"Still thinking of yourself."

"I wasn't at all. I was digging for bodies. I think there are a lot of people buried in that dump. I can see their faces, kind of shrivelled, peeking out now and then. Little grains of sand run down out of their nostrils, they look like shrunken heads from the Amazon."

"It's nice to have a talk, isn't it," he said. "Maybe all these sandpiles, rosebushes, fireflies, and ponds and shrubbery ravines are just fantasy."

"You can't do that to me. You can't tell me what I've been thinking."

"Not unless you want to know."

"Well, give me the pitch. I don't like the way Nature parodies human life."

"Maybe it's the other way round."

I preferred not to think too much about that. I am never sordid in cold blood. "I'm delighted," I said, "to find you so conversational. I thought you were just an undertaker's mute at the funeral of civilization."

188

I must have been gaga, it seemed to me he grabbed a firefly from the sultry air and used it to light a cigarette.

"Conversation is too exhausting," he said. "I mean for the people one talks to. As for civilization, don't worry about its funeral. It will move on, to another star, or another sandpile."

"Bushwa," I exclaimed. "I don't buy this astronomic ever-expanding universe. I take a clear view of man within his artistic limitations. All he can achieve is mortal hunger and mortal curiosity, perfectly expressed. If that's what you did in that MS. you left with me, I'll get it published."

"I'm sorry you're so argumentative. You've given all your other friends such a run for their money, I was hoping you'd give Me a few sides."

I didn't like to say that I hadn't ever thought of him as a friend. (Though I admit, a murderer has a peculiarly intimate feeling about his victim.) I was cagy and didn't say anything. No one can call me argumentative without a struggle. He surprised me by a gesture of courtesy. "Let me give you a Light," he said, and handed me a dry cigarette and a twitch of flame.

"Thanks," I said. "Sure, Man is beset by unimportant details. How else would he learn how trivial they are?"

"Nothing is so trivial as you think."

"I don't like this conversation," I said, "each of us seems to be saying what the other one ought to say. I don't like this talk about Man and how he behaves. But I tell you what I'll do, I'll take expert advice and report back."

He got up, shook some of the sand of mortality off his clothes. I gathered that I had bored him. I can bore anyone if I try to be honest. The night had stopped dripping, it was that peaceful middle dark when only the 3 A.M. prowl-car goes through and startles the bedroom with a flush of headlights as it gently turns the corner. The beam caught the polished lip of my shovel, and the birch-white clothes of my visitor. I wondered if the cops would pause to inquire; they halted, and then went on. I was peevish, because I needed sleep; all men do, and will never get enough of it until they get nothing but. I put away the shovel

189

and fell on the mattress. I think even then I knew what had to be done.

✒ I reread, for the many-th time, Dobson's description of Dean Swift in bed—I could even smell the singe of his candle where it scorched the bed-curtain. He was saying good night to Stella in his Little Language; God pity those who have never had Little Languages of their own, and I think I have a closer guess at breaking Swift and Stella's code than our prof in English 88 (Prose Masters of the Eighteenth Century) ever imagined. PDFR, as Swift signed himself, looks like a broadcasting station, and indeed he was. . . . I was remembering by smell, because once at Rosy's Place she lit a candle to look for a book on a shadowy shelf, and accidentally held the flame against a dingy old curtain.

Memory is special pleading. Whatever you remember, dream or fact, has been screened in your own interest by the Brownies.[1] "The past, whether feigned or suffered, is all of one texture." I wonder? Surely the dream is more vivid? Its rich furnish and detail; meticulated mimicry of sounds and sights, accents and gestures, arts and lusts and sciences of which consciously we knew nothing. We saw "no longer blinded by our eyes" (Rupert Brooke). And all those privily packed possessions, those tunes and rhymes and godlike glimpses, memories and musette bags, what becomes of them at the end?

✒ I remember now, where I used to see Young Doppel. It was at Rosy's Place—R.S.V.P. we called her: Rosy Sotto Voce Picasso, because being both unmoral and unconstitutional she always spoke softly. (I was telling the Girls, I mean Gin and Ginger. It's wholesome, when you have a chance, to tell things to people who won't, or can't, correct and contradict. Bless them, they are still knee-deep in reality; yet because they come from Philadelphia they still have innocent faith.)

[1]The allusion is to Stevenson's essay *A Chapter on Dreams*, of much interest to psychologists, but not easy to find except in the Collected Works or in the file of *Scribner's Magazine*, 1888. Z. E.

190

It was at the old Grillparzer Club, the original Rosy's Place, long ago. Philadelphia had its tenderloin, too, and more tender than the vanished New York slum. (In N.Y. they turned the naked Tenderloin into a garment center, by way of evening things up.) The long brown velvet curtains were across the windows, and it had a comfortable 1910 feeling—the last time the world ever felt comfortable. I thank whatever gods there were to have known just once such a resort of Rabelaisian relief. It must have been there I saw him, because we were young and pure and happy. But Rosy's wasn't a pure kind of place—and then when she moved to New York and some Viennese artist renamed her speakeasy the Grillparzer to flatter the after-supper crowd, it became corrupted with ambition. It became fashionable, as places do in New York, even built a fir-tree forest (made of strips of varnished nylon) and the waiters had to fight hard to keep their South-Teuton trills on the tip of their tongues. It wasn't necessary for any producer to put on Grillparzer's plays, because they had been done so often already under other names. We still had to "take" Grillparzer in German 31 at Wisconsin, but after 1914 he went down the sink.

"Never heard of him," said the girls, "but a wonderful name for a chophouse."

Yes, it sounds like a Rostbratstube. But I'm thinking of *Der Traum ein Leben*, or *Des Meeres und der Liebe Wellen*. I used to go swimming in Lake Mendota and think it was just like Grillparzer's Hellespont. But that mammal-girl from the School of Animal Husbandry couldn't understand that Hero was feminine. She would remember now, if I reminded her; but that isn't real remembering?

I'm filling this in afterward, I'm sure that Minnesota Mammal wasn't part of my swoon. Dreams deal with essential significance. They telescope time, collapse the diseased lung of fact, and blue-pencil themselves. But when I talk, or even imagine I'm talking, to Gin and Ginger, I get excessive. Twins, so diverse and so sympatica, are not an audience but a megaphone.

I guess it really was Philadelphia, because (the way I feel it, thirty years later) it was a north-south street. In New York the pleasanter hideaways, like the police stations, were set east-west? I know there was some association with Edgar Allan Poe who once lived in that neighborhood. White Trash Poe, Rosy called him, for reasons of her own. Our little crowd worked on a foundering newspaper—there once was a time when Nearly Everybody in Philly didn't read the same paper—and spent our most profitable hours at Rosy's. It needed tact, though, because you couldn't sit very long in the dining room downstairs without noticing that something was going on above. There were visitors we called the shelly horns and promontory goats (we were all reading Meredith then)[2] who came in and whispered sotto voce to Rosy at the desk in the hall and then went furtively upward. It was so long since the place had been cleaned you could see puffs of dust under their footsteps, always (I used to think, in my young horror) like smoke under the hooves of Mephisto. Rosy smiled and made a memo in her desk. It was a rolltop.

Rosalie Picasso, a grand old overlapping structure; if still alive she must be past eighty, but I expect eggplant parmigiana and osso bucco and veal scallopini with saffron-risotto burst her sutures long ago. Picasso in her name was just an accident, the important thing was Rosalie. She maintained, and after a few Schuylkill Scotch would sell you a case of, that she was a pirated second-reprint of Tom Chivers, the mysterious figure who kept writing the same poems that Poe did, only funnier. To hear her recite *Rosalie Lee* (Chivers' version of *Annabelle* ditto) would have stumored the cops; more than once, it did. We used to gravel her by saying that no great poet ever had such a loyal friend as Poe had in Chivers, who showed how great Poe's poems were by burlesquing them,—sometimes even before they were written? Wasn't there something the same that happened to Keats, that lady called Mrs. Tighe? As I said about Sarah Bernhardt's wooden leg, I must look it up. It happens in politics, too, the

<hr />

[2] It took me a long time to check this: *Phoebus with Admetus*, Stanza VIII. I always thought it good that R. T. kept reading Meredith long after Meredith's publishers did. Z. E.

jocose rehearsal of an event before it actually takes place. Hazlitt wrote something about that, I think in his essay on *Cant and Hypocrisy*—did I ever read it to you?

Yes, you did, the girls said. We were badly confused, we thought it was about the philosopher Kant, and we got flunked in Ethics at Bryn Mawr for saying Kant was a hypocrite.—Tell us more about Rosy.

Inherited from her grandeditor, I suppose, she was crazy about poetry and without severe discriminations. She was mighty cute about petty cash, but a book reviewer or a poet could hang up a check on her. I was doing poetry reviews for the paper so if I didn't have money I'd take her a book instead, or even write her something. "A mellow Cydonian sucket," we would say (quoting T. H. Chivers) and hand her a lyric typed in purple on yellow copy-paper. She had a passion for poetry that never really got across, like Meredith's *Ode to the Comic Spirit* (which was worth to me several platters of ravioli and baked shad) or Henry Frank's *The Story of America Sketched in Sonnets* (copyright, 1911; Sherman, French & Co.). She used to sit in that dingy little hall—the place was two old Victorian houses straddled into one, the fusky carpeted stair went up behind her into a heavy twilight of patchouli and chypre and b.o.—and turn from her accounts to the latest volume of verse. As the grand-daughter of a Southron she was always pleased by Confederate sentiment. She seemed to learn other people's poetry unconsciously (like her gaffer?) and I remember her putting forth Henry Frank's sonnet on Appomattox:—

> Dull o'er the dolorous land the painful thud
> Of failure's final volley fell unheard. . . .

(Some lines intervened, I forget, and then with an upstairs gesture she went on:—)

> Comfort could
> Be found in winding arms of love, who gird
> Their loins for lowlier ambitions' sway.

"Rosy," I said, "arms can't gird their loins. But I could gird a jolly good bowl of spaghetti if you think Henry Frank rates it."

"What happened upstairs?" said the girls. "The chypre and the goats?"

"Upstairs was professional, but Rosy was one of those wise delicate-minded old madams who knew I wasn't interested. She was really a sort of managing editor for young men; I remember she had Toulouse-Lautrec lithographs and Felicien Rops and pre-Raphaelite posters in the hall and dining room, but the light was so cautious it took me a long while to appreciate them. All my art education has been that way, in the most casual and vulgar studios. You can't learn about art in the college library. They wouldn't let you even if you wanted to. But after we got on terms, one evening Rosy invited me upstairs. She waddled ahead along various corridors; I remember how startled I was when a door opened and a beautifully naked redheaded girl came out and crossed the passage with a towel on her neck. 'Excuse me,' she said, 'I just want to get in the bath with Eunice.' As Keats said (*Letters*, II, 467) I had never seen a redhaired girl before. She opened the bathroom door and Eunice was rising from the tub streamy with foam. Like Venus from suds.

" 'Come on in, treacle tart,' said Eunice (who was brunette, *passim*), 'I'm all through.' Eunice must have been English, to mention treacle tart? But that's exactly what the other looked like a wedge of."

Bill Mickle was with me; he was about to be fired from the paper for literary allusions, but we didn't know it then. He turned to me and said "Stendhal stuff, Le Rouge et le Noir."

"When I take a bath," said old Rosy, "I like to take it by myself."

I suppose all this must have happened. It couldn't be so clear in my mind if it wasn't actual? Every time I think about Rosy's I see that lovely white-and-gold figure cross the hall, and the door open on the dark and soapy tanagra in the crummy old bathroom. The girls took their baths so hot, the ceiling-plaster was always flaking off into the tub.

"Just a fantasy," said the twins. "If a thing recurs again and again, it's a signal, it means a wish-frustration."

194

"So everything is Freudian now," I said sourly. "Nuts, I've never had a frustration; only what old Canon Spooner called a half-warmed fish. I know it was real, because Rosy said her mother told her that as a child she (her mother) saw Edgar Poe and he complained of a headache. She was only twelve years old, and innocently put her hand on his forehead and was horrified. She said it was red-hot."

"I bet there hasn't been a hot forehead in Philly since then," said Gin.

"Except in political conventions," said Ginger.

I continued. "Rosy turned a right angle, or outflanked it, and led me to a room at the back of the house, looking over the yard and a ragged ailanthus tree. A real overstuffed 1900 sitting room with heavy curtains and gas-lamps and a cosy-corner, and there was her husband, Mr. Picasso. Now I knew why she was crazy about Toulouse-Lautrec.[3] Mr. Picasso was also a misshapen dwarf. He had been the great Professor Phil Picasso, the midget magician in vaudeville, but arthritis had bent him like italics. He sat in a dusty Morris chair, wearing a derby hat, and surrounded by all the appliances and props of his old career. He had a basket of glass balls in his lap, and when we came in he gave us the patter and started to throw the balls in the air. Poor soul, it was like a poet laureate trying to write an occasional poem for duty and the London *Times*. The balls rolled round the floor, but he was just as pleased. He cocked his hat sideways on his big-dwarf head and said 'How's that?' The room was stacked with bookcases of poetry, including even the Philadelphia ½oets who had to publish at their own expense. Rosy sat down, poured snorts of bourbon, and said, 'Still the showman.'

" 'Have we had First Warning?' Phil said. 'The trombones get here? Tell them grease their slides.'

" 'Sure,' she said; and explained. 'Mr. Winkelsteen, the theater manager, is coming tonight, that's why I had Eunice and

[3]So was Richard. He used to annoy me by asking if I remembered the Toulouse-Lautrecs at the Art Institute, Chicago. I have never been in Chicago. Z. E.

Treacle take baths. I thought they were a little strong after lunch. It's the Italian food, makes them perspire.' "

We used to talk about poetry, or Toulouse-Lautrec, for hours. The subject of Picasso was barred, because old Phil was jealous of his namesake. If the name was mentioned he would make a paraplegic attempt to repeat some of his professional conjuring and juggling. The tricks always failed, he would take off his derby hat and cry into it, and Rosy shouted downstairs for another pint of Cobbs Creek, an urgent local snakebite. She would turn to her crowded bookshelves, she had the greatest collection anywhere of the Forgotten Poets of Philadelphia but the light was beamed on Phil, it was hard to see the books. She even remembered Ezra Pound when he was a student at the U. of P. She had an autographed copy of *Quia Pauper Amavi* (it must have been worth at least a charger of ravioli) and quoted in moving tremolo:—

> God, how swift the night,
> And day comes on.

She insisted that the Philadelphia influence was just as important, in Ezra, as the Provençal.

"No one ever told us there were any poets in Philadelphia," said Gin.

"Nor any whorehouses," said Ginger. "All we ever knew was, the Symphony and the Hotel were on Broad Street, and the Paoli Local left at 15 and 45."

"I wonder if Chelton knew about all this," Gin muttered.

"Philadelphia keeps herself to herself," I said.

"There were always a lot of young men in this neighborhood," said Rosy, "who intended to write poetry, but it never got round to them."

The house-phone rang, from the little Filipino pimp who took the desk when Rosy was off duty. "Not a chance," I heard Rosy say. "You know damn well, no credit upstairs. Not even a bath without cash."

I don't think I was ever more happy, or more perfectly in-

196

terested in literature, than in those evenings. Names, publishers, bookstore sales, meant nothing to our dear fat Rosy. She liked the sound of intelligible words in a congenial voice. I remember giving her, in exchange for a bowl of minestrone, one of Vachel Lindsay's earliest books. She read *The Broncho That Would Not Be Broken of Dancing*. She said to me, "You can eat on that as long as you need to." Another nourishment was the greatest of Philadelphia's Forgotten Poems, Charles Leonard Moore's *Elegy on Edgar Allan Poe*, Rosy gave me her copy.[4]

Rosy gave all her girls a talk about both poetry and prophylactics, every week. It was a pity when she moved to New York (Mr. Picasso had to go to a hospital and she needed more money; she said neither a whorehouse nor a poet could ever break even in Philadelphia) and sold her first editions to a wealthy collector on the Main Line.

Phil's face had fallen into his bowler, and Bill Mickle was telling about a friend of his who wrote poetry while he was supposed to be working for Campbell's Tomato Soup in Camden; and I think Rosy was going to tell us about other naborhood poets—I'll be as prudent as their publishers and not mention their names. But I was tired. Nothing wearies a young ½oet like hearing about poets. Little did I know how much more tired I was going to be, a manhood later. I said: "Rosy, I gotta go, but I don't want to embarrass anybody in the corridor."

She looked at her watch. "All clear, Dick. Nobody in the bathroom now, they should all be in bed, earning their keep. If you see anyone, don't mind. The girls are only self-conscious when they have their clothes on."

But I was embarrassed; there was that same lovely divisible figure triangled in gold—she can't have been in the tub all that time?—but I didn't need to apologize. Young Doppel appeared (from where?) and snapped a nickeled gadget in front of me. "Let me give you a light."

[4]Noble and beautiful little book: *Odes* by Charles Leonard Moore (1854–1923), "published for the author," Philadelphia, 1896. "To America" is one of our few great patriotic poems. R. T.

I caught one of those grinding old Philadelphia trolleys, thinking of Meredith's Ode to the Comic Spirit. You can think of Meredith's poems, you can't remember them. But Rosy herself was the Comic Spirit. Perhaps she also, in her own smoky way, gave me a light. But what's the use of it until you know where you want to go?

᠊᠊ I sent Gin and Ginger indoors: I said I heard the telephone and it sounded like Wilkes-Barre. I had remembered another dream, a lovetime later. But it's better for uncles and nieces to keep their dreams apart. I was in a very wide bed in a chrome-and-crystal withdrawing room, more like Park Lane than Park Avenue. The double-duchess bed was in a vast salesroom-salon that sparkled with jewelries and bangles and bibelots; for patrons to take home as conscience-gifts? There were luxurious toys and trinkets in glass cases, priced in hundreds of what the English call gns., meaning guineas. I was in one of my sardonic moods, and kept saying "They must think I'm an American publisher." Then, as I was turning over to get fresh cool from the linen sheets —the kind of sheets you only get on Park Lane; America rolls on cotton—she came running like a child, light as hinnuleo, young and silky-gold as corn-tassel, flung herself burrowing into my surprise. I never felt so many arms and legs at once, they were slendered and cruppered all around me. It was Treacle Tart (I never had any other name for her, except Hinnuleo, which she thought I made up on the spur of the moment).[5] But like the glass show-cases she had a tag round her neck, which she had quite forgotten —it was beautifully hand-lettered and said Treacle Tart, $1000. It lay between her baby breasts and I said, "What's this?" She tore it off and said "That's a joke from Rosy; it doesn't mean a thing."

So it was sweet? So it didn't mean a thing? So it cost nothing but a memory? The girls came back to the garden and said (doubly innocent), "It must have been Wrong Number."

[5]Vitas hinnuleo me similis, Chloe. Horace, Odes I, xxiii.

CHILD OF GREED

One of those blazing days, like the one (years ago) that split my thermometer. I put it out on the sundial to see how high the juice would rise. It went above 120 deg, but when it sank again it left a smidge of red fluid up there, which has stayed ever since. That was tops. I guess everyone's memory has a little red wine-stain like that, way above normal scale, when they hit high flood-mark. Remember?? You said: "I have beauty for you, come take it. Oh child of hunger, I can give you rest." We left a little broken bubble of living, a stain of volatile scarlet, high in the crystal tube.

My bathroom has a window that looks over the woods; and as I was in my late tub I looked out and saw Sharpy Cullen glooming on my sandpile with his grandchildren. It must have been one of his babysit days. The children were frolicking in the yellow mound. He was like God, who loved apples and serpents and found Adam and Eve tiresome. His pipe drooped over his chin. The Retreat must have cut him down.

Cat and kitten were there too; they're always on that sand-pile; they were playing with the children, or vice versa; and Sharpy, poor ironmonger, was paying no attention. He looked as helpless as a man when the drawstring of his pajamas snaps inside the hem.

When the tub is cold and deep enough it really makes me

feel springbok. Mealie had laid out clean underwear, and I put on Ironer 5's fresh laundried duck pants, and my creaky crisscross Mexican huaraches, and went down to show Sharpy how much at ease I felt.

He likes to pretend that my part of Wending Ways is miles from everywhere, so I play up to him.

"What are you doing way over here in the slums?" I said. "Your monastic interlude fills you with indulgences?"

"I walked the kids over because the undertaker's van was next door. They're taking away Joe Gamble, he died early this morning."

"I'm sorry," I said. "I hardly knew him."

"I was coming along, eyes on the ground and sort of a gloom in my mind, and I got the fright of a lifetime. Big black wings suddenly swooped round my head and I thought now the Dark Angel is after me. It was going to light on the handle of the stroller. You should have heard me yell."

I couldn't help smiling. "That's the tame crow, belongs to some boys down the road. He's all over the place round here. Perfectly friendly. If you drink outdoors he'll take the cocktail glass right off the table."

"That's neighborly, isn't it. He's got a beak like a chisel. I thought he was going to pick our eyes out, we took refuge here. I had Cass in the stroller and Servia kept pushing and hauling. A regular little woman. Life sticks to pattern."

The stroller or kiddie-kar was pushed up into the foothills of the sandpile. The cats, a little gaga (they love a hot day), were making gymnastics on the coarse yellow mound. Castlemaine and Servia (I like their names, parturition fantasies of Betty's) were crawling and scrabbling, flinging cats at each other, having a wonderful time. Not so poor Sharpy, the changeling soul. But no matter how down he is, there's no percentage in letting him use you as a trellis.

"You look like the Sandhill Stag," I said, remembering a book of our youth.

"Listen," he belled. "It's tough. You don't know what it's all

200

about. Here are these unspoiled kids. What a long road they have to travel."

"That's *their* hard luck."

"They live day by day, innocently happy. Why can't we?"

"What have you done to be innocently happy?"

"Plenty," he shouted. "I spent a week-end once in the Indiana dunes. South of Chicago. A hell of a lot more lovely than North of Boston. These sandpiles make me think of it." He started digging with his heel, getting deeper than I liked; I tried to calm him.

"Everyone has to find his own beauty," I said. "Maybe you were good at that. I suppose that was a long time ago."

"I can tell you exactly when it was. We were all singing *Here in my arms it's adorable! It's deplorable—That you were never there.*" He actually sang it.

"As lyric, it's champion bathos," I said. "But copyright anyhow, 1925, by Rodgers and Hart."

"Well, I had the copyright of it on the dunes. You should see that country, Dick; that's my idea of Sandy Arabia. And Lake Michigan, with no tides and a little imitation television surf. You keep a whisk brush handy to scour the sand out of bed in the morning."

I raised my eyebrows at him; something Sharpy can't do effectively, his brows are so blonde and scanty.

"Well," he said defensively—Sharpy goes on the defensive almost as quick as I do—"the sand sort of rubs off of you during the night. That's real fine sand, not like this stinking lowtide gravel."

The children were getting bored. The little girl, Servia, handed one of the cats to her brother and said what must have been an echo from Betty. "You take baby now, I'm bushed."

"I don't know anyone else around here," I said, "who gets supersonic about these sandpiles."

"Damn all, I wasn't being romantic, I was thinking about the Oily Land. Here's my outfit running a Big Inch across Sandy Syria. As fast as we get it laid some Ayrabs or Irguns tear it up. Or the government cancels our export licenses. We could have a through-put of several thousand barrels a day. Then they talk about another steel strike. It's a stalemate."

"A steelmate," I suggested.

"Judas Priest, I wish I could roll up these grandchildren in steel pipe and put 'em out of harm's way."

"Nobody put *us* out of harm's way? As soon as you get to be a human being you're just surrounded with harms."

"They seem to come thicker and faster than they used to. Maybe something's gone wrong with our time-sense. There ought to be some way of slowing things down?"

The children had wearied of sand; they rambled off into the woodlot and were trying to scale my hurricane jungle gym, a huge fallen tulip tree. The warm summer noon must have cooked Sharpy's brains to critical temperature. The red liquor in his tube was ready to break away and leave a floodmark. He moved in on a soliloquy. Was it the Retreat, or his Hicksite ancestry seeping out? He was almost Walt Whitman. Worse still, he was almost Me. I kept quietly brushing sand back on the pile so Doppel wouldn't hear——

SHARPY'S SOLILOQUY

I have lived here a long time (said Sharpy). You live long enough in one place you adapt yourself as best you can.

I have lived here through forests of newsprint (commuters who buy the papers twice a day use up about a cord of pulp per week) and through real estate frenzies and floods in the cellar. I have lived through several cesspools and quite a bunch of nouveaux neighbors who were ambitious to take over the Community Chest, the Firehouse Block Party, the Garden Show, and the Neighborhood Nurse. I might have thought of that myself if she hadn't been so shrivelled and antiseptic. It was a pity to have such starchy and twirly skirts around such meager gams. She had safety pins all right.

It's no use putting on plumes in a place like Wending Ways, the hillsides are so steep all social drainage falls right into the

Sound. That's why the bathing has been declared doubtful. We have a few old lace-collar girls who still try to serve tea instead of martinis, but they were checked up for Unamerican Activity.

I've lived here a long time. I've seen our old forest trees naked like fishnet in winter dusk, and I've seen them thick with leaves and squirrels in summer. I'm the man who has to nose out the corpse of the squirrel that dies under my garage every winter; or sometimes it's a rat. Did you ever see the brown Norway rats running along the railroad tracks the first warm day of spring? That's when they move from the Grain and Feed Warehouse up to the High School. The rats are crazy about American children because the kids throw away their crusts. It's funny, because American kids are crazy about garbage in the comics or on the radio.

(People who have had children are always too hard on children, I thought.)

I've lived here a long time (Sharpy continued). Twenty-eight years. I've seen a whole generation turn on its axle. The mischievous children of twenty-eight years ago are now the parents of the mischievous children who make highway through my yard. They throw their lunch-papers and popsicles on my lawn, their English compositions and Roman catechisms marked C-plus, and one each of their mittens and galoshes. I've watched a generation of kids wheeling on their bicycles like flocks of birds, humping up and down on the pedals; they go round and round that slough at the bottom of my hill, ecstatic with life unawares, just the way I was. Isn't it awful, when you get to be about forty, or fifty, or never mind, you realize life isn't going to go on indefinitely.

Copyright has to be renewed after twenty-eight years, I said.

Sharpy was thinking strong and not to be diverted. As Conrad said, how moving it is when the mutes find a voice. Was it the ghost in the sandpile that had him in thrall? He really Got Through—into that other element that I call God's Country, or the Square Root of Minus One. Zoe would call it sublimation? Or the Id? The sense of livable peace that is so near and yet so hard to reach; because it is not beyond our reach but inside it.

We blunder and stumble, and pursue it down dead ends of sense
—well, not always dead ends, but detours—winding ways—Wending Ways——

Sharpy was going on:—

. . . seen lighted windows in the middle of the night when
some harmless neighbor was ill. Or the decent black hearse waiting quietly to roll him away. There are no whitewall tires on a
hearse. Death is even more protocol than Emily Post.

Sharpy sniffed. "Zounds, I don't like the smell of this damn
sandpile. I don't like the smell of anything these days. If they
wouldn't strike or lockout on me I could sell sewer pipe all the
way from Nazareth to Nijni-Novgorod, and I could fill it with
people who belong there. Men of distinction, quite a lot of
them."

Then he startled me. "Your Miss Zoe said radio is a succuba.
The only dictionary I have is one published in Philadelphia,
Somebody's Simplified, and it hasn't anything between *succotash*
and *succulent*."

"They belong together," I said. "But except for Philadelphia, a dictionary should never be simplified." I wondered when
Zoe had said that? "She shouldn't have been so psychiatric, but I
know what she meant. A succuba is a female demon who cohabits
with helpless men while they are asleep—in this case while their
minds are asleep. As most minds are."

"Wait a minute, the kids are getting into your lovely poison
ivy——"

He hauled the children back and told them to play in pretty
sand while Grandpa smokes his pipe. That was evidently Cullen
family code.

I kept unusually silent. Forenoon was droning sweet,
stealthy sugars of honeysuckle loitered along the road and
mixed with damp sandy corruption from beneath us. I wished
some historian could have been there, but they are always fatally
late. I thought of a wonderful idea for a series of articles: *What
To Do Before the Historian Comes*. I think I could sell that to
Penguin Books? . . . or if Manly and Hidden Page could have

been there (those earnest austere men, one from Chicago, one from Dartmouth) who put poetry in pickle for my generation. . . .

"No kidding," Sharpy was saying, "I'm in a bad way."

I thought, as one does between someone else's sentences, what right has he to be in a bad way just when I am??

"I think I'll get myself analyzed. Maybe it's a good thing to have a dictionary under the bed."

He suddenly broke off and leashed up the children.

How did he know that??

He looked embarrassed, but I give him full marks for what he said, after dragging Servia from a clump of poison ivy:—

"In the old days, the only dictionary we had under the bed was Chambers'."

Well as I know Sharpy, I had never heard him in this vein before. I wished Miss Tally could have been there to take him— in stenography, I mean.

Just then Cass handed a squirming cat to his sister and repeated, "You take baby, I'm bushed." Sharpy grabbed the sodden child (too late), put the little girl in the carriage, and began pushing hastily toward the Electric Side. I swept up the topsand and retreated to my study.

⏤§ That Man was there; wearing his whites, brushing sand off like Sharpy Cullen in the Dunes. The cats followed him through the screen door. I pushed them into the cellar.

"This is a good excuse," he said, "for you to have a drink."

"I haven't any gin; it was too hot to go down to the village. I've only got some all-purpose sherry."

"A bottle of sherry and a cold chicken. April 10, 1798."

"On Going a Journey?" I exclaimed. I looked again at his lean, lightfoot, evasive, ulcerated demeanor; the long flexible nose, the scrub and rough-chopped hair. The angry eyes, the miraculous muscled liver-wing hand, trained for the volley, both writing and racquets.

205

"So you're Hazlitt," I said. "Have you written *Liber Amoris* yet?"

"I am everyone you ever loved. Even yourself."

I was embarrassed by his being so plain. And I felt guilty, there was still sand in the cuffs of his trousers. He had a cool corpsy smell too, but maybe the sherry would improve it? There was a great gash in the back of his head, but I didn't have bandaids big enough for that.

"Here's to you," I said; "both Plain and Ringlets. Recto and Verso. I'm glad you're Hazlitt."

"You love to pigeonhole things, don't you."

He had me there. "Well," I said clumsily, "you might have been several people. You're not big enough to be Conan Doyle. Don't you think it was tragic, Doyle was only knighted when he should have been sainted?"

He said nothing, but shook off more grains of gravel on my rug.

"I'm sorry about that," I said. "I guess that sand wasn't heavy enough."

"A sandpile is like an hourglass," he said. "You can always turn it upside down. Even gravel isn't heavy enough to bury the truth."

"It should have been stickier," I suggested. "It should have been quicksand. Or quicklime. Or printer's ink. Am I talking nonsense?"

"Nonsense goes very deep," he said. "When reality misses the bus it has fun in the corner pub, waiting for the next one."

"But it's so ghastly," I cried, "the more the mind cries for solvency and peace, the more disastrous ugly slapstick it utters. What is it, somewhere in the Sonnets, about my erected wit and my infected will?"

"The pure Pauline paradox" (he gave me a wicked leer on the triple alliteration). "Who shall deliver me from the body of this Death?"

Who indeed, I wondered, but my faithful instinct kept blundering for what worried me most. I turned to pour him another goblet of that proletarian sherry, saying, "What about that manuscript you left in my office? Have I got a release on that?" I remembered a phrase of Mealie's. "I'll give you a toast," I said, "Let's burn through to the story."

I offered the wine and there was no one there. I had a shooting pain as though there was a calculus in my bladder.

Queer, though, there was an echo in my mind—it floated there the way the last sentence you read (when you break off in a book) lingers until you pick up the text again:—

"There's no sand thick enough to stifle human hunger."

و§ Just to make sure, I went down and dug up the whole sandpile, by flashlight that night. Nothing. I said to myself: Man in his autumn is besieged by insects.

I was gruntling the cats, came a telegram:—

MEET US GRILLPARZER SIX PM TUESDAY REPLY PAID.

Z.

The *Reply Paid* griped me; I answered:—

BLESSINGS OKAY BUT WHO ARE US AND WHY DOUBLE QUESTION.

INSTINCTUAL ID.

I was just thinking about not getting to sleep when still another message:—

CHILD OF GREED STOP PHONE ME RENEW COPYRIGHT TUESDAY.

Z.

DEFENCE IN DEPTH

§ Mealie has been complaining about my accumulation of books; she says they attract cobwebs. (Man in his autumn is besieged by spiders.) In line of duty I get a terrible lot of tripe—not only file copies of my clients' works, but courtesy consignments from publishers. I used to give them away to the parish rummage, but Dodie Pikestaffe complained so many of them were bawdy. So that warm Sunday I set up a table on two sawhorses at the bottom of my lawn, like the vegetable stands along the highways. I lettered a sign: SUMMER CLEARANCE—FRESH BOOKS FOR SALE—YOUR PICK 25¢—*Benefit African Methodist Deaconess Home.* I carried down the old kitchen rocker, and persuaded Mealie to sit there (she is a deaconess herself) to make sales. I gave her two glass pitchers; one to put money in (I salted it at 9 A.M. with five dollars in quarters) and the other full of lemonade spiked with gin. There was a lot of quite legible stuff, including detective stories, some nice first editions of ½oetry, historical novels with bosomy jackets, and (just to puzzle the customers) a pile of the new railroad timetables. I was proud of my placard for them: "These Are the Times That Try Men's Souls. If Train Is Late, Read a Good Book." I even sneaked in a copy of one of my old imprints (35 Sonnets, by R. T.) inflating it to 35 cents. Then I went off to spend the day at Jones' Beach.

When I got back, in the warm hebetude of late afternoon, Mealie was asleep in the rocker under the maple tree. She said

208

she had a wonderful day. Everybody stopped, but they did more talking than buying. Most of them wanted to know the way to Great Goitre. Many took timetables, many wanted to hire Mealie herself. That was how she learned that General Housework in Great Goitre now is worth $1.25 an hour.

"Now, Mealie," I said, "let's not be morbid. How much actual cash did you take?"

We counted it, deducting the salt. $4.75 for the Afro-American deaconesses. Mealie put the money in her wonderful old scuffed handsack, and then remarked: "Village trustees was around too. They say you can't do business in residenting zone without a permit. Fine you five dollars for first offence.—I try hard to sell that 35-cent book but they seem suspicious it ain't regular reading matter."

"They were quite right," I said.

"Most of them hanker for fresh corn," she said. "They terribly puzzled to see all those books out there."

"If we do it again, that's what we'll label them. But we have fun, don't we, Mealie?"

"I wouldn't work anywheres else, not even for dollars and quarters. I'm sorry I fell asleep, but that lemonade was a mite strong. While you got the car out, you might as well run me down to the Landing. I don't like to walk past the liquor store with all this money on me. This for our mission fund, we got an outpost for poor heathen in China. Maybe this bring me luck to hear from Salmon. I have to wipe out my eyes when I think of that boy. I guess he nothing special, but you know how it is, everybody is somebody's somebody."

I left Mealie down in our village Heart of Darkness. The cabins there have the deep yellow shine of kerosene lamps, because the Electric Company doesn't think them good risk. I drove back uphill singing one of my impromptu lyrics: Oil for the Lamps of China, to the tune of Deep in the Heart of Texas. I forget the copyright line.

Bewildered with egotism, I said to myself, "Tolman, you should be on a quiz program."—Maybe we all are.

209

Disastrous as my vacation has been, I have learned from Mealie more attentive observation; a few curiosa of the great ecology. I remark, for instance, how the gaunt rabbits come loping from the woods, especially after a shower, and hang about my driveway.

"Don't scare them off," says Mealie. "They eat tuffs of grass off the drive. That grass mighty sweet because it have to grow through gravel. Like Colored People."

I complain about the big setters that come streaking through my flower beds.

"Nuisance dogs sure enough, but we get bigger manure from them than any others."

I was going to throw out a can of fuel oil the furnace man left here after some check-up on the burner. "Don' throw out that erl," Mealie exclaimed. "Thass good for tools. That's creeping erl, it go up as well as down." I never knew there was oil that went both ways. Think of having lived so long and knowing so little about the actual physics of the world. I would call it capillary action, or Zoe might call it Instinctual Id, and think we had explained it.

I remember a sign I used to see, long ago, on a warehouse downtown. I always thought I could shirttail it onto a sonnet— *Crude Drugs and Spices and Essential Oils.* Perhaps for my unwritten pamphlet, *God in Brooklyn:*—

> *The half-grown beauties of those Brooklyn goils*
> *Like drugs and spices and essential erls.*

Off-rhyme is fashionable now, but won't be by the time I get the sonnets written.

I am grateful to learn from whomever (whoever?) will teach. (Give me a forward parse on that, Wisconsin?) As Sharpy said in his Walt Whitman mood, we are all dying of the same disease, Ignorance. At least I die angry. . . .

But just to use eyes and nose and ears, on a summer day, makes life so terribly short: the big yellow butterflies that crave coppery zinnias; and why do the other blue-selvage butterflies prefer pink phlox.

Or the smell of boxwood on a hot dry day, like a translation from Latin prose; faintly sour, like a maiden aunt not too lately bathed. Also, like the aunt, with a cobweb chambray scarf.

Strengthened, too, by the loitering acrid whiff of Topsolito's coarse tobacco, as he shambles across the toasted gravel of the drive.

Or, in the colorless ether before dusk, two army planes in stark formation, busy-flying nowhere like a husband and wife walking, one just behind other. They turn up their tails like scorpions.

Or a mass of sunset phlox, reflected in one of our rustic ponds. Or my hour-late sundial, the only one in the world that shadows correct Summer Time. I set it for Magnetic North, not knowing that variation here just makes it exact for Daylight Saving. And does anyone else but me never sleep secure until he sees the dawn-light brighten on the garden? How can anyone sleep safe until he sees the dark is past? Then I turn on the other side (never mind which) and say we are safe again, until the 9 A.M. News.

Mealie and I were working on a supper menu for Rev. and Dodie Pikestaffe; Mealie has such respect for the cloth, our annual duty, it makes the two days beforehand a misery. I was going to make Eisenhower Soup: Ike knows that a Soup, like an Invasion, needs a big marrow bone and a lot of cooking: but Mealie said the weather was too warm. So I invented *Poached Eggs au Spinegar à la Pikestaffe*: eggs poached in a bouillon broth and then dropped on triangles of toast with mashed spinach acidulated with vinegar. We were giving it a dry-run, hovering over it like a couple of helicopters, when Mealie overflowed.

"If that boy really dead and gone I thought you'd give me your old Navy cape that hangs with the moths in closet. I could stitch myself a good memorial coat and skirt, that's heavy pre-War stuff if you want to wear mourning and it's a cold winter."

She gulped away from the stove, and spun the roller towel.

"I never did know we were going to have wars, at least not in hot countries. That Salmon, he just young enough to get smitten.— You go outdoors, Counsellor, let me broach those eggs."

I went, and watched rabbits and roses. Life wambles on in its glory and despair, its ingenious triumphs and disasters. I better get back to work, the anaesthetic for man who is the only creature capable of discriminating glories and despairs. And only print, my fumbling concern, can wrap and deliver them—the United Parcels of the mind. Fortunately lots of the agonies of the mind haven't been packaged in print—but the margin decreases.

◄§ Summer plunges on. We have killed July, the month of murder (or at least mayhem) and not only of emperors. From this lobe of woods I can sometimes hear the rubber yowl of tortured tires, the crash of collided metal, the ululation of the ambulance. To live within sound of an Arterial Highway is a fable in citizenship.

Time is no longer an ancient with a scythe, but a high school boy with a jet-plane.

As he goes faster, I go deeper. I can hear the tapping on the shell of the foundered submarine, where the thoughts of poets clink their last appeal. Already locusts, the vedettes of frost, wind their watchman's rattles.

Zoe warned me, the Mind has Defence in Depth. It conducts evasive and delaying action through a whole maze of think-traps. One of its expendable echelons is comedy. It withdraws under a smoke-screen of ridicule. There are always good reasons for retreat. I pass on Zoe's ideas to discipline Urban or Seldom. I told one of them, or probably both, a writer mustn't try to make life ridiculous. Life can do that for itself. Art mustn't try to Tell All, any more than fireflies do.—I paused a moment in dictation, to think up an effective wisecrack, and said to Miss Tally "What am I trying to say?"—She looked at me with her lucid, Italian-vermouth eyes, and said, "Sam always says Art should be unobstrusive."

212

I was so pleased with Miss Tally that I went on in high spirits. "Forget," I dictated to Mildred Chezelle, "your idea of writing another half-million-word novel about the Gamut of the Grand Republic. Remember that patient editor who drew a line across poor Tom Wolfe and said This is the End. And don't talk back about Walt Whitman; I know him better than you do. He wasn't writing a book but a bible."

"Mr. Tolman," said Miss Tally, "you should spend more time dictating, you do enjoy it so."

(I think it a great tribute to my natural dignity that even after our intimate parentheses she still calls me Mister.)

"I can tell when it's good dictation," Tally said, "I get a rash on my chest."

"Better than caterpillars. You'll find some bubby-powder in the Lucknow."

"This hot weather, you do get them in the funniest places. If it weren't for the mirror you wouldn't even know."

"I just can't get on without them any longer," I said.

She looked instinctively, or defensively, inside her blouse.

"No, no. I mean the two volumes of the Oxford Dictionary. I'm coming back to office-work tomorrow."

In this pleasant ribbing I can see I was doing exactly what I forbade Urban Block. But then I don't think Urban is mature enough to be allowed to take anything lightly.

"He wired us his new address," said Miss Tally. "Pranksome Brae Motel, Talcum Terrace, Beverly Hills."

"I suppose he's sleeping on somebody's running board. If you think I ought to dictate more, I will. Take a letter to Urban Block:—

My dear Urban:—
I can write to you with even more than usual candor because during my so-called vacation I have not only read your new script, but even tried to do a little writing of my own. In both cases I found myself reminded of the story of Mrs. R. L. Stevenson who came to her husband's bedside (he was ill, but writing as usual) and found a mass of ashes on a tray on the floor. It was the first draft of *Jekyll and Hyde*.

Paper burns easily and makes beautiful wafery ash.

I have a picnic grill in my garden, it is useful for burning notes for sonnets. I think sadly of those notes: each had, in its moment, the thrill of annunciation, the joy of man's finest energy. But so also does the old shrunken cake of soap remember the bubbles the children blew.

Reflect that as long as a thing isn't printed you still have power over it. It is perfectible, and how beautiful, in your own mind. As soon as printed, you are in its power.

So I agree with you, I am probably not a very good Agent; but I can always be cancelled at the drop of a Homburg. I should add that I submitted the MS. to my partner. Her comment was that "most successful novels are written either to pacify or infuriate women. This does neither. The theme of Boy gets Boy only baffles them."

Some of the writers I most admire show occasionally such astounding lapses of taste, I can only assume that either they lapsed on purpose, or they became too friendly with their publishers. If an author forgets that his publisher is first of all a merchant, he is doomed. If the publisher forgets it, the author is twice doomed. (The agent, you may be sure, never forgets it.)

I am not trying to be witty. One should never write a wisecrack to get even with anyone else; only to get even with oneself.

Miss Tally has forwarded the books you wanted (André Gide, Cyril Connolly, Eric Gill, Thomas Merton) and we have charged them to your account—which needs a little support. I am glad you are going uphill, as you say, for altitude and solitude. If a man lived alone he could write all the time, but what would he have to write about? Me, I am going back to Town tomorrow—to the city (as Merton says) that "lived 400 years, with nickels running in her veins." (Alas, *nous avons changé tout cela.*) It is going to be a wonderful day, with New York leaning over my shoulder.

I'm not at all sure that H'wood is a good place for you to be just now, not even in a Motel. Cancel me if you wish, but prove me wrong. What bothered me most about H'wood when I was there, they don't know how to make iced tea. They put a jug of tea in the frigidaire and let it get all sour and tannic. It should be fresh boiling tea poured over ice and drunk at once. So should writing.

I am thinking of a European philosopher who came over here (no client of mine) and found to his horror that he was famous, and most of all among the wrong kind of people. It caused him much woe and fatigue. When I met him at a publisher's pandemonium I

said "If I had been your agent you would never have become famous."
He was dragged away then by squads and squids of photographers
and publicity gals, but I met him again going down the elevator. His
chin was low and his eyes injected but he was still at least bosun of his
soul. "You Americans do say the most astounding things. Hyarr,
hyarr! No intellectual background, if you mean what I know, but the
most unspoiled ideas. Hyarr, hyarr!"

"Which are you now," I asked, "Plato or Panurge? Let's go round
the corner to the snorthouse and have a deep one. I beg you, realize that most of what America shows you is pure mischief. You're
their plaything and they're having fun. If I were you, I'd hurry back
to Buda-Prague or Belgrade-Pesth and be serious. Scholars can't afford to be famous."

What I say to you, my dear Urban, is only $\frac{1}{2}$ mischief:—

Pour your boiling elixir on the coldest dryest ice; come home to
unprofitable despair.

Yours, etc.

"End of Take," I added.

"I itch all over," said Miss Tally.

I sent her away, earlier than she expected. "Take care of talcum terrace. Have another sprinkle. I'll make my supreme sacrifice, I'll put on socks and shoes and drive you to the Electric
Train. But keep your notebook handy in case we get an idea. Powder your nose, too, it glistens."

"I'm sorry it's End of Take," she said.

"Back to the office tomorrow," I said sternly. "Have the
safe open, there's a lot of things I've got to look up in the dictionary."

We have a three-way traffic light toward Marathon, it always agitates Tally whose father was massacred by one like that
near the Bronx Concourse. I drive better when I wear socks and
shoes, and I calmed her by saying that a three-way light is good
theology. "You do think of the nicest things," she wept. "Now
my Sam, the grandest guy in the world, but he doesn't seem to
comfort me like you do."

"My poor dear, Sam has got to live with you."

"Does that go on indefinite?"

"Certainly," I said. "You be kind and firm with Sam, you'll

have him on all fours for at least ten years. After that he can work on his high school textbook."

"How did you know he wants to write a textbook? He's going to dictate it to me after we're married."

"I hope you'll have many and many a rash on your chest. Got your notebook? Put something down. Many a man buyeth hell with so much pain, he might have heaven with less than the half."

She wiped a splash off the page. "I'm sorry, Mr. Tolman; is there quotes on that?"

"Yes, quote and close quote. Sir Thomas More, M-O-R-E. Here comes your train, honey. Be seeing you."

⊸§ I had it in mind to get back before sunset. I wasn't expecting Mealie (it was her day with Old Grandad or Southern Comfort) and I thought I better have just one more look in the sandpile, to make sure if I had really scoured it. Perhaps, in that coarse brown-sugary sand, by flashlight, I could have missed Salmon's ankle or shoulder if he was buried there. But I also told myself, the desire to go back again and again and check something you've already assured, is a first symptom of mania—like Dr. Johnson returning to count the fence palings or step on every crack in the pavement.

Listen, Tolman, I said, you can't afford any symptoms of mania. I slowed down and drove by a roundabout way. New houses are being built, over Scathingtown direction, (for much less than they cost) and there are fresh damp sandpiles. Maybe we're all buried in sandpiles. That's a fine fat one below Sharpy's house, there's room there for Sharpy and Betty both, stuffing it in each other's ears. Frank Mullaly's private sandpile would be hard to fight out of, it would be rolled with hot tar? Or Dodie Pikestaffe, poor soul, would have a whole Bible School and parishhouse to tamp her down. Sandpiles of sliding civilization. The wet harbor gravel was steaming up into our golden sunset light, like the fume of burnt offerings from abandoned altars—sandpiles of horror and habit and—anything that doesn't begin with h, I snarled, as I came to the three-way light, dangerous as any treble alliteration.

Waiting for the light to change I gave myself defence in death. Tolman, I said, undoubtedly you're manic-depressive, but you have as much fun with your own mind as anyone who ever lived. Compared to you, in the Court of Special Pleas, Saint Paul was an amateur.

The least pain in Salmon's little finger was more important than anything that ever happened to me. If Salmon is dead, like Ozymandias, stifled in sand, it is my guilt and everyone's. Just to have written filthy inscriptions on the wall is more of pure subconscious protest than most newspaper editorials. Maybe every dirty word men know has the poet's anger behind it?

Anyhow I'm going back to work tomorrow. I was mad to take a holiday. Man is not strong enough to live at ease like a god. Man has glands and conscience. Gods can dictate the textbooks, but man, lewd man, has the rash on his chest—the light changed

——

I got home, noticing that my overchurned sandpile looked as ragged as a sonnet on the second day out, and there was Mealie waiting for me on the drive. She was yelling with excitement and Southern Comfort. She grabbed the sill of the car and practically hauled me to a stop:—

"I hear from Salmon. God in Brooklyn, what do you think, life sure piles up on us folks. He alive and some, not in jail neither. He write me two days ago, but Post Office so surprised the way he spell his own name it take time to deliver. I so drunk with mother's sentiments I can scarcely recite."

I thought she was going to faint, but I grabbed wherever I could catch hold and dragged her to the chair on the kitchen porch.

"I wouldn't come up here so stinking and motherhood" (she blew a few deepbreasted yawps) "but where do you suppose Salmon working at? He got a job washing dishes at your Grillparch Club. He hear me mention Mr. Meyerbeer who run that club, you always making reservations with him. Salmon walk by there just on chance and they need a strong boy with basketball hands who can tear loose spaghetti and cigarette stubs caked on dishes. He get himself a dormitory at the Colored People Y, and he swear his oath he never take a pencil in the Men's Room."

"Mealie, that's wonderful. I'm going there tomorrow night, and I can check up on him. If he has a pencil, I'll take it away. Why don't you go with me? Miss Zoe will be there."

She mopped herself, took a look at the pot where she was messing me an impromptu slumgullion of shrimp, and said with dignity:—

"Counsellor, you can tell me about it afterward. Any club where my son works in kitchen and my employer sits in reservations, I don't spend the evening hiding behind someone maternity gown in the cloak room. When Salmon want to describe about society on 8th Avenue he can come home and beller it out. Just you tell him, don't cross his ankles and fall on his face. He always stupid with his feet."

⤎§ I slept. I really did. You never know how dangerous consciousness was until you wiped it out. It is man's Vergeltungswaffe, his revenge weapon, but no matter how high it screams into the ether it falls back on himself. I was too tired, or too happy, even to sneer at Wending Ways, poor blueprint of human absurdity. All the neighbors I see, giant forms of patience and mercy, are better salvage than I, or Me. Every one of them has triumphed over the steeplechase of the railroad, over the cesspool and the radio commercial, the Parent-Teachers and the putting-up-screens, the January blizzard and the laundry list. I was tired, and I had earned my fatigue, and I slept. The glass door at the Commodore bar was going round in glittering quadrants, and the lip of my shovel was bright with useless digging, and the toes of my feet were turned the wrong way for prayer, but I slept.

Only those who have loved life so clumsily can sleep like that.

218

T HE TRESTLE

⸫ It seems strange, my deepest greatest day, to find myself going to town by the Electric Train. Sheer accident, my old tin heap wouldn't start—jealous perhaps, she has got used to having me round the house. I had to cab to Marathon with a quartet of the Wending Wayward matrons who rush to New York City for a lunch of lettuce, pineapple, green maraschino, and whipped cream with chopped hazelnuts. Then they go to the Ladies' and rinse it out, so as not to grieve the Dentist.

If only they wouldn't gabble in the cab, and be jocose about a man going to town at noon. I reply austerely, "Yes, I'm sorry to go in so early but I have to play a matinee this afternoon." Then they wonder, just as I do, who the hell I am. They probably say to themselves, vaudeville must be coming back. Many comedians and radio jockeys live on the Electric Line, because they can get back at any time of night.

The cab is crowded, somebody's wife or mother is thighed up against me, and I'm afraid her girdle must be riding, but I'm having amusement. Women are like the Scots, they have two rebellions, at fifteen and forty-five. Both times they zizi like cicadas; the first is hormones, the second is Six Weeks to Frost. Really noble women have a final rebellion at seventy-five; then they are ripe to write history, but they have struggled too long to believe what they've been told. They worried so about runs in their stockings they never noticed runs in their minds.

This, I thought, seeing the ladies slithering out of a flux of cabs, is what the Marathon train does to me in its high tide of meridian muliebrity. Could one of them be Lot's Wife, the mystery matron who had been subsidized? Local rumor, among anxious husbands, was that the Three-W-Club (Wives of Wending Ways) had drawn lots (hence the name Lot's Wife) for one of their number who should go to town, at joint expense, and singe her lovely wings. The not-quite-so-young matrons, bored by the endless drudgeries of life, clubbed together to baby-sit and alibi-sit and buy lascivious lingerie for their cruising moth. She was to be Worse-than-Death by deputy. Her only obligation was to report, in cynical secrecy, whether it was really Worse. As a precaution she was to go to town fast, by Electric, and come back slow, by Steam. I never would have known about this—and it is still only rumor—except that the husband of the Three-W-Club secretary happened to see his wife's cautious entry in the minutes, while she was heating a bottle. She wrote: "All members were thrilled, it was like something from Cazenovia." That puzzled him, and he consulted me. We put our heads together, as men sometimes do. When husbands and wives put their heads together it is so often the wrong husband and wife.

The Electric Train is always to me a *mystique* of disaster. It comes jarring and grinding, volting and revolting, through the narrow cutting, like a magnetic or manganese eel. (I love metathesis, an arterial habit of our crippled human speech; I am never so happy as when the brakeman cries *Matharon* for Marathon.) It isn't even a frank fuming train, just a tram. Sometimes there are two-story cars, built by efficiency engineers in East St. Louis, in which passengers are racked on double trays, like leftovers in an icebox.

But the women are really wonderful as I see them waiting for the train, modestly shrugging down their elastics, panting a little as they tighten the gaps, putting on fresh white gloves. They have left the children with some sturdy Polish mammal

and their spirits, like their corselets, will creep and pucker upward until they get home for supper. They chirrup together in
ecstasy of escapade. They have achieved their little flutter from
the facts of life. There were two of them in front of me, and I
heard one triumphing: she had seen a popular play (to which the
other one was now going) before the Police Department had
taken out the dirty words.

The other rallied and boasted that her husband threatened
to divorce her because he was an Englishman. I wondered about
that (I can wonder about anything) but there was no difficulty
in hearing the coda. "He spells *pajamas* differently, he spells them
pyjamas, so we get all mixed up. I never make out a list, there
never was a man worth making out a laundry list for? Unless
maybe Gandhi. When my husband found he had six pajama
tops, and no pants at all, he said I was an atheist. I said that was
better than the other way round, but I guess we don't understand each other."

It never occurs to the Three-W's that somebody might be
a quidnunc lurking and listening. On the Pennsy, or the N.Y.
Central, or the New Haven, almost anyone might be a congress-
man or a professor or a padre. On the Marathon line they're just
wives on furlough, or husbands tottering home. One thing about
commuting, it certainly knocks out the old Malthus. Our birth-
rate is the lowest in the almanac. If we starve first it will be a
breakdown of the grocery chains, not because we are philopro-
genitive.

On the Electric Side dismay and radioactive disease are
much more evident. You see (at noon) people going to Town
because they don't know what else to do. The appalling gim-
crack trestle is only too plain a parable of humanity on its tight-
rope. Why, I think with closed eyes, doesn't the train roll off
between Marathon and Great Goitre? There's a wonderful combe
or ghyll or gully with plenty of room for a thousand smashed
commuters, without spoiling anything but a few roadhouses.
But it doesn't. Ballistics are strangely patient with their pupils.

Steam trains, I reflect, don't take you to town for tiffin.

Lunch is fatal to the mind. Steam trains are the trains for husbands, puffing and loitering. Electric Trains are for the well-shapen wives, with fuses ready to melt.

Even at midday the Electric Train is overcrowded everywhere, except at the naked platform of United Nations, with its humble little vermilion signboard, like a Philadelphia suburb. Then even faster and more feverish than others, the Nonce and Noonaday Special goes voltage through the tunnel. Did you ever stand at the rear end of the train seeing the white glare of Sunnyside diminish as the brittle boxes-on-wheels pour down the tube? Like a thread of fever, like a stream of light, like a needle in the brain; like an afterthought of Plato's, like an unprintable joke, the Electric Set are vomited, roaring and screaming, through the gullet of New York. I always wish the trainmen were uniformed in white like internes; some day, when rail and wheel and wattman and rheostat granulate with fatigue, they could at least pretend to give us Last Aid.

Tolman, you're full of uranium. You're a master of double-talk. You know you could make out just as good case for it being a ride of glory.

It was. I remembered, this is how Sharpy goes to Town; I wonder what he thinks about? The little salt-smelling harbors, the inflationary realtors' billboards, the brassbound marine cadets off azimuth from Great Goitre, gave me joy and laughter. Perhaps partly because, to my astonishment, I saw That Man get aboard the train. We turned into different cars, but he gave me a recognizing grin. He actually waved his hand in a friendly salute. How would one express friendship without a hand? It was my first build-up in quite a while and I was pleased.

It's good for one of the old Steam Train crowd to ride, occasionally, with the Electric Set. It makes you put yourself into their peculiar horrors, and I dare say one person's horrors are as fierce as another's. I think the Electric Set will collapse sooner than us poor Steamers, because they are more decorative and Dow-Jonesy. They have much smarter garden furniture, with colored umbrellas and lounge chairs and barbecue pits. But as

Mealie says, the pits aren't deep enough for bomb shelter and you can't afford to barbecue anything unless it's the dog.

I comfort myself across the trestle by considering the saddle-shoed high school kids, with their highblowing chintzy skirts, going to Great Goitre for peanut butter and cola and movies. What could happen to them, so beautiful in assurance? I load my meager coefficient of survival on their huge confidence of life. If they can skim the gulf, so can I. In my worst horrors of Wending Ways (Incorporated Village) one summerbrown child coasting on his bike gives me an airlift. He is not whipped, nor has it occurred to any of these children that they could be. Salute, Lone Rangers of the Prairies of the Future.

There was once a bearded youth, Lincoln Steffens, who cried in the flush of 1919 (year of beautiful numerals, beautiful hopes, beautiful Grillparzer Nights; then the century left its teen-age forever; it's hardly worth while talking to anyone who doesn't remember 1919; why on the Electric does one's whole life rush through the great canals of the brain?)—that was when Steffens exulted, as Wordsworth did in 1789 (watch out for years that end with a 9, they're getting ready to decimate something), "I have seen the Future, and it works."

It made a swell headline, but I wonder. It looks to me, now, man is too young for his future, he mayn't have time to grow up to it. I took a gander at Sluicing Main Street, where the will to Death and Realtors is specially strong, and drew a row of asterisks in my mind.

⊷§ I couldn't help overhearing two talking men behind me (my ears are always sharper backward than forward). There was something about their Oxford-Harvard phonetics that made me suspect who they were: a lingering on diphthongs, a slurring of palatals, the complete absorption of the r's,[1] and a kind of whistle in the fricatives. They seemed also unaware of the Great Vowel

[1] See Jespersen: *Essentials of English Grammar*, Allen & Unwin, 1933, which means as much to me as Fowler to Zoe. R. T.

Shift that took place about Chaucer's time. (He didn't know it was His time; he thought it was just living.) When they began to talk about Acceleration, and the Rhythm of Disintegration, I was sure of their identity; I wanted to ask if either of them needed an Agent? But I am modest and shy, and though I think I understand what they were talking about better than they, all I did was say to the ticket collector (who came through just then), "Please ask the gentlemen behind me not to talk about such important things on this train, it might run off the rails. Please," I begged, "let's not get serious, everybody just wants to get to town without disaster. They should save that kind of talk for the New Haven or Princeton trains; it's not safe here where the surface is worn so thin."

"Okay, buddy," he said, and punched my ticket. "Everybody's on a train going somewhere." I looked at him and was disturbed to see it was That Man. I don't know where he changed into railroad uniform, with bright nickel clipper and a deep leatherlined pocket for coins.

"You don't even stop for United Nations," I said sadly. We were rocketing past that pathetic naked platform.

"Who does?" he said ironically.

"Even the railroad has a veto?" Then I did something very ill-mannered, I made a remark loud, to be overheard by the philosophers behind. I thought it might abash them into silence. I didn't want to hear any more of their academic rifacimento.

"This part of the ride," I proclaimed, "always reminds me of De Quincey's Dream Fugue, the Vision of Sudden Death, rushing toward the loom of those metal-blue terraces, that awful reredos on the sky."

He leaned confidentially and whispered, "Let's not be morbid," then went on punching. I could feel the horrified magi quizzing the back of my head. I was glad I had a village haircut the other day; a cry of anguish is less gauche from a well-trimmed skull.

There was a silence from the seat behind. I don't suppose either of them had read any De Quincey since Tom Brown was at Rugby. I was ready to sneer at them on the slightest provocation. A couple of Learned Men who would talk like gibbons (who are apes as well as historians) under the very terror and glory of our man-made sierra. Most proud, most doomed, most savage of all mortal sights; town of bravura traders and imitation arts, and I was going to turn her geometry to purity and joy. I had a horror they would soon say something about existentialism, or whatever was the literary bowel-movement at that date. I prayed, as the tunnel drew us smoothly fatally in, I prayed: Oh, God in Sunnyside, let them not say anything (in those high sweet Back-Bay Balliol voices) to make arses of themselves.— We plunged into the tunnel, the blessed ghastly tunnel. If the magi muttered to each other I couldn't hear. The ladies in front buckled like jelly as the cars reeled on flaky piecrust edges of tired steel rail. But they were approaching their mayonnaise and matinees, they were as innocent as a couple of statistics. Dead or alive, none of us mattered. Oh, my roaring and destroying tunnel, I sang quietly. Fundibular! Who else, but De Quincey, ever came to town in such a Mail Coach?

People stood up in the aisles, waiting to shuffle out in queue. I could hear the philosophers saying how much easier it is to get out of a European train. I thought of the great American Cry, the wild and angry paean of the Western folk: "If you don't like it here, why don't you go back where you came from?" Oh America, land of corrosive comedy (I was trying, politely, not to bump the afterworks of the ladies), I should be subpoena'd by some Congressional Committee. I love you, I love life, too much to attempt the truth.

The two intellectuals behind me, bent over with scholarship and stout British luggage (full, I was sure, with woollen small-clothes and singlets, for the bitter frost of a Long Island summer; and English harness-makers emphasize all corners of luggage with steel braces), were wondering how they could get away from each other. They must have met, by horrid chance, at some banker's North Shore estate; what could be more awful? We were held up, as usual; the tail of the train was beyond the platforms, and

225

we had to crocodile a long way, through several cars. I was in my worst malicious mood. I kept exclaiming, just to grieve the magi, "*Fatti maschii, parole femine.*" I couldn't remember whether that was something Mussolini said, or the motto of the State of Maryland? But I knew it would perplex the scholars. When foreigners come over here, one of their notions always is that the U.S.A. is a low-class country because it has no Eccentrics. They learned different.

I could see they didn't know how to say good-by; struggling to evade, they found themselves adjoining in the Men's. I always go there, too, as the Duke of Wellington advised, and I could see them wondering how to elongate from each other. They were really frightened by now, they thought I must be F.B.I. or Scotland Yard or the Committee on Unamerican.

Man, proud man (Shakespeare and I said to ourselves) is so polite he doesn't know how to get away from King Bore in the washroom. Englishmen, entwined in protocol, on rival missions in the Plantations, what a problem! How many times I myself have been stricken just so; some friend with a loving heart pursues me so I won't be lonely. Humanity resents nothing so much as other people's privacy. I waved to them both and flitted. I was on my way to simplicity and beauty and fulfillment. They couldn't know that; they would have been furious. They were going to lecture about life at a Publishers' Lunch Club. I was going to live.

I paused to get my shoes shined—one of the few places in New York one has a chance to sit and think. From there I scanned the newsstand, a tesseract of color. Newsstands in railroad stations ("bookstalls" in London) are to me professional shrines; there Our Lady the Press is worshipped with most devotional juggling. A study of the different kinds of newsstands in the octopus exits of Times Square would astound historians. What billions of words, even some of them true; even some of them beautiful. As Sharpy would say of his pipelines, what through-put.

Watching the newsstand I feel like a Geigerman, one of those radiologists with a Geiger-counter that enumerates radioactive trouble. I see the papers, I hear the radio-voices: day by day they draw the tensions tighter, they turn the little screws of resentments and rivalries, with merry ha-ha they hustle up costs and depress values. News, born free, is everywhere in chains, or networks. I wondered what would happen (I never had the courage to try it) if one went to a newsstand and asked for a copy of the Bible?

They would say, of course, "Go hire a room at the Statler Hotel or the New Yorker, you'll find one in the bureau drawer."

Only people from Out of Town are supposed to need the Bible?

Then I think, as I see the headlines (*Night Extra* is on the stands by noon), of the horror of people who find themselves in the headlines, but I console myself to consider that This Afternoon is Yesterday's Future. I remember Yesterday so well, or at least I think I do; the Future can't be so terrible? With what relief, what a wiping of the forehead, an editor must welcome Death? My shoes are glossy now and the Mediterranean has even brushed out the death-sand of Wending Ways from my trouser-cuffs. I have enjoyed and relished and taken breath in this great shining cave of profusion. I cry (to myself) my other magical word: Speluncophile! Amateur of caverns! I give the man an extra nickel because he lends a hand as I teeter down from the high stirrups, unbalanced by my briefcase full of the heaviest story in the world. I mustn't forget to put it in the safe. A little closer to the gin than to Shakespeare, but Shakespeare would understand.

I am horrified to see the two philosophers still mutually beset, quavering at each other beside the cigarette counter. They can't remember the name of any cigarettes except British Virginian blends, and they don't like our loose-packed fags. These leave shreds on the tongue, and the Englishman likes to have his tongue clear for criticism. They were in argument; in their struggles to separate they had been looking in a drugstore window, searching novelties to take home to their nanniekempt nurselings.

"I am not amused by these micturating dolls," I heard one complain. "It's odd, don't you think, the Americans have such a zest for physical facsimile?"

"It's really Egypt under the eighteenth dynasty, isn't it. Climate and architecture very much the same, and everyone says the Hudson along Riverside looks exactly like the Nile." He gazed at the vivid newsstand. "What a papyrus dump they will have."

"They do have the most extrordinry passion for spoiling facts by insisting on them."

In a few moments they'd both be giving the same lecture, even clipping the same syllables. I rushed up to the counter, put out a 4-bit piece, and said: "Give these gentlemen a couple packs on me. Chesterfields for good manners. Tell them one can go through the dimestile to Seventh Avenue, the other better walk the cloister under Gimbel's to Sixth Avenue; otherwise they'll never divide, they're so rigid. Me," (I said) "I'm going up the escalator to 34th. Tell these historians it's likely the only time they ever had any decisive effect on human destiny. Tell them I love them, but they better go their different ways. Tell them, we call a singlet an undershirt. Tell them I won't go to my office now, I'd have to traipse along that Gimbel corridor behind Professor Allsouls with his horsehide dispatch case."

They were really on Whitehall guard, with plume and cuirasse. Bravely they said "Quite." They looked at each other, but not at me.

It is hard luck for a high horseguard bracketeer when he happens to encounter the most clownish man in North America. It gives him a fatal sense of security. That was why I didn't go to the office, as I had planned. I went straight to Zoe.

For what is so important as renewal of copyright? Renewal, Redemption, Rebirth, I hummed on the escalator, to restrain from pushing past the lady Charge Accounts on their way to the great bazaars. I felt like Manly's English Poetry in trousers. From

somewhere, from nowhere, perhaps from Manly, p. 122, I heard
myself intoning:—

> Fair stood the wind for France
> When we our sails advance
> Let escalators prance
> But nothing showy;
> Tolman, don't be a crab,
> Here is your chance to grab
> Some yellow taxicab
> Landing on Zoe.

That smooth upward slide of the escalator, methodical as
a college curriculum, or an assembly line, fills me with mumble.
It's like a mechanical Bartlett's Quotations. I was so happy I
would have liked to back downward and prolong the procedure,
but I was blocked by Charge Accounts behind. I was thinking
what an English Teacher I might have been if English wasn't
such a shy language, but the steps flattened and shilled me off.

And there, Miracle on 34th Street, I was just timed for the
pull-up of the yellowest taxi I ever saw. It was a chromosome on
wheels, canned orange juice deified with gin. Anyone would
sparkle in that cab. I jackknifed aboard. It was the fastest-looking
hack I ever rode, but even privacy detectives have to fight traffic.
In the slow treacle of New York noon it crawled like a golden
scarab. I felt for confiding in the driver—it is the taximan's occupational hazard—so I leaned forward to shortsight his name on
the license. *J. Doppelganger.* I hadn't recognized him, because
his head, as always, was a little askance.

"You're really taking care of me today, aren't you," I said.
"How did you know I would take a cab? I meant to go to the
office first, I was going to open up your manuscript."

"That's okay. If you took the subway you might spoil the
timing."—He turned warily, in a pause of red light, and said
softly, "Timing is all."

I felt I was being drawn on and on, as by a tunnel or an
escalator or an interviewer. I assumed my well-stropped profes-

sional manner. "I hope it's a good book, after all this horseplay."

"It's one of the most important books you ever handled. The kind of book that's quick to read but a long time to live."

Lights changed and we scooted across Proletarian Platz, that great area where they used to sell Birth Control papers; the one place in New York City where B. C. would have been most useful a generation earlier. Man's ingenuity is usually a lifetime late; we fight the wars that are already over. Our devices never catch up with our desires. The Prayer Book? I'm so happy, I could graduate from wisecracks into wisdom? I saw a comely Charge Account, whom I had noticed on the train, going into the side entrance of a great cashporium, and thought I could have gone just as fast walking as in this gelded cab. Doppel was poising gears to turn left into uptown flow, Magnetic North. We had squeezed out of crosstown stricture, flanked downtown diastole, we were in Uptown Systole. I was thinking of Zoe.

"She won't be Hypatia, will she? The Lady of Learning? I've just eavesdropped two demographers or geopoliticians. I don't need any Learned Women."

"She'll be whatever you need. She's good that way."

How can a saint, or a cynic, be so lucid on both sides? And a wonderful driver too. He spun round excavations, and women with their tops down, like an Arab hajji on his way to an arms cache.

"I'm in a simple Swinburne and Saroyan mood," I said. "I might get pooped."

"I'll warrant she'll taxi you home. Polonius, Three, three."

"Say, how would you like a job at a State University, as an English chauffeur? I'm one of the alumni trustees."

"How would you?" he said sourly. He slowed, and added, "Be careful what you say when you're happy. People don't like it.—Here we are: how's that for timing?"

We stopped at the near corner.

"Does he see what you see?" He pointed, and through the large window of a florist's shop across the street I saw Sharpy.

"I hope not," I said. "Not in this part of town. Let me out

here. Never mind the change. And good-by to you, old multiple phantom."

"Nearly but not quite," he said. "I'll pull over and pick up Mr. Cullen. He'll be needing a lift. The way he tells it, he was never north of Columbus Circle in his life."

He took the words right out of my head. I went grimly into the flower shop. Sharpless M. Cullen was supervising the wrap of a great sheaf of tiger lilies, and writing on a card. He covered it with his hand, which I noticed was hairy-ape between the knuckles. I give him credit, he looked startled.

"You are doing here so what?" I asked. "Who is for buying pipe in Yorkville?" And why tiger lilies, I thought? Sunlit stripes on a tawny rug.

"I saw the sign, *Flowers by Telegraph*. I always wonder how they do that."

I outfaced him. His jowls gapped at the corners. He kept his hand over the bottom of the card, but I could see that the address he had written was Zoe's office.

"If you must know," he said, "I've had a session with my analyst. She has given me so much help I thought I'd send her some flowers." Unconsciously he lifted his hand to wipe sweat from his forehead, and I saw he had signed the card S. M. C.

I was relieved, but still frigid. So were the flowers, just out of the icebox. I looked contemptuously at them, and picked out a dead bee that clung to one of the tilted stigmas.

"Pistils for two," I said. I flicked one of the tremulous pads of pollen that balance on the stalks. They are the most miraculous of all botany, sensitive as the bristles that grow in men's ears to sieve out commercial radio. I was at my best, and Sharpy hadn't got further uptown than initials.

"Give them to me," I said as the bundle was papered. "I'll deliver them. Analysts don't like flowers in the office. It distracts the Instinctual Id."

Sharpy was feeble. He was far above the latitudes he understands. "She's having us to dinner tonight. I thought it was the least I could do." ·

"Also the most," I replied heavily. "Funny thing, the first time I ever see you in town it has to be round here. I've got a cab waiting for you."

Thrifty as I am, I was shocked to see what Madison Avenue charges for tiger lilies. I took the paper cornucopia and led Sharpy out. The golden scarab was waiting; S. M. Cullen never had such service. Doppel's ear was akimbo for instruction. "Take Mr. Cullen down town," I said. "A long way down, where they sell pipe."

That Driver had switched on his dashboard radio. "I've made my fortune," he said. "They're offering a car, a washing machine, a lawnmower, a marriage on-stage and honeymoon in Bermuda, for the best rhyme about a laxative. All you have to do is send in a cute rhyme for *Ginger Cubes are simply great.*"

"I've *been* to Bermuda," said Sharpy. "Lilies are cheaper than here."

"I've got a swell line," offered the driver. "*For yokel or sophisticate.* That's worth a laxative, ain't it?"

"Well, here's yokel," growled Sharpy. "Take me back to Canal Street. See you later, Dick."

"As much later as possible," I suggested. I watched the golden scarab swing round and beetle off. I watched it out of sight.

PLENTY OF TIME

⁄§ "These are from Sharpy."
I handed the tiger lilies to Zoe. "I saw him at the florist. Even if
he doesn't know your address he'll damn near stumble on it."

"Sweet of him," she said. "The comical old shikari. Is he
on your spoor?"

Then I knew everything was all right. When she uses dictionary words, with that green grimalkin flash of the eye, I know
she's ribbing and expects to be ribbed back. She isn't Hypatia
or Minerva but just Female Girl.

I cajoled her toward the light, crossbarred against New
York's jungle sun. "You've got a new hair-do."

"Do you like it?"

"Give me time," I said.

"I imitated it from a Persian miniature at the Museum."

"Where's the dictionary?" I asked.

"In the usual place. Good goods, are we going to make
semantic love? Which volume do you want?"

"N to Z," I said. "We've been through A to M."

She brought the big blue book in its pink wrapper. I was
pleased to hear her puffing a few goofer feathers off it.

"Check," I said. "Urdu, that's Persian. We can call it your
Urdu hair-do."

"How like you, to look it up in the dictionary before you
study the phenomenon itself."

"I was trained for scholarship."

"Divorced old barren Reason from your bed, and took the Daughter of the Vine to spouse. Omar Khayyám was Persian too. It's a branch of Sanscript, isn't it?"

"I love you so, I won't even correct you."

"That isn't love, that's just laziness."

"Thank goodness there isn't a dictograph here."

"I wonder. Sometimes I think you're a dictograph yourself."

We were having our own kind of fun. We invented it. I have sometimes thought, but am too prudent to say, it exists only in alumni of State Universities, where humanism, diabolism, and dairy farming, are in three-way stretch. She was arranging the tiger lilies (with needless care) in tall vases.

"So what put tiger lilies in his mind?" I asked. "They're terribly Freudian." I reacted (about as subtle as a summer-stock apprentice) to the stripes of gold and shadow on the settee.

"I suppose you'd rather he sends me a furlong of drain pipe. I get plenty of that in my profession."

"I've never been to a psychiatrist's office, but if I saw lilies there I'd flee at once."

"My poor Richard. Everyone isn't as pure as you are. You don't know what trouble is. I cancelled a clinic for you this afternoon, a perfectly horrible case. A patient who suffers trauma from reading D. H. Lawrence. Now I've got to read all his books before I can give her an intelligent consultation."

"I suppose you have to read the files of the *Iron Age* before you can counsel Sharpy."

"Think if it had been Henry James."

᰸ Was it laughter, or beauty, or our own mingle of the two? I could see my imagined Old Woman Historian, rocking and nodding and tapping her slipper in approval, knitting for someone a hair-shirt of steelwool. This is the way it should always be (she whispers) but keep it to Yourselves.

I had a vision, in her kindly mischievous old grand-historian's face, of all the overplus middlemice of earth, screaming for

234

their consoling solemnities, fleeing like roaches from the blasting light of comedy. I thought of Meredith, and a lecture on him when he died, his doctrine of the hypergelastic, the laughter beyond mirth. I wanted to be sure, was that the word, hypergelastic? the fatal caress of excessive laughter? but we had forsworn volume A to M.

Silly to be thinking at large, and so not marking the world's wizardry of timely beauty. Zoe was wearing a flimsy (but opaque) widespread green-and-white gown that had large coverage. Particularly, in a little strict vestee or bib, were two unused buttons. The whole effect was the more delicious because we both knew it was only temporary. One of the loveliest things about women's clothes in the past twenty years (I have heard them say) is how quickly they can be got out of. Marvellously their intricate chrysalis sharpens the mood of clumsy man. Zoe sat on an antique milking stool, but always modestly sideways; a zoetrope, a turnaway of Zoe.

"That stool reminds me of one of the ridiculous things that happened to me at college. I was offered a scholarship in the School of Dairy Farming. I might have had a diploma in Lactation."

"A pity you missed it. I expect cows give down easier than publishers."

Zoe is life enriched by antiseptic. She has iodine for every wound. And how little she says of her own.—How sad (my thought went on) if one had to die before pointing to one's lacerations. At least it won't happen to the young modernist poets.—Do they still put pennies on dead people's eyes? I wonder about that, because an American penny isn't heavy enough to close the busy American eye? It would need at least a quarter.

"Inflation," I said; but she was rattling ice-trays in her kitchenette. I heard the poom, the extorsion, of a brandy cork (deeper than the squeal of a gin cork, less metallic than the downzag of a zipper).

"Break out some ice," she said. "It won't last long this weather."

"Ye pretty cubes, we weep to see you haste away so soon. Herrick, On an Ice-Cube Dying as Soon as Born."

"Have a drink," she said. "Miss Tally must be lucky, at least she doesn't recognize your foul parodies."

"They give her the itch," I said.

We drank a toast, and slacked off the lines. "Okay, no more rickrack," she said. "We're going to have Beef on the Roof."

That is her name for a card-table lunch on her tiny penthouse terrace. We like to quote one of Keats's ½oetries, about "One who has been long in city pent." (A small poet feels wonderfully at ease in quoting the lesser things of the great.) It always delights me that her city pent is overlooked by the huge obelisk masses of Park Avenue. From those great shelves of masonry, far aloft both in rent and arrears, come sometimes the screams and cigarette stubs of Zoe's patients. The brokers and butlers of those percentage Alps rarely guess that in the small duckboarded veranda far below is the commandatura of their mistresses' tantrums. Zoe, nothing if not humorous, never resents the jetsam from above unless it scorches her garden-box of chives. That meager sprout she crops and cherishes for the iced soup of Vichy, which (she used to say) should be served as cold as Collaboration. I have sat with her, receptive in summer dusk on her little balcony, when she could recognize the hysteria tones of different patients, and even distinguish their cigarette butts. The stubs lipped dark magenta were Mrs. Mixogam's; the lighter pink were Mrs. Yeshadoč. Once an ember landed on my head. "Butt me no butts," I protested, but Zoe said it was corny.

Gingerly I examined the stub. Dark red, I observed. "Mrs. Mixogam?"

Zoe made one of her rare gestures of sauve-qui-peut. "I've underheard, from here, so many screams and crashing bottles, I get frightened. I know it's unethical, but I sent in my bill to her lawyers the first of the month. Home, Home, Saylor & Seabright."

"I always trust them, they're so alphabetical."

We sat postponing delights and despairs until all the lawyers had gone home, or wherever lawyers go. After Zoe's account had

236

been rendered, Crena Mixogam cast herself from the parapet. She came down faster than stubs, either cheque or cigarette. Poor soul, she saw an Instinctual Id about twenty stories below.

"One of the great advantages of your profession," I said, "is that rich patients prefer to pay out of Household Account, they even have checks printed for it, than remand it to The Estate, which might involve testimony."

Zoe says, "Why should a psychiatrist be more sentimental than a Police Commissioner?"

ᴥ§ When not yarking out her good heart on debile patients Zoe loves to spend a few hours in creative cookery. There she rises to simple greatness; except for the chives, which (to me) always taste of soot. But with wild Carolina rice and mushroom sauce and fatted kidneys, or a few beefbones and oxtails and baked squash, she can make something that would pacify Freud. She does more of the eating, I do more of the drinking, but we have fun. When we diverge it is in the pleasantest way. She gets more like an etching and I more like a cartoon. She gets placid and I get impatient, or vice versa; the sun lays his cards on the table, everything is simple. Is it often in life that living is as evident as that? I can only guess what others have lost by what I have gained.

I think it may even sometimes be a relief to her not to be (for a little while) Minerva and Psych. D. While she is sopping up that mushroom-kidney gravy, and Mrs. Mixogam's butler (twenty stories above) is hanging out his green-striped stomacher to dry the spray of champagne, I am gently sipping watered cognac. The sun creeps west behind some pilastered powerhouse complete with chimneys and cinders. I get out the brush now and then to dust ourselves. It is the pure dip and loin-gold slope of afternoon. I can even hear the sycamore trees scaling off their bark. Zoe looks at me as if I were human——

I am. I am released for the moment from fever and futility, even miraculously from desire. I am serene, even possibly witty. Richard is himself again. Time has grown large, and Space is unimportant. We talk most about Space where we get least of it, in Pullman cars.

"I feel the way human beings so rarely feel, like a human being. My copyright is renewed."

"Good," she says. "We're both at our best. I've had something to eat and you've had something to drink."

I am trying to hold everything. Trying to get a fix on this moment, before we swing off again onto the great circle of living. I review in my mind the furniture, the pictures, the bathmat, the generously transparent shower-curtain; the heavy Viennese brain-books, the bed-lamp, the green silk coverlet, all the daily decorum she has when I'm not there. The black vulcanite telephone handle, a double dicebox in which our voices are so often shaken for a lucky throw. Two minds never wholly interoccupy, but they can get transit visas. What wonderful little raids can be made across the frontiers. . . .

"You must be thinking," she said. "Poor Richard, you have no idea how confused it makes you look."

"I was thinking of all the things I think and don't say. I wish I knew more of the things you think and don't say."

She didn't say them, but poured coffee instead.

"I was wondering about swallowing my tongue, the way the yogis do, induce a trance of meditation; like the Master of Ballantrae. I tried it once, but I only got a kink in my uvula. I was speechless."

"When was that, I never noticed?"

We sometimes get so amused in our mutual frontier-raids that we forget (or do we?) everything else. I had to hold back from repeating a sweet old gag of ours, "Let's not be quizzical, let's be physical." But I did hold back. Zoe, the always onward spirit, hates anything said twice. Say it once, or like historians, say it always.

"I was thinking of Sharpy," I said. "Maybe I've underestimated him."

It's really a privilege to get off on the wrong fin with Zoe, she plays you so exquisitely. "In what way?" she asked calmly.

238

"He's the kind of guy who thinks the greatest compliment he can pay you is to make a pass at your girl."

"Perhaps it's me you're underestimating."

I was so neatly hooked, right in the slack of the jaw, it was better not to make any flurry. I sounded as deep as a trout, and got behind a snag. She was pleased by my caution.

"You can't swallow your tongue with a psychiatrist," she said. "What were you really thinking?"

"One day Sharpy and I sat on the sandpile. A car came by and asked the way to some corkscrew address. Regular callers like Señor Don Borden y Sheffield, or United Parcels Esquire, or Mr. Cesspool, know the turnings, but any casual visitor is lost like a whiffenpoof. Sharpy said, 'You took the wrong turn on Alameda. Better go back to the fork and then left. If you try to find it from here, you're sunk.'——

" 'Wending Ways,' said the man in the car. 'What a name for a village. Whither do they wend?' "

"Uncork us another squeak," said Zoe. "I know what's coming. This is the second time today I've heard this story."

"Even so, it might still be true. I'm just asking, when did we all take the wrong turning? Is it too late to get back to the fork in the road?"

"You sound like Emily Post. She was always worried about forks. Every moment in life is a fork. You can't parlay your bets on different prongs."

"So we have to go on regardless? I was watching a newsstand while I had my shoes shined. I could see how every day we get more contaminated. I feel like a Geigerman, reckoning radioactive poison. I wrote it down ½oem in my spiral notebook:—

> I am the Geigerman
> I carry my little listening box
> And eavesdrop the radiant waves of doom.
> I hear them on the air
> Click click click
> I hear them in the papers, in people's minds,
> Tick tick tick tick tick."

"I think your shoes were better polished than your verses," she said, "but you got deeper into the subject than Sharpy ever will."

We went back indoors. The shadow stripes were gone with the sun, but poor Sharpy's lilies renewed the theme. She was never so beautiful; it was hard to tell in summer afternoon, but I think at least part of her face was laughing at me. Love, and the absurdity love understands, lift silliness to sacrament.

We said it simultaneously, but maybe she thought it first:—

"Are we Geigers or tigers?"

The deep, the deep embrace.

COME TO NOTHING

ક્ઈ Later, the sun gone be-
hind Radio City, the world's most glorious Egypt of geometry.
Euclid alone has looked on Beauty bare. What immortal hand or
eye Could frame thy fearful symmetry. I was thinking more of
Zoe than of the RCA building, but I renewed copyright (in my
mind) to Edna Millay and William Blake and John D. Rockefeller.

"Queer," I said, "those straight-cut buildings giving out with
so many sloppy words. The great beehive of slovenly English."

Silence.

"Is that irony, or paradox?" I asked. "I always forget what
irony really means. Is the volume A to M still under the bed?" I
started to rummage for the dictionary, but was taken by a sneez-
ing fit. Zoe usually has kleenex handy, but I couldn't find them. I
blew my nose with my shorts. Life is blessedly ironical, or para-
doxical.

"Why is literature so dignified?" I exclaimed. "It is fre-
quently vulgar and shameless, but why does it neglect the tender
delicacies of mortal delight? Deliciae meae puellae! Oh Catullus,
little tomcat! Oh Euclid the Lone Ranger. I am Euclid Second.
—Are you awake?"

"No," she breathed. Perhaps she had swallowed her tongue?
I knew she would want coffee, so I lit the burner under the

cold percolator. After the sweetness of the body comes the sweetness of the mind. Also the sweetness of a cigarette. I pulled the Venetian blinds so I could blow zeroes of smoke toward the radio programs. I even did the unforgivable, opened one of Zoe's dressing-table drawers, and found the box of kleenex. To open a woman's bureau will rouse her when nothing else will. She stirred. She was a lovely moulding under a sheet, perfect as one of Lord Elgin's marbles. She whispered Love's consummate pitiful question:—

"Are you all right?"

I lifted the sheet, always selfish, so I could cover her better.

"I'm wonderful. I am Euclid's favorite child. I am copyright renewed, until we anchor in the bay where all men ride."

"Sonnets," she murmured. "In the safe. 137, isn't it? Horrible."—She struggled up, like Venus coming ashore out of a cotton surf.

"Thank goodness," I said, "none of your Park Avenue hetairai have read the Sonnets. Boy, would that set off the *Time* and *Newsweek* researchers on a steeplechase."

She blinked her eyes wider open. "Coffee," she said. "Cigarette."

I served her, cool as any butler. "Is this life?" I said. "Is life like this? You told me to let myself go."

She was silent a while; seemed to go deeper and deeper away into some Wienerwald, the dark pineglades and pineal glands of Krafft-Ebing, where the only safety is the stark little hyphen between.

"If you're carrying something precious, say maybe an idea," she said slowly. "People do have them sometimes.—You've got to walk carefully.—You've got to say it acceptably.—Don't be just *half*-safe."—(She gave a beautiful imitation of that poor spook on the armpit program.)—"Remember that people who don't understand are more dangerous than those who do. The people who understand too much fling themselves off high buildings and are finished. The others stick around and crucify you—not with

242

spikes and vinegar but with thumb-tacks and peroxide. Much slower and more painful."

I was thinking how I had struggled to dig in sandpiles. As Uncle Remus said—Uncle the deepest and darkest America ever had—He diggy-diggy-diggy, and no meat dar. Nervous Americans, broken or distracted men, have almost forgotten their own great fables. Like the ancient wine-caves of Europe which were dug for convivial fun, but the twentieth century finds mortal refuge in them. The cave men who have no cave but a wine cellar. Like Sharpy on retreat?

Zoe, all fission spent, is patient to let me muse. Beyond the intimacy of ourselves is the sting and brandy sweetness of a spirit distilled in truth. (Spirit is mostly *She?* How would one define Spirit except as what can both Give and Take?)

She was speaking again, with the help of coffee dregs, which I had heated too fast. The dregs of anything are always bitter.

"I'll always give you what you want. But you want so little; such accidental delight. Don't you think, my old Richard, you could learn to want more, much more; infinitely more?"

Silence, from me.

"You're getting nowhere terribly fast."

I agreed with her, the wisest way to agree with a woman; on your knees, in silence.

"You play around with sharp words, first thing you know you've cut yourself, and cut a lot of other people too."

I can't remember anything I've ever said that was the least bit sharp? But people one loves are savagely ingenious to sharpen blades against themselves. My own Zoe, I thought; she has to hone so many edges for others, how horrible when she tries, with such practised hand, to keen the razor, or nurse the viper, at her own innocent breast. I editorialized by thinking what beautiful breasts they are. Leaning back against pillows, she held the saucer high so the cup wouldn't drip.

My knees were aching, I thought I better say something to relieve them.

"I was only trying to be pure. A kind of worship, like, well, like Chaucer. He was highly praised, 500 years after, for being so plain."

"If pure is pure, you don't need to lay so much stress on it," she said.—She sipped more bitter coffee.—"Try giving. Giving everything. Not just lending yourself a little while."

I got up off my cramps. "My weakness as a lover," I said, "my knees get tired so soon."

"Think what a rest they'll have presently."

"You drink so much black coffee," I said, "some of it gets into your mind." I don't think she even heard me. She had gone into her own far places, the wine cellars of unselfish love. West of the RCA monitors, west of radio, west of language itself.

"I'll take one of your ice-cold showers," I said brightly. "Then you'll have plenty of time for soapytub."

She finished her cup and held it out brusquely. "The things you say. Oh God, the things you say." She slid down and buried her face.

I even knew, in the shower—which was only a crystal shellac over heat within—what I had said. "Plenty of time" is fighting words for lovers. I didn't mean it like that, I screamed silently, groaning under the prickling chill.

I towelled myself into sanity. Nothing of Zoe was visible but a swatch of dark hair on the pillow and an unconscious half moon lower down.

"Are you all right?" I said.

"I'm asleep."

"When are we due at the Grillparzer?"

"I changed it from six to seven. So we'd have plenty of time."

"Then I might run down to the office and come back. I'd like to clean up a few things and open that MS. I'm sort of anxious about that."

"Not a chance. Phone Miss Tally, she can bring it up here."

"It's too late. She's gone by now. Listen, honey, only take me a half hour while you're in the tub."

"If you call me Honey I'll analyze you. I'll do a Rorschach inkblot on you. Don't you think a woman likes to have a man around to admire her while she's bathing and dressing?"

Of course she's perfectly right. That cold Croton water is enough to kill the Keats or Kafka in any man. We can stop, on the way down town, for me to pick up the script.

"I've got all my papers in my briefcase, I'll leave it here and take them down in the morning. You might like to look them over."

"That sounds like sense." It sounds like she's going asleep again. Psychiatrist, yes; but woman, double-yes. I prowled around and saw with pleasure that there was dust on the Berlioz records. The pages of the D. H. Lawrence books (on Mrs. Mixogam's account?) were too stiff to have been opened. Finally I felt it my duty:—

"Sweetheart. Sweetheart. Better take your bath. Then I'll put that little whiff of atomizer on port and starboard."

"Why?" she breathed, like the inaudible exhale of a goddess dying.

"You know damwell why. I like to have something to think about while we're sitting in that night-club. Something Sharpy wouldn't think of in his wildest dreams."

She seized me as she never did before. "Oh, darling, don't let's talk about wildest dreams. That's my business. They can be so terrible."

"And they come down on your terrace in the form of cigarette stubs."

"I'll take my bath."

The apartment, rebuilt on the top floor of an old house, has a skylight over the tub. When the glass is washed by rain, and not too speckled with cigarette butts, you can look up through it and see the tall cliffs of human waspnest, or frames of reference, surcharged with sunset, the only thing they get for free. Even Zoe, submersed in bubbles (her bath seems as much soap as water), caught a faint refraction of nipple-pink light. And looking up from the C.D.N. (code again: not a newspaper nor a poem, but

245

Chalet de Nécessité) I could see the rectangles of Park Avenue Petrified.

> "Amid a place of stone," [I quoted]
> "Be secret and exult,
> Because of all things known
> That is most difficult."

Zoe was languidly flippering a washcloth to and fro through warm slosh. Only women can *lounge* in the tub?? They regard it as a liquid chaise longue.

"I really do love you," she said.

"You're not loving me. You're loving Yeats."[1]

"But your mind is more accessible."

"Come on now, Savonarola. Wash off all that soap in the shower. We should be under way. Remember we'll have to hunt for a cab."

⊷§ It was already seven, the feral hour, the hour of wolf and headwaiter. New York burns in sunset parallel while New Jersey tries to shrug the senile day off her bony shoulders. Fresh gloved and pettypanted, we set off in Quest of the Golden Cab. To my amazement (I should have foreseen, but I'm not a foreseer) one was parked under the shedding sycamores. Zoe, with not only two but four erotic bombs atomized on her, was in high. "You left your hat," she said, "but that means nothing. When you left your sacred briefcase, Oh, Doctor Geiger, I knew. You're definitely contaminated, click, click, click."

Of course she didn't recognize the taximan, but I did. Proudly but modestly I squired her in. The little hollow behind her knee never looked silkier.

"You want to stop at the office?" said the driver, sideways.

Zoe thought this just a gag.

"Of course he wants to stop at the office," she said. "That's

[1] *To a Friend Whose Work Has Come to Nothing.* I didn't want to grieve her by mentioning the title. R. T.

246

why I got all dressed up. It's just this side of sunset, Standard Time. No, Greenwich, that's where they have a Mean Time."

I don't think Zoe should have had that Rob Roy after her bath. I was glad J. Doppelganger was in a tactful mood.

"I was waiting for you. This is my last trip, I'm back to the stable."

He's good at traffic lights, That Man. Even in New York's appetizer hour he juggled the red and green apples of the lamps like a trained serpent in Eden. South and then West, South and then West, like a political or theological candidate he avoided full stops. Even Zoe, student of forks in the road, noticed it.

"One block under and one block over," she hummed, "Brings the little dog to Dover. Did you tell him the address?"

"He knows my address."

"It was one of the most thoughtful things you ever did, to engage him beforehand. A woman hates to go on safari for a cab when she's all smarted up."

My street was quiet, buttered with melting sun. That flume of light puts the wretched little diamond chips into hiding; even jewelers go home, aching in one eye. Ah sunflower, weary of time, I thought, stepping out into the burnish of the hour. William Blake?

"Will you wait a few moments? I've just got to run up to the office, get out that manuscript."

"I better not," he said. "If you're going to open that up, I'm shy, I might be embarrassed. I'll go back to the sandpile," he said, with a sideways glance at me.

"What's he talking about?" said Zoe. "I'll go up with you, I haven't been at the office in ages. Miss Tally won't be there, will she?—Driver, you'll wait?"

"I'm sorry, lady, I'm through. Will you take care of him?"

"I don't know who will if I don't."

"Bye now." He swam off, jetting gold from every curve.

"Something funny about that driver," she said. "There was such a dazzle I couldn't really see him, but he sounded familiar. Does one ever get the same cab twice?"

We surged up in the elevator. The evening operator was pleased. "Mr. Tolman! Haven't seen you lately."

I was pleased too. If I had been one of the jewelers he would have said "Long time no see." I gave him a cigar, and said "I've been in the woods, fishing." That is what one says to barbers and elevators, it always satisfies them. Miss Tally had left a memo on the desk:—

MR. TOLMAN:——

Home, Home, Saylor & Seabright phoned, said the paper will compromise $500 for breaking release on Mr. Block. I looked up the ledger, that will just about clear his a/c.

Miss Knox phoned, says she heard Calamines badly need a Book Drive selection for January, why wouldn't her novel be just the thing.

I waited until 5, thought you wouldn't mind my leaving promptly; Sam came up to tell me he got promotion and wants to celebrate.

TALLY

I looked warily round the office. I was sheepish about Zoe noticing things, I fear she thinks it ought to be as trained-nursified and clinical as a Viennese crankhouse.

I believe Sam *had* celebrated. It looked to me there was a sag in the old couch; but I admit the springs are tired. Still more libertine, he must have used my typewriter: two of the keys were stuck together, the ½ and the p. And that, I thought, was my private specialty. I corrected these irregularities without remark. Zoe went behind the modesty-screen and was doing inscrutables. Ten minutes in the cab had probably shaken her make-up.

If Miss Tally's morale had crumbled a little, whose fault was it? Everything that ever happened, every cruelty committed, every kindness bypassed, is everyone's fault?

"You've got some new *affiches* since I was here," said Zoe, muffled from behind the screen. "I'm glad you keep this one out

248

of sight. *No one is so tedious as an Author with a Grievance.*
Who said that?"

"Any publisher. Any agent." But my mind was entirely on
the immediate concern. I crackled my hams down to a stiff-spavin
crouch beside the safe (I haven't the genuosity of Miss Tally). I
groaned, and Zoe asked what was the matter.

"Every ham once had a twin, but mine seem to be change-
lings."

"Let's not be elfish," she said, in the lipstuck utterance of
applying cosmetic.

I opened the safe. The parcel was there, correctly between
gin and Shakespeare. The gin, I thought, was a few sucks lower
than I remembered, but I have no right to grudge Sam anything.
Think of a young stalwart man, incessantly tossed between Addi-
son and Swift. He must be quite frenzied in his interims? Isn't
that the gruesome truth about teaching literature to children,
there's so much you daren't tell them that you are obsessed to
verify it for yourself?

I took out the package. This was a Moment. Dishonorable
in much, this I had held unblemished in escrow. The cord was
knotted, neat and strong, scurfed with shards of crimson wax; the
rubber stamp with the pinpoint autograph of Aaron Gutenberg
who does most of the notarizing on my street.

"Come out, come out, wherever you are," I called to Zoe.
"This may be important. Here's the script I've had hidden all
summer. I have a hunch it's just what we need. Calamines are
crazy for a Book Driver in January. Oh Female Freudian Girl,
this might make up for Mrs. Mixogam's Fatal Obsession. Char-
ters and Accountants, my side of the business might kick in yet.
I've got publishers' prickle in my thumbs. Kiss me for luck, before
I open it."

She had put on one of those cold-caustic mint-julep lip-
services that women love in the early hours of the evening. They
like to wait until near sunset, because if the crosstown light
catches them the lips are corpse-livid. But no woman realizes how
late sunset comes in crosstown streets. Sonnet on the summer

sun: Linger, and loiter, and late to lie down, The sun lies level across the town. Sideways I could see the light in golden fuzz through coruscated Urdu hair-do.

I sheared the parcel open, slicing through brown paper, wax, and string.

Zoe seemed minty and frosted over my shoulder. "Do we have to open it now? Why not wait till tomorrow?" I realized that she had had not four but six atomizer bombs. I had forgotten the lobes of her ears.

"Don't be silly. These may be my unwritten sonnets."

"I don't like those shears. They're terribly long and sharp. Let's wait. Let's have our happy evening. I'm afraid of unwritten sonnets."

Already I had slit the thick wrappers. I had the feel of the script, well packed, sharp and four-cornered as a baseball diamond, full of someone's agony but irrelevant to me; I felt as assured as an umpire in a blue serge suit.

I hefted it, prolonging the editorial gusto. "Feels like 100,-000 words," I said, like De Soto smelling the fresh clam-beds of the Mississippi. "Fine; that's as much as any publisher can afford. Oh beautiful squadron of pages, black with work and woe, what this must have meant to some qwertyuiop½. What he drudged and grudged to say, his ribbon running paler and paler. . . . Oh manuscript, I open thee with reverence—it might even be 120,-000, but we can always cut—a Three Dollar Item, unless we get a Book Drive Selection."

Zoe was smelling sweet over my shoulder. I opened the last fold of wrapper. There was a title page, ribbon-clear and fresh.

"Good title," I said. "Seven words; that's always lucky; they need to take an extra line for advertising space. We'll just take a gander at the text."

The pages were blank, about 400 of them. A great pile of empty paper.

I don't want her to read that by accident at the foot of a page. People—even Zoe—can give too much value to what they see by chance, leafing over the textbook of life.

250

"Accept it at once," I said. "It's my unwritten sonnets. So all my life is blank pages. A Friend Whose Work Has Come to Nothing. I suspected that."

Zoe looked troubled. She put her hand to her forehead, in a way she doesn't often do; as though something was going on behind there which she didn't want to escape.

"Richard," she said sharply. "Richard! Put it away. We'll think about it later. Not now. Richard!"

"Miss Tally was saying we should buy some typewriter paper. Now we have plenty. For free."

"We haven't much time," she said. I left the blank sheets on the desk, neatly squared up. We found a cab on Seventh Avenue.

"Dreams you had, what happens to them if you die?" I think I said that as we drove downtown, but I'm not sure. "I've had some wonderful dreams. They were sweet, but they'd need a lot of blank paper."

T HE VASTY HALL

⟫ Mr. Meyerbeer, that little round fat oily man of food, is delighted to see us. Fräulein Doktorin! he exclaims, pleating his torso forward. Herr Tolman! *Laengst sehe Sie niemals* (or something like that). Then, remembering I have no gift of tongues, he says with pride, "Long time no see."

I have for him my loving smile, pinched with crowsfeet. How different this is from Rosy's Place of bygone days.

"Your guests are already here," he said to Zoe. "They are at the bar." He twitched his eyebrows a little, like Venetian or Viennese blinds, suggesting to me that Sharpy might be using the whip.

"I'll find the Cullens while you're in the vestry," I said to Zoe.

Mr. Meyerbeer escorted me in under the balcony. He is observant as a maître d'hôtel needs to be. "No hat, no briefcase?" he said. "This is your Night Off, *wahrscheinlich?* I am sorry you find us like this; we are rebuilding. We should be closed, we reconstitute our kitchen, I show you. But the tourist business, the conventions, the United Nations exiles, I felt we should keep open at all cost. We enlarge the kitchen and Ladies' Comfort, build in under the balcony on this side. I know Miss Else" (Miss Elza he calls her) "likes a quiet table, I reserve her your favorite, the one so quiet at the back. I am sorry about the scaffolds, they cut a new kitchen door. By the way, we have a friend of yours in the kitchen, a gemuetlich black boy. He gives your name as reference. A strong worker if he doesn't stumble on things."

"Oh yes; I must speak to him.—But later," I added, for I saw Sharpy waving at me. I could tell by the way Betty was grooved and saddled on the green stool that she was trying to hold Sharpy in harness by sheer force of will.

"So there you are," said Sharpy. "Where is Lady Freud? And what kind of a place is this? I ask for a shot of rye and they want to give me a glass of Hungarian wine as a folktale. Tokay is tokay is tokay, but I need an airlift to get me over the hump."

"Sharpy is behaving badly," said Betty. "He keeps telling them he wants a Wienerwald on toast."

Mr. Meyerbeer was going to say something, with his patient politeness, but I threw a face at him and he faded.

The Wienerwald, of course, was what made the Grillparzer famous. When other restaurants were going in for Cocoanut Groves and Palm Gardens, the old Grillparzer built its Firtree Forest. The great barn of a place—it may have been a trolley-car roundhouse, I never knew—was built into the likeness of an evergreen grove. The trees, of some synthetic stuff but they looked just like tannenbaums, were set in concentric array round the dance floor, there were even two of them coming up through the long bar. Music was on an island in the middle, profiled to suggest a Danubian or baroque castle. That prevented a sargasso of static dancers in the center of the floor. Wherever you were, you saw aisles and alleys of radiating distance, always with a table (and a pretty girl) in white linen down some spoke of temptation.

So the trees, lifting up through the dance floor, looked (after a couple of Rob Roys at the bar) like perfect Wienerwald, if like me you never saw the Wienerwald; and the music was Mozart, the Strausses, Lehar's *Lustige Wittwe*, and Haydn, the most perfect waltzer of them all. In my dictionary he alphabets next to Hazlitt.

Mr. Meyerbeer made a specialty of his Sunset Effect. Every day he checked in Maritime Intelligence the time of sunset, and at the correct hour he put on a battery of baby spots, over at the west corner of the floor, to flood the hall with amber gelatines. And in late summer, when the girls were wearing their floating flimsies, you got some wonderful bifurcated teasing down those translucent slopes. Mr. Meyerbeer was smart, the only place he ever advertised was the Next to the Last Page in the papers; there, after strumming through Temperature, Precipitation, Fire Record, Women's Help Wanted, Tide Table, and Arrival of Buyers, you would find a small notice: *Sonnenuntergang Today at Grill-parzer, 7.33 P.M.* People who never even guessed that the Sun was part of a System used to go there just to see the lights shine through the skirts.

It didn't take long for Zoe to put Sharpy under professional discipline. We were disturbed to see that the whole kitchen side of the house was under scaffolds, and evidently some of the Tannenbaum Forest was being sacrificed for enlargement of the laboratory. A whole copse of mimetic fir trees was being felled to make more room for new ranges, iceboxes, and sinks.

"This is really quite a place," said Sharpy beaming toward the synthetic pinewoods where a few dancers were already floating gently in the sunset effect. "It's almost as woodsy as Wending Ways. Must take some skill to weave round all those trees without bumping a fender. Where has this place been all my life? I see the United Nations have discovered it, look through those Hindu ladies in wrappers. I want to see what those trees really are."

He got up and went to examine one.

"Let him work off some of his energy," said Betty. "I don't want him to drive me home from Marathon with one eye closed."

"Betty is a psychologist too," I said to Zoe.

"Every wife has to be," said Betty.

"As I suspected," said Sharpy returning, "they're only plywood columns with bark glued onto them. Structurally speaking,

I don't believe they're adequate. The game is afoot, Dr. Else, will you give me a spin through the balsam?"

I don't think Zoe was very keen, but she graciously assented. Her private smile, as she confided me her handbag, was my consolation. The heavy handbag of the day had been discarded; this was the light little mesh purse of a golden evening. I felt sorry for poor Betty, who must have been in town shopping, I could guess the weight of her large gripsack. (How they grip them!) What an essay could be written on the atomic weights of women's bags —— It was my obvious courtesy to invite Betty to a balancelle, but she said let's wait awhile.

"It's this tinkle-music," she said. "It makes Sharpy think of an old Swiss music box he had as a child, he never got over it."

"Well, I don't suppose a man gets many opportunities to dance with his analyst." Sharpy was doing his twirls, but rather stiffly (legs like steel pipe) round the most remote tree trunks.

"He gets farther and further away," said Betty sadly. "I always use both those words because I never know which means more distant."

"That bothers me too. I think *farther* means more distant in space, and *further* more distant in thought. We must ask Zoe, she'll remember from Fowler."

"Zoe knows everything, doesn't she."

"I'm glad we got this table in the corner," I said. "It's farthest, or furthest, from the traffic."

"Yes, it's nice to be under the balcony. I like to have something overhead when we eat. Then Sharpy doesn't make such an echo."

We watched the distant dancers, caught in flushes of Consolidated Edison. "She doesn't seem to be saying much to him," Betty observed. "Poor soul, I mean Sharpy, I was hoping maybe she'd tell him how wonderful he is as a grandfather and how lousy as a consort."

"I guess it takes a generation longer to learn to be a grandfather," I said. "Grandparenthood is pure egotism, and that comes easy?"

I was absurdly happy. Why had I so long secluded myself from the innocent patterns of human concourse? I saw Zoe gently steer Sharpy away from collision with one of the tree trunks. Every float of her wide skirt, as she controlled his free-enterprise cycles, gave me humble pleasure. I must have been happy, for I found a line of Chaucer coming into my head; which is as good luck as a head can have.

"The life so short, the craft so long to learn. Chaucer."

"Chaucer!" exclaimed Betty. "What put him into your mind? When I was at Beaverbrook we were specially forbidden to read him. You couldn't do it unless you were an approved English Major. We used to borrow the texts from the literary grinds, but we couldn't understand that middlewestern German or what had he?"

I knew very well what (and who) made me think of Chaucer. Love should be irradiated with a glory of simple and personal and unquotable jokes. Zoe and I had a special one, you'd have to read the *Canterbury Tales* from top to bottom to guess what. I must say love is more tolerable when it has a little literature mixed in it.

"Anyhow," I said, "nobody ever got a trauma from reading Chaucer."

"I suppose he had no idea his stuff would ever be printed."

Cool, collected, and considering God knows what, Zoe preceded Sharpy back to the table; her long frail dress tossing out in front of her advancing slippers; Sharpy mopping his brow. She looked as beautiful as any of Chaucer's heroines, and smelled sweeter. I think she was nettled to hear the name of Chaucer, whom we regard (and so would he) as one of our privacies.

She sat down, repossessed her vanity bag, and looked at herself, selfishly, in a minuscule glass. With the detachment that a woman pretends in the oblique of a pocket mirror, she said:—

"I don't remember much about Chaucer except that he had to apologize, at the end of one of his poems, for being vulgar."

"Sure he did. It was just an act. According to the formalities of his time, he wanted to be on the safe side."

Sharpy wanted to sing; he had already started on *Yip-I-Addy-I-Ay* (one of the formalities of *his* time) but Betty beat him down.

Mr. Meyerbeer had come to the table, and was flexing himself from the midriff. He wanted to be sure we were being taken care of.

"Every artist is on the safe side, always," he said. "He overbids the fact with the perfect word. He knows in life there is No Trumps, so he doubles No Trumpers and then redoubles Spades."

"Three carousing cheers for you, Steward," said Sharpy. "Your bridge is out of date, but your Wiener Waltz is full of Schmalz."

I could see Chaucer sitting on the edge of Zoe's bed, the blessed old boy in his gray robe (not unlike Sharpy's) and his tall cap and forky beard. I could see him coming in to the Grillparzer, escorting Emily Post (handy with forks) and so dignified no one would dare laugh. He might have been someone from Paradise or Pakistan. Out of the dry sandpile of dead speech, or out of the wine-and-bomb cellar, rises the noble ghost of human courage. Anguished in imperfections, glorified by abject mirth——

"What a wine cellar for refugees," I exclaimed. "I mean Chaucer."

"I guess you get a lot of refugees here," said Sharpy. "I see plenty of foreigners. Zounds! Look at those femmes in sarongs. Oh rare!"

"We get refugees from the United States too," said Mr. Meyerbeer with just the slightest sauté of double-meaning. "They don't always know from what it is they seek refuge."

"Perhaps it's a flight from Free Enterprise," said Zoe mischievously.

"Or the flight of a Tartar Tribe," I suggested ditto.

"I went to the dentist today," said Sharpy.

"What a day you had," said Betty; "your teeth and your mind both cleaned. Dental and mental."

"I ought to do that too," I said, as my tongue unconsciously

257

explored a weak spot. "The dentist, I mean. If Sharpy's man enough, so am I. I'll call up for an appointment, first thing tomorrow. But I never seem to have any time."

"We never have time to do things we don't want to do," said Sharpy. "I bet even God doesn't get more than two-three hours a day for real work."

"What does He do the rest of the time?" asked Betty.

"Decides what to do about requests for His Autograph," I said.

Psychiatrists, Parsons, and Maîtres d'Hôtel are always uneasy at allusions to Deity. Zoe, with subtle tact, caught and queried Mr. Meyerbeer's eye. She has a special feeling for him because his father was a barber in Vienna who used to trim Dr. Freud's beard. It was very wiry, he reports.—Even psychologists don't always realize how rich life is in small jigsaws of reference.

"Gnaediges Fräulein. I just wanted to be sure you get exactly what you wish for dinner. In spite of the kitchen torn apart, tonight we have soufflé potatoes and breasts of guinea hen."

"Sounds fine," said Sharpy. "I knew a wonderful guinea hen in Kentucky."

"I always remember Doktorin Elza likes Kartoffeln soufflés," said Meyerbeer. "She said it abolishes the body of the potato and leaves only the soul."

It's the Flight from Eros to Agape, I whispered to Zoe. I was feeling wonderful and all sorts of philosophical eavesdroppings were coming into my mind. I am not a philosopher, but I have had beggars' handouts from her kitchen door. The flimsy Wienerwald was sparkling with kilowatts, and the silk robes of the Hindustani or Indonesian ladies were not as opaque as their maharajahs may have supposed. By this time most of the little tables had ordered their meal, and were dancing for appetite; the zingari on the bandstand were weaving elbow-patterns round their fiddles.

"Soufflé potatoes," I said. "I haven't had them for years. Mealie always says she hasn't got kettles big enough for the boiling grease."

258

"*Schon gut. Bestimmt!* Now you excuse Mr. Tolman for a moment, I show him our alterations, and he can speak to his blackamoor. Without young Salmon we couldn't have the soufflé potatoes, he is the only one on the staff can heave those great cauldrons. He is so strong in the hands.—But for your sweet, Fräulein?"

"Do you have a special drive for anything?" Zoe asked Betty.

"I do," cried Sharpy. "I have an instinctual yen for Crêpes Suzette. Flamboyant and full of curaçao, like World War One."

Mr. Meyerbeer took me through the scaffolding, where they had made a new opening into the enlarged kitchen. "At last, you see, we can serve the balcony without waiters running past the downstairs tables. Nothing annoys customers so much as to see other people's meals on the way."

I wondered where the draught came from.

"Yes, it's the new opening, and the emergency door into the alley. I am sorry everything is so bouleversé, but the inspectors come tomorrow and the contractor was trying to catch up. Also we have put air-conditions in the cellar, and with these doors open it blows through. I made inventory in the cellar and found we had still a few bottles of the echt Schoenbrunn Tokay. I send up a bottle for your table; better for Mr. Cullen than whiskey. A man must age gradually, like a wine. Not fall on his face."

"If he does fall, we're not far from the *Herren*."

"We had to make alterations there too. During the conventions so many gentlemen went to relieve themselves, and then relieved themselves of the check also by climbing through the window into the alley. You wouldn't believe how many lovely ladies we had hung gup on our fiscal chivalry. We make a wire netting on that window."

I wished Mealie could have seen Salmon, wearing a white overall and busy at the dishwashing end. He was glistening with heat and pride, and his great basketball hands were bronze for a sculptor. He wiped them carefully, which gave me a chance to palm a bill into his clasp.

"You always good to me, Mr. Tolman. I sure congratulate with you."

"Salmon got here just the right time," said Mr. Meyerbeer. "We needed a boy with strong arms. He's the only one can lift those kettles. You know, you must have both a hot one and a boiling one or the potatoes don't puff. Only thing bothers me is his feet."

"Always have stumble feet," Salmon cackled. "Mother said feet was the last she ever saw of my father and they must have stuck in her mind. The way we got it here, all electrical cables and carpenters' dornicks and new range not connected, you's likeable to trip. I sure keep my mind on my footwork, but the way those waiters run it's keep your legs to yourself."

He got a peremptory gesture from the chef and obediently hoisted a huge aluminum pot of boiling fat, from which I saw them seining up the pale shining pods of ballooned potato. Then another cauldron was put on the fire. The place was a frenzy of crackling steam and fry, and I didn't want to interfere. "I'll give your love to your Mother," I said. "When things quiet down, maybe Mr. Meyerbeer will let you come out and speak to us at the table. We're not on the main floor, in the corner just outside this door."

Fans were spinning, great pans of cutlets hissing, waiters sweating and grabbing dishcloths, drying their faces. Nowhere is so full of participles as a restaurant kitchen in height of service.

"Few customers," I said to Mr. Meyerbeer, "know how much perspiration they get with their soup."

"It saves on salt," he remarked, and ushered me back to our table.

"I was just saying," Betty greeted me, "Sharpy and I can give you a lift home."

"Thanks a million, no. I'm not going back tonight. I have to go to the dentist first thing in the morning."

The waiter came with the bottle of Tokay, and Sharpy was so fascinated by the upside-down wooden bracket in which it was placed—so you can serve yourself by gently pushing the bottle upward—that there was no need for argument.

"While you were in the kitchen," said Sharpy, "we've

changed the order. The waiter said the guinea hen had been frozen too hard, the breasts had chilblains. He suggested Casserole of Tripe, or Wiener Fleischschnitt, Vienna Steak, he says it's wonderful."

"It is," Zoe agreed. "Chopped and creamed with onion rings in white of egg and fresh parsley."

"No chives or cigarette stubs?"

"I like this place, it makes me feel foreign," Sharpy announced. "I feel like shooting the moon. I feel like footprints on the walls of Time."

"You don't have footprints on walls," Betty corrected him. "You have handwriting."

I tried to lighten the pressure. "Not Salmon's I hope."

"I'm on a party," said Sharpy. "I give everything the tipsy switch." He lifted his goblet under the wine bottle and sang:—

> "Quand j'étais sur mon père,
> Zing zing zing and a boom boom boom,
> Quand j'étais sur mon père,
> Garçon n'a marié——

"That was one of our French-Canuck numbers in the Harvard Business School Glee Club," he apologized. "I used to try them on the poules in Normandy, but they couldn't understand Canadian French. Say, I haven't told my analyst about my French undertow, have I?"

I understood why psychiatrists don't make social engagements with their clients. Even a podiatrist doesn't want to spend the evening with people who have corns.

"You're not on the couch now, old boy," I said. Sharpy, mellowing his ethers, was charming. "I'm sorry," he said. "I agree with you. Like we used to say when I was a cow-hand in Texas, let's mammy-up. That's when you sort out the cows and their calves. Betty, let's do a fandango."

They went off among the sunset forestry. I saw him jamming against various obstacles. The floor was crowded now, and workmen's scaffoldings and great screens of muslin reduced the space. Mr. Meyerbeer said they were closed until 5 P.M. during the alterations, but they couldn't afford to miss the night business.

"Sharpy is in fine fettle," I said. "Your treatment has done him good."

"Good for me too," said Zoe. "In my line I get lots of artists, journalists, ham actors, not many tycoons."

"Mostly their wives, I expect."

One of the delights of the Grillparzer is that delicate sadness of old Dual-Monarchy melodies, done with harpsichord and strings. It is music after my own taste: wheedled or plucked or tingled, not blown and pounded. It is music for those who have more to remember than to anticipate. Of course at midnight they bring on a new crew and play gipsy czardas, but that requires better knees than mine—or Sharpy's.

"Let's keep him off his French reminiscences," I said. "He loves to tell when he first landed in France he saw freight cars marked Hommes 40, Chevaux 8. He knew Hommes meant Men, so he assumed Chevaux were Women. He kept shouting: 'Put me among the Chevaux.'"

Zoe seemed thoughtful. We drank a mutual in cool Tokay, and I kissed both her hands, a Dual-Monarchy gesture.

"You mustn't mind Sharpy's bawdy talk," I said. "It's like Salmon writing things in the Men's Room. It's just an instinctive protest against a civilization they don't understand."

"Thanks for explaining to me. Still I'd rather have *Shakespeare's Bawdy*—you promised it to me for Christmas, didn't you?"

The great crowded shed, made to look almost real in orange jello light, was thrumming and quavering with the music of lorn Hapsburgs.

"That was the Hapsburg trouble: I mean, they'd do anything for a sigh. Their Danubian dance tunes make me think of dirndls (which just means servant gals) in wideflung skirts with an underflash of petticoat. Like girls on bicycles round Lake Mendota forty years ago. If you geared a music box to the

262

sprocket of a bicycle, it would be as lovely and impossible as Betty Cullen at Beaverboard Junior College."

"I'm sorry you've got into this Old Home Week mood. Everything is as lovely as everything ever was."

Laufen, our usual waiter (his name is correct, he's always on the run), was serving the cold soup. He waited until he saw Sharpy and Betty, glazed with exercise, returning from the balsam forest. I thought how real Sharpy is, complete with wife and grandchildren and toidy-seats. He kerchiefed his brow; I envy him his wonderful big linen handkerchiefs. I always envy men who have such perfect equipment. Compared to Sharpy, I am like a script of blank paper.

"Sharpy has the brightest eyes and the best buttoned vest I've seen in years," I said.

"Because I've been dancing with my wife. It's part of my treatment."

"Soup!" exclaimed Betty. "How one needs soup after a rendezvous with Sharpy."

"If we're going to be intimate French," said Sharpy, "it's a *rendstoi*. That's what I said when I first got into a Ladies' cattle car at Brest (Brest without the a) and found myself among the horses."

"I never heard you tell it that way before."

"Did I tell you about the Legs Magnifique de Madame Bellechose?"

He had, repeatedly. "Yes," I defied him. "That was World War One, remember?"

"Vichyssoise?" said Zoe. "Yes, Lady," said Laufen. "We use the outsides of the potatoes for soup, so we have the tenderhearts for soufflé."

From the navel of music in the belly of the floor came the first heavenly lamentation of that Haydn waltz. I don't know its name, but it is girls on bicycles and archdukes off thrones, every sweet disaster of human feeling: that pain of forgetting, since one can't forget until he has first had it to remember. I took Zoe kindly but firmly by the wrist. "They're playing Our Tune."

⋅§ "I wonder if Chaucer was a good dancer?"

"I'm sure he was, when he didn't think about his feet."

"He sang his didn't, he danced his did."

"That's e.e. cummings, isn't it?"

"Yes; Duell, Sloan and Pearce; 1940, I think."

"There's good psychiatry in that line. We make music of our defeats, and choreography of our achievements. That's what I like about lower-case cummings: he puts so much into a line, and then keeps quiet about it."

"I'm planning to do that too."

She looked at me so tauntingly, or smoky-gray, that I didn't need to say what we were both thinking: Let's not talk. Zoe is exactly the size that my chin fits on the hollow of her temple (close to the instinctual id?). By pulsating my jaw I can semaphore, or muscle in, all sorts of ideas. I tried to ask, by facial asymmetry, how would a composer feel when he was about to invent a waltz like Haydn's? Was he singing it in his head? Timing it in his feet? Breathing it (like Zoe) on my shoulder?

We said nothing. You don't know whether you ever danced until you've danced your did, in silence, with Zoe. Yes, in that magic, malicious, malingering air of Haydn's. Like so many of life's loveliest things I can only hum it to myself, never communicate. It has in it the sunset, and old photographs, and the sweatsoaked scarf of the weary fiddler chinning his violin. It comes from volume A–M, the one we thought we knew. It says to me that terrible sandpile speech of some Elizabethan, who was it?—

But that was in another country.

And, besides, the wench is dead.

O equipoise of reluctance and desire! You are visa'd beyond the frontier; you are over the hill to the crankhouse. The sunset is Consolidated Edison, the forest is plywood and nylon and glue.

Then comes, if you are still human and mostly brandy for lunch, a tickle of hunger for the schnitzel you haven't yet had. As we walk back for it, through the torrent of Mr. Meyerbeer's searchlight, I am glad that Zoe always wears a specially heavy slip at the Grillparzer. Those unconscious mercantile maidens at Rosy's Place, long ago, didn't seem nearly so forky as some of these Eighth Avenue silhouettes.

Later, Mr. Meyerbeer puts on his Moon Effect, a white cascade from a cluster in the roof. You move in a crossword diagram of shadows. Nachtmusik indeed: the melody loops and traces upward, in a lifting bellyache of Viennese woe, half tearstains and half soupstains, until it belches over the sharp moonlit edge into an abyss of black notes. I suppose this is all adjusted for what (I think?) musicians call Equal Temperament: small calculated discords on a rigid scale, to compromise practical harmony for the customers? What a wonderful political analogy! I wish I could tell it to the ladies in Burmese wrappings and that footproud South American who is dancing livelier than anyone else. A man as flexible as that is up to no good, not even at Lake Success? I am suggesting to Zoe, nipping her under my jaw the way the fiddler does his shiny carton of chords, that this is all a gorgeous ½arable.

I don't know how long we had been swaying and swooning on the cataract edge of Time. Zoe smelled like mint through the kitchen steps. I had steamed myself out of crude citizenship; I was a beggar at life's back door, grateful for any handout. Even grateful for our noblest enemy Time, God's mercy to man, the measure that lifts us above beasts and tradesmen. What would we be without sense of passage, cracking the atom or cracking doom? Time stretches before us like a sheaf (about 400 pages?) of blank paper; and when pages are blank the editor has to count them one by one.

I gently compressed her thumb. I could still remember code: that means (one of the sweetest things we ever said, and we've said many): A thumb is only a thigh, on a smaller scale.

Time giveth, and Time taketh away, but I didn't say so. I suggested it by gently chewing her shoulder. I always try to ingratiate myself with Zoe by using technical terms.

"Since I can't kiss your feet," I mumbled, "I'm just biting your clavicle."

"Known, in volume A–M, as the merrythought," she whispered.

"Better still," I said in her mint-laden ear, "as the wishbone."

❧ Now the vasty hall was shaking with crowd and music; lighted and darkened like a shuffle of dominoes. The men looked sure of themselves, and the women looked sure of them both. People came streaming down from the balconies, where they were hidden behind screens and scaffolds. The orchestra had forgiven Sharpy for insisting that they should play the Parker House Roll, which they finally decided he meant the "Barcarolle" from *Tales of Hoffmann*. I suppose a barcarolle is something you sing in a boat? They outed oars and pulled hard. They caught a few crabs, but then they eased off into the "Blue Danube," which is Mr. Meyerbeer's Dow-Jones Average Up. It brings the rotarians from the balcony, and they grind their old cogs round the slippery floor. I love it. I pass into my wohlgemuth of synthetic Wien. Mr. Meyerbeer once told me, the Grillparzer was established to carry on, among the new barbarism, the Viennese Weltanschauung. This had only three fundamentals: to play music by strings and reeds; to cook veal cutlet in a lather of Gruyère cheese; and to discuss international agreements among gentlemen, accompanied in the evening by dancing. The Peace Congress of Vienna was famous for dancing and cooking; even for Peace, its agreements (said Meyerbeer) lasted over thirty years.

"I'm only quoting Meyerbeer," I muttered. "I'm not a historian. That's what he said. But he said cooking and dancing last longer than treaties. He still serves Nesselrode Pudding; but Metternich and Talleyrand never had ices named after them."

"The Russians always get things named after them; wasn't there a Molotov cocktail?"

"It's all a matter of *Racing Form*," I said (we were wheeling round the second violins in drei-viertel Takt). "I used to play horses at Belmont and Aqueduct before I discovered that authors run more true. I've done very well with second-rate authors, but you don't get anywhere with second-rate horses."

"Horses have four legs," she said. "There's twice as much chance of a stumble."

Bloodstreamed by middle-aged hoydens and consorts from Forest Hills, Dongan Hills, and maybe Cypress Hills, we were achieving a barcarolle of our own. Nothing thrills me so much as to see elderly people (like my friends) achieving escapade. There is no beauty in escape unless you really have something to escape from? The diggety-dig of kids from Balliol or State Normal or Rocky Ridge Agricultural means nothing. But when a grandfather like S. M. Cullen does *All policemen have big feet* in the middle of a cover-charge, it means he has escaped. Into what, of course, is a problem.

Zoe and I moved, in ½arity and ½oetry, round the circle of imitation life. The grove of trees was artificial; the light blazed ambiguity, blank or black; the music howled its loving pretence like a Department of State, hoping for the best and favoring its adhesions. How tragic that the earnest men who are willing to sacrifice themselves for human weal haven't always got minds or even stomachs that are worth sacrificing. I carried Zoe into a terrific swingletree movement with the second violins (my dancing is best at submelodic) and she broke a shoulder strap.

When a woman rummages her shoulder, and has only one pair of straps there instead of daytime two, you might as well pay the telephone bill. Then you will begin to think, with seventeenth-century Sir Matthew Hale (carefully copied out in my Musette Bag) There is no wisdom *sub cingulo*, below the belt.

My blessed Zoe said: "That's why you don't hit there."

What is merciful about Zoe, not even historians would know what we talk about.

She leaned away from my palm (her tender backriff was warm). She looked at me curiously.

I said "I think we better go back to the table. I just heard Sharpy saying he was laughing like a cantor. He meant stentor."

She said "You're thinking. I can tell by the way your jaw champs. I told you not to."

"I was only thinking, I'm glad I never went to Vienna. It would be either too Freudian or too Theatre Guild for me. I don't dare be emotional. It bristles every follicle."

"You're always mixed up about follicles. They're small sacs full of wind; like soufflé potatoes."

"Let's have some," I said. "I see the Vienna Steak coming in."

"And don't forget Tolman's Second Law."

I had forgotten. It was one of my aperstrophies to the demi-scrutable Law of Life.

"How did it go?" I asked. "I don't seem to be remembering very well. I'm so happy just to be Now."

"If you consciously put yourself at the mercy of any power or person, what happens is as much your own fault as theirs."

"Did I say that? I don't like that use of the pronoun."

"In Heaven all pronouns will be abolished."

I whispered to her, the shortest-longest message I ever say: "God bless."

&§ The Vienna Steak was luscious, and the soufflé potatoes like redhot bladders of oily sunshine. "How would a potato imagine this could happen to it?" exclaimed Sharpy, tossing up a follicle and snapping it out of the air. "I am so glad this isn't the kind of place that serves Good American Food. What Good American Food is there but Clam Chowder, Corn on the Cob, and Old-fashioned Cocktails?"

"Sharpy's French undertow is carrying him away," said Betty.

"Sharpy is really a character from Balzac," I said. "Perhaps everybody is, except Balzac?"

"I'd like to be a character in a book," said Sharpy. "I'd like to be a Modern Library Giant. I've always been jealous of people in books, Betty has so much fun with them."

268

I could hear Zoe listening. After all, Sharpy is now one of her clients. Was this a transference or an ego-involvement? But even a psychiatrist gives precedence to a mouthful of Vienna Steak.

"People in books have it easier than people in Persian Pipe," Sharpy squawked. "There's always an Author to tell them what they think about things."

"I disagree," I said. "If people in books are alive they begin pushing the Author around."

Mr. Meyerbeer's Moon Effect was in perigee, we were mostly in dark shadow, but when Sharpy leaned over to retrieve his napkin I thought he looked paler than usual.

"This is when we shoot the moon," he said. "Or something."

"You've forgotten," I said, "shooting the moon is old English slang for leaving your lodgings without paying the bill."

"Something I never do," he mumbled. "Excuse me a moment." With his napkin to his face he tottered off to the lighted sign that said HERREN.

"We pay in full for our pleasures, don't we," said Betty. "At least Sharpy always does."

"Do you think I should go with him?"

Zoe put a quiet unseen hand to restrain me. I knew she meant, in her wisdom, don't embarrass the guy. After all, he'd had several kinds of humiliation already. Even mahatmas don't take that many?

"The dentist gave him novocaine," said Betty loyally. "You know what whiskey does to you after that. Once after I'd had novocaine I took the wrong subway, I found myself in Harlem by mistake. It was the first glimpse I ever had of the American Problem."

"Sharpy is wiser than he realizes," I said. "He's quite right when he says Americans only fry the fat while the French boil it."

"That's what purifies all the Schmalz."

Through the builder's opening into the kitchen behind us came Salmon. In the chiaroscuro of Grillparzer moon his overall was whiter, and his face darker, than usual. He spoke with the bashful courtesy of his proud race.

"Mist Mybare say come do my manners. He say there's three steps in learning to wuhk here. First you pair of hands; then you pair of feet; then if you stick it out you can be service. He want to know did you like them soofle potatoes? I take one myself on the sly, it was real tasty."

We assured him we agreed.

"He say he give you a little time to catch breath, then he whip out your crapes. This all new to me, Mr. Tolman, but those big grease-kettles in kitchen, I'm the only one can heft 'em on and off stove. I tole you, it's basketball hands."

"You don't write anything on the walls, do you, Salmon?"

"No, suh! When you wuhk in hightop kitchen like this you got no time for nonsense."

He bowed to the ladies to show that he was talking to them as much as to me. His face was beautifully dark and honorable in the broken light. Perhaps the darker the angel the kinder.

"I sure do congratulate Mr. Tolman to utilize his name. This here a swell place to wuhk. You should see me show those frogs how to swing a grease bucket." Salmon went back, full of drama and assurance, to the kitchen.

"Isn't it swell to see a triumphant human being," said Betty.

Zoe put her hand, ever so lightly, on mine; I had left it hopefully adjacent. I whispered to her, "Duchess of Malfi." That is code, it means the line "That curious engine, your white hand."

"Mealie will get a great kick out of this," she said.

"Good old Mealie. Let's drink her health." I filled the glasses with beautiful blonde wine.

"Why not drink to all your women," suggested Betty; "just one gigantic bowl of punch."

"Black, white, and ribald," said Zoe.

I weaved under these. It was my turn to dance with Betty, but I couldn't until Sharpy came back. I wouldn't even offer my jocular toast: Blondes in wine and brunettes in women. As the vulgate says, I didn't want to Start Anything. I simply said, "To Mealie." We were drinking——

In the kitchen behind us was a clang of metal, a scream, a

270

low booming billowing puff, a flash of light. Against the blaze I saw Mr. Meyerbeer in silhouette, mixing batter in a chafing dish and Laufen hovering with ingredients. There was a universal hush, then more screams, and a rushing trample down from the balcony. A violinist on the dais lifted his bow from the strings and held it like a wand. Unbelieving, I saw a running rib of fire searing up the middle of one of the muslins. A man coasted down from upstairs feet foremost. The other side of the ballroom, fighting for exit, looked like a football scrimmage from behind. On the fake branches overhead flame ran, roared, rioted. The dry synthetic Wienerwald sang and seethed with fury. I felt the blast of heat on the bare top of my head; a cinder fell with a hiss into Zoe's wineglass.

Salmon grabbed us. "This way, this way," he shouted. One leg of his overalls was charred and rimmed with burn. He dragged us through the kitchen. The whole other end was a leap of fire —the terrible element: so familiar we patronize it, so awful we use it as emblem of purification and disaster. Through its fierce joy, poor dense matter achieves release into other forms. Salmon, weeping with his own pain, wrangled us through the bottom of the kitchen into the back alley. We stood appalled in the sound of fire and frenzy. Betty was screaming: "Sharpy! Sharpy! Sharpy's in the john."

"I'll get him," said Salmon, and I followed. Mr. Meyerbeer's chafing dish had been knocked over, the spirit lamp was burning blue on the floor, and he was pointing a fire extinguisher at it. "It won't be fit to eat," he screamed at me. I rushed, after Salmon, into the blazing hall. The spinet player, Viennese to the last, was playing twangles on his keyboard.

Somehow I always knew it would be like this.

POSTSCRIPT BY S. M. CULLEN

       ෯ Dr. Else says it's part of
my treatment to write a note about the Grillparzer Fire. It was
played up in the papers, but the next day there was a big airplane
crash, and then some international Molotov, and I guess the
building inspectors were glad to see it eased off the news pages.
I don't think it got careful coverage anywhere except in that
neighborhood sheet, *The Villager.* The afternoon papers invented a new angle, LITERARY AGENT LOSES LIFE
TRYING TO RESCUE AUTHOR. This identifying me as an
author was certainly part reason for my crack-up.

  I was sick quite a while, in my mind I mean. As Dick used
to say when I hounded him to go to the dentist, "I know where
to go for a toothache, but where do you go for a heartache?"

  There were thirty people burned or suffocated or trampled
to death in the stampede, but two of them lost their lives trying
to save mine, and Zoe says I should make a plain statement. It's
humiliating but I suppose that's part of the medicine.

  I was drunk. I was in the Men's, sitting in a stupor, actually
I was humming to myself "I'll Go No More a-Roving," which
is probably true. I heard a noise, and yells, but I was too bushed
to worry. Then in rushes that nice colored boy Salmon and drags
me off the Church Seat. "Pull up your pants, Mr. Cullen, the
place is on fire." He looped my suspenders over my shoulders and
looked out the door. There was a great whirl of smoke with

brightness and crackling on top of it. "Can't get through there," he said. "Try the window." He struggled with the wire grating, it had just been put on, and strong. He couldn't do it. But while brooding in the alcove I noticed a workman left a wrench on the floor. I handed it to Salmon, he was able to get a purchase and tore out the screws.

He bent up part of the netting and pushed me through. My suspenders and trousers caught on the jagged edge but he squeezed me out. I fell into the alley. I staggered to my feet, I heard smashing glass, and the fire seemed to be yelling louder than the people. I could see Salmon's hands bleeding, very white on the palms, where he had torn out the screen. Those were the basketball hands.

"Take care of the ladies, outside kitchen," Salmon shouted. "I got to find Mr. Tolman." Dick had tried to follow him in.

"Put a wet towel on your head," I cried, but he was already going through the door.

I was dizzy and sick, but I groped down the alley and round the corner. There were Betty and Zoe and a bunch of waiters milling and shouting. One of them had a champagne bottle with a napkin round it, he threw it into the blazing kitchen and I could hear it explode. Betty had a wineglass in her hand, but she had lost her bag with her commutation ticket. Zoe said "Where's Richard?"

She wanted to go inside and look for him, but it was impossible. The Villager said afterward that someone spilled a cauldron of boiling fat on the stove, the flame ran up the dust-screens and plywood partitions. The screens and scaffolding and all those scenery fir trees went holocaust. Maybe there was some escaping gas too, from the alterations being made.

It was useless to try to go in. We heard the Fire Department sirenes about then. The skylight shattered and the flame went up like a brush-fire. I could feel the indraft on the back of my legs as we stood there in horror. Then the balcony let go.

Dick didn't have to go to the dentist after all.

The people who were lucky were in the Ladies' Room. The

273

firemen started work from that side. *The Villager* reported some of the ladies said their clothes smelled of smoke for weeks. They gave them to the Salvation Army. A cop came and moved us away from the alley. There was nothing we could do. We waited till dawn, it was a mass of wet stinking steaming ruins. My trousers were ripped in half and I had left my coat hanging in the washroom. Zoe took us uptown to get some rest in her apartment. Betty slept in with her, and I lay down on the couch in her living room. There were tiger lilies in vases on the mantel.

Zoe hasn't let me read the story that Dick left in his briefcase. She says it's better for me to make my statement without any influence. She says she had to do some editing and cutting, because Dick was likely to go off the rails here and there, but she thinks as a psychological document it is interesting. Dick was sometimes a bit of a corntreader, and I dare say (if he was really saying his ideas) he might annoy all sorts of people. I don't doubt he made some remarks about Sharpy, the old pipemonger. That won't bother me. Fundamentally he was as sound and solid as any of the National Association of Manufacturers. I don't think I could always play ball with him, he had his screwy moments, but he certainly gave me more than I ever gave myself. He would be amused if he knew that on his account I find myself a character in a book. A Modern Library Dwarf.

Urban Block offered to take charge of the Agency, but Zoe hired Miss Tally's young husband; she says she always had great confidence in English Teachers. One of Dick's nieces was able to take over the house, there is still a white ring on the piano that I feel responsible for. Mealie calls my attention to it, but it hasn't been refreshed in a long while.

The anxieties of politics, and steel pipe, to say nothing of grandchildren, don't leave me much energy to be analyzed, but Zoe has me well under control. Sometimes I think she encourages me a little too much to talk about Tolman. I loved the guy, but the one I need to make friends with is myself. She did say something that startled me, because I was always curious about his background. Tolman, she said, wasn't his real name. He had a foreign name, and he was afraid people would be prejudiced. He changed it when he went into the literary business. His real name was Toulemonde. Everybody.

Betty has got quite fond of Zoe and talks about being analyzed herself, though I don't think there's anything there that would make a rich sediment. She thinks it's very sweet that Zoe wants to come and see us when the tiger lilies are out in Wending Ways.

Sincerely,
Sharpless M. Cullen.